I BE

Damn!

By: Dawn Barber

Facebook: Dawn Barber
Instagram: damn_dawn3
Twitter: Dawn Barber
Snailmail:

Dawn Barber
PO. Box 2942
Baltimore, Maryland, 21229

Printed in the USA

ACKNOWLEDGEMENT

Thank you, God, for teaching me that things don't happen on my time, they happen when it's time.

My Mother Jean Marie Nelson, you are the absolute best. I love and adore you. To my family, friends and readers, thank you.

Chapter One

"*One time for the Birthday Bitch..* Everybody cheered, sang an yelled music blasted through the loud speakers. Holding my Chanel gold metallic clutch in one hand and a slew of birthday cards in the other, I shook my size-eight ass all around the dance floor. My party was packed! Everybody from who's who to who is that was celebrating my twenty-ninth birthday, and every single person was dressed in white just as my invitation had requested. I was going to wait for my thirtieth birthday to have a white party but for two reasons I decided not to. First reason being, there is no guarantee I will live to see thirty, although I pray I do, and second because white to me symbolized light, and I had been in the dark for so long, Not only was I celebrating my birthday, I was also celebrating a new beginning. Although Ahmaun didn't know it, I was leaving his ass! And this time, muh, I was for real!

The DJ slowed things down a little. A few couples stayed on the dance floor, others gathered and mingled, but most headed over to the spread that adorned the table of food fit for a queen.

I made my way over to the bar feeling as sexy as the song that played sounded, and ordered my third Sex on the Beach, swaying to the music and visualizing myself stripping in the middle of El Dorado's Stage, until Mea's loudmouth startled me.

"Happy birthday, my Sollie!" she yelled in my ear and then hugged me tightly, kissing me on both sides of my cheeks. You can't tell her ass she's not a star.

Five-Six, light skin and drop-dead beautiful, and I must say she was wearing the hell out of her new short cut.

"You're looking really cute!" I said, checking out the backless white ruffle dress Mea was wearing, that damn near showed the crack of her ass.

"Yeah, yeah tell a bitch something she doesn't already know!" Mea said as she reached inside her red Louis Vuitton clutch and pulled out my birthday card.

Mea is my girl; we've been friends since junior high school. When you first meet her, your first thought would be she's a conceded bitch! But that's not true; she's cool as a fan, people just have to get to know her and stop judging her upon meeting her. And I must admit I have much respect for her, because she is definitely handling her business: she owns a very successful hair salon, buying her house, and just bought a brand new black Lexus Coupe, all before the age of thirty and how could I forget that she's a single mother and doing the damn thing on her own. Now, that's what I'm talking about. But two things pissed me off with Mea: one, she thought a man and sex was the answer to every woman's problem, and two, she talks too much! Tell that ass something, and all of B-More would know about it, which is exactly why Tyra and I don't tell her shit.

"Girl, that nigga spent some coins!" Mea exclaimed as she looked around the club. "Now that's a nice touch, and very classy." Mea said staring at the five chic's that Ahmaun hired to carry around the Hookah pipe; they were all dressed in black tight tuxedo pants, and white shirts with black bow-ties.

"Is that lobster over there?!" Mea asked looking over at the table of food. "Girlllll nothing but the best for Sollie, it's too bad he such a whore."

"Yeah, too bad," I frowned.

"Sollie, are you really going to leave him this time or are you just talking shit again?" Mea asked, pulling money out of her clutch.

"Yeah, I really am. I can't take anymore," I said eating one of the cherries that garnished my drink.

"I feel you, but girl, that's going to be a mess! Because one thing I know for sure, when you do leave it is going to be pure hell! I myself would stay put. You ain't wanting for shit. Let the nigga do what he do," Mea said waving her twenty dollars in the air to get the barmaid's attention.

"Maybe that's your take on it, but it's not let him do what he do. Hell, he's been doing what he wants for the last eleven years!" I said, pausing to greet more guests that had just walked up to me. I turned back to Mea. "Anyway, like I was saying, I'm done!"

"Yeah, you say that now. But wait until you see the birthday gift he bought you," Mea said, right before ordering a shot of 1800, and then cut her eye over at me smiling, because she obviously knew what Ahmaun was giving me for my birthday.

"You wench," I blurted, grabbing her arm, "you know what it is, don't you? And put your money away. You know how Ahmaun gets down. It's an open bar."

Mea looked at me with a devilish smirk, throwing her hands in the air.

"I didn't say one word. Don't try to get me in trouble. Y'all already say I talk too much."

"And yes, you do. Mea, just tell me!" I pleaded. And just as I went to plead some more, the DJ blasted Cardi B. *Bodak Yellow* which just happened to be one of Mea favorite songs, and obviously everyone else's. Within seconds the dance floor was packed.

She quickly took her shot straight to the head and danced her way over to the crowded dance floor, turning back and looking at me smiling, knowing she had just piqued the hell out of my curiosity.

I looked up and stared at the huge banner that hung from one end of the bar to the other, reading "Happy 29th Birthday Sollie." Refocusing on my drink, I ate the pineapple, and slowly stirred the liquor. I couldn't help but wonder what he could have

3

possibly bought me; hell, I already had everything. And just as that thought came, another came behind it. Materialistically, I had everything. But the one thing I needed and longed for was happiness within myself. Something I knew Ahmaun, or no one else could give me. And where the hell is he at anyway? I thought looking at my Vintage Rolex. Just as I looked up, there he was walking through the doors, with his entourage on his heels, 'cause the nigga can't go anywhere solo.

He noticed me standing at the bar and proceeded to walk over to me with a swagger that I love.

"Much love, Shorty," he said, leaning over and kissing me, he backed up and looked me up and down. "Shorty you're wearing the hell out of that Dolce and Gabbana suit." He said licking his lips. "So you good?"

"Yeah, I'm good. Where have you been?"

"I had to take care of some business, look I need to make another run." He said, glancing at his Rolex. "I just wanted to stop through and make sure everything was good. I'll be back in about a half hour. Love you, nigga," he said. Kissing me again, he headed out the door.

That's Ahmaun, my boyfriend of eleven years, and unfortunately the love of my life. Even though the rumors are true about him having mad bitches, it didn't matter because as long as I was with him, I was not wanting for anything. I was the one with three karats on my finger, and the only thing those bitches did get was the dick! But I just couldn't do it anymore, and after going to his mother's last week unannounced and catching him in bed with another woman was just a bit too much.

I headed over to make me a plate and noticed Tyra and her fine husband, Terry, coming through the doors, holding hands as always, looking like twins. They say when you're with a person for a long time you begin to look like one another. Thank God I never turned into Ahmaun! Don't misunderstand me. He's fine as hell. He just looks so mean; mugged stayed broke. I made a quick detour and walked over to greet my bestie and her husband.

4

"Hey, Sollie, I'm loving that suit. Where did you get it?" Tyra asked.

"Nordstrom. I'll buy you one for your birthday, little sister," I said greeting her and Terry with a kiss, taking a few steps back and smiling at them both. "Y'all are looking all fresh in your all white." Tyra had on a simple, yet cute poplin dress and Terry was wearing white linen pants with a white shirt.

"Oh God!" Tyra blurted, looking over at the entrance of the club. Remi stood there looking around, wearing a white one-piece hooded jumpsuit, and her hair weaved into long wrap with pink streaks.

"You didn't tell me she was home. When did she get released?" Tyra frowned.

"Tyra, you say it as if she was on lockdown or something. She came home yesterday. I went with B. to pick her up. You have to admit she looks good, but I don't know what's wrong with her. She's been acting really strange since she's been home. Maybe she's just scared; you know this will make her third time coming out of treatment."

"Whatever! And yeah, she looks good, but for how long! And childhood friends or not, I don't trust her, and I keep telling you to watch that girl. And when is B. going to realize she's just using him?"

"I don't think she's using him. You know I wouldn't have that! I do however think she still has feelings for her ex, but using B., I don't see it. And as far as you telling me to watch her, I know how she used to get down. But people do change. And besides, I can't see her crossing me, because she knows how I get down! And I really don't think Remi wants that in her life. Anyway, hopefully she will stay clean this time."

Remi was not one of Tyra's favorite people. Tyra always goes on her intuition when it comes to others, and she makes it known that she doesn't trust Remi as far as she can see her. Remi at one time was something else. I must admit.

Fuck everybody else, she looked out for only herself and did whatever she needed to do to take care of Remi. I remember the day I met Ahmaun. And when he approached us she thought for sure he was trying to holla at her, but it was me he wanted. Ahmaun is a real slick nigga, has very expensive taste and swag, So it was understandable that he would want someone that matched his fly.

"Okay, Sollie, if you say so," Tyra continued. "But if I were you I would deal with her with a long-handled spoon. She's a snake! And clean or not, she has always been envious of you."

"Hi everyone," Remi greeted nervously.

Tyra half spoke, and Terry being the nice guy he is, shook Remi hand and wished her good luck on her sobriety. Tyra handed me my birthday before walking away.

"What's up, Remi. You look cute, ass all fat and shit." She definitely had her shape back, because for real when she's out there on that shit, that fat ass disappears.

"Thank you. B. took me shopping earlier. I have gained so much weight, I needed a whole new wardrobe."

"Well, that's a good thing. Where is B. at anyway?" I yelled leaning closer because the music was blasting.

"He was on his way in, but he stepped back outside to answer his cell," she yelled back.

Remi ordered a Sprite and nervously looked around the club. I asked her if she was okay being in this environment.

"I'm fine, Sollie," she responded. "And besides, alcohol was never my drug of choice."

"So is everything good with you and B.?" I asked.

She hunched her shoulders carelessly "I guess." She responded.

The first time Remi came out of treatment she asked if she could stay with me and of course I said yes. Ahmaun had a fit, which I really didn't care. That was my girl, and I was going to look out for her. But when I mentioned to my mother that she would be staying with me for a while, she didn't like the idea. And because it was her house, I had to respect that. So when she batted her big brown eyes and switched her fat ass by B., they hooked up. And yeah, at first I was a little skeptical; B. was a business man, whose mind was constantly focused on climbing that ladder of success. When they met, he had just graduated from Morgan State with a bachelor's degree in business administration, and Remi was straight out of treatment. And here they are again for the third time; B. has stuck right by her side. I just hope through all of this that he doesn't end up hurt.

"Karen!" Remi yelled, "Over here." She waved her hand in the air to get Karen's attention.

My eyes widened. "Oh hell no, what is she doing here?" I asked, slamming my drink down on the bar, because I sure didn't send her raggedy ass an invitation! And then she has the nerve to show up wearing a ten-dollar red suit. As I attempted to walk toward her to tell that ass to turn around and get the hell out, Remi grabbed my arm.

"Sollie, I invited her. I didn't think you would mind."

"You didn't think I would mind? Let's see, why I would mind," I said placing my index finger on the side of my chin. "First of all, she is not my friend. Secondly, you obviously forgot she stole four hundred dollars from me two years ago. And you didn't think I would mind. Well, guess what, Remi? I do mind."

"But Sollie, that was then, people change, I mean look at me; I have changed." Remi whined.

"I get people change, but you never stole from me, because if you did, you wouldn't be here. I can't stand a thief. And why are you hanging with her crack-head ass anyway?" I said angrily as I watched Karen head over to us, but not before stopping and bumming a cigarette from one of my guests.

"Look at her, she's high now." Remi began to laugh, and although I was pissed, so did I. But I still could not believe that Karen had the audacity to show up at my party. And wearing red!

"Heyyyyyyy, happy birthday, Sollie," Karen said, looking simple, putting the cigarette she just bummed inside of a full pack that she already had. That's the shit I'm talking about. And then acting as if nothing ever happened, like her and I rock with each other like that. Here I was still pissed that she stole four hundred dollars from me, and this wench was ready to dance at my party wearing red!

Remi grabbed my hand and uttered the words please let her stay.

I took a deep breath and turned to Karen. "Check this out, the only reason you're here is because Remi invited you without my permission," I said, cutting my eyes over at Remi. "And the only reason I'm letting you stay is because of Remi, but if you do anything, start anything, or say some slick shit out your mouth to anyone, your ass will be going south!" "I ain't going to know DC."

I shook my head. "The door, the door is facing south!"

Karen started to respond but I quickly stopped her.

"Don't say it. Tonight, this club is open strictly for my party, so don't think it can't and won't be done. Because for real I can make it happen right now!" I said with my eyes widened and eyebrows rose.

"Okay, okay," Karen said, "I'm going to be cool. I don't want no problems. I just came to have a good time and get my grove on, that's all. I don't want no trouble."

And just as she said that, the DJ blasted Neyo *Independent.*

"Heyyy . . . that's what I am, a mother-fuckin independent women," Karen yelled out, which could not have been farther from the truth. Karen turned to me and smiled, looking like she really wanted to cuss me out, as she danced her ten-dollar ass over to the dance floor.

"Thanks Sollie, for letting her stay," Remi said, sipping her soda.

"Yeah, whatever, and if she wants to eat, please fix her plate. I don't want her nasty hands in my food!"

I looked over on the dance floor and Karen was gettin it in. I told Remi that I would be back. I headed outside to see what was taking B. so long to come inside. When I got out front, B. was still on the phone, looking like Morris Chestnut.

"Heyyyy, happy birthday, cutie," B. said, kissing me on my cheek and handing me a card. "Look at you, looking all sexy and shit!" He grabbed me by my hand, and turned me around.

"Thanks, B. When are you coming inside?"

"I'm coming. I'm talking to my brother. Yeah man, that's the one and only Sollie. What! Is she fine? Fine isn't the word. Let's see. She's five feet five, caramel complexion, long beautiful hair, and yes, it's all hers, big pretty brown eyes, dimple in her chin, and oh yeah, how could I forget, she's fat to deaf!" B. said, hugging me tightly.

"Shut up, B.," I said, playfully slapping him on his arm.

"Sollie, my brother wants to say hello, and wish you happy birthday," B. said trying to hand me his cell. I pushed his hand away and told B. to tell his brother hello and thank you, and headed back into the club. I did wonder if his brother was as fine as B.

Once back in the club, I went over to make me a plate. Just then I noticed Ahmaun coming through the door, and watched as he walked over to DJ.

Ahmaun knows that seafood is my favorite, but wearing all white I had to be very careful not to get any on my suit. And thank God the food was catered, which meant I wouldn't have to do any cleaning up. There were so many options of food to choose from, everything from whole lobsters to clams on a half shell. The centerpiece was an ice sculpture shaved into the number twenty-nine, and the five-tiered pink-and-white birthday cake was beautiful!

Now, check this out. Ahmaun wasn't no Nickey Barnes, but word on the street was he was getting paid big time! He stayed out of town a lot, claiming to be picking up money from his other contacts, especially down Atlanta, where he visited the most. Now, Atlanta I don't mind, because right before he would fly back to Baltimore, he would always stop at Gladys Knight Chicken and Waffles to bring me back my favorite dish.

Just as I sat down with Tyra, Terry, Mea, and some other guest and I was about to crack open my lobster, the DJ turned the music off and yelled into the mic.

"Sollie where you at?"

I looked at Tyra and Mea, leaning over and whispering, "I know y'all didn't get me a stripper." Thank God, they said no. I wasn't crazy about strippers and Ahmaun would have a fit. I turned to DJ wondering what he wanted with me, and then looked at Mea, remembering our conversation from earlier. With the look on her face, she knew exactly what it was about. "Go ahead, go Sollie, I'm about to go LIVE on FaceBook." She said excitedly. I quickly wiped my hands and got up, at the same time noticing my brother, Salique, coming into the club. He was very well respected by others, and if you ever had the chance to talk with him, it was always a pleasure. He was one of those brothers you wanted to listen to when he talked. And there's nothing like talking to an intelligent black man. Hate was a strong word for Salique, but when it came to Ahmaun, it was definitely in his vocabulary. Salique whipped his ass a few years ago for all the dirt he was doing to me. And he hated the fact that I chose to still be with him knowing how he cheats on me. But he will be happy to hear that I'm finally leaving him. I hurried over to Salique and greeted him with a kiss, and watched as he cut his eye over at Ahmaun and mugged him.

I walked back over and sat down in the chair that Ahmaun had placed in the middle of the dance floor and watched as everyone began gathering around us. Nervously, I began twirling my hair around my finger. I then looked over and saw Tyra standing there, looking as if she wanted to yell, "hell no, she will not marry you." I then noticed Mea standing there, smiling, and showing all her bleached-white teeth. Everyone's eyes were wide with curiosity and excitement. I turned back to Ahmaun. *I know this boy is not about to ask me to marry him. I might be crazy, but I'm not stupid. Here I'm getting ready to leave his cheating ass, and he's about to pop the question. But wait he's not on one knees,* I thought as he stood there.

"Sollie you my baby, my life and I will do anything in the world to make you happy and I hope this does." Ahmaun said pushing away a balloon that had floated in front of him; he extended to me a small silver box with a white bow on top of it.

"Ahmaun, what is this?" I asked curiously, slowly taking the box out of his hand.

"Just open it," he said, looking over at Salique, making sure he was paying attention to what he was about to give his little sister.

I slowly opened the box, and inside was a black car key with chrome Mercedes Benz symbol on it.

My eyes widened "Ahmaun, is this a joke?" I asked removing the key from the box.

"Nah, Shorty, it's not a joke. Come on," he said taking me by my hand and pulling me through the crowd, toward the door.

And just as we were leaving out, I spotted Karen standing over there by the food looking very suspicious. *"That bitch"* I thought. Excited as I was to get outside to see my present, I tried to pull away from Ahmaun to go over and see what her sneaky ass was up to, but he wouldn't let me.

"I know that nigga ain't buy my girl no Benz!" I heard Duce's loud mouth say.

When I walked out the doors, there it was parked right in front of the club, a brand new silver two-door SLK Mercedes-Benz with a huge white bow attached to the roof of the car. The inside was filled with white and silver balloons. I thought I would pass out, and everyone along with me was in disbelief.

"That nigga rolling like that?" I heard someone ask.

"Oh yeah, I heard the boy was getting money! Say he got all of Bmore sewed up," someone responded.

"That pussy must be da bombbbbb!"

"I know one thing. He love dat girl!" I heard someone else say.

As I ran over to the car, I still couldn't believe my eyes. I ran around to the driver's side and pressed the unlock button, and as I opened the door the balloons came out and we all watched as they floated into the air. "It's beautiful, Ahmaun, and oh my god, it's a stick! I love it," I said jumping into his arms and hugging him tightly.

"And I love you, nigga, for life!" he said as he hugged me back.

Excitedly I jumped into the driver's seat, looking around the car; I than looked over at the club, and noticed Tyra and Terry. Tyra shook her head and turned and went back inside the club. I guess she knew my plans on rolling out on Ahmaun just rolled out the window. Remi stared while listening to whatever Karen was whispering in her ear. Salique stood there with his arms folded, staring at me disappointingly as I pulled off.

"How much was this?" I asked as I quickly went into second gear realizing that the car was fast. I wished I could have jumped on 295, and really opened it up! "Is it paid for?" I asked, still very excited.

I jumped when one of the balloons popped, and Ahmaun almost jumped out of his skin; living the life he lives keeps his ass paranoid. "So Ahmaun, answer me. Is it paid for?"

"Sollie, calm down," Ahmaun said, still nervous from the balloon bursting. "And yes, it's paid for, to answer your question. I drove it right off the showroom floor!"

"Are you making that kind of money?"

"Shorty, believe me when I tell you, we about to millionaires!"

What, millionaires! Sorry, Tyra, Check this out y'all; fuck what I said in the beginning. I changed my mind. I'm staying. I'm not going anywhere! I thought, shifting into fourth gear.

Ahmaun laid back in the seat, mugging as he rocked his head to the music. "I'm going to go on Monday and take care of the rest of the paperwork. Right now, it's still under the dealer's insurance.

"Are you putting it in my name?"

"Nah, its staying in my name!" he snapped, looking at me with that controlling look on his face.

Yeah okay, we'll see whose name it goes in. One thing about me— I was with a nigga that's in the game, and I know just how to play it! I thought.

"So you love it?" he asked.

"Yeah, I do. Thank you, Ahmaun," I said staring at him and realizing more than ever that despite his cheating, he really did love me. I silently hoped he would change.

After driving the Benz around the block a few times, we pulled back up in front of the club. A few of my friends were still standing outside talking about the car. As I got out, I noticed that Ahmaun stayed in the car, finally answering his cell that had been ringing off the hook.

"Sollie, you must put it on his punk ass." Duce said, leaning up against the club's door and trying to give me a high five.

Duce was six feet tall, dark skinned, thin built, kept a fresh cut and fine! He had definitely grown into his good looks. When we were younger, he looked like "Buck-Wheat" from The Little Rascals. Unfortunately, his good looks are coupled with immaturity. And for him to be turning thirty soon, I wonder if he would ever grow up. I loved Duce, but sometimes, well, most of the time he could be a little overwhelming, especially when he and Jodi go at it. But I must admit when it came to Tyra and me, he didn't play.

"Duce, shut up!" I said smiling.

"Sell me the Beamer?"

"Duce, I don't know. I may give it to Remi."

"Fuck that freak! Let that nigga B. buy her a car."

"Duce, be easy now. Don't talk trash. If I can remember correctly you used to want Remi and another thing, watch your mouth. That's my girl you're disrespecting and you know that I don't play that. "

"Yeah, whatever, you're right I did try to hit it. But that's before I knew everybody else was hitting it!"

Ahmaun got out of the car and walked over to me. He took me by the hand, and we headed back inside the club. As he walked by Duce, he slightly gritted on him, and Duce gritted on him right back. Little did Ahmaun know that Duce has wanted to whip his ass for a very long time. The only reason he hasn't was because of me begging him not to. As we walked inside, everyone was still partying. I told Ahmaun that I would be right back. I had to use the bathroom before I pissed myself from excitement. I rushed into the bathroom stall, relieved that I made it. And guess who comes in the bathroom talking on her cell phone.

"I don't believe he bought that bitch a Benz!" I heard Karen saying, sounding like she just drank a whole bottle of methadone. "She already thinks she's the shit! I can't stand her cute ass. That's just why I wore red. Fuck her, muh. And like I was saying earlier, she gotta know that nigga ain't no good! And as a matter of fact he had one of his girls up here last week. I heard she's from Atlanta. At least that's what the boy Dino told me. And guess what? The sister is bad! But it was something about her, something crazy almost. She came into the corner store, and I told her she look nice. She had on a slick-ass Gucci suit, and you know me, I ain't got no problem giving a bitch a compliment. And you know, I know about that couture, I runs cross that shit when I be in the department stores throwing it in the bag. Anyway," Karen said smacking her rotten teeth, "Immediately . . . you hear me, immediately, she handed me a twenty-dollar bill, almost as if she was paying me for the compliment I gave her! I started to tell her that her hair was tight. She mighta hit me off with another one," she said as she slapped her leg and fell out laughing.

I had heard enough. Pulling a little toilet paper from the roll, I quickly patted myself dry and pulled up my pants. When I burst out of the stall, I was in total shock. I thought Karen was on the phone, but to my surprise the girl I thought was my home-girl was standing there quietly listening, and allowing this wench to speak bad about me. I could have bought both their asses for a penny. I looked at her as she stood in shock, knowing she was out of order. I walked over to Karen and got as close as her odor would allow me to.

"I told you, if you start running your mouth, you were leaving!"

"I ain't gotta go nowhere. Dis ain't your club!" Karen snapped with her illiterate talking ass.

I smirked. "Okay, wait right here." Little did Karen know that the guy doing security was one of my closest friends, a police by day and a bouncer at night. I told him to just mingle and act as if he was one of the guests. Ahmaun had a whole lot of enemies so if something went down, Kane, along with his coworkers, would be here. I looked outside of the bathroom door and managed to get his attention. While waiting for Kane, I stared Remi down, I couldn't believe it.

"What's up cutie?" Kane asked, now standing at the entrance of the bathroom door looking sexy in his all white. And the brother's body was cut up!

"She needs to go," I said pointing to Karen, and that was all he needed to hear, no questions asked.

"Miss, you need to leave," Kane said walking into the bathroom and over to where she was standing.

"I ain't gotta go nowhere! I think you the one who needs to leave! Dis a girl's bathroom. Dis some bullshit right here! Y'all is really trippin!" Ignoring him, Karen walked over to the mirror and began fixing her tired ass ponytail.

"Look, let's not make this out to be a problem," Kane said walking over and standing behind Karen. "Either you can leave on your own or you can be assisted. The choice is yours." And with the look Kane gave her, she knew he was not playing.

Karen was heated. Rolling her eyes, she snatched her knock-off Louis Vuitton pocketbook off the sink. Just as she did this, a napkin full of steamed shrimp came flying out and landed all over the bathroom floor. As pissed as I was with her, it took everything in me not to laugh. Kane stood there shaking his head. You would have thought it was money from the way Karen's ass dived on the floor scrambling to pick up the shrimp and placing them back inside the napkin.

She looked up at us. "They ain't dirty, shit! They got a shell on them!"

"Give it here!" I said snatching the napkin full of shrimp out of her hand and throwing it in the trashcan.

Karen got up from her knees and walked to the door. She turned back to me.

"I can't stand your ass!" Karen yelled.

Quickly I walked over to her. "And guess what's great about that Karen; I don't give a fuck! And one more thing, what I choose to take off Ahmaun is my business, and as you saw tonight, bitch, I get mine," I said dangling the Benz key in her face. "And the next time you see the side-chick with the Gucci suit, let her know that his main girl has twelve of them!"

"Bye Remi!" she said, walking out the bathroom door and Kane followed behind her. I walked over to the sink to wash my hands and looked over at Remi.

"Remi, what was up with that?"

"What do you mean?" Remi asked.

"You know exactly what I mean. I know you and Karen are cool, but I was supposed to be your girl. And I can't believe you stood there and allowed her to speak bad about me. As soon as she came out her mouth wrong about me you were supposed to have checked her ass!"

"Sollie, I was about to . . ."

"Remi, for real, don't even go there, but it's cool, I now know where your loyalty for me stands." I walked away and left her standing there.

I had heard before that Ahmaun was seeing some chic that lived in Atlanta. I was upset, but I was not going to let that ruin my night, however, I was still in disbelief about Miss. Remi. And I was feeling some kind of way about it. I wondered could Tyra have been right.

"This song is going out to the owner of the silver Benz !" The DJ yelled into the mic. Everyone cheered and I headed back over to the dance floor and whined my body to favorite song, while Ahmaun watched from the side with that I'm-going-to-tear-that-ass-up look on his face. He then walked over and stood in front of me, two-stepping, 'cause he sure couldn't dance. I slightly pushed him away.

"Ah shit, what's wrong now?"

"Nothing Ahmaun, I'm fine."

"Shorty, I know you, which one of your girlfriends been running their mouths again? Those bitches hatin that's all!"

"Ahmaun, who is this person you are seeing that lives in Atlanta?" This is the second time I have heard this and I'm sick of it. And you had her up last week, is that why you go there so often? *My mind quickly shifted back to leaving his ass.*

Ahmaun got closer to my face.

I looked around to see if anyone noticed us, and yes, my brother Salique was on his way over to us and Duce was right behind him.

"You okay?" Salique asked, with his eyes pinned on Ahmaun.

I assured Salique and Duce that I was okay, and they both hesitantly walked away. As Mea danced by us, Ahmaun said to her, "Hi hater!" Because of the loud music, Mea didn't hear him. She would have definitely responded if she had.

"Ahmaun, you're out of order!"

"Yeah, and you're out of touch! Keep thinking those bitches are your friends."

"And just what is that supposed to mean? You know what . . . forget it. I'm going to get another drink, move!" I said pushing him out of my way. "We'll talk about this later."

I went over to the bar and ordered another Sex on the Beach, which I really didn't need; my head was starting to spin. Oh Lord, I said to myself looking over and noticing Duce heading in my direction. I threw my hands in the air. "Duce, please, not now!"

"Sollie, I ain't said shit yet!"

"Yeah, but I know its coming."

"All right, I'm going to leave that alone, but that nigga is going to make me fuck him up for real. And look at this pussy-eating motherfucker coming in here all late and shit," he said, looking over at the entrance of the club watching Jodi as she came inside.

"Duce, don't start it!" I tried not to laugh at him.

"I don't know why you even deal with the little man."

"Because we have all been friends since we were kids. And that's my girl, that's why! Check this out, Duce. What Jodi does is her business. Just because she's gay doesn't mean anything to me. She's a good person and a good friend, and that's what I judge a person on the content of their character, and not their sexual preference."

"Yeah whatever Martin Luther King." Duce walked away, but not before giving Jodi his middle finger. I laughed as she gave hers right back to him.

Jodi is a pretty girl, long beautiful locks, shape-up stayed fresh, dressed her ass off, and the women loved her. But there is so much sadness in her spirit, I first noticed it when we were younger, one day Jodi came outside to play and she was no longer the happy person that she once was; I often wonder what changed her. Most of her family has turned their back on her since she's come out the closet. And for some reason she hates her mother, and I really didn't believe it was because her mother didn't accept her lifestyle; the hatred she had for her mother came long before Jodi came out.

"Hi Jodi. Why are you so late? You missed my birthday present from Ahmaun."

"I knew you were getting it a few weeks ago."

"How?" I asked.

"Mea, who else! Anyway, I saw it out front. It's hot," Jodi said looking and sounding depressed. "Yo, Duce bitch-ass gets on my nerve," she admitted, watching Duce as he walked across the floor. "Anyway, sorry I'm so late," she said turning back to me and handing me a card. "Man, I have been arguing with that girl all night," she said taking the rubber band from her wrist and pulling her locks into a ponytail. "All that bitch wanna do is fight, fuss, and fuck. And why she gotta always be accusing me of seeing other bitches?"

I could barely hear Jodi because of the loud music, but from the scratch on her forehead, I guessed she and LeLe must have been fighting again.

"Jodi, why don't you go and get something to eat before the caterers start putting the food away, we can talk later."

"Yeah, I think I will. Do me a favor. Order me a bottle of Ciroc." Jodi said, walking away.

"Jodi!" I yelled over the loud music. "Did you say a bottle?"

"Yeah, I did!" she yelled back.

Oh, she's going through it for real! I thought ordering Jodi's bottle of Ciroc as she requested, and had sent over to her. The party was almost over, and I was feeling those drinks. The caterers had begun to clean up and most of my guests were leaving. Remi and B. came up to me; B. kissed me goodnight. Remi stood there looking at me with a sad face as if she had lost her friend, and maybe she did.

"Sollie, my brother said to tell you he can't wait to meet you," B. said smiling.

"I can't wait to meet him either, B. If he's anything like you, I know I'm going to love him."

My two favorite people, Tyra and Terry, were leaving.

"Did you two enjoy yourselves?"

"Yes, we did," they both responded. "We needed this night out badly," Tyra said, as she bent over and whispered that she wanted to talk with me.

"Okay, Tyra," I said. I knew just what it was about—me leaving Ahmaun. "Did you see your girl Jodi?" I asked.

"Whatever! I talked with her for a minute. Her and LeLe has been fighting again."

"Yeah,. Did you see the scratch on her forehead? Look at her she looks so sad." We both looked over at Jodi sitting there eating her food.

"It's ridiculous! Somebody is going to get hurt."

"I hope not."

"Love you," Tyra said, kissing me good-bye.

"Love you too. Kiss the kids for me, and don't forget I'm taking you shopping for your birthday."

"Love you, Sollie soul," Terry said, affectionately kissing me good-bye.

I said goodnight to all of my guests as they were leaving. Wow, what a night, I thought sitting at the bar while waiting for Ahmaun to finish carrying my gifts to the car. However, I did manage to carry my cards, and I couldn't wait to hit the malls in the morning. Yes!

Whooo, I thought, getting up from the bar stool and realizing I had definitely had too many drinks. Ahmaun walked over and gave each of the five barmaids a one-hundred-dollar tip, took me by my hand, and we headed out to the car. I said to him, "I hope Dino isn't driving around joy riding in my new car." He held the door open for me to get inside.

"Dino don't play with me when it comes to my shit! That nigga knows what's up. If you wasn't so fucked up, you could have driven yourself."

As soon as we turned the corner of my street, there it was—my brand-new Benz parked in front of the house.

"Look at that nosy motherfucker," he said.

"Who?" I asked, looking around as I opened the car door.

"That lady next door," he said getting out of the car.

"Who, Mrs. Johnson?"

"Yeah, I guess that's her name." And then I watched him put his middle finger up to her.

"Ahmaun! I know you didn't just do that!" I said as he attempted to help my drunken ass out the car. When I looked over to Mrs. Johnson's house, she quickly pulled the curtains closed. "Ahmaun, don't you ever do that again!" I snapped. "I'm not crazy about her either, but I wouldn't dare disrespect her. Your ass is going straight to hell!"

"I'm already here, Shorty, I'm already here!" He mugged.

"Why do you talk like that?" I asked frowning, because his attitude was the worst.

"Sollie, just come on!" he said, as he opened the front door.

"Don't rush me. I'm coming, and I'm in no condition for birthday sex, so don't even think about it!" He helped me over to the couch and then retrieved the rest of my gifts from the car.

"Sollie, come on, Shorty," he begged as he was bringing in the last of my gifts.

"Sorry, me speak no English," I laughed, as I stumbled my way up the stairs and into my bedroom.

"That's fucked up. You think everything is a fuckin joke. Five minutes, Sollie, I promise!" He said following me up the steps.

"Baby, I'll be asleep in two."

Once in the bedroom, I flopped down on the bed and asked Ahmaun to take my stilettoes off. He did although pissed because he couldn't get a quickie. I stood up and began coming out of my clothes, and he watched as they dropped to floor.

"Shorty, please! Come on," he whined, watching me stand in the middle of the floor wearing only my black lace panty and bra set, while the one karat diamond stomach ring he bought me accessorized my stomach.

"Goodnight," I said, climbing into the king-size bed and pulling the covers up over my head. I pulled them back just enough to see what he was doing, and he was still standing there, holding the imprint of his big dick, looking like a sad puppy. God, men act like babies when they can't get any ass. I laughed again which really pissed him off even more. All I could do was think about my head that had begun to spin out of control once it hit the pillow.

Chapter Two

Oh my god, my head is killing me, I moaned the next morning, reaching for the pillow and placing it over my face trying to block the irritating sunlight that made its way through the curtains. I attempted to get out of the bed. I sat up hoping that my stomach would stop turning, but it didn't, and the taste of those Sex on the Beaches lingered in my mouth, which made me remember just how many I drank and I felt even worse. My head was still spinning, and every time I tried to open my eyes all the way my head pounded even more. *Here it comes,* I thought grabbing my stomach. I snatched the pillow from my face, jumped out the bed, and quickly stumbled my half necked hung-over ass into the bathroom, just making it. I leaned over the toilet and threw up all seven of those drinks!

God, please stop the room from spinning, I whined, I promise I will never drink again. I slowly got up off my knees and turned to look at myself in the mirror. My beautiful roller rap was now looking like a mo-hawk, and my eyes were bloodshot red. I reached over and grabbed my toothbrush. After brushing my teeth three times, I still had the horrible taste of those drinks in my mouth. I washed my face with cold water hoping that it would make me feel a little better. But it didn't.

When I returned to the bedroom, I noticed that Ahmaun wasn't there; I didn't even know when the sneaky bastard left. Did he even stay here last night? "Ahmaun!" I yelled down the steps to see if he was here, and the loudness of my own voice irritated my head even more. As I went back into the bedroom, I noticed he had left several crisp hundred dollars on my dresser, I began to count them. I counted out fifty one-hundred-dollar bills. As much as I love money, the way I was feeling, I wasn't impressed; all I could do was climb back in the bed. I lay there with my eyes shut and my arm stretched across my forehead praying for the pain to ease. I wanted to hit the malls later, but the way I was feeling I wasn't going anywhere anytime soon. I reached over and retrieved my cell from my purse to see if he had called. He hadn't. I dialed his cell, and of course, there was no answer. I decided to call his mother's house. I dialed her number. Ahmaun's mother said he was not there, although I didn't believe her, and I was certain he wasn't alone. If my head didn't feel like it did, I would drive my ass right over there and find out for myself. But I didn't need confirmation; my intuition had already given it to me. Why do I stay with him?

I looked around my room, at the Italian bedroom set he bought me, the walk-in closet full of high-price clothes, shoes, pocketbooks. I looked over at the mahogany jewelry box that sat on my vanity with very expensive jewelry inside, the money, and now the Benz. I laid my head back on the pillow. *That's why.* I thought. I then made another promise to God that I would never, ever drink again.

I eventually dozed off, and then it started: everyone began calling about the car. But the call that irritated me the most was the one from Tyra. I loved Tyra, but she was really getting on my last nerve.

"Sollie, I know you're not keeping that car. And I hope you have not changed your mind about leaving him."

"Tyra, he'll change!" And just as I said that, although knowing I didn't believe it myself, the other line beeped. Thank God for two-ways. "Tyra, hold on. I have to get the other line."

"Hello."

"Sollie!" Jodi yelled, making my head hurt worse than it already was.

"Jodi, please stop yelling!"

"Yo! The bitch just stabbed me!"

"Who just stabbed you?" I asked quickly sitting up in the bed.

23

"LeLe!"

"Where are you?"

"I'm on my way to St. Agnes."

"Okay, I'll be there."

I clicked back over to Tyra and told her what just happened. She said that she would meet me at the hospital. I hung up thinking that this was not what I had planned for today. I jumped out of bed and walked into the closet and grabbed a pair of jeans and a T-shirt, took a two-minute shower, threw my hair and a quick ponytail, and headed out the door.

Mrs. Johnson was in her yard picking flowers from her rose garden. I wanted to apologize for Ahmaun's disrespectful ass, but I knew if I started a conversation I would never get to the hospital. I said good morning, jumped in my car, and left.

For a Sunday morning, the traffic was heavy, and it seemed as if I was never going to get there, catching every light as it turned red. I waited nervously tapping the steering wheel, and praying that Jodi was okay.

Finally! I thought, pulling into the ER's parking lot. I walked inside the ER and waited in the information line, wishing that the little girl standing behind me with her mother would shut the hell up with that irritating whining.

"Hi, I need to get some information on Jodi Reed," I said to the registration clerk. God! Could she type any slower? Everything was getting on my nerve. I raked my hands across my hair feeling very insecure, knowing full well I had no business out in public looking like this.

"Ms. Reed is in triage; let me check to see if it's okay for you to go back."

While she checked, I walked over to the vending machine and bought a ginger ale in hopes that it would settle my upset stomach.

"Sollie, Sollie!"

Please, don't be, please! I heard a voice that I hadn't heard in eleven years—that prissy ass, Jennifer Thompson. I hadn't seen her since high school, and of all days, she had to see me looking like this.

24

I slowly turned around trying not to give her a full view of my face. As close as she came to me, I thought she was going to kiss me.

"Girl, how have you been?" she asked excitedly.

"Hi, Jennifer," I said slowly lifting my head up.

"Girl, you look a damn mess! Are you okay?"

I could have dropped dead right there. Why is it that you always see people you shouldn't when you're not looking your best? She was steadily running her big mouth, talking about absolutely nothing. I noticed the registration clerk trying to get my attention. I quickly told her I had to go, and headed back over to the patient information desk.

"Sollie, wait. Take my number!" she yelled.

I kept walking as if I didn't hear her. I didn't deal with her in school, and I sure as hell wasn't about to start. My circle of friends was small, and she was definitely a square, which meant she didn't fit.

"It's fine. I checked with the nurse. You can go back. I'll buzz you in."

Just as I was going back, I noticed Tyra frantically walking through the emergency room doors.

I smiled, because although Jodi and Tyra did not get along, she was clearly worried.

When we walked into Jodi's room, she was lying back on the bed with her arm all bandaged up, looking like she was half asleep. She slowly lifted up and looked over at Tyra. By the look on her face, she was not happy to see her.

Tyra and Jodi have a love-hate relationship. When Jodi came out of the closet, Tyra hated it.

"What happened?" I asked.

"Yo, last night, after your party, I went home and the bitch started talking about how she knows I was at the party with someone, and started accusing me of cheating again," she stopped said looked over at Tyra to see what her reaction was to what she was saying.

"So me being tired of hearing that bullshit." she continued. "I began to pack my shit! She started crying and saying she was sorry, so I unpacked my clothes. We did what we do, and went to sleep. We woke up this morning, and she started that shit all over again! So, once again, packed my shit, and this time I was rolling out for real. The bitch started really trippin, and as I was leaving out the front door, she ran into the kitchen, grabbed a knife, ran back, and stabbed me. I didn't know it was this deep until I got into the car, and that's when I called you." She looked at Tyra again waiting for her to say something, so she could cuss her out. I knew Jodi like a book.

"What are the doctors saying?" I asked, leaning over and taking a tissue from the box, and wiping the sweat off Jodi's forehead.

"They saying I might need close to twenty stitches," she said sadly, resting her head back on the pillow.

"Ah, Jodi, that's ridiculous."

"Yes, it is," Tyra co-signed, standing there with her arms folded, mouth twisted, and shaking her head.

"Tyra, what the fuck . . ."

The doctor knocked on the door just in time, interrupting Jodi from cursing at Tyra. Following behind him was a tall, slim, freckle-faced police officer.

"Excuse me, Ms. Reed. I need to speak with you for a moment, privately," he said, looking over at Tyra and me.

"Nah, nah," Jodi said. "They ain't gotta go nowhere." She cut her eyes over at Tyra.

"Okay, fine," said the small-built Korean doctor. "This is Officer Myers," he said pointing to the officer who was standing there holding a pen and pad ready to take notes. "He needs to ask you a few questions concerning your injury."

"Come on, what that bullshit, doc. You know how I got it."

"Ms. Reed, this is why the officer needs to speak with you."

The officer cleared his throat "Ah, Ms. Reed," the officer said walking over to the bedside. "You're obviously aware of who assaulted you. Would you like to tell me what happened?"

"No, I would not like to tell you anything, and besides, I didn't call for no police anyway!" Jodi snapped, gritting on the officer. "I don't fuck with y'all!"

"Ms. Reed, its hospital policy for us to notify proper authorities when victims of assault…"

Jodi angrily glared at the officer.

"Here she goes," I whispered to Tyra.

"Nah, fuck that," she said, "and fuck hospital policies. Only thing this hospital needs to be concerned with is that I have insurance to cover this visit, which I do!" Jodi said angrily, trying to sit up. "And I know my rights, and I don't have to say shit! So, officer, you can go back and finish freeloading off McDonald's, and doc, you can stitch my arm up so I can get the fuck outta here!" She yelled angrily.

The doctor's eyes widened, appalled at Jodi's language. The officer reached into his pocket slightly shaking his head and attempted to hand Jodi a card, which she refused to take.

"Officer, I'll take it," I said reaching for the card.

"Thank you ma'am. Please have her call if she changes her mind," said the officer. As the doctor and the officer were leaving the room the doctor turned back and said "Ms. Reed we are just trying to help you"

"Ah, whatever. Jodi said waving her hand in the air. You wanna help me, bring Nicki Minaj up in this mother fucker, do dat!"

"I can't believe she said just said that," I whispered to Tyra.

"I can!" Tyra said looking at Jodi, once again shaking her head. As soon as the doctor and the officer left out the room, Tyra asked Jodi, "Was she crazy?"

"Nah, why you ask dat?" Jodi mugged.

"You need to have her arrested for stabbing you. That's why I asked that," Tyra said, while emphasizing the word "that," trying to teach Jodi proper English.

Jodi sat up again.

"Fuck you, I aint no rat, I don't care what she did. And for real you need to mind your business. And just like the police, I didn't ask you to come either. So you can get the fuck out too."

"You know what, you're right. Sollie, I'll call you later!" Tyra got up, grabbed her purse, and left

"Jodi, you need to calm down. Tyra is just concerned."

"No, she's not! Why would I get that girl locked up, I don't get down like that? Tyra is full of shit, always acting like she's better than everybody, 'cause her husband is a lawyer, and they got a few coins! We never got along anyway, and ever since I came out, she's really been throwing shade! And you know it Sollie—her, my mother, brother, and sister, and I'm sick of this shit! I'm sick of everybody," she said, picking up her cup of chipped ice and throwing it up against the wall.

I watched as Jodi's eyes welled up with tears. She tried with everything she had in her not to let one teardrop fall. I pulled my chair closer to her bedside and reached for her hand.

"First of all, Tyra doesn't think she is better than anybody, and you know it. Yeah, you two have had your differences, and that's okay. Friends go through that. If she didn't care, do you think she would have been here? Now, true she has been throwing shade since you came out, but like I told her, this is your life. And until what you are doing affect's Tyra, your lifestyle is none of her business. But I will say this—Tyra loves you, Jodi, and her love for you is much stronger than her hatred for your chosen lifestyle. Unfortunately, she just doesn't know it. And stop trying to fight back your tears. Guess what Jodi, you can bop, wear your men's clothing an even act like a man, but it doesn't change who you are internally, and by nature, most women are emotional, and it's okay, look at you, your trying so hard to holed back your tears the veins in your neck are bulging, and I guarantee if you keep trying to cover up and keep what you're feeling inside, you're going to explode!" I gripped her hand tighter and told her that it's okay to cry.

And just as I finished that statement, she did just that, uncontrollably. I leaned over and hugged her tightly, and she hugged me even tighter, and the way she was bawling I was convinced that it was a whole lot more going on with my friend emotionally. But now wasn't the time to ask. I was just glad she was getting some of that pain out.

"Listen, Jodi, I'm not going to tell you what to do about this situation. I don't like it, but this is your decision. But I do know that whether you are with a male or female, it needs to be a healthy relationship." *Listening to myself,* I thought *I should take my own*

advice because there wasn't a thing healthy about my relationship
with Ahmaun. I had no room to give advice to anyone.

Jodi wiped the tears from her eyes, once again looking like the lost little girl that I often see in her. After getting her armed stitched, we left the hospital. I made sure all of her prescriptions were filled, and I was able to talk her into staying with her aunt for a few days, just until things calmed down between her and LeLe. She agreed. I took her car keys and told her that I would ask Duce to pick her car up later. Since she's hurt he may do it. Truth be told Duce really did love Jodi.

Driving to her aunt's, Jodi began crying again. I reached over for her hand and told her everything would be okay. When I pulled up to the house, I turned off the car, and we just sat and talked for about thirty minutes. I thought now would be a better time than ever to ask why she hated her mother so much.

She stared at me strangely, and then asked me where that question came from.

I told her I was just curious, and she said she didn't want to talk about it. I didn't pressure her; I just said okay. She gathered all of her prescriptions and proceeded to get out of the car.

"Thanks, Sollie. You and my aunt are the only ones who have accepted my lifestyle."

"Jodi, it's going to be a whole lot of people that may never accept you being gay, but you can't worry about that. Life is too short to worry about what others think! Jodi remember this. Those who judge don't matter, and those who matter don't judge!

Chapter Three

R ight before pulling off I checked my cell to see if Ahmaun had called. Where the hell is he?! I dialed his number and still no answer. *Oh well, I guess I'll go home and get ready to start this new job tomorrow,* I thought, pulling off.

When I arrived home, I went straight upstairs into the bathroom, took a long hot bath, and tried not to think about Ahmaun. After my bath, I slipped on something comfortable, gathered all my gifts and cards, and sat in the middle of the bed and began to open them. The first gift I reached for, I immediately thought this had to be a joke: who would give me a cheap plastic-ass purse? The card had fallen to the bottom of the gift bag. I reached down and pulled out the card and read it. "Happy Birthday Auntie Sollie" and the words written in crayon, we Love You! Terry Jr. and Trinity, Tyra kids, who I'm proud to say, are my godchildren. I felt terrible thinking badly about their gift. There was an arrow at the bottom of the card, instructing me to turn the card over. Ha, ha, the kids picked this out with their own money! I immediately called and thanked them.

After talking with Tyra and the kids, I got back to opening the rest of my gifts; they were all really nice. Reaching down inside the last gift bag, I pulled out a black doll wearing an all-white suit, holding on to a gold clutch, and wearing a pair of gold stilettos, almost as if someone was mimicking me, because that's exactly what I wore last night. The gift would have really been cute, and I may have even sat the doll on my vanity, but the weirdest thing was that the doll's head was missing. I immediately thought about Karen's ass. Who else would give me something like that? I picked up the gift bag and looked on the card dangling from the handle, and the nausea that I felt earlier quickly returned as I read what was written. Hope This Is Your Last, Bitch! I reached for the headless doll and placed her back inside the gift bag, trying to shake the eerie feeling that came over me. I gathered all my gifts and put them away thinking that Karen had taken her dislike for me, a little too far. But wait, I remember when Karen came into the club the only thing she was carrying was her knock-off Loui. And how were they able to dress the doll like me? The only one who knew what I was wearing was Ahmaun.

I called Ahmaun again and still got no answer. Out of frustration, I tossed the phone across the bed and began thinking about my new job. I wasn't ready to start, but I was twenty-nine, and it's time to stop playing and start getting serious about my future.

I made my way down to the kitchen, tossing the gift bag with the headless doll into the trash. I began searching the cabinet shelves for a can of soup, because that's all my stomach would allow me to eat.

Opening the can of chicken noodle soup, I thought about how I would much rather have my mother's homemade soup, but this would have to do. I sat at the black-and-white marbled breakfast bar, and watched the five o'clock news. I already feel bad—don't want to start this job tomorrow, can't find my lying, cheating, no good-ass boyfriend, and to top it off the weather man is talking about a hurricane that's coming through Maryland.

I called to check on Jodi, and her aunt said that she was back at LeLe's place.

Now in the living room I stared out the bay window. Suddenly the wind began blowing with such force, and just that quickly, the storm began. "Oh well, I guess I'll go to bed."

I laid in bed and watched the episodes of Insecure that I had missed. I fell asleep around nine and before I knew it the alarm clock was going off. I pressed the alarm button, and immediately reached for my cell and saw that he still hadn't called. I reached over and grabbed the cordless phone off the base looking at the caller ID to see if he called the house phone; I even checked to see if the ringer was on. *Sollie focus on your new job. That's right, my new job!* I thought.

I began thinking about the interview, and how impressed Mr. Melbourne was with my résumé. I chuckled, remembering how I told that man everything I knew he wanted to hear. I'm detailed oriented, team player, a very hard worker and can multitask, I said to him, knowing the only thing I could do at the same time was shop, and talk on the cell. And then he asked about "attendance" and I answered just the way he wanted me to. With my past jobs, I would call out in a New York minute, but not anymore, remembering how becoming responsible was on my list of to dos.

It's not that I didn't want to work, even though between Ahmaun and my mother, I didn't have to. But I knew that in order for me to accomplish what I have dreamed of since I could remember, I needed to work to obtain it. I could have it right now if it was up to my mother, but this was something I had to do on my own.

Anyway, after the interview, I was offered the position. I accepted. Now Monday is here already! As I attempted to get out of bed, the house phone rang. *"Who the hell is calling at six in the morning?"* Probably my mother making sure I'm up, I thought reaching for the phone and looking at the caller ID. American Enterprises. What do they want? I'm not due at work until eight.

"Hello," I answered curiously.

"Good morning, I'm trying to reach Ms. Carr."

"This is she."

"Hi, Ms. Carr, this is George Melbourne calling from American Enterprises."

"Hi, Mr. Melbourne, how are you? And please call me Sollie."

"I'm fine. Thanks for asking, and by the way please call me George."

Okay, now what the hell do you want?! I wanted to ask. But I needed to remain as professional as I was during the interview.

32

"Sollie, the storm that passed through last night caused an electrical outage in the building and surrounding area, and the electrical company says it may be a few days before it can be restored."

Yes! Say it ain't so, say it ain't so, Joe! I wanted to yell right into the phone. But I held my composure.

"So to play it safe," he continued, "and to make sure that all systems are running effectively, unfortunately, I'm going to have to push your start date back a week. And I truly apologize for any inconvenience this may have caused. So hopefully I will see you next Monday at eight."

I can't believe what I just heard. It's a miracle!

"George, I was really looking forward to starting today, but I guess we have no control over nature. And yes, you will see me on Monday."

"Great! I'll see you then."

I love it! I yelled jumping out of bed grabbing my purse to recount my money. A whole week! I can't believe it, I said, flopping back down on the bed. My paper was stacked and I knew exactly where I was headed. Who is this? I said looking at the caller ID it was my mother.

"Helloooo," I sang.

"Well, well, glad to hear you're up and cheerfully ready to start your job. That's a very positive attitude."

"Actually, Mother, a miracle just occurred," I said, laughing and explaining the whole story to her.

"Sollie, you're a mess! Oh well, so what are you going to do today?"

"What else? Why, do you want to take me?"

"Sollie Carr, I just took you shopping for your birthday and spent almost three thousand dollars. You are ruined, but there is no one to blame but myself," my mother admitted. "Why don't you take your birthday money and put it in the bank and begin saving for your restaurant, that you don't want my help with, although I must say, I respect that."

Dawn Barber

"Ah, did you say something?" I asked, acting as if I didn't hear a word she just said.

"Sollie, listen. I have a few errands to run, and I will call you when I'm done. We may go out, but I'm not promising you. Love you, and I'll talk to you later."

My mother is not rich, but she is well off. She's a retired school principal, and just bought a beautiful five-bedroom colonial home in Randallstown, Maryland, and left me this one. I'm supposed to pay water, electric, and yearly taxes, but I don't. Between her and Ahmaun, it gets paid.

I decide to call, you know who, again, and still didn't get an answer. I left a message. "Ahmaun, were the hell are you? It's been almost two days! Call me!"

I took a shower and put on my very comfortable boy shorts and a wife beater and literally dived back into the bed, curled up under the sheets, and listened as the rain hit up against the window. I couldn't help but think that this was the weather for making love, eating, and staying in bed all day. Ohhh! I wanted to scream! Where the hell was he? I said grabbing the pillow, folding it, and placing it between my legs. I was so horny! And I hated the visions that had begun in my mind of him being with another female.

I lay there tossing and turning for about an hour and decided to get up and go fix breakfast. Down in the kitchen, I decided to have steak and eggs. And guess who should walk through the door as if nothing was wrong? I looked over at him angrily. "Where the hell have you been for a day and a half?"

"Shorty, I'm sorry. I had to take care of some business out of town," he said walking up behind me and grabbing my ass. "I see you got on my favorites. I missed you," he said kissing me on the back of my neck.

"You could have at least called and told me. Why do you do that? Where did you go to Atlanta to see your side-chic?"

"Shorty, don't start that shit. I had to take care of business. I'm sorry. You forgive me?" he asked turning me around to face him, and then began gliding his tongue down my neck, making his way to my breast.

"Move, Ahmaun!" I said pushing him, knowing I really didn't want him to because I was horny as hell. "I'm trying to cook my breakfast."

Shaking my head, I took a deep breath. "Are you hungry?"

"Yeah, I am," he said grinding that big- dick against my ass.

"Ahmaun stop! Let me finish cooking."

"Come on, Shorty, you owe me from the other night."

I laughed, remembering how angry he was the night of my party, although I was quite certain he had already released his anger. I turned and faced him, and just stared at how fine he was. He had that sexy thug look, you know, like he just stepped from behind the walls of the state penitentiary. But every time I looked in his eyes, all I saw was pain. When and where it came from, I had no idea, but one thing I did know—all that pain equaled anger! An angry brother, fine! But angry brother equals one thing—a dangerous motherfucker! I had heard stories of how he slow-walked a few dudes to their death. If he wanted you gone, he could and would make it happen; it was just that simple.

"Shorty, come on, my dick hard as shit! Ahmaun pleaded. You want it, don't you?" he whispered in my ear. "You love it, right?" He said, pressing against my ass even harder.

Fuck it! I thought, can't stay mad forever. I turned off the stove. There goes breakfast, and here comes pleasure, I thought, as I quickly ran up the steps to get a condom from out the draw. Yeah that's right, a condom. On my way back into the kitchen he stood there with that look of disappointment he gets every time I got a condom. Bracing his hand around me, he backed me up pinning me against the kitchen wall. His tongue was warm, as it entered my mouth, and then he began sucking both my breasts like a mad man. The bones surrounding my pussy began to ache with pleasure in anticipation of what was about to come. With his help I wiggled my ass out of my boy shorts, placing my hands on the top of his head as he slowly moved down to taste me. Finally! I thought closing my eyes and feeling nothing but intense pleasure as he began licking, sucking, and devouring my pussy nonstop! "I love you, shorty," he said pausing for just a second.

My eyes rolled back in my head "Ahmaun, stop! You're going to make me cum," I pleaded while trying to get out of the firm grasp his hands had around my hips.

"Go ahead, cum right in my mouth."

Now face-to-face, I anxiously unbuckled his belt, unbuttoned, and unzipped his jeans. As they dropped to the floor, I slid my hand down his boxers, gently stroked his shaft, softly messaged his balls and watched as his head fell back with pleasure. "Awwww," he moaned, right before I put the condom on. "Turn around!" He ordered.

Now facing the wall, he went back down, spread my legs, and licked every part of my ass. Feeling my juices running down my inner thighs, I could no longer take anymore. After he was done, he stood up and lay his head against mine and asked, "You ready?" and began putting inch by inch inside me. And once fully inside he became my "bitch" One thing I did well was to know how to make Ahmaun feel like he was losing his mind! The walls of my pussy gripped his dick like suction! "Awwww, shorty, this pussy so motherfucking good," he whined, as I began rolling my wet ass around and around, in and out. "That's what I'm talking about!" he said as his breathing became heavier. "Shorty, why you fucking me like this? Damn." I didn't respond. I just continued riding the hell out of his dick!

"Wait a minute, greedy," he laughed trying to catch his breath. I turned around and backed him into the kitchen chair and straddled him.

"You all right?" I asked.

"Yeah, I'm good," he panted. Placing his hands on my hips I slid down on his dick, I wrapped my arms around his neck, feeling chills run through my body. Gripping his dick tighter, I slowly began riding it again. I raised my head and looked him in his eyes. "Whose pussy is this?" he asked.

"It's yours," I whispered staring into his eyes.

36

"You are the only one I'll ever love. I know I be fucking up, shorty, but I promise you're going to be my wife. Believe dat. You hear?"

"I hear you, Ahmaun," I said but I knew hearing and listening were two different concepts, 'cause I had heard it all before. He held me tighter and whispered for me to cum with him.

My head fell back; my body felt as if it was contracting and was once again feeling the pleasure that I always felt when I was with him. In unison we both came, holding each other tightly, bodies drenched in sweat, both trying to catch our breath.

"And you wonder why a nigga ain't never letting you go? You're mine for life. I love you, nigga."

I rested my face against his "I love you too, Ahmaun. God help me, but I do. And stop calling me nigga, nigga."

Chapter Four

W e took a shower, and I finished cooking breakfast. As we were eating, I asked Ahmaun was he putting the car in my name.

"Nah." he mugged, "That ain't happening!"

"Why!" I snapped almost choking on my juice.

"Sollie I'm not putting shit in your name!"

"You know what, Ahmaun," I said jumping up and throwing my unfinished breakfast in the trash, "Forget that car! You bought it for me, but just so you can be in control you want it to stay in your name. You drive it! I'll continue to drive my BMW."

What is he thinking? I wondered, as he sat there quietly staring at me.

He shook his head "All right, Sollie! You're right. I bought it for you. Fuck it. I'll put it in your name, but the first time I hear or see a ni. . ."

I quickly cut him off. "I would never disrespect you and have another man in that car. When are you going to start trusting me? And just for the record, Ahmaun, your distrust has nothing to do with me, and has everything to do with yourself, because of what you're doing out there. So try that bullshit on one of your other bitches, not me."

"Sollie, I said okay! And why aren't you at work anyway? Weren't you supposed to start a new job today? What you do, quit before you started again?" He teased, laughing.

"Whatever, they pushed my start date to next week."

"You know I got you. You ain't gotta work nowhere, for real!"

Although it was good to hear, and I had taken him up on that offer many, many times, for some reason that offer didn't seem as appealing to me as it once did. I was really ready to try this independent thing.

After getting dressed, we finally left the house. The rain had stopped and the sun was shining. I looked over in Mrs. Johnson's front yard and the roses from her rose garden were scattered all over her front, obviously from the storm last night.

Ahmaun followed me to my mother's house, and I'm so glad she wasn't at home. I hadn't told her yet about my birthday present from Ahmaun. I parked my BMW in her garage and we left. We then drove over to the insurance company and then we headed to the DMV.

"Oh my God" I said walking through the DMV doors, and looking at the long lines.

"I told you we should have gone to the Motor Vehicle in Glen Bernie!"

"Just come on! I got this," Ahmaun said, reaching for his cell and dialing a number. "A friend of mine works here. She'll push this transaction right through," he said walking away.

Within five minutes a beautiful woman came walking over in our direction, and with her looking at me side-ways immediately told me what was up! Ahmaun rushed ahead of me and said something to her. She said hello to me and directed us to her office with a fractious smile on her face. Once inside, we all sat down and I watched as she nervously typed the information into her computer system. She couldn't seem to keep her eyes focused on the matter at hand; instead they were focused on me. And I politely asked her if there was a problem. And of course she replied, "No."

"Sollie!" Ahmaun snapped.

"What?!" I snapped back. The woman cleared her throat, picked up her cup of coffee, took a sip, and said that she was just admiring my outfit, which she probably was; but that was bullshit. The truth was he was sleeping with her too. See what these women need to realize is that Ahmaun doesn't care anything about them. All that nigga trying to do is, go! As she went to hand him the registration, I pushed his hand aside and said, "I'll take that!" I took the papers out of her hand. I had just become the proud new owner of a Benz! And besides, what Ahmaun was doing was starting not to even affect me anymore. And that quickly I decide that until I leave his ass, I was going to get all I could. I got up and walked out the door, and he quickly followed behind me, not before telling the broad "good looking out!"

"Didn't I tell you Shorty, we wouldn't be in here long?" he said putting his arm around me as we left out the DMV.

Whatever! I thought.

"Ahmaun, I need some money," I said, as we walked to the car. And he looked at me as if I was crazy.

"Money for what Sollie? I left you five stacks the other night. You spent it already?"

"Yeah, I did," I lied.

"Shorty, check this out. You know I don't have a problem giving you money, but you spend that shit entirely too fast. All your little-ass want to do is stay in the mall, and you don't need shit." He reached into his pocket, counted out two stacks, and handed it to me. As we drove up Edmonson avenue, as usual Karen's raggedy ass was standing on the corner begging for money, she's lucky I didn't tell Ahmaun how she was running her mouth the night of my party; there is no telling what he would have done to her, or should I say have someone else do it. He always has someone else to do his dirty work.

As we pulled up to my house, poor Mrs. Johnson was out front trying to salvage what was left of her rose garden.

"Hi, Mrs. Johnson," I said, getting out the car.

"Hi, Sollie, that's a beautiful car," she exclaimed, cutting her eyes over at Ahmaun, afraid to look at him directly.

"Did you speak to Mrs. Johnson, Ahmaun?" I asked as he rushed by me, opened the door, and went into the house.

"Fuck her!"

"Why are you so nasty and rude?" He didn't answer, he walked into the kitchen and grabbed a bottle of water out the refrigerator.

Ahmaun leaned over and kissed me, and said he would be back later. It didn't matter because I wasn't going to be here when he returned, I thought as I reached for my cell, thinking it was probably my mother calling. But no, it was Aunt Bessie calling to see if I could pick up her medication. I told her yes.

I drove over to Wal-Mart. After getting the prescription, I was on my way to Aunt Bessie and decided to stop at Lexington market and buy her some hog maws and chitterlings, which was one of her favorite foods. Aunt Bessie was eighty-four years old. She used to be very independent but having knee-replacement surgery has slowed her down a bit. So I always try to help out as much as I could.

As I turned into Aunt Bessie's block, it was live as usual; each corner always seemed to have some type of activity going on. One corner, a sharply dressed Muslim brother walked back and forth with a bean pie in one hand and the Final Call in the other. Across the street a minister preached the word of God loudly into his mic. The other corner a cop sat inside of his patrol car, but I really wasn't sure how much patrolling he was doing, 'cause on the other corner were the hustlers, doing what they do. Aunt Bessie neighbors sat on their front eating crabs and drinking beer. And as I parked they all stared.

"That's a bad ride, miss!" the lady said as I got out the car.

"That's my car! And my mother!" a little girl declared dropping her jump rope and stared as if I was their idol.

"No, it's not!" the other little girl snapped, placing her hand on her tiny hips. "That's my car, and my mother!" She rocked her head back and forth, while pointing her finger in the other little girl's face. I smiled because when Tyra and I were young we would say and do the exact same thing.

I called Aunt Bessie and told her that I was out front. I stood patiently waiting on her steps, knowing it takes her a little longer to get to the door.

"Hi Aunt Bessie."

"Hi baby, thanks for getting my medicine for me. I was going to call the sedan, but these knees are aching something terrible today," she said kissing me and slowly walking into the kitchen. I followed her. Aunt Bessie was small built, short, bowlegged, with curly gray hair.

"Aunt Bessie, I brought you something good!" Aunt Bessie turned to me, and her eyes lit up!

"Oh, Sollie, my favorite!" she said with her eyes gleaming. "Give me a fork baby, give—me—a—fork! And hand me the hot sauce and the vinegar."

She quickly put out her cigarette, and sat the little stump inside the ashtray. She always says that cigarettes were too expensive to waste, even though she always talks about quitting. She smokes about a pack a day and drinks, and she's still hanging in there. I guess it's true what they say—you're not going anywhere until it's your time.

"Sollie, whose pretty car you driving?"

"It's mine. So Aunt Bessie, do you want me to bring you some more hog maws and...

I was trying to change the subject of the car, but it didn't work.

"Who bought you that car?" Aunt Bessie interrupted. "Your mother, didn't she? That doesn't make any sense in the world. All Marie has done since you were a little girl is spoil you. Don't make any sense in the world!" she repeated angrily.

I wanted to let her continue to believe that my mother bought the car but I went on and told her Ahmaun bought it for me.

"Sollie!" Aunt Bessie said wiping her mouth and angrily shaking her head. "I told you to leave that drug boy alone! He don't mean you any good! And your mother done told me how he still running with those other women! Sollie, listen baby, look at you. Not that looks mean everything, but you're beautiful! You could probably have any man you want and would treat you like you suppose to be treated. I know why you like him, 'cause he buys you all those expensive gifts, and now that car. Why don't you start your new job and keep it this time, and take care of yourself and stop depending on your mother and that boy. It doesn't make any sense Sollie, none at all. I know it's hard to become independent especially after having everything handed to you, but you have to learn to take care of yourself. And messing with that drug boy is going to lead you into a world of trouble. I can't stand him, with his sneaky-ass self. And keep his bigheaded ass out of here. He ain't welcome here no more. Your mother told me what he did," Aunt Bessie said, shaking her head. "Now, that's a dirty man baby, a dirty man!"

Oh my god! I thought I would die. *How could my mother tell that!*

"That don't make any sense," Aunt Bessie continued. "And I can't believe you still with him, and it ain't no hearsay. You saw it with your own eyes. Sollie, you—have—to—learn to—love—you!"

"I do—"

"Uh uh! Don't even say it," Aunt Bessie said cutting me off. "Because if you did, you wouldn't allow that boy to treat you the way he does, and you think 'cause you wear all those expensive fancy clothes and keep your hair all done up all pretty, it don't mean a thing. It's a cover up! That's right, that's what you are—a cover girl! Because I know deep down inside you're not happy with him or yourself. Yeah, everybody wants somebody and everybody wants to be happy but at what cost. All that material stuff ain't worth it. And it sure ain't love. Be by yourself," she said slamming her frail wrinkled hand on the table. "When do you start your job?"

"Next week."

"Good. And stop running to the mall every chance you get. Start saving your money. You keep talking about the restaurant you want one day. You will never get it spending unnecessarily the way you do. Baby, listen," Aunt Bessie said reaching out and gently holding my hand, "you're still young. Start now and begin building. And the way you can cook, your restaurant would be a great success. Once you get established, then you can start spending a little money. It's okay to like nice things but take care of priority first. And if the good Lord let you live to be my age you will have something to fall back on, and live comfortably. And remember when God is ready He will send you someone, a decent man, not a bum, like that dope boy," she said looking up to the ceiling. "My Kirkwood was a good man, God rest his soul. And don't start that crying!" she said noticing my eyes beginning to well up with tears.

Aunt Bessie was right. I had no business with Ahmaun. I should have stuck to my plans and left him.

"How's Tyra and her family doing?"

"They're fine."

"That's good. She's a nice girl. I always did like Tyra. I remember when she was a little girl, she would always talk about becoming a criminal lady. Too bad about that unfortunate accident, but God knows best, God knows best," she repeated with such certainty.

"Aunt Bessie, it's not a criminal lady. She wanted to become a criminologist," I said, laughing.

"Don't be funny, Sollie. You know what I meant!"

I sat with Aunt Bessie for a few hours longer, and listened as she continued to fuss with me about Ahmaun. After hearing all I could take, I told Aunt Bessie I had to go, but I would call and check on her later. As I was leaving out the front door a fine brother pushing an all-black big-body Benz slowed up and stopped in front of her door.

"What's up? Can I holla at you for a minute?" Before I could say no, Aunt Bessie said it for me.

"No, you can't!" Aunt Bessie yelled out. "She don't want no more drug boys!" I was so embarrassed; the guy looked at her like she was crazy as he drove off.

"Aunt Bessie, how do you know that guy was a drug dealer?"

"Wisdom, baby, wisdom," she said smiling, leaning over and kissing me good-bye. "Now you remember what I said, okay, puddin?" I said okay and left.

Before pulling off, I dialed Tyra number to tell her the latest, and also to see if she wanted to go to the mall.

"Tyra, why the hell did my mother tell Aunt Bessie that I caught that bastard in bed with another woman?"

"Girl, get out of here! No, she didn't," said Tyra.

"I can't believe she did that. Anyway, are you free?"

"Actually, I am. Terry just took the kids out for ice cream. Why? What's up?"

"Let's go to the mall. I want to get some things and also buy you the suit I promised."

"Sollie, you are not buying me that expensive suit!"

"Whatever, I'll be there in about thirty minutes."

I pulled off, While driving to Tyra house I thought a lot about what Aunt Bessie said and I still could not believe that my mother told her about me catching that boy in bed with another woman, I'll never hear the end of it. I just needed to get to the mall and clear my head. *Please be ready* I thought, as I turned the corner and pulled into the cul-de-sac. Thank God, Tyra was standing on her front steps waiting for me.

"I must admit you're looking really cute in this car," she said as she got inside. "But you look even better in your BMW!"

"Tyra, please don't start it. I got an earful from Aunt Bessie."

"Good!" she said handing me a school picture of the kids.

"Awwww, they look so cute. I'll buy some frames for them while we're out. Oh yea, I bought you something. Look in my pocketbook." Tyra excitedly reached in the backseat and grabbed my purse.

"This?" she asked smiling, and holding up Kendrick Lamar CD.

"Yeah, that's it. I knew you wanted it."

"Girl, I just said I was going to get it while we were out. Thank you," she said leaning over and kissing me on my cheek. Tyra immediately put the CD on. I smiled as I sat there and watched Tyra sing along word from word to her favorite cut.

Tyra was my very best friend, and has been since we were ten. I call her my little sister because I'm five days older. She's a very pretty girl, beautiful dark brown complexion, about five feet four and rocks a short natural afro. She married right out of high school. She and Terry had planned to wait until they both graduated college. Terry wanted to become a lawyer and Tyra wanted to become a criminologist, until everything changed when she was almost killed by a drunk driver. While in ICU for two months, she endured eight surgeries; no one expected her to survive, not even the doctors. And Terry stayed by her side the entire time, even putting off his dream of becoming an attorney; now you talk about love! Terry loved Tyra to death.

I remember visiting Tyra one day, and before I entered her room, I saw Terry crying as he sat by her bedside, holding her hand, asking God not to take Tyra from him. He talked to her in hopes that even in her unconscious state she would somehow hear him. I remember the loving words he said to this day. That's when I knew that's the kind of love I hoped to one day have.

.I walked into the room and placed my hands on his shoulder. He reached around and placed his hand on top of mine.

"Sollie, I can't lose her. I just can't."

"You won't lose her, Terry," I said as I stared at my best friend, praying she would make it, because like Terry, I didn't know what I would do without her either. Terry and I sat there quietly; Tyra parents came into the room. Mr. Jones walked over to Terry and patted him on his back. Mr. Jones was crazy about Terry. From the day Tyra introduced him to her parents she had their approval. But one thing has not changed; Tyra mother looked at Mr. Jones with such hatred. The same look that would send Tyra running to my house in tears when we were younger, saying that all her parents did was argue.

We all sat quietly, until we heard what we had been waiting to hear for two months—Tyra's voice.

"Hi," Tyra whispered, as she tried to open her eyes.

"Tyra! Tyra!" Terry called out to her. He softly kissed her all over her swollen face. "Mr. J., get the doctor!" he yelled

The doctor rushed in and asked us to step out while he examined her. We all went to the family waiting area, anxiously waiting for the news of Tyra's current condition. After about fifteen minutes, the doctor walked into the waiting area smiling, and told us that Tyra was going to be fine. Excitedly we all went back to her room, Terry immediately reached into his pocket and pulled out a box with a diamond engagement ring inside.

"Please, marry me." Terry proposed as he opened the small box.

Tyra softly whispered, "Yes, Terry, I'll marry you!" Mrs. Jones and I cried, while Mr. Jones stood there tapping Terry on his back, and proudly saying, "That's my boy!"

After Tyra recuperated, they were married and started a family, Terry went to law school, obtained his law degree and has recently been made partner at a very prestigious law firm.

Tyra loved being a stay-at-home mom and being able to spend time with her kids while they're in school, unfortunately both children have learning disabilities. So between going to school with the kids and volunteering at the department of social services Tyra stays really busy. Although deep down inside I think she still longed to become a criminologist.

"Sollie," Tyra said nudging me, "where is your mind at? Are we going to the mall or are we going to sit here?"

"Oh damn!" I said.

"What were you thinking? You were a million miles away," Tyra said, looking at me curiously.

I smiled and reached for her hand, and said, "How thankful I am that you're in my life."

"Awwww, that's so sweet. I feel the same way," Tyra said, snapping her fingers and rocking to the music.

I was about to jump on the highway when my cell rang.

"Yes Ahmaun!"

"Sollie where you at?" Ahmaun said, yelling into the phone.

"I'm on my way to the mall. Why?"

"I left my wallet in the car, and my driver's license is in there. I'm at your crib. Can you bring it to me?"

"Ahmaun, can't it wait?"

"Shorty, if it could wait, I would not have called you. Just bring it to me," he demanded.

"I'm on my way. Listen for the horn. God, he gets on my nerve!" I said throwing my phone on the dashboard. I quickly made a U-turn

"I'll never get to the mall! Tyra, look inside the glove compartment, and see if that bastard's wallet is in there." She reached opened the compartment and held up a black leather Armani wallet.

"Is this it?"

"Yeah, now open it!" I said, with a very serious look on my face.

"Sollie, I am not going in that boy's wallet."

"Give it here!" I reached over and snatched it from her, causing me to swerve over into the other lane of oncoming traffic.

"Give it here, wench, before you kill us both!" Tyra snatched it back from me.

"Open it, Tyra."

"Wait a second!" she yelled, as she reluctantly opened the wallet. "I don't know why you're looking through his wallet, 'cause even if you find anything you're still going to be with him. So you see, Ms. Sollie, it's really a waste of time."

"Ha, ha, real funny. I'm going to surprise you one day."

"Please do!" she said as she went through his wallet.

That no-good bastard had several business cards. And the names on each of them were names of women, all except one.

"Atlanta's Mental Treatment Center," Tyra said reading the card that was tucked away from the others. "Who does he know there?"

"I have no idea."

"And why does he stay in Atlanta so much anyway?" she asked curiously.

"Well, I know he has friends there. He was sent to live with his aunt by the juvenile courts system when he was a teenager 'cause he was bad-ass kid. It was either go stay with his aunt in Atlanta, or do time here at a juvenile detention center. His mother said after explaining to the judge that Ahmaun's behavior changed drastically when his father walked out on them the judge was sympathetic and gave him those two options. She said Ahmaun did everything he could to get back to Baltimore, even went as far as saying some guys were trying to kill him. Anyway, a few months after he was there, his Aunt was brutally murdered, so the judge allowed him to come back to Baltimore just as long as his mother sought counseling for him. But of course, she didn't. His mother says when he returned from Atlanta that his behavior became worse and that he hasn't been the same."

"I don't know, Tyra. I just want out!" I said, as I looked at all those women's business cards.

.I pulled up in front of the house and tooted the horn several times.

"I know he hears this horn! Tyra, do you want to come inside?"

"No, I'm going to call my babies, I miss them." she said, smiling.

"Ahmaun." I yelled, as I walked through the front door. "I know you heard the horn."

"My bad, Shorty," he said coming down the stairs. "You loving that car, ain't you, Shorty? Nigga's told me they saw you on Pennsylvania Avenue. Give me a kiss?"

I slightly turned my head as he leaned over and tried to kiss me, still thinking about all those business cards.

"Awwww, shit! Now what?"

"Just move!" I said, pushing him away, and laying his wallet on the entertainment center. I walked back over to front door getting ready to leave.

"Sollie! Come here," he said, grabbing me by my arm. "I asked you what was wrong. Who's in the car?" he asked pulling the blinds back, and looking. "Yeah, your other bitch-ass girlfriend . . ."

"Hold up!" I snapped, as I quickly cut him off. "I told you before you are not going to disrespect my girlfriends. And make sure this is the last time you do. If that's how you feel, keep it to yourself. And trust and believe, she's not crazy about your ass either!"

"All I'm saying is we was cool earlier. Now you got a fuckin attitude and about what I don't know."

"You know what, Ahmaun; none of this is cool anymore. I'm sick of this shit. You walk around doing whatever the fuck you want, and my simple ass continues to stay with you. I'm tired of you," I yelled. "But that's okay, 'cause being tired brings about change, and change is definitely coming." I reached for the doorknob.

"What the fuck does that mean?" he said snatching me by my arm, staring at me with that look that scares the hell out of me.

"You're hurting my arm!" I said, ready to get on the phone and call my brother. He let my arm go, and apologized.

"Shorty, just stop talking like that. I hate when you talk like that. Take this," he said reaching into his pocket, and handing me several one-hundred-dollar bills.

I took the money and left. I climbed in the car. Tyra was still on the phone with the kids. She covered the mouthpiece, and asked, "What, you got a quickie?"

Chapter Five

O nce at the mall, I swear, when I walked through the doors I felt like a kid in a candy store!

"Okay, first stop, Nordstrom!" I said, reaching into my pocketbook to retrieve my ringing cell that had been ringing entirely too much in one day. "Who the hell is this? If this is Ahmaun, I'm going to scream," I said right before I looked at the ID, and then wondered, what the hell she wanted? "Yes!" I answered hastily.

"Hi, Sollie, it's Remi. Are you busy?"

"Actually, I am. Why?"

"I was in your neighborhood, and I wanted to stop by and talk."

"Well, I'm not at home, and I won't be for a while."

"Where are you?" she asked.

"Why, Remi?" I said. Remembering what happened the night of my party I immediately became pissed all over again. "Look, I have to go," I said ending the call.

"What did she want?" Tyra asked with her lips curled.

"I don't know. Asking was I home. She said she was in the area, and she wanted to stop by and talk to me. Fuck Remi."

"Did you say, fuck Remi? Whatttttt?" Tyra exclaimed.

I told Tyra what happened the night of my party, and once again, the I-told-you-so began.

"Sollie, she's not to be trusted. It's something about her. I can't put my finger on it, but it's something about her. That's why I don't deal with her at all. I speak and keep it moving, and I know I keep saying it, but I will never understand how she got such a nice guy like B."

I heard Tyra talking, but truthfully I really wasn't paying her any mind. All I wanted to do was get inside of Nordstrom. As I walked through their doors, I thought, "finally!" as I happily walked by and smiled at the gentleman playing the piano.

"Something is really wrong with you," Tyra said, staring at me as if I was crazy.

"Tyra, you just don't understand," I said heading over to the designer collections.

"Oh yes, I do, 'cause I feel the same way when my happy ass walks into Target and Wal-Mart!"

"Whatever, wench! Come on," I said playfully pulling her by her hand.

Tyra, and I began to look through Alexander McQueen collection, and I thought Tyra was going to pass out! After looking at the price tag that was hanging off the sleeve of the suit, I chuckled, as she removed it from the rack, to get a better look at it.

"Sollie, this suit is fourteen hundred dollars!" Tyra blurted holding the price tag. "And that's the sale price! I wish I would . . ."

"Shhhhh! Wench, you're all loud!" I exclaimed looking around to see if anyone heard her loud mouth. "See if they have your size. I got you," I said as I continued looking.

"Sollie, no thank you. I do not want you buying me a suit this expensive! This is ridiculous," Tyra fussed, placing the suit back on the rack.

She followed me over to the Ralph Lauren section, and I found the perfect shirt to go with my jeans my mother bought me the other day.

"And why are you buying that shirt again? You already have one exactly like it!"

"Tyra, let me do me! For your information, I have it in black. This is white. Thank you very much!"

"I'm going to the café to get me a cup of tea. Call my cell when you're ready," she said, shaking her head as she walked away 'cause I didn't make any sense. And admit I didn't. What is wrong with me?

For four hours, I shopped, not even answering my mother call.

I did text Tyra to see where she was, she text back and said that she was doing her own shopping. By the time I reached the cash register, I had all of my friends with me: Ralph Lauren, Alexander McQueen, Becca, Armani, Chloe, BCBG . . ., Gucci, Juicy Couture, and my very best friend, Jimmy Choo! As the cashier was ringing up my selections, Tyra walked in carrying a bag with a dog on the front and a red ring around his eye. "What's that?" I asked.

She rested her hand on my shoulder. "Girllll, a slick shirt that's going to go great with my new jeans that I got from Target!" she said, emphasizing the word.

"Real funny Tyra." I turned back around and focused my attention on the prissy sales women.

"These items you chose are exquisite! There's nothing like quality clothes and shoes," she said while admiring my Burberry Metallic Leather Hobo. "And it's so nice to be able to afford them. Don't you agree?" she asked very properly, as she began folding each of my items to perfection, looking at Tyra and me smiling.

Oh no, I don't agree was the look Tyra gave the sales woman.

"Nothing for you today, ma'am?" she asked Tyra.

"No, this really is not my kind of store," Tyra responded, speaking in the same proper manner as the woman.

The woman smiled, and then looked around, and leaned closer to Tyra, like she was getting ready to tell some top-secret shit, placing her hand up to the side of her mouth, batting her eyes and whispering softly.

"I really shouldn't be saying this, but Lord & Taylor is having a fabulous sale, darling." The women giggled.

Dawn Barber

"No, darling, Lord & Taylor is not my kind of store either," Tyra said, batting her eyes, marking the woman.

"Well, what is your kind of store?" she asked curiously. "Sachs, Neimans, which one? Oh, let me guess. Barney's of New York. You look like a Barney's girl." She giggled.

"Well, actually," Tyra said leaning closer to her, "I'm a Target and Wal-Mart kind of girl," Tyra blurted loudly, proudly holding her Target bag up to the woman. The woman was appalled. "You know, my husband is an attorney, and he loves the neckties Target carries."

Tyra let the woman know she had paper. And she still shopped at Target. Tyra and me stood there dying laughing at the look on the woman face.

"Come on," I said wrapping my arm around Tyra's. As we were leaving, we turned and looked back at her. The woman rolled her eyes, making us both laugh even harder.

As we walked by Jared Jewelry store, Tyra noticed a pair of earrings in the display window that she liked, and I convinced her to let me buy them for her birthday.

"What is he staring at?" I asked walking out of Jared.

"Who?" Tyra asked, looking around.

"The guy over there at the smoothie stand, although he is really cute!"

"Girllll, that brother is gorgeous!" Tyra exaggerated.

"Come on now, he's all right!" Please don't come over here, I chanted, noticing him walking over to us. I grabbed Tyra by the arm and tried to pull her in the other direction, but that wench pulled me back. And before I knew it, we were face-to-face with him. And yeah, Tyra was right. The brother was gorgeous.

"Hello," he said smiling. He was about six feet two, well built, light brown eyes and beautiful smooth brown skin tone. And the long locks he wore were neatly pulled back into a ponytail. I figured he must have been in the medical field; he had on a white lab coat, and I noticed a pair of stethoscopes hanging out the side pocket. My eyes made their way to his shoes. *"Salvatore Ferragamo"* I thought

I leaned over just enough to read the writing on his lab coat. Alexander Morgan MD.

"I'm Alexander, and you are?" he asked, taking the napkin and wiping his full sexy lips.

"I'm Sollie, and this is my girlfriend, Tyra."

"Pleased to meet you both," he smiled extending his large masculine hands out to us. "That's a beautiful name, Sollie. Listen I don't mean to be so blunt, but are you married or involved?"

"Yes, I . . ."

Tyra quickly interrupted me, and said, "She's very much single!"

He looked at Tyra and laughed. "I like your girl already," he said reaching into his pocket. He then pulled out a business card, turned it over, and wrote something on the back. "But if you are single," he said looking at Tyra and smiling, "call me. I would like to take you to dinner." He handed me the card.

"I will," I said, knowing I was lying. Walking away, I looked back to make sure he wasn't watching and attempted to throw the card in the trash.

"Give it here, wench," Tyra said, snatching the card out of my hand, and turning the card over. "Girl he even wrote his home number on the back, oh yeah, you're calling him for sure!" Tyra said with such certainty. "Fine, a doctor, and appeared to be very interested in you."

"Well, guess what? He can get uninterested," I said snatching the card back from Tyra, and quickly ripping it up.

"Sollie!" Tyra snapped and stood there with one hand on her hip looking at me as if I was crazy. "Why did you do that? You get on my nerves. You didn't have to call him right away. You could have just hung on to it. You need to start dating other guys and stop sitting around waiting for Ahmaun to change, something he is never going to do. How do you expect to find Mr. Right when you won't leave Mr. Wrong?"

"Whatever! Come on, you hungry?" Still with that disappointed look on her face she said yes. "Good, let's go, my treat."

As we exited the mall, I stopped in front of the large fountain of water, reached into my pocketbook, pulled out a quarter, and tossed it into the water. I silently wished for the peace and happiness that I so desperately longed for. 'Cause the truth was, even with my hands filled with all these bags, I still felt terrible. This too was no longer making me as happy as it once did.

The ride over to restaurant was quiet, with the exception of Tyra humming to the music as she stared out the window.

Once inside the restaurant, we were seated. Tyra sat across from me with her elbows on the table, resting her chin on her hand, and I sat there tapping my nails on the wooden table looking right simple, because I knew my girl was upset with me. "Elbows off the table young lady!" I said marking her father. He would say that to Tyra when we were younger. I remember the first time I heard him say it. We were at the dinner table, eating, and I had a mouthful of peas, and when he said it I burst out laughing and the peas came flying out of my mouth. Tyra began laughing. Thank God, because I hated when she was mad with me. The waitress came over to our table and handed us the menus, although we didn't need them. We both knew exactly what we were ordering—the same thing we order every time we came here. The waitress returned with my hot crab claws, and Tyra's stuffed mushrooms and salad.

"So, Tyra, what's up for tomorrow?" I asked, taking a bite of the sliced apple that garnished my drink.

"I have to help out at social service," Tyra said, cutting up her salad. "Why, what do you have planned?"

"I'm not sure, but I think my mother is taking me shopping."

"Come on now, Sollie, that's ridiculous. This doesn't make any sense," she said looking at me as if I was crazy. "All that money you just spent, something is really wrong. Why are you spending money like this? Terry and I are well off, and we don't spend money like that." She sipped her Chardonnay.

"Well, guess what, Tyra, that's you and Terry. You have a family, and I don't!" I said hastily, because Tyra was really starting to get on my nerve.

"Whatever, Sollie, it doesn't matter if you're single, married, kids or no kids. You still need to watch how you spend money. Sollie, you maybe you need to seek therapy or something."

"So what, am I crazy now? And besides I just finish having therapy."

"Huh?" Tyra responded with a confused look on her face.

"Retail therapy." I smirked.

Tyra shook her head.

The waitress came back over to our booth and took our order.

"Now, back to what I was saying. So you think I'm crazy?"

"I'm not saying that, and you know it. But it's evident that there is a problem. Maybe you have some issues that you're not aware of and shopping excessively is how you're dealing with them."

"Tyra, please! It's nothing wrong with me wanting to shop just like the million other women in the world, so would you stop trying to make an issue out of this. And besides, you know my motto, money ain't—"

"Uh, uh, don't even go there. You have been using that tired-ass excuse since we were teenagers, and I'm sick of it. Ever since you found out that your little so-called friend was screwing your so-called boyfriend, buying her clothes and giving her money, is when you started saying money ain't shit! We were how old then? Thirteen?" She pushed her half-eaten salad to the side, looking over at the couple sitting at the table next to us. Realizing she was talking loudly, she turned back to me. "And news flash," she continued, in a lower tone. "Money is something, and it must be respected or you will continue to be reckless with it. So you can stop using something that happened years ago for an excuse. All you're doing is trying to justify your irresponsible behavior."

Seconds passed as I stared at Tyra. "Well, I guess you told me!" I smiled.

"Yeah, I guess I did, wench!" Tyra said beginning to laugh. "Listen, Sollie, I'll see if the kids can stay over at my parents' house a little longer tomorrow, and when I'm done at social service, maybe instead of going shopping, me, you and your mother can go see Black

Panther I heard it was excellent. My treat and besides, it would be nice to hang out with Mrs. Marie."

I told Tyra I would think about it. We cleaned our plates and we were stuffed, and my greedy ass had the nerve to order another chicken alfredo, to go. I paid the check, and we headed out to the car.

"Drive," I said tossing the car keys over to Tyra.

"My pleasure," she said excitedly catching them, anxiously she jumped into the driver's seat. "Girl, I don't know, I may have to get one of these. She said adjusting the seat, and getting comfortable. But of course, it would have to be a four-door." She turned the key in the ignition, reached over and pressed the button for the sunroof to open. And I swear, I think I was bipolar. By the time we reached Tyra house my mood had changed drastically. Just thinking about all that Aunt Bessie and Tyra had said, the fine brother in the mall, and all those women cards I found in that boy's wallet had depressed me. Tyra pulled up in her driveway. I got out the car, and walked around to the driver's side.

"I love you," Tyra said hugging me.

"I love you too," I said hugging her back tightly.

"Are you okay?" she asked.

"Not really, but I will be."

"You sure will, Sollie. I know I can talk too much sometimes. And I realize that nothing in your life is going to change until you make the change. I just want you to be happy. And you can start by getting rid of that sorry-ass boy! Okay, okay." She threw her hands in the air. "I'm not going to start." She got her bags out the trunk, and told me to call her if I wanted to talk.

When I got to my house, I noticed Ahmaun's car was gone, which was good because I really didn't feel like dealing with him right now. Here she goes, I thought to myself watching Mrs. Johnson breaking her neck to get out of her front door. I stared at her as I retrieved my bags out of the trunk, and just as I walked up the walkway, she asked me if everything was okay, saying that she heard loud noise inside my house. I told her thanks, unlocked the front door, and hesitantly walked inside; I sat my bags on the couch, stood there for a second, and looked around. I immediately called Ahmaun's cell.

"Ahmaun, did you have someone over here?" I asked.

"Nah, why you say dat?" he asked with his none talking ass self.

"Mrs. Johnson said she heard some loud noise earlier."

"There she go; tell that nosy-ass lady to mind her fuckin business! That was me on the phone beefing with those stupid ass nigga's fucking my money up!"

"Where are you?"

"I'm over east. I'll be there in a few. You good?"

"Yeah, I'm good." I hung up, still thinking about all those business cards I saw in his wallet, and immediately became even angrier. Why get angry, Sollie? I asked myself. You accept it, so just deal with it. Getting up and snatching the bags off the couch, I headed up to my bedroom.

Dropping the bags in the middle of my bedroom floor, I flopped down on the bed and reached over on my nightstand for the cordless phone. I noticed the display screen indicating I had two new messages. "Hi Sollie, its Remi . . ." I didn't even listen, and quickly pressed the delete button. *"Next!"* I thought, *"Hi Sollie, it's your mother, I was wondering why your car is in my garage, and the credit card you wanted me to order for you came today. Love you! Call me."*

Hearing that message quickly perked me up. I'll call her later. Right now, I want to put my things away, take a shower, and relax.

"Sollie where you at?" Ahmaun yelled as he came in the front door.

"I'm upstairs." God! I didn't think he was coming this soon. I really didn't feel like dealing with him right now. Well, maybe it's a good thing. It was time to tell him that I was done!

"I brought you something. Shit, you don't need anything," he said stopping at the entrance of the bedroom door and looking at all the shopping bags on the floor. "Here," he handed me the bag. I looked at him strangely. For some reason he looked weird. I took the bag from him and opened it. It was a Burberry raincoat.

"You like it?"

"It's okay," I said hanging it up inside the closet.

"What's up sexy? You put it on me this morning Shorty." he said, leaning over trying to kiss me.

Walking around him and picking up the other bags, I told him that I didn't feel like kissing.

"What you still mad from earlier?"

"I'm just not happy with this relationship. I try to act as if you're seeing other women don't bother me, because that's supposedly what all men do. But that's bullshit. All men don't cheat. B, Terry, and several others of my male friends are good guys, and I know for a fact that they don't cheat! And I'm getting really tired of settling, because I don't have to! I meet guy's everyday and won't give them the time of day because all I want is you, hoping that one day you will change. It's just this last time catching you in bed with that girl, the chic I keep hearing about down ATL, the chic up Motor Vehicle and God only knows who else."

I looked at Ahmaun thinking he was going to at least try and deny the chic up Motor Vehicle, but he didn't. "You know it's all getting to be a little too much. Ahmaun the money, clothes, jewelry, sustained me for many years, and now the car, but it's no longer enough. I want so much more. If I keep holding on and waiting for you to change, my life would have passed me by. I have set goals and I'm ready to do whatever needs to be done to make those goals a reality. And when I do, I want a good man by my side, one that's going to uplift my spirit, not constantly bring it down. And another thing . . ." And just as I was about to continue, a rage came across his face, one that I had never in the eleven years that we have been together seen. He walked slowly over to where I was standing.

"What the fuck!" he snapped. "Who the hell you been talking to? Pumping your head with all that bullshit! A good man, what the fuck am I? Look at this shit! All this shit!" he said looking around the bedroom, and walking into the walk-in closet, and began going through my wardrobe with such vengeance. "Gucci, Jimmy Choo, Chanel, Prada . . . all this shit," then turning and walking over to the dresser, and opening up my jewelry box that had nothing but diamonds, necklaces, tennis bracelets, and God only knows how many rings inside of it. "Diamonds, Rolex, you ain't wanting for shit! I'm out there hustling, and grinding for you and me and your ungrateful ass talking all this bullshit, half these bitches out here wish they were you!" He slammed the cover of the jewelry box down. "And trust, and believe, the other nigga's you talking about, them motherfucka's cheat too! It's been done, it's being done, and it's going to continue to be done long after we are fuckin gone!" he said, throwing his hand in the air. "It's the fuckin way of life. That's— what—nigga's—do, cheat!" Pausing for a second, he lowered his head as if flashbacks had invaded his mind, looking like the hurt little boy his mother has often told me about. *What is he thinking?* I wondered, as I stood there terrified, biting down on my bottom lip, uncertain of what to say to this person that I thought I knew. He slowly raised his head, held his hand out, and began counting on each finger. "My grandfather, my father, my uncles, cousins, all of them nigga's cheated! Shit, I remember my father punk-ass taking me over to different bitches' houses when I was younger. They be upstairs and I would be downstairs, hearing them fucking and giggling and shit! I remember days my mother would leave out for work he would have them bitches in our house. And guess what, miss, I—want—a— good—man! She knew about it! She allowed it, she tolerated it. You know why?" he asked with the tone of his voice becoming much louder. "Because—the—nigga—took—care—of—home! That's why!" He said staring off, he turned back to me "Until one of them bitches got the best of him, and then he rolled out on us! Fuck him!" he yelled, hitting the wall, hard enough to leave a dent, scaring me even more. "And another thing, stop talking that bullshit about rolling out on a nigga 'cause it ain't happening! Only way it will, if I'm six feet fuckin under!" He said staring at me with such anger. "I'm out of here!" he said furiously walking out the bedroom and mumbling, "A good man" He went down the stairs and left out slamming the front door behind him.

I was trembling, as I stood there in complete shock. My heart was racing, and my palms were sweaty, and I realized that what I just witnessed was a portion of Ahmaun's pain. What was I going to do? I thought beginning to pace the floor. This boy was crazy. How was I ever going to get away from him? I wanted to call Tyra, my mother, Salique, someone, but I didn't. I sat down on the edge of the bed, still in shock, rubbing my sweaty hands realizing now, more than ever, that he was never going to let me go. I went into the bathroom and ran my bath water, sitting down on the side of the tub with my head in my hand wondering how I got here.

After my bath, I climbed into the bed, and lay there tossing and turning as the words Ahmaun spoke resonated in my mind.

Around two in the morning, Ahmaun came in the house. I sat up and reached over and turned on the night-light, uncertain of what his mood was going to be. My heart began racing as I listened to him make his way up the stairs.

"Sollie, you woke?" he asked.

"Yeah, I am." I said getting out of bed to go to the bathroom, and as I walked by him he grabbed me and held me tightly. "You're my life," he whispered. "That's why I love you so much, Shorty, 'cause you're strong like my mother."

God, please help me! I silently thought while still in his arms. He released his hold, and I headed into the bathroom. When I came out he was still standing there. I walked by him and climbed back into the bed. And would you know it, that big dick came right behind me; after we were done, everything was forgotten. I laid in his arms and thought *"Fuck it, let STOPPED, CUT AND PAST him do what he do."*

We woke the next morning. He didn't say anything and neither did I. He took a shower, got dressed, laid some money on the dresser, kissed me good-bye, and left. I got out of bed and walked over to the dresser picking up the money and counting it. Two thousand dollars I counted, shaking my head. I was confused, and lost. Angrily I threw the money back on the dresser. And just as I did, my mother called.

"Hi, Mommy," I said trying to sound as normal as possible.

"Hi, baby, did you get my message I left?"

"Yes, I got it."

"You don't sound too happy. Is everything okay?" And why didn't you tell me about your birthday gift from Ahmaun?" Your brother told me after I called him to see if he knew why your car was in my garage."

"I was going to surprise you. I hope you didn't mind."

"Not at all, so what about the BMW?"

"I'm not sure what I'm going to do with it." I said sadly.

"Sollie, you don't sound like yourself. Is everything okay?" she asked with that motherly intuition in her voice.

I began to cry.

"I'm on my way over there!"

"Mommy, no! I'm going to be okay, it's just that for some reason I'm so unhappy, and I don't know why." I said wiping my eyes.

I heard my mother take a deep breath, and then asked God to please help her child.

"Listen to me, Sollie. I know for certain that a lot of what you're feeling is stemming from your relationship with that boy. What is keeping you with him? Are you afraid of him?"

"No, I'm not afraid of him."

"Sollie, listen, you know how I have felt about that boy from the first day I met him. And you also know that I'm aware of the life he lives, which we both know is no life for you. I have preached and preached to you about him, but the truth is until you're ready, you're not going to end this relationship, regardless of what I or anyone says. But know this, the measure of love you feel for yourself, determines exactly how you will allow him and others to treat you. Baby, I wish I could take your pain and endure it myself, but unfortunately, I can't. All I can do is pray that God protects and gives you the strength and courage to move from this, and that he will allow me to live long enough to see you truly happy one day. But one thing I am sure of, this too shall pass!"

For the next two hours I found comfort and reassurance in the conversation we had. We talked about everything, not just about Ahmaun but the other necessary changes that I needed to make in my life as well. And of course, one of them was the irresponsible way I spent money, and for some reason, this time it seemed to register with me. Before hanging up I told my mother that I was going to put the rest of my money in the bank and began saving. she chuckled, saying, "See, God is working already." I laughed, and thought, He must have been. I even promised her that the credit card she ordered for me would only be used for emergencies. I asked her to put all the bills for the house into my name; I lived here, so they where my responsibility, not hers or Ahmaun's.

And I vowed to myself that as long as I was with Ahmaun, however long that may be, every dime he gave me was going into my savings.

After getting out the shower, I put on some old-school Mary J, sat down at my vanity, and curled my hair, thinking that if Mea cut it again instead of trimming it like I asked her to, I was going to take my business to the Dominicans. "Why do hairdressers do that?"

I got dressed and headed down to the kitchen and grabbed a pop tart and a soda; looking down at my hips spreading, I should have grabbed a rice cake, and a bottled water. Oh, well, that will go on my to-do list with the other life-changes I was getting ready to make. As I walked out to the front, everyone one was out sitting on their porches enjoying the beautiful weather. I waved to a few of my neighbors, and watched as the guy across the street stared as he always does; and I laughed when his girl angrily pushed him. And of course, he responded with that million-dollar question, "What I do?" Dumb ass! I thought.

I looked over at Mrs. Johnson's and wondered what she was up to; she's normally out front doing something with her rose garden.

I climbed in the car, and looked into my pocketbook for my sunglass case, slipped on my white Prada shades. I looked through my CDs and popped in my old school Beyonce CD and pressed the button until I got to "Ego." I pulled down the sun visor, checking to make sure I was good, pressed the button for the sunroof to open, and headed off to the bank. But I first had to stop at the post office and get a PO Box address, 'cause I didn't want Ahmaun seeing any of my bank statements. After purchasing a mailbox address, I went to the bank, opened my savings, and walked out the doors staring and smiling at the total on my deposit slip.

Now what do I do? I thought getting into the car, and just that quickly I came up with the perfect idea—I called Tyra to see was up for it. As I went to dial Tyra's number, I noticed the small envelope in the corner of the screen flashing informing me that I had a new text. Who the hell is this? I thought puzzled as I read the words *I Hate You Bitch!* What was this about? To my knowledge, I didn't have any enemies. I checked to see what the number was that the text was sent from and it read unknown caller. I stared at the words and I knew that the person that sent this text was the same person that gave me the headless doll. I dialed Tyra's number.

"Hey Tyra."

"Hey, Sollie, I was just getting ready to dial your number. What's up? Are we going to the movies later?"

"No. I have a better idea."

"Sollie, please, for God's sake don't say shopping."

"Girl, be quiet. Let's have a cookout."

"Have you forgotten its Tuesday?" Tyra asked.

"Okay, it's Tuesday, and it's eighty-nine degrees outside. Come on it will be fun, and besides I'm going to play the rest of the week, because, come Monday when I start my job, it's going to be all about the business."

"Okay, okay, I like the sound of that. So what time, and what do you want me to bring?"

"Bring nothing and I guess around five-thirty everyone should be off by then."

"Girllllll! I have something to tell you!" Tyra blurted.

"What?" I asked anxious to hear the tea.

"My coworker's cousin's boyfriend's homeboy told his sister's aunt's nephew baby mother, who happens to be pregnant for the sixth time and she's only nineteen."

"Tyra, please! What is it, shit! After that long ass grape-vine, it's probably not true."

"Remi is back out there on that stuff!"

"Whatttttt!" I listened as Tyra went into the details about what she had heard, although we both knew how rumors and lies could spread. But anything was possible when it came to Remi.

After hanging up with Tyra, I just sat there hoping that it was just that, a rumor. I still had much love for Remi, as crazy as that may sound. I wondered if that's what she wanted to talk to me about yesterday when she called, and I brushed her off. I thought about calling her to invite her to the cookout, and to find out if what I just heard was true. I'll just do what Tyra said, and deal with her with a long-handled spoon.

I called Remi, when I said hello, she didn't say anything. I said hello again and then I heard her take a deep breath and then nervously say hello. She obviously thought I was calling to discuss the night of my party. I kept the conversation short and to the point. Remi sounded very relieved to know that I was calling to invite her to the cookout. She excitedly accepted. I didn't question her about what I heard; I would wait until I saw her. Although it had only been three days since she has been out of treatment, I would still be able to tell if she was using again.

After hanging up from Remi, I called the rest of my friends and they all said they would be there. I pulled off and headed to the market.

Chapter Six

"W hat the hell is going on?" I thought, pulling into the market's parking lot, noticing a group of people gathered in a circle staring and pointing at something on the ground. I parked and quickly walked my nosey-ass over to where all the commotion was. I tapped the elderly man that I was standing next to on his arm and asked, "What's going on?"

The elderly man pointed to the ground and said that the young woman lying there was leaving the market when the security guard approached her and accused her of stealing from the meat department. And just as they grabbed her arm, the meats fell out from under her shirt and when security went to escort her back inside, she collapsed, and the poor thing had a seizure.

I walked around to the other side, stood up on my toes trying to see through the crowd to get a better look. And wouldn't you know it; there was Karen lying on the ground faking a seizure, with three packs of T-bone steaks lying next to her. The angry security guard stood over the top of Karen with his arms folded and mouth twisted, knowing that the whole seizure move was stunt. She has done this so many times before. If she gets caught stealing, she will slip an Alka-Seltzer in her mouth, suck on it until it dissolves making it look like she is foaming at the mouth, and figure that they will transport her to the hospital and not Central Booking.

Hearing the emergency sirens, I turned and watched as the ambulance sped into the parking lot. They stopped, got out, rushed through the crowd over to Karen, and began taking her vitals. I swear that Karen deserved an Oscar; she made her legs shake as if she just had the best fuck in the world! One of the paramedics rushed back over to the ambulance and retrieved the stretcher, as the onlookers watched and whispered. Once back over to where Karen was lying, they placed her onto the stretcher, and draped a white sheet across her; Karen was making her eyes blink and neck jerk so fast you would have thought she suffered from Tourette's syndrome. Just before the paramedics put her inside the ambulance, I yelled out her name. She rose up slowly and looked directly at me. Then she sneakily eased her hand out from under the white sheet and gave me the flip, and then smiled. I chuckled, grabbed a cart, and headed inside the market. Strolling down the aisle, I began putting any and everything in my cart and I prayed that the little boys in the neighborhood would be outside playing so that they could help me carry the bags into the house.

Sitting at the red light, I thought about Remi, and if there was any truth to what Tyra had heard.

I've heard that drug addiction is a hard habit to break, and I thank God I never got caught up. But I guess one habit is no better than the other, and I'm pretty sure everyone in one form or another has a habit. I guess mine was spending money, shopping, eating and Ahmaun's dick!

While waiting for the light to turn green, several people came running from different directions over to some guys standing in the alley that were obviously waiting for them. I watched and listened as the guys began ordering the people to form a straight line.

"Get in the line, bitch!" the tall slim dude yelled with a mouthful of gold grills.

"Come on, y'all. Shit, please get in the line! A nigga trying to get high, I'm sick!" the disoriented guy from the group yelled, vigorously rubbing his arm as if he was cold, with a look of sheer desperation on his face.

The light turned green, and I slowly pulled off, still hearing the guy's yelling and talking to the others as if they were nothing. One thing I don't do is judge people, because none of them were born addicts. And I have no idea what may have happened in their lives to bring them to this point. And it's crazy, the majority of the women that are caught up, you can look at and see the beauty that was once there. I felt so very bad for all of them. But I guess being a woman, I felt really bad for my sisters as I watched the two guys continue to verbally degrade them and even kicking one of the women in her ass.

Finally, making it home, I pulled in front of the house, and wouldn't you know it, there wasn't a child in sight. I got out the car, popped the trunk, and stared at all the grocery bags inside. I was supposed to be buying only a few items, and look at this!

Finally! I thought, sitting the last grocery bag on the kitchen counter. I was tired as hell, trying to catch my breath. I sat down at the breakfast bar, realizing I better join somebody's gym quick! But that didn't stop me from reaching for the bag of Lay's potato chips. Eventually, I got around to putting the food away. I headed upstairs changed, then came back downstairs, turned on the radio, and headed back into the kitchen. And that was it; I was in a place I always seemed to go when I was in alignment with my purpose, which was cooking.

After dicing, cutting, seasoning, boiling, chopping, and marinating, I was almost done; the only thing left to do was make the potato salad and deviled eggs. So while the potatoes and eggs cooled, I went and took a quick shower. I decided to wear a simple black one-piece short set and I loved the way it hugged my curves.

I was heading back downstairs to finish preparing the side dishes when I heard some noise out back. I walked over to the window, pulled back the curtain, and watched nosey Mrs. Johnson struggling to bring some old rusty grey chairs down her back porch steps. What is she doing? I grabbed the bag of charcoal and headed out back to find out what she was up to.

I walked out on to the deck and spoke as I began dumping charcoal inside the grill. She smiled and said, "Hello, are you putting your dinner on the grill?" with an excited look on her face.

"Actually, I'm having a few friends over for a cookout." I can't imagine why Mrs. Johnson would be setting up chairs; she never has company. I don't even think she has any family. "It looks like you're getting ready for company yourself."

Tirelessly, she placed both hands on her hip, and reached into the torn pocket on her housecoat. She pulled out a tissue and wiped the sweat that trickled down the side of her face. I told her to wait a second and went back inside to get her a cold bottle of water. I walked down the deck steps over to her fence and handed it to her; she took it and drank the whole bottle nonstop.

"Thank you so much, Sollie. That really hit the spot. Now, to answer your question, my church electricity is still off from the storm Sunday night and we didn't have any place to have our Tuesday night Bible study. So I told the saints they could use my house, and I could sure use the company. It gets pretty lonely over here. And since it's so nice out today, I decided to have Bible study outside," she said, walking over to the yellow recycling container and tossing the empty bottle of water inside it.

I'll just ask everyone to keep the noise down until she's done. I wondered how many people she's expecting. The small corner stone church she attends only has about eleven members and that's including the pastor and his wife. Oh well, we will just do our thing inside until their bible study is over.

Chapter Seven

I   was outside stocking the outdoor bar when a few of Mrs. Johnson's church members arrived.

"Praise the Lord! God is good!" the loud mouth woman said, as she switched her fat ass into Mrs. Johnson yard. Tirelessly she flopped down in the chair, and fanned herself with her handkerchief.

"The king is her!" Duce exclaimed as he walked out onto the deck.

"God is good! And praise the Lord to you too, Sister!"

"Hello, I'm sister Betty." The lady said to us, we both said hello.

Duce leaned over and whispered "Sister Betty got a big ass!" Duce exclaimed.

"Duce shut your mouth! Will you ever grow up?" I whispered.

"Whatever, you just mad because Sister Betty ass fatter than yours, punk!" Duce said.

Later, Duce and I hooked up the speakers, and then set up the gazebo; he lit the grill and when the coals were ready, he began cooking. Tyra came in shortly after.

The food was cooking and smelling good and Mrs. Johnson's church members wasn't paying any attention to the scripture that she was reading from her Bible. They were too busy trying to see what was going on the grill next.

Mostly everyone I invited was there. I told them that for now, just chill out in the house. Some of them went down in the basement and shot pool; some was in the living room, and the rest went out on the front porch. Duce took care of the grill.

Furiously, Tyra stormed into the kitchen telling me that Duce had just invited the group of hungry members over to the cookout when they were done with Bible study.

I walked over to the back door and Tyra stood behind me pissed! We both watched Duce blow kisses at the lady with the loud mouth and big ass. The women sat there watching him blushing from ear to ear. Mrs. Johnson knew the lady was flirting and she didn't like it one bit. After no longer being able to take the flirtatious woman, Mrs. Johnson cleared her throat rather loudly, quickly getting the woman's attention, and giving her a very nasty look. Mrs. Johnson continued to read. The lady tried to stay focused but she couldn't; from the look on her face I could tell she wanted Duce. And little did she know she could get him.

"Sister, you is wearing that hat!" he told the lady while flipping the Turkey burgers over.

"Thank you," she muttered, patting her chest, while conveniently unbuttoning a few of the buttons on her dress.

"Like I said, Sister and Brothers, feel free to join us when y'all are done studying the good word of the Lord." Duce looked back at Tyra and me and winked his eye.

"Ohhhhh! Sollie, he gets on my last nerve!" Tyra fussed. "You shouldn't have even told him to come. He really needs to grow up."

As smell of the grilled food filled the hot summer air, I noticed the church members becoming more and more restless; and I watched one of them stare at Duce as he opened another ice-cold Heineken taking it straight to the head. "Awwww," he said enticing the man that was staring. He then took a porterhouse steak off the grill and held it up long enough for them to get a good look at the thick, juicy steak. I knew Duce was crazy, and now, so did Mrs. Johnson. I watched as she cut her eyes at him as if he was the devil himself.

They all tried to stay focused on bible class, but unfortunately, after seeing Duce put the shrimp kabobs on the grill, the members could no longer take it.

"Ah, Mother Johnson," the lady with that I-need-some-dick written all over her face said, interrupting Mrs. Johnson from discussing the topic the devil is a lie. "Do you think we could finish this up next week? It's really scorching out here." She took off her pink straw hat and gently patted the invisible sweat from her forehead, being extra careful not to touch her adult baby-hair that extended from the large finger waves in her hair that fit her round fat face perfectly, looking like a fake-ass Betty Boop. A man with a gray beard and very thick bifocals, took a hard swallow, licked his lips as he stared at the frosted cold bottle of Heineken that Duce had set down on the table, shaking his head yes, fully agreeing with what the lady had requested. Mrs. Johnson was so upset, she saw right through their fake-asses.

"Fine!" said Mrs. Johnson closing her Bible shut. She stood up and sat the Bible in the chair, leaning over and picking up the plate of uneaten sugar cookies. She then gathered the five chipped porcelain tea cups that they never even got a chance to drink from and carried them into the house. She wasn't in the house good, before they all jumped up and hauled their ass out her yard and over into mine; one of them even took a short cut and jumped the fence. They didn't even help her carry the chairs inside. I have known Mrs. Johnson all my life, and that was the very first time I have seen her upset.

I told Duce to ask her if she needed help with the chairs. He did, and she angrily replied, "No, thank you!" And right before taking the last chair inside, she turned and disappointedly looked at her church members. Then her eyes slowly made their way over to Duce, giving him a look that could kill. She then stormed into the house, slamming the backdoor behind her.

"What the fuck is her problem?" Duce laughed.

I headed back into the house to let everyone know that it was okay to go out into the yard and it was on!

"Yo-yo where the ho at!" Duce asked walking in from out the back.

"Please, don't start that Duce!"

"Well, it's the truth, B. gotta know that you can't turn a *Ho* into a housewife!"

And just as I looked up there was Remi walking through the front door, wearing a pair of black-and-white Coco Chanel boots that I bought her, tight white shorts with the cheeks of her ass hanging out, a black T-shirt that read *Thank My Mother an none of us could ignore the* black and white bandanna tied around her twenty-six inch lace front.

I chuckled as I heard Mea try to whisper to Tyra, that Remi looked at hot mess. And yes the fuck she did.

"Hi, Remi, glad you could make it," I said walking toward her. Normally, I would have greeted her with a hug. But I wasn't feeling it, and I could tell she wasn't either, but I remembered keep her close! And so, I hugged her and acted as if everything was cool. We both knew that it wasn't. For the life of me, I couldn't understand what was up with this shade she throwing my way. Only thing I could think is that she was cheating on B. and she knows how I feel about him, and if that was true, I was determined I was going to find out. She walked into the living room and spoke to everyone. I think that what Tyra said earlier was a rumor. She still looked really good, and as a matter of fact, she looked like she'd gained more weight since I saw her three days ago. She sat there looking around clutching her pocketbook. I asked her if B. was coming. Twisting her mouth and poking her lips out she said B. was not going to be able to make it, she almost seemed glad. My attention was taken by the noise in the yard. I told Remi I would be back, and headed out back.

"Girl, did they forget it's a Tuesday?" Tyra laughed as I walked out on the deck to join her. The yard was packed! Everyone was eating, talking, and dancing. I began dancing and snapping my fingers looking out at everyone enjoying themselves; they even had a game of spades going on under the gazebo. I was loving it, and so were the church people; they was tore up! One of my good friends, Black, pulled up in his white Lexus, and close behind him were his homeboys, each pushing something real slick. They got out of their cars, and every last one of them was fine as hell. Black walked to the back of his car, popped the trunk, and took a large box filled with nothing but top-shelf liquor, then walked to the corner and directed a guy who was driving a large white truck over to the yard. The man got out and walked to the back, raised the grate, and took out four bushels of hot steamed crabs; and that was it—the cookout had turned into a crab feast. I went down and greeted him and the others, and we all laughed as Duce and Sister Betty began to dance and that old ass woman was getting it, I mean really getting it! *I have to get this on camera* I thought as I ran into the house and up the stairs to get my camcorder.

I rushed back down the stairs and out the back door, and pressed the record button. The other church people yelled out with delight, Go Betty, go Betty. After the song went off, everyone was dying laughing at them both, and her ass was tired! Making her way back over to her seat, she flopped down on the chair, panting. "Let me see, Shorty," Duce said walking up the steps, reaching for the recorder. I pushed his hand away and told him to move and went into the house to finish my conversation with Remi. Just as I was headed into the living room, Tyra came in behind me and said that we needed more ice. I detoured and headed down the basement stairs to get a bag of ice from the deep freezer. A few of my friends were still in the basement shooting pool so I pressed the green button to record them as well, and just as I pressed the record button, I lost my balance. I tried to grab the banister, but it didn't matter. Before I knew it, my happy ass went tumbling down all sixteen steps. All the guys ran over to me asking if I was okay. I held my hand up and told them to let me sit there for a minute and get myself together. Although my ankle was killing me, I couldn't help but laugh when I realized that with all that tumbling I had managed not to drop my camcorder. Tyra and Duce ran down the steps, and after Duce saw that I was going to live, he stood there laughing, and really laughed when he reached over in the corner and picked up the heel of my Jimmy Choo stiletto.

Duce took the camcorder out of my hand and began recording me lying there on the floor. But after Tyra removed my shoe, and he saw how swollen my ankle had become just that quickly, he didn't find it funny anymore. He quickly sat the camcorder on the shelf and asked with a very serious look on his face, "Are you okay."

"Sollie, your ankle may be broken!" Tyra said with concern. "I think you need to let me take you to the hospital."

"Tyra, move, I got her." Duce said.

He picked me up and carried me up the stairs and into the living room sitting me on the ottoman and elevating my leg with throw pillows.

"Where is Remi?" I asked.

"She's out on the front porch. I told you once a ho, always a ho!" he exclaimed while watching Remi standing just a little too closely to her ex-boyfriend.

I lifted up just enough to see, and Duce was right. The way she was up on Tavon, something was going on with them. Tyra filled the ice pack and placed it on my ankle. Duce headed back out into the yard to finish entertaining.

I sat there talking with Mea, Tyra, and few of our other girlfriends and smiled when I saw Jodi walk through the front door with her cute self. LeLe frail ass followed closely behind her looking like the tramp that she was, and I didn't open my mouth about them being back together. LeLe asked if she could use the bathroom and Jodi headed outside to make their plates.

LeLe was a nuisance, I thought, watching her as she switched her narrow ass up the stairs. She really didn't know who she wanted, a man or a woman. I guess as long as she was getting fucked it didn't really matter.

A few minutes later Jodi walked back into the living room carrying her and LeLe plates. Duce was right behind her and with the look on his face, I knew he was getting ready to say something stupid out his mouth. LeLe returned and just as Jodi handed her the plate of food, Duce started.

"Jodi, can I ask a question?"

I looked over at Mea, Tyra, and the girls. I knew that boy like a book, and so did Jodi. Sitting her hot dog back on her plate, she mugged and said, "Ask, nigga!"

"Now, check this out," he smirked. "I can understand a nigga being pussy whipped and might go nuts about the pussy, but tell me how the fuck can two broads be pussy whipped. Y'all ain't feeling anything. Y'all don't know if the pussy good or not, and y'all running around stabbing each other. Now that's some dumb-ass shit if I ever seen any!"

While Duce and Jodi were arguing, I watched as Remi and Tavon walked by. She looked over at me with a devilish smirk on her face.

Jodi stood up from her chair. "Fuck you, nigga." She spit!

"Nah, fuck you! And you better sit your little ass down," Duce said, walking toward Jodi.

"Look now, please will y'all stop it, Duce, leave Jodi alone. You don't have anything to do with her lifestyle. I keep telling you that!"

"Whatever!" he said turning and walking out the room. Jodi sat back down and finished eating her food, and LeLe didn't say anything. But her eyes said it all, staring at Duce as he walked away, like she wanted to show him the business.

Mea leaned up from the couch and rested her chin on the back of her hand. With a very curious look on her face, she asked Jodi why she didn't like men. Jodi bit into her hot dog and said, "Because their dicks stink!" And we all fell out laughing. "Fuck a man!" Jodi snapped. And there it was, that look that tells me something more was going on with my friend.

"Do you ever think you will be straight again?" Mea asked.

"Didn't I just say fuck a man? Look, check this out. I'm gay!" Jodi proclaimed with a very serious look on her face. "Ain't no crossing over. It is what it is. I'm gay! And Mea, you need to stop worrying about me getting some dick, because you get enough for us both!"

"Whatevrrrrrr," Mea said throwing her hands in the air, laughing.

"Oh, yeah, Mea, that reminds me, Sollie met a doctor the other day. He was fine as hell but of course she wasn't interested, maybe you would like him, I remember his name. I could look check to see if he's on Face Book." Tyra smiled.

Mia sipped her wine "Yes hunnie, you do that, let's see what's up with the brother with M.D. behind his name."

"Oh, you would really think you the shit if you start dating a doctor." Jodi mugged.

"Him being a doctor doesn't impress me. That nigga can have a G.E.D. a C.D.L. it doesn't matter, I don't discriminate, long as the dick is good and I wrap it up!"

"Girl, you're crazy!" I said laughing.

"I ain't crazy. I just love sex!" She laughed. "Anyway, yeah, I'm interested. Try to locate him Tyra and hook a sister up." Mea reached into her pocketbook and pulled out a small mirror and a tube of MAC lip gloss. Just as she went to glide it across her lips, she looked up at us and asked, "Do y'all think I'm a freak?"

"Yeah!" everyone said in unison.

Tyra and the girls went back outside. I told them that I would be out, but I first wanted to call Ahmaun to see if he was coming to the cookout. But he didn't answer, and knowing him he probably would have said no anyway. I slowly got up and hopped into the kitchen. As I walked past the basement door, I heard what sounded like someone crying; trying not to put any extra weight on my swollen ankle, I slowly walked down the basement stairs. And when I got to the bottom step I could not believe what I was seeing. Remi and Tavon had just finished having sex on my pool table.

I threw my hands in the air and angrily asked, "What the hell are you two doing?! Have y'all lost your minds?" Remi jumped up from the table, reached for her T-shirt, and struggled to get it over her head. She then reached down and pulled her panties and shorts up from around her ankle, Tavon turned his back to me as he pulled up his jeans.

"My bad, Sollie," he said turning and facing me. I went to lay their asses out and just as I did I heard the basement door open.

"Sollie, are you down there?"

This is not happening. Shaking my head in disbelief of what was going down, I took a deep breath and looked at them both and said, "It's B.!" Remi didn't know what to do. Her eyes looked as if they were going to pop out of her head. Nervously, she looked around and then stared at the door that led out into the backyard.

"Don't even think about it." I snapped. Tavon attempted to go around me, not even caring that B. was upstairs. I pushed him back and asked, "Where the hell do you think you're going?"

With my eyebrows raised I told Tavon he had a lot of nerve and that there was no way I was letting him go up those stairs! I leaned over the banister and yelled up to B. that I was coming. I turned back to them both and told them to wait here. Nervously, I limped up the steps. B. was standing right there at the door smiling as usual. He leaned over and kissed me on my cheek asking if everything was okay. He said he heard me yelling. I told him everything was fine. Truth was I wanted to take him right down the steps so he could see that Remi was still a tramp. I pulled the basement door shut. B. said that his meeting ended earlier than he anticipated and he didn't call Remi because he wanted to surprise her. He admitted that with him trying to get his business started he hadn't been really spending quality time with her. God, I wanted to tell him what had just happened, but I knew it was not the time.

I told B. Remi was out in the yard. I hated lying to him. B. walked over to the back door and looked out into the yard.

"Sollie, among all these people I may never find her." He laughed. "She's probably somewhere eating. My baby's appetite has tripled since she's been home."

Yes it has . . . I silently thought. I watched B. walk out the door, and I quickly made my way back down the stairs. Tavon tried again to apologize, and I wasn't trying to hear or accept any apology from him. "Just leave my house," I said. Tavon headed out the basement door that led out to the yard. And I stood there staring at Remi once again with disgust.

Chapter Eight

"Y   ou have obviously lost your fucking mind!" I said walking over to her. "I should have let B. come down here and see for himself the slut you still are, and then in my house! What kind of person are you?" Remi stood there leaning against the pool table smoothing out the wrinkles in her shirt, as if she could care less about what just happened. "Listen, B. went outside in the yard. Just go upstairs. And the only reason I'm doing this is because the house is too crowded for a bunch of drama, but rest assure he will know about this tonight!"

"What, are you going to tell him?" Remi asked with such coldness in her voice.

With my eyebrows meeting and curiously shaking my head I was thinking I no longer knew this person that I once called my friend. "What the hell is up with you?" She just stood there with a remote look on her face. "And to answer your question, I'm not going to tell him anything. You are!"

Once at the top of the stairs, she stood behind me. I peeped out of the door making sure B. wasn't around. I slightly moved to the side and told her to go ahead. I walked over to the back door and B. was standing on the deck talking on his cell. After hanging up, he walked down into the yard. I looked through the crowd and noticed Tavon was still here, and obviously, telling Duce what had just happened. I watched as Duce listened and gave the handshake; you know how dudes do when they're bragging that they hit. B. was making his rounds greeting everyone, and I literally became sick to my stomach as I watched B. extend his hand to the man that had just fucked his girl. And they say woman ain't shit!

I opened the door and yelled out to him that Remi was upstairs in my bedroom watching TV. He came back inside and went up to check on her. And I quickly made my way out into the yard and told Tavon again to leave.

After telling Tyra what just happened, I had to practically beg her not to step to Remi, and then I had to listen to Duce with his I told you so's. I must admit I was relieved that she finally let her true colors show, and that she would soon be out of B.'s life; and after today she was definitely out of mine.

B. yelled up the stairs to Remi, she told him that she would be doe and a few minutes. I got up and walked back up the stairs. Just as I made my way to the top, I noticed Remi lying across my bed, gripping my pillow tightly, and slowly rubbing her hand back and forth on the comforter.

"Please get off my bed!" Startling her, she jumped up and walked out. I snatched the comforter off the bed, and put it in the hamper. I left the bedroom and closed the door behind me.

Back downstairs in the living room, B. was talking to Tyra about a business proposition that he wanted to discuss with her and Terry. Tyra listened, although I could tell that she was still very agitated from what Remi had done.

Mea reached for my photo album with pictures inside of all of us when we were younger. Passing the album around, we all laughed at the old photos, and you couldn't tell Tyra and me that we didn't have it going on. And we died laughing when we came across the picture of Duce crying, because his mother had just finished combing his knotty hair.

"Those were the good old days," I said, flipping through the photo album. "Listen at me like I'm so old." Tyra bit into her peach and said, "You're getting there!"

"Whatever, Tyra, don't forget, you will be twenty-nine in a few days! And you know what that means: one more year before the big three-zero." I laughed moving my hands and fingers in a ghostly manner. "That's crazy how all of us will turn thirty in the same year."

Our attention now focused on Remi as we watched her come down the stairs asking B. if he was ready. He told her he would be soon; he wanted to wait and speak with Terry. Remi frowned and then asked if she could have a soda. Tyra took a deep breath trying to contain herself from saying anything to her. I followed behind Remi as she walked out on the deck and got a soda from the cooler. She then sat down at the table crossing her legs as if she was a lady. She reached inside her purse and pulled out two cell phones, placing one of them back in her purse and dialing a number with the other. Whoever she called, didn't answer, but she continued to call repeatedly. *"Crazy bitch!"* I thought walking back into the living room, and wondering why she had two cell phones. I sat down on the couch and dialed Ahmaun's number again. "Where is Ahmaun at?" I asked out loud.

"His bighead is probably down Atlanta," Tyra said flipping through the photo album.

"Yeah, why does he go there so much?" Mea asked.

"I have no idea. Oh, I forgot to tell you what Karen said at the party."

"Yes, you did," Mea said leaning closer to get the gossip. While telling the story I laughed. She was happy that I was even telling something, 'cause Mea runs her mouth too much. But this was different. Everybody in Baltimore knew Ahmaun had woman, and unfortunately so did I. "Tell Karen to go to hell!" Mea said waving her hand in the air and taking a sip of her wine. "Her crack-a-jack ass needs to mind her business. You know she came in the shop the other day trying to sell my clients some food stamps. She needs to take them stamps and buy food for all those kids she has!"

"Time to go," B. said, getting up and leaving out the living room, I guess, knowing we were getting ready to start.

"Yeah, Mea, but this time Karen was right. I have heard that before, but it's whatever." I shrugged. "And there's no need to keep complaining, but believe me I know I keep saying it but I'm done. It's just a matter of time. All I know is that I want to be happy. I thought for sure that the car would have kept a smile on my face, but thirty minutes after the nigga gave it to me, I was sad. And you know what else? I had a long conversation with my mother this morning, and with the conversation Tyra and me had over lunch yesterday I'm beginning to realize that, obviously, I am lacking something in my life. Could I have low self-esteem?"

"Oh, hell no! "Mea said raising her hand in the air. "Wait just a minute, Sollie. Look at you. You're beautiful, with a banging body, a nice house, stay fly, and now your pushing a Benz, girl please, you got it going on. I know you can't be thinking your self-esteem is low."

"See, Mea, that's where the mix-up lies, with most people not understanding low self-esteem and what it entails." Tyra interrupted. "Yes Sollie is all that you just said; however you need to understand that a person with *self esteem* has personal value, self respect and most importantly self worth. Although this is not my level of expertise, it doesn't take a rocket science to realize that something is going on with Sollie to feel as though she has to continue to stay with his cheating ass, because none of us need to be with any man that cheats!"

"But Tyra that's what they do." Mea said looking at Tyra as if she was crazy.

"No not all of them, and for the ones that do, we need to stop excepting it like its okay, and then keep using that sorry, tired excuse that you just said. And yes, I know Sollie loves herself, but to what degree?! Because once she really truly loves Sollie and realizes her self-worth, that's when and only when she will realize she deserves much, much more than what she is settling for!"

"Tyra is right." I sadly agreed

"You'll be fine." Tyra said reaching out for my hand.

"Well I still say let the nigga do what he's doing. Get yours and while you're getting yours from him, have another nigga on the side," she said reaching over and giving another one of our friends five. "Fuck that, I get down just like them, cause it don't take a rocket science to know that two can play the same game!"

"Whatever Mea, and another thing, you talk about this house. It's not even mine. It's my mother's. The truth is I really don't have anything except the Benz and that's 'cause it's in my name, but I didn't work hard for it. It was given to me just like everything else Ahmaun and my mother has bought for me. I have nothing to say I sweated for. Mea, you should understand. Look at all you have accomplished and you're not even thirty yet. Don't misunderstand me. I'm very thankful for all that my mother has done, but I want to be able to look at some shit and know that I obtained it on my own, and if I can't do that then it's meaningless." I stood up, reached over on the table for the bottle of Moscato, and poured a little in everyone's glass. "I toast to learning to love me, leveling up and accepting nothing less than what deserve!" We all put our glasses together and toasted.

"Here, here!" Simple Duce yelled, jumping from around the corner and scaring the shit out of all of us, which sent my wine flying into the air and landing on my plush cream carpet! I could have slapped him. "Is this a cookout, or a fuckin woman's rap? Y'all in here talking bad about the brothers!"

"Shut the hell up, nappy head!" Mea said showing him the picture of him when he was a kid.

"That's cool but look at me now, Shorty," he said looking in the mirror on the living room wall.

"Yeah, you grew up fine, I give you that. But you still stupid!" Mea laughed.

"Check this out. I have to go, and my church friends left. They told me to tell you thanks for everything."

"Why are you leaving? It's still early."

"Just because you got it like that, some of us have to work! And besides, I have a date with Sis Betty tonight," Duce said laughing. "I'm going to tear that old ass up!"

Terry finally came, looking real sharp in his Armani suit that Tyra got straight from the Salvation Army. The way Tyra and Terry greeted each other you would have thought they hadn't seen each other in months. I smiled as I watch Terry hug Tyra tightly and kissed her all over her face.

We all went out in the yard, and Terry went around and greeted everyone. Terry was so cool, down to earth and everyone loved him.

B., Tyra, and Terry sat down at the table and Remi sat there impatiently looking at her watch as B. discussed the business he was trying to get started. I wanted to tell her to walk home.

Around ten thirty, everyone was beginning to leave. Tyra and Terry stayed to help me clean up. B. offered to help but I told him no thanks. I just wanted him to leave so that Remi could get out of my house. Before leaving, B. told me that his brother's job was relocating him to Baltimore to oversee a hotel that was being built downtown and he was thrilled that his brother was going to be moving here.

After we were done cleaning up, I walked Terry and Tyra out to the front and watched until they pulled off. I turned to go back into the house and noticed poor Mrs. Johnson staring out of her window as if she had lost her best friend. I waved, and thought, what she would do if she knew Sis Betty's hands weren't in the air, her legs were. Yuck! Just the thought made me sick, and I couldn't wait until tomorrow to get the gory details from Duce.

Chapter Nine

I   went upstairs to my bedroom, got undressed and headed into the bathroom, ran a tub of hot steaming water and sprinkled Jasmine-scented beads inside of it and couldn't wait to climb in. I was beat. Sitting on the side of the tube I ran my fingers through my hair, thinking about all the events that occurred today, and wondered if Remi had told B. yet about her indiscretion. With the aroma from the beads dissolving in the steamy hot water, I closed my eyes and quickly became lost with the thought of making love to Ahmaun, although knowing that in my quest to leave him, sleeping with him was not making it any easier. I became aroused just thinking about how I wanted it tonight, doggie style, which was one of my favorite positions, and with that thought my juices began flowing. After having a mental orgasm, I opened my eyes and noticed the tub was full. I climbed inside, and took several deep breaths. Soaking my sponge, I released the hot water all over me and watched as it trickled down my breasts, still thinking of Ahmaun. I slowly began washing my pussy, and with every stroke slightly touching my clit made me want him even more. Where was he, I thought, determined not to call him again, but obviously thinking him up, because I heard him come in the front door.

He came up the steps not even offering one of his tired-ass lies, and it didn't matter. I had one thing on my mind and that was to tear his ass up tonight. He got undressed and anxiously joined me in the tub.

Sitting behind me, I rested my head back on his chest; he reached over for my warm vanilla body wash saturating the sponge with it. I felt so relaxed as he began rubbing the soapy sponge all over my breast. His hand made its way further down and he began sliding his finger in and out of my pussy, licking me all over my back, and whispering everything I wanted to hear; I turned around and stroked his neck with my tough, placing the palm of my hand on the side of his caramel-colored face, kissing him, and pulling him closer as every inch of his tough entered my mouth. I reached my hand down into the hot steamy water, gently stroked his dick, and watched as his eyes rolled back in his head when I softly caressed his ball's. And there went that stare he gives me right about the same time, and that's when I know even with all his shit, he loves me.

"Baby, I love you to deaf!" he whispered, confirming my thought.

Now holding both of my breasts in my hand, my head fell back with pleasure, and I moaned as he began sucking them. Unable to take it, I lifted my head and whispered in his ear for him to come on. Ahmaun climbed out first and then with his help so did I. Standing behind me with his arms around my waist, and his very hard dick up against my ass, we walked into the bedroom, leaving a trail of water behind us. I laid my wet body across the bed and watched as Ahmaun walked over, dimmed the lights, and then over to the dresser picking up the bottle of oil. Without even saying a word, he opened the dresser-draw and took a Magnum out the box.

Once over to the bed, he lay on top of me, and began to lick every part of my body. He then gestured for me to turn over, and I happily abided. I folded my arms, rested my head on them, and closed my eyes. Ahmaun began pouring the body oil all over me, feeling the warm oil run down my ass drove me insane.

"Sollie, promise me you will never leave me?" I didn't respond because it would have been a lie, although we were here once again getting ready to make love. I didn't forget anything I said earlier. But hell! I couldn't help it. The dick was just so fucking good! "Sollie, did you hear me?" he moaned, now putting every inch inside me, "promise me, baby, promise me!" With every thrust, I felt his dick becoming much harder inside me.

My eyes quickly widened. I raised my head up and slightly turned looking back at him, noticing that look on his face.

"Ahmaun, you better not! Ahmaun," I whined, "why did you cum?" I asked disappointedly. "Move, move," I said trying to push him off me.

"Baby, I'm sorry, shit! I couldn't help it. The pussy so fuckin good. I'm sorry, boo." He rolled over and laughed. "Come on, we can still finish."

"No, we can't!" I said looking at his limp dick. I got up from the bed and stomped into the bathroom to wash off. While I cleaned the tub, Ahmaun went downstairs and made us two big bowls of butter pecan ice cream. With the lights still dim, we sat in the bed talking until two in the morning. We talked about everything, but as soon as I mentioned him living in Atlanta as a teenager, the conversation ceased. And I saw once again the pain that lay so deep in his soul that not even I could touch. And I finally realized why he inflicted so much hurt on me. *Because hurt people, hurt people.* He got out of bed and took the empty bowls down to the kitchen. He returned, climbed in the bed, and lay in my arms as if he was a little boy, and asked me never to ask him again about the time he lived in Atlanta. I said okay, although I wondered why and what could have happened there to make him feel the way he did.

My house phone rang about seven in the morning, waking me up. When I said hello they hung up; I turned the night-light on to look at the caller ID and it read "Out of Area." I lay there unable to fall back asleep. I got up around eight and of course, Ahmaun woke up and tried to make up for last night. However, I wasn't in the mood. I took a shower, and decided I would go over to my mother's since I didn't make it yesterday. Walking back into the bedroom with my huge pink towel draped tightly around me, Ahmaun was sitting up watching the morning news and surprised the shit out of me when he asked if we could spend the day together, even giving me the option to do whatever I wanted. I reasoned with myself that shopping was okay; because it was his money I would be spending, not mine.

I got dressed and went down into the kitchen, put a pop tart in the toaster and wondered what was going on over at B.'s apartment. I picked up the phone to call him and see if he was okay. Changing my mind I hung up figuring I would wait for him to call me.

I wrapped my pop tart up in a paper towel, grabbed a soda from the refrigerator, yelled up the steps to Ahmaun that I would see him later, and left.

Another beautiful day, I thought, walking out the door. I climbed inside and just as I turned the ignition key, I jumped, quickly looking to the left and right. I looked up in my rearview mirror and didn't see anyone, but I could have sworn that someone was standing outside of my car door. I know I'm not crazy. I shrugged. I then heard a car start up. Looking in my rearview mirror I watched as the car pulled off and quickly turned the corner. I pulled off. Just as I drove up the street the same car came screeching out of the alley almost crashing into the side of me. I swerved into the other lane to avoid the speeding car. Stupid bitch! I thought wondering how terrible an accident that could have been. Noticing the car driving fast behind me, I pulled over to let the lunatic motorist go by because they were obviously in a rush. I slowed down, and so did they. I pulled back into traffic, and then noticed the car driving closer. Stopping at the red light, I inched up just a little, and so did they. I watched as they began slowly drifting back and forth. "Okay, I have a stick too, and what?" and I began doing the same. Squinting my eyes looking in the rearview mirror, I was trying to see the person driving but the tint on their windows was entirely too dark. I raised myself up to get a look at the tag but there was none on the front of the car. The light finally turned green, and I noticed the other lanes around me were clear. I drove slowly thinking maybe speed racer would go around, but they didn't. There was nothing but open road that surrounded us. So I figured if they wanted to play, okay then, let's play! I pressed down on the clutch quickly shifting into third, fourth, and then fifth gear crossing three lanes over, making a sharp right onto Cooks Lane. The tire squealed as I made the turn, but the Benz handled the curve like a racecar! With the car still on my ass, I began driving faster, and so did they. I swerved to the right and then to the left, and watched as they followed, making a quick left onto West Hills; they were still on me. *What the fuck!* I thought. I sped around the corner and then another making my way back out to Cooks Lane. The car was still close behind me, and then even bumped my car. The impact was hard enough to throw me forward, and that's when I realized this wasn't a joke, and the cat-and-mouse chase wasn't fun anymore. It was now scary; someone was trying to kill me. I nervously reached over to the passenger seat and reached into my purse frantically digging around inside trying to feel for my cell. I located it, pulled it out, and tried to dial Ahmaun's number. *What am I doing?* I thought, forgetting that all I had to do was say his name into the phone, and it would automatically dial his number. Holding the phone up to my mouth, my voice trembled as I yelled his name and waited for the connection, nothing. I looked at the phone and it read NO SERVICE. Remembering I was on Cooks Lane and everyone who knows this area for some reason most phones loses service. I glanced up and they were still on my ass. I drove faster. "I know," I said with relief, as I sped down to the bottom of Cooks Lane and prayed that the police would be sitting in the alley where they normally do; but they weren't there. My relief quickly turned back to panic. I looked over, ready to pull in the nearby gas station. What the hell is going on? I thought looking at the large sign that read "temporarily closed." I sped out the gas station, and noticing the light ahead turn yellow, I slowed down as if I was going to stop, looking to my left and right to make sure there was no oncoming traffic. And just as the light turned red, I sped through it, thinking that the car that was following me wouldn't run the light, but they did. Taking the speedometer to ninety, I sped up Security Blvd. My hands trembled as I picked up my cell, and thought fuck Ahmaun realizing this obviously had something to do with his grimy ass! "Salique!" I yelled into the phone, making it up to Woodlawn Drive. I quickly turned toward the gas station noticing a woman on the other side pumping gas; I drove into the gas station and came to a screeching halt, startling the woman. She immediately placed the pump back in the holder, jumped in her car, and pulled off. I looked in the rearview mirror, my legs shook uncontrollably; with the phone still ringing I prayed for Salique to pick up. Noticing the car door slowly opening, I pressed in the clutch and went into first gear and sped off, not even seeing a group of guys pushing a broken down vehicle into the gas station, and almost hitting them head on. I slammed on the breaks, avoiding the collision. The guys ran over to my vehicle asking if I was okay. "That car is following me," I said with tears streaming down my face. Just as the guys looked up, the car made a U-turn and sped out of the gas station. Holding my chest, I breathed a sigh of relief as I watched the car speed up Security Blvd.

"Sollie, Sollie you there!" It was Salique. He was at the track doing his morning run. I explained to him what just happened. He told me to call the police and that he was on his way. I called the police.

Minutes later Salique came flying into the gas station, looking around, and ready to hurt someone. He jumped out of his car, and ran over to my driver's side window asking if I was okay. I explained to him what happened and he was also certain that it had something to do with Ahmaun. We walked around to the back of the car to see if there was any damage and thank God there wasn't. Getting back inside the car, we waited for the police to arrive. I could only give the 911 operator a description of the vehicle, since I didn't get a tag number or even a look at the person driving.

"Look at them," Salique said, shaking his head with a very serious look on his face as he watched the police officer arrive thirty-five minutes later." Did you call them when I told you to?" I nodded yes.

"That's ridiculous!" he said glancing down at his watch. We both got out the car to talk with the officer.

"What seems to be the problem?" the officer asked while adjusting his uniform pants, pulling his wooden black nightstick out of the holder and letting it dangle from his finger, suspiciously looking at Salique.

"Everything is under control, officer," Salique said, although still pissed at how long it had taken him to get there. And he had definitely planned on doing something about it.

"What do you mean everything is under control?" the officer said to Salique, in a very nasty tone. He turned to me. "Ma'am, are you okay?"

"Officer my . . ."

"Now, wait a minute boy!" the officer said raising his voice, and pointing his nightstick at Salique.

"Boy, boy!" Salique snapped, leaning toward the officer, with his eyebrows now raised. "No! you wait a minute. My name is not boy. It's Mr. Salique Washington, and don't you ever speak to me in that manner again. I am not your child, and I'm damn sure not your boy. And on the contrary to what you're obviously thinking, I'm a very intelligent black man, and just like you want respect, I demand it. And as I told you a few seconds ago everything is under control, which you would have known if you had been here right after the 911 call was placed, and not thirty-five minutes later. And by the way officer, I'm going to need your name as well as your badge number."

I reached into my car window and inside the glove compartment and pulled out a small notepad and a pen and handed it to my brother. The officer chuckled and smugly asked, "What, are you going to call Internal Affairs?"

"Actually, Officer Chadwick," Salique said while looking at the officer's nametag, "that's my place of employment. I'll be there in one hour, and you will be hearing from us."

We could have brought his fat white-ass for a penny.

"Well, sir . . ."

"Oh, now it's sir."

"I was just trying to get more details about the incident."

"And from the tone of your voice, and in the manner in which you addressed me, you obviously thought I was the assailant. This woman is my sister, and as I told you a few minutes ago everything is under control. You have a good day. Let's go, Sollie."

Salique followed me to our mother's. When I parked, I walked over to his car and asked him not to mention to her what had happened. I didn't want her worrying. Angrily, Salique told me that I needed to leave Ahmaun alone, and that he was going to end up hurting him. I kissed him good-bye and walked up the pathway of her neatly manicured lawn and went into the house.

I rushed inside and quickly locked the door. I yelled up the stairs, letting my mother know that I was there. I walked down the four steps that led into the living room and sat down at the baby grand piano, gently running my fingers softly over the keys. Unable to keep still, I walked over to the huge bay window staring out at the water garden that my mother had built on her front lawn, watching the water stream down the large universal cascade rocks that surrounded it. I would have loved to go out and sit on the concrete bench and watch the beautiful Jamaican fish that swam around inside, but I was too terrified. Taking a deep breath, I turned and went into the dining room, and over to the étagère staring at all the pictures of Salique and me when we were younger; and for a moment, I wished I were a child once again when everything seemed much less complicated. *Who was that following me?* I wondered walking into the kitchen, sitting down at the Euro cherry-colored kitchen table distraughtly resting my head in the palms of my hand.

I almost fell out the chair when my mother touched my shoulder. I didn't even hear her come down the steps.

"I'm sorry, baby. Did I startle you?" my mother asked, leaning over and kissing me, while pushing my hair back out of my face.

"Yes, you did. You look pretty," I said smiling at her. My mother was seventy and looked nowhere near her age. Looking at her standing there in her floral pink housecoat and her locks up in a bun, I hoped that I would age so gracefully.

"What's wrong, Sollie, and why are you looking like that? Are you sure you're okay?"

"Mom, I'm fine," I said, getting up to go back into the living room unable to keep still.

"Come back in the kitchen, and let me fix you some breakfast." My mother said as she followed behind me.

"I'm good. I had a soda and a pop tart earlier."

"A soda and pop tart, Sollie you need to eat some food, putting that junk in your body early in the morning. And look at you. Your hips are starting to spread. What are you wearing now, a size ten?" she asked, tapping me on my butt. "All right, keep on and you're going to lose that beautiful figure."

My mother asked if I wanted to go to lunch later. I told her, maybe, another day. I didn't want to take a chance on that car popping up again. I agreed to eat breakfast and picked over most of it. After, we went into the living room.

"Oh, before I forget. Not that you would let me." She chuckled. She reached inside her housecoat and handed me the credit card and I assured her again that I would only use it for emergencies.

Later, I called Ahmaun and told him to meet me at my mothers. While waiting for him to come, my mother and I went out front and I showed her the Benz. Needless to say, she wasn't impressed; and truth be told, no longer was I. Just as we went to go back inside, Ahmaun pulled up. "There's your son-in-law," I teased.

"Not in this life time!" she said rolling her eyes at me. Ahmaun rolled down his window and spoke and she vaguely spoke back. I got my purse, kissed my mother good-bye, and left.

Although Ahmaun followed directly behind me, I was still very nervous, constantly looking in my mirrors for any sign of that car. We pulled into my block; I parked the car and quickly jumped inside Ahmaun's car. Immediately, I began questioning him about knowing anyone who drove that type of vehicle, and knowing him for the last eleven years, I knew he was lying just from the look on his face. He was actually beginning to make me sick.

As he drove to the mall, his cell rang off the hook. I didn't say anything. I just stared out the window hoping Nordstrom still had that Prada jacket I had seen two days ago. Once inside the mall, he handed me some cash. He walked a few feet in front of me to answer his phone that hadn't stopped ringing. Although I couldn't really hear him, it sounded like he asked the person on the other end, "What the hell is wrong with you?"

Fuck Ahmaun, I thought. I walked by him and went inside Nordstrom, and headed straight to the area where I had seen the jacket.

Yes! It was still there. Ahmaun finally joined me; I turned and looked at him leaning against the mirrored beam and rolled my eyes.

"Sollie, you sure you're okay?" he asked with guilt all on his face.

"Excuse me, I need to look in the mirror," I said trying on the jacket, and it fit perfectly.

"Man, shit!" he said, becoming annoyed that his cell phone was ringing again. "Shorty, I'll be right back. Go ahead and get whatever."

I walked slowly through the store, ending up in the shoe department and purchasing two pairs of Jimmy Choo's. Looking at my Rolex, I wondered where he was. I dialed his cell. He answered, and I told him I was ready. A few minutes later Ahmaun came walking in the department store carrying a Lord & Taylor bag, with my favorite perfume inside of it. He said that he had noticed the bottle I had was almost empty. He took me by the hand and led me over to Jared Jewelry store.

"You like that one?" he asked pointing at the five-karat teardrop diamond ring.

"It's all right," I replied, still pissed.

"Good. It's yours."

"Ahmaun, look at the price." I said.

"So what? That price doesn't mean anything, but I don't have that much cash on me. I'll come back and get it on Saturday. Sollie, check this out. I'm going to start giving you two grand a week."

"What!"

"You heard me. That's eight thousand a month and that should hold you. And besides, Shorty, that's a small thing. You remember the night of your party when I told you that within a year we were going to be millionaires?"

"Yeah, and . . ."

"Well we there!"

His cell was ringing again; he told me to wait a second and walked away to answer it.

What was I going to do, I thought, staring at the five-karat ring I was about to get; do I stay and let him do whatever as Mea suggested, or do I leave and wait for true happiness, and besides everybody knows that the drug game doesn't last forever. Maybe, I'll stay load up on the money, and then bounce! Still gazing at the tumor-sized ring, I contemplated in my head, money or peace, money or peace. A strange feeling came across me. I turned around and there was Remi, standing outside the jewelry store staring inside as if she hated the sight of me. Ahmaun walked back into the store, telling the salesmen that he would be back on Saturday. The man anxiously handed Ahmaun his business card.

"What's up Remi?" he mugged, as we walked out the store.

"Hi Ahmaun," she said smugly, and not even speaking to me. But ask me if I cared. I just wanted to know one thing. I told Ahmaun I needed to speak with Remi and that I would meet him at the entrance of the mall. He looked Remi up and down and then proceeded to walk away. I turned back to Remi and watched her as her eyes stared with envy at the shopping bags in my hand.

"I hope you told B. about what went down yesterday."

"Sollie, for real, you need to mind your business!" Remi snapped.

"What!" I walked closer to her. "First of all, trick, you made it my business when you decided you wanted to fuck Tavon in my house. And secondly, like I said yesterday, I wasn't going to allow you to use B. I have no idea what has been your problem for the last week, and come to think about it, for the last several months. All I have done was help you and now your ten-dollar ass wants to try and get slick with me. Well, guess what, Remi, fuck you! And obviously you didn't tell B. anything, so let me take care of that for you." Pulling out my cell, I walked away to do what I should have done yesterday. Remi stood there staring looking as if she really didn't give a shit.

Disappointedly, I listened to his voice mail saying he was flying out of town for an emergency business meeting. I left him a brief message and marked it urgent. Remi stood there with a smirk on her face, but it was cool. I would talk to B. soon enough. I walked back over to her.

"You better start looking for a place to lay that head. Oh, I forgot, you don't even have a job. You really fucked up a good thing."

"Whatever! I got a good thing going on," she responded sarcastically, pulling for a strand of her hair and twirling it around her finger with a very devious look on her face. She winked her eye at me, turned, and walked away.

"Yea, whatever, slut!"

"I got your slut," she retorted.

I shook my head thinking after all these years our friendship had come to this, and the crazy thing about it, I had no idea as to why. I turned and noticed Ahmaun walking to me with urgency.

"Shorty, come on, we have to go. I need to stop at my mom's house for a minute," Ahmaun said angrily. "I just got a call about someone fucking with my money, and for his sake I hope it's not true!" he said quickly walking toward the mall exit. Once in his car, he began driving like a maniac to get to his mother's house. I told him about what Remi had done, and he was pissed that she would even do something like that in my house.

He pulled up in front of the house, jumped out the car. He went inside, straight down into the basement, and I followed. As I got to the bottom of the steps, visions of him and that girl surfaced in my head; that morning was crazy. I remembered how I had slapped the hell out of both of them. I wouldn't have slapped her, only him, but when she started talking mad shit, it was warranted.

Looking at the picture of his mother that sat on his dresser, I wondered how in the hell she did it—allowing his father to cheat on her the way Ahmaun said he did. I guess the same way I do. I reached over and picked up the picture and thought about how I should have listened to her when she told me time after time to leave her son alone. Now, you know, any time the mother says that, he must not be shit! And I wish to God I would have listened. I then noticed a medicine bottle sitting on his dresser with the word e-pill written on it. I knew he was still using those pills. And I also knew when he used them, because it always seemed to bring out a rage in him. I turned toward Ahmaun and watched as he got down on the floor and reached under his bed.

"I hope it ain't true," he said pulling out two large red suitcases from underneath the bed, "that punk-ass nigga taking from me!" He picked both suitcases up, sat them on the bed, opened them, and pulled back the covers.

"Oh my God," I muttered. I saw nothing but hundred, fifty, and twenty-dollar bills, rubber band together. I stood there leaning against the dresser staring in disbelief. He walked over to the closet and pulled out a money counter and sat it on the table. One stack at a time he took the rubber band off and placed it into the money counter. He reared back on the black leather chair and rested his arms behind his head. "That nigga better pray it's all here," he said looking over at me. Removing the money as the machine finished counting it, he rubber banded it back together and repeated it the same steps until it was all counted. When he was done, the machine had counted a half million dollars. He folded his arms and looked over at me, disappointedly, shaking his head. "Why did that nigga fuck with my money?"

"Ahmaun, who are you talking about?" I asked curiously.

"The boy, Dino," he said, with a look of revenge on his face. "He fucked up." He put the money neatly back into the suitcases, and asked me if I could open an account and deposit this half million. I asked him if he was crazy. The IRS would be on my ass, depositing that kind of money without any kind of legit documentation as to where it came from. *Stupid,* I thought to myself.

"Okay," he said getting out of the chair. "I'll buy a safe and keep it at your crib."

"You trust me like that?" I asked.

"Yeah, I do. You are the only one I do trust. Well, you and one other person."

I didn't bother to ask who the other person was. His cell began to ring. He looked at the caller ID and mugged. I headed up the stairs to get something to drink, and just as I got to the top of the stairs I heard him answer the call. I stood quietly by the basement door and listened.

"Yeah! Why the fuck you keep blowing my phone up? I'm busy. Look, I don't want to hear that bullshit. You did what you did, and it's whatever. Yeah, okay, and that will be the worst mistake you ever made. Now run your mouth if you want, and see what happens! Talk to me about what. We ain't got shit we need to talk about! I'm gone!" He said ending the call.

"Who was that?" I asked coming back down the stairs, "and don't say it was one of your boy's! I heard you."

"Shorty, come on now, it was nothing. She's nothing."

"Who is she?! And what was that conversation about?"

"Sollie chill out! I told you she's nothing." I turned to walk away, and he grabbed me by my arm.

For the next hour we argued about the phone call, and whoever she was had to have called back at least twenty times in a row. He later turned his phone off and we eventually fucked. But this time it was different; somewhere in my spirit told me that it was the last time I would ever sleep with Ahmaun.

The ride home, I said absolutely nothing. My head was hurting so bad from the arguing and stressfulness of the relationship. I stared out the window and silently asked myself again, money or peace, money or peace? Sitting inside the car, waiting on Ahmaun, while he went inside a store and purchased a large steal safe, I thought about the Benz, money, jewelry, clothes, and most of all, the cheating. By the time we pulled in front of my house, I was mentally drained. I got out the car and just as I walked by the Benz, I stopped and stared, again, wondering if this was all worth the bullshit. Slowly walking away, I went into the house and straight to my bedroom. Flopping down on the bed, I thought, *peace.* That's what I wanted.

Ahmaun had to make two trips to bring everything in the house, and I watched as he began transferring the money from the suitcases to the safe.

"Ahmaun, you have to let me go!" I said as a tear fell from my eye.

Stopping for a quick second, he looked at me. "I ain't ever letting you go. Here," he said as he handed me the code to the safe. He stood up and briskly rubbed his hands together, asking me what was up for the rest of the day.

It's useless, I thought, not even responding. I headed down into the kitchen and made a bowl of ice cream. On my way up he was obviously talking to whoever had called him earlier. I stood on the top step and listened.

Didn't I tell you, I was busy? Nah, nah, ain't shit we need to talk about. What?! What the hell did you just say? Awwww bitch, that's some bullshit! You done lost your fuckin mind if you think I believe that shit! Where you at? stay right there. I'm on my way. Man, shit!

When I walked into the bedroom, Ahmaun was holding his head, and pacing the floor. He looked up at me and said, "I have to make a run. I'm taking your car. I'll be right back!" Just as I went to follow him, my cell rang. Noticing it was B., I answered.

"Is everything okay, Sollie?" B. asked with concern in his voice.

I told B. no, and that I really needed to see him. He asked if we could meet later; flying out of town last night on such short notice really wore him out, and that he needed to get a few hours sleep. Although he sounded tired, I could hear excitement in his voice, and I asked why he was so happy.

"My brother is flying in from Atlanta this evening. But Sollie, if it's really important, I can shoot over there now."

Thinking how much this was going to hurt him and how excited he was about seeing his brother, there was no way I could tell him, not right now anyway.

"Sollie, how about, once I pick up Lamar from the airport, we can stop over? That way you can finally meet my big brother, and we can talk then."

"B., don't worry about it. It can wait. And I really do want to meet Lamar, but tonight isn't a good night. Tell him I said hello and hopefully we will meet soon," I said and hung up.

That bitch was really lucky. It's cool though. There's a time and place for everything.

I lay across the bed and ended up dozing off, and woke up around seven that evening. Reaching for my cell, I looked to see if Ahmaun had called; he hadn't. I headed down to the kitchen to fix something to eat. As I walked by the living room, I noticed his car keys were laying on the glass table. I picked up the keys and went out to his car searching for anything I could find. But I found nothing but numbers, business cards, the usual. I opened the trunk, looking inside, and then thinking Ahmaun had to be the dumbest nigga in the game. Why would anybody ride around with a scale and other paraphernalia? I looked further to the back of the trunk and noticed a Nordstrom bag. What is this another surprise? I thought, reaching inside the bag, and it was the exact same suit he had bought me for my party, same color, and everything. That bastard! I went back inside and waited for him to return. Sitting on the couch and I was thinking I wasn't the only one he was lacing in couture. I heard the front door open, and he wasn't in the house good before I jumped up from the couch ready to lay his ass out. But when he walked through the door, all I could do was stare. He had a look on his face that I had never seen before. I wanted to question him about the suit in his car, but he was looking so weird, I decided not to say anything. Leaning up against the wall, with my arms folded, I asked, "What's wrong?"

"Nothin, Shorty," he said, walking over to me and grabbing me tightly.

I reached for both of his arms and pushed them from around my waist, and looked him in his eyes. "Ahmaun, what's going on? You're scaring me." Ahmaun stared back with a blank look. He said it's nothing and that he needed to lie down. I stood there staring as he slowly walked up the stairs. And for some reason I felt that whatever it was, it was going to affect me, and my heart couldn't take another blow from Ahmaun Moore.

Chapter Ten

N o longer hungry, I sat in the living room and drank a glass of wine and flipped through the TV channels trying to find something to watch. "Nothing," I thought turning off the TV and headed upstairs to the bedroom. Ahmaun was stretched out across the bed, asleep. Noticing his cell in the palm of his hand, I quietly walked over to him and slowly eased the cell phone out of his hand, and walked into the computer room. Pressing the scroll button looking for names and numbers and there were none, he covered his tracks very well.

I walked back into the bedroom and placed the cell next to him, put on my nightclothes, climbed in the bed, and moved as far away from him as I could. The next morning when we woke he rolled over and pulled me closer. Opening my eyes and pulling away from him, I noticed he still had that look on his face. He reached down for his cell, and seemed very relieved that no one had called. "I knew it was bullshit," he mumbled as he climbed out of bed and walked into the bathroom.

He took his shower, got dressed, and kissed me good-bye. About two minutes after, he came back inside yelling up the steps that he needed to take my car, because his car had a flat. He asked me to call and have the car towed.

"A tow truck, why don't you change it yourself?"

"I don't know how to change a flat tire, just call the tow truck."

That's a got damn shame. I thought googling a tow truck company. I called the tow truck company, and they said that someone would be out within the hour. Just as I was getting out the shower, the phone rang. It was the tow-truck driver telling me that he was out front the house.

The morning air was cool. I wrapped my arms tightly around me and shivered as I walked over to the side of the car where the man was standing. And I couldn't help but notice the look of certainty on his face.

"Is this your car?" The old man asked with a Salem100 dangling from his mouth.

"No, it's my boyfriend's car."

"Well, your boyfriend must have another girlfriend," he said, right before taking a long drag off his cigarette, and then blowing the smoke directly in my face. He bent down and slowly rubbed his finger along the tire.

"Excuse me!" I snapped.

"Oh yeah, this tire here ain't flat! This tire has been slashed!" Quenching his eyes from the smoke, and then taking another drag, he said, "And I tell you another thing," he continued, "Men don't do things like this, only y'all damn women."

"It's a flat!" I blurted, rolling my eyes at the old man.

"Listen, pretty face," he said licking his ashy lips. "I have been towing cars for the last thirty-nine years, and I know a flat from a slash. And this here is a slash!" He pointed to the tire, seeming to become somewhat offended that I would question his knowledge of a damaged tire. "And whoever did must have a terrible cut. "Look!" he said pointing down to the ground at the blood in the street. "Now listen," he said leaning up against the car door, "if he ain't treating you right, I will, with your pretty little self, mmhhh." He smiled showing all three teeth in his mouth.

"Yuck!" I didn't even feel like cursing him out. I signed the invoice and went back in the house.

That bastard, so whoever he is seeing knows where I live. I called Tyra to wish her happy birthday, and to tell her the latest news. She couldn't believe it. Then again, yes, she could.

"Girl, I'll be so glad when you leave him alone," she exclaimed. "It won't be long now anyway."

"What are you talking about won't be long?"

"I met your future husband yesterdayyyyy," she sang.

"What are you talking about, future husband?"

"Girl B. and his brother stopped by the house last night, and Sollie he is fine. You think B. is fine. Child, please wait until you meet him, and he seems like such a nice guy. And girl, you know, I asked him a million questions. He's single, no kids, never been married, has a good job, knows the Lord, and oh yeah, did I mention fine?!" Tyra said excitedly without taking a breath in between.

"No, no, no, hell no! Don't even think about it, Tyra. The only thing I want to do is get rid of Ahmaun, and be by myself. I don't care if the brother looks like Idris Elba, Hill Harper, and Laz Alonso rolled into one. I'm done."

"Okay, I like the first part, and I know it would be too soon to get involved with someone, but you two can just be friends."

I quickly changed the subject because there was no way I was meeting anyone. I told her about the car that was following me and like she said this whole thing was starting to get really ugly, and I must admit, it was. She invited me to her house for dinner. She said the kids were cooking for her birthday; I declined, but we made plans to hook up later to go out and have a drink. The way I was feeling maybe two or three drinks.

All day I struggled with the temptation to go shopping. So to keep myself busy I ended up cleaning the whole house. Around eight, I spoke again with Tyra, and we laughed at the dinner the kids made for her birthday. French fries were the appetizer, and fish sticks and onion rings was dinner, which just happens to be the kids' favorite meal. And for dessert they each had a strawberry shortcake ice cream. Tyra was cool with it. She's never been one that had or needed to go way out for her birthday as long as she was with her family. They could have made mud pies for dinner and she wouldn't have cared. That's one of the things that I loved about her.

I got dressed, went down into the living room, turned on the radio, and waited for Ahmaun to bring my car back. Just as I began putting a coat of clear nail polish over my nail, he came through the door. And just as he did I looked up and asked God to help me keep my mouth shut; all I wanted was the keys to my car, so I could get out of there.

"You look real slick," he said in a depressing tone walking into the living room. "Where are you going?"

"I'm going out with Tyra," I held my hands out for the car keys and his simple ass reached in his pocket and handed me money. I kept it. "The keys Ahmaun," I said frowning.

"Where are y'all going?"

"Why?"

"Sollie, don't start. I just asked you a simple question."

"Yeah, and I just asked you a simple question yesterday, and still haven't gotten an answer."

He stared at me and asked, "Marry me?" I asked Ahmaun if he was crazy. Our shit was already raggedy. "We can make it work," he pleaded. I shook my head, and left out the door, leaving him standing right there in the middle of the floor. Hearing him call my name, I continued walking.

God, I wish when he uses my car he would put the seat back like I had it. And who in hell was in here? I thought looking over at the passenger seat that was laid all the way back. I told him not to be having them guys in my car anyway.

The ride to Tyra house was very uncomfortable; I was constantly looking at all my mirrors to make sure I wasn't being followed again. Once there I pulled into the driveway, relieved that I made it safely. I sat there for a moment to get myself together; being on edge like this was driving me crazy. I got out of the car and headed into the house. The kids were so happy to see me, and I was as equally happy to see them. Trinity, who looked just like Tyra, was four, and little Terry was nine, and the splitting image of his father. Trinity was a pretty little girl; she inherited Tyra's free spirit, brown complexion, big brown eyes, and thick black eyebrows. And when she smiled the dimple in her right cheek would appear. And she looks so cute wearing the tiny brown bifocals that at one time she had refused to wear because the kids in head-start teased her so badly, and every time Tyra would pick Trinity up from head start she was always in tears. But as always Tyra came to the rescue. She went in purchased a pair of bifocals from the dollar store, and glued them to the face of Trinity's favorite doll; and the doll just happened to be the envy of all her class mates, because the doll sings and dances, and ever since Trinity had no problem wearing the glasses. Little Terry inherited his father's curly hair, light brown complexion, and hazel colored eyes. Although they both had learning disabilities, they were very smart children.

"Aunt Sollie, can I go?" Trinity asked jumping into my arms.

"No, I'm going," Little Terry said, pushing his little sister slightly out of the way.

"Listen, your mommy and I are going out for a little while, and it's only for grown-ups." I smiled pressing down her pony tail that was sticking straight up in the air. I put her down, and she stood on her toes, and said, "I'm a grown up. Mommy says I'm a big girl."

"And you are a big girl and a very pretty girl too." Watching Trinity blush, I promised them both that I would get them soon, maybe even overnight and have a slumber party.

"Cool!" they both said, jumping up and down.

Tyra kissed her family, and we left.

"Sollie, you're going to kill me," Tyra said, getting inside the car. "I think I may have broken your earring." She reached down and picked up the cheap gold-plated earring.

Taking the earring from her and feeling my pressure rise, "This is not my ugly-ass earring! I wouldn't wear anything like this. I know, that boy didn't have a Bitch in my car! I know he didn't!" I said, hitting the dashboard causing me to break a nail. "Now this is too much. I going to find out who the hell this broad was that's bold enough to get in my shit, come to my house, and call my phone. And her ass will be dealt with accordingly! And Ahmaun, I'm going to take that cheating, lying, disrespectful-ass nigga for all he's got. No more being nice. He wants to play. Let the games begin." Angrily gripping the steering wheel, I lay my head back on the headrest and my eyes began to well up with tears. As I turned to look at Tyra, a teardrop slowly rolled down my face. "Tyra, I'm tired."

Tyra reached into her pocketbook and pulled out a tissue handing it to me and said, "As much as it hurts me to see you in pain, this is exactly where you need to be. All these years I have never seen this look on your face. You're ready," she said with certainty.

"Ready for what?" I asked wiping my eyes.

"For change. Now I suggest we go to your house, pack his things, and end it. But knowing you, it's not going to happen that easy especially with you finding this earring. So let me call my contact." Tyra said pulling out her cell, "and see if she can make some things happen." Looking at me with that detective look in her eyes.

Although Tyra never pursued her dreams of becoming a criminologist, it was still in her blood. She loved shit like this. I started the car and slowly began backing out the driveway. Tyra dialed a friend who worked for a cell phone company and she could pretty much do anything to anyone's cell phone. Tyra gave her Ahmaun's cell number, and asked her if she would be able to change his pass code, so he would be unable to check his messages. She said yes, and would take care of it as soon as she got to work in the morning.

"We got him," Tyra said, raising her hand in the air giving me five. "Tonight, when you get home, try and get his cell if you can."

I looked at Tyra curiously and asked, "What do I do with it?"

"Girl, I don't know. Throw in the trash, just as long as he can't answer it. If she calls and he doesn't answer, she may leave a message. Remember she's going to take care of this in the morning, so you have to get the phone tonight." Tyra's attention was taken when our favorite song began playing on the radio. "Hayyyyyy, here's your song, Sollie," Tyra said turning up the volume, and snapping her fingers.

What the hell? Are they giving something away? I thought pulling up in front of the club. It was packed. I drove around the block several times before finding a parking spot. After parking, I popped in a club mix, hoping that it would pump me up a little, 'cause truthfully I wasn't feeling this tonight. But it was Tyra's birthday . . .

"You know, it's ladies' night," Tyra said pulling out her tube of chocolate-colored lipstick.

"That's right," I said looking over at the long line in front of the club.

"Do you really want to go inside?" Tyra frowned.

"Not really," I admitted. "But it's your birthday."

"I have a better idea," she smiled.

I asked Tyra where we were going, and she said, back to her house. As we drove to Tyra house, we really didn't say much. Tyra knew that I had a lot on my mind, and yes, I did, glancing down at the earring; I don't know why I found it so hard to believe he had a female in my car considering everything else he has done. I pulled up into the driveway and all the lights were out inside the house.

"Okay, give me a second," Tyra said taking off her heels, running up the side walk and up to the door. She put her key inside the lock and slowly turned the doorknob, looking back at me smiling as she tiptoed into the house. A few minutes later she came running out the house with two wine glasses, a bottle of Chardonnay, a box of vegetable crackers, extra-sharp cheddar cheese, and my Phyllis Hyman CD that she refuses to give back. I opened the sunroof and with the warm summer breeze blowing, the stars shinning over us, and Meet Me on the Moon playing, I had to admit that this was much better than a hot, crowded club. We poured our wine, toasted to Tyra's birthday, laid the seats back, and ate our cheese and crackers. And for a short time it seemed as if all of my worries were gone.

Tyra said that she was cooking dinner for B. and his brother tomorrow night, and they were going to discuss possibly backing B. on starting his group home business.

"Why don't you come? I'm cooking your favorite."

"Tyra, come on now, please! I don't want to meet him. Maybe he is a nice guy, but no thank you."

Before we knew it, it was two-thirty in the morning, and those two glasses of Chardonnay had us acting really silly. And I guess, the Chardonnay had me not thinking clearly, because I finally agreed to come to Tyra's for dinner and made her pinky swear that she wasn't going to play matchmaker.

Tyra tried to get me to stay the night, concerned that I may have drank too much, but I was good; my concern wasn't the police, but the person driving that car that was following me. Once again, while driving, I was constantly checking my mirrors. Thank God I thought, pulling in front of my house. I parked and quickly got out. Terrified every time I heard a car go by, I hurried up the walkway and up the steps, unlocked the front door, and quickly went into the house.

I heard the shower running, so I rushed up the steps. Good, I thought I rushed into the room searching everywhere for Ahmaun cell. Where the hell is it?! I thought looking around the room. Snatching his jeans from off the bed, I quickly searched his pockets, but the cell wasn't there. I heard the shower turn off so I reached for the remote and sat down on the bed and acted as if I was watching TV.

"Hey, what's up baby. I didn't hear you come in," he said walking into the bedroom with a brown towel wrapped around his waist. "Did you have fun?"

"Yes, I did. What, are you high?" I asked as I stared at him, making sure I didn't see any signs that he was pooping those e-pills again. 'Cause the rage I was harboring, and how those pills have him would not have been a good mixture!

"Yeah, I'm a little fucked up. I smoked a little loud earlier," he admitted, taking the towel from around his waist, and looked at me as it dropped to the floor.

Whatever, you won't get this ass again! That big dick was no longer worth this madness, I thought rolling my eyes at the sight of it. I got up and headed into the bathroom. "Yes!" his cell was lying on the sink. Stupid ass, he must have smoked a lot of loud, forgetting his phone was in here. I quickly scrolled through the phone and once again he had cleared all the numbers. I turned on the faucet and accidentally dropped the cell under the running water. "Oops," I chuckled walking out the bathroom.

When I returned to the bedroom, Ahmaun was lying across the bed with a wife beater on and Ralph Lauren plaid boxers. I got undressed and climbed into bed. It took everything in me to keep my mouth shut about the phone calls, the slashed tire, the suit in his trunk, and the earring I found in my car. "I love you, nigga," he said moving closer to me. Moving further away from him I rolled over and stared at the safe sitting in the corner. Little did his disrespectful ass know I was about to be half a million dollars richer. Yeah, that's right, like the old saying goes, it's a thin line between love and hate! And Ahmaun had crossed it!

Chapter Eleven

T he next morning, I prepared myself for what was about to come, as I lay there and watched Ahmaun walk into the bathroom.

"Sollie! How the fuck did my phone get in the sink?" he yelled, walking back in the bedroom holding the damaged phone.

"I have no idea. Maybe you knocked it in there," I said, rolling over and trying not to laugh.

Ahmaun sat there literally taking the phone apart, but it was no use—the cell phone was ruined. He picked up the cordless and dialed his cell number, "Shit I have messages on here." He attempted to put in his four- digit pass code. "What the hell is going on?" he snapped. "It's not accepting my pass code, and I still would like to know how my shit ended up in the sink." He looked at me suspiciously.

"Don't look at me like that, you was so high last night . . ."

"Yeah, whatever." Sitting the phone on the dresser he walked back into the bathroom.

Tyra called and said that her friend had just faxed a copy of Ahmaun's phone bill, and had even reset his pass code.

I whispered to her that I knew.

Tyra said as soon as she dropped the kids off at her parents' she would be right over. Ahmaun got dressed and called one of his homeboys to pick him up. Thank God, I thought, hearing the horn blow. He headed down the steps angrily saying he would call me later.

I took a quick shower, put on my robe, and went down into the kitchen to fix Tyra her favorite meal of the day, breakfast. Just as I finished cooking the last pancake the doorbell rang. I rushed to the door and opened it. "Good morning, Detective Palmer," I said laughing and grabbing Tyra by her arm, pulling her inside the house. With urgency we both sat down at the breakfast bar, removing the phone from the wall mount, and sitting it in front of us. Tyra handed me the new pass code. I put the phone on speaker and began dialing his number, praying that the bitch had left a message.

You have thirteen new messages.

Tyra and I looked at each other and smiled, but not for long. Eleven of them were hang-ups. Disappointed, I rested my chin on my hand, realizing there were only two messages left.

Twelfth Message.

Tyra and I crossed our fingers in hopes that this wasn't another hang-up.

Ahmaun, this is your mother. Why aren't you answering your phone? I wish you would call that girl. She is very disrespectful calling my house all hours of the night looking for you. And I have told you time and time again about giving my number out. Call me when you get this message.

Thirteenth message.

We heard a clicking noise, but that was it. "Oh well, maybe she will call later," I said getting up to fix Tyra's plate. And just as Tyra went to end the call a very chilling voice came through the speaker.

"Sollie, Sollie," Tyra said waving her hand for me to come back over to the table. She pulled the phone closer to us and turned up the volume.

Ahmaun, it's me. You could have at least called to make sure I made it back safely. I'm sure you are aware that the job was done, and everything went smoothly. As they always do. All these years I have done everything you asked of me, and you keep saying we're going to be together. But when? You keep lying to me. And I can't take it anymore, being alone, and living in seclusion like this. Only thing you seem to be concerned with is that stupid-ass bitch! And you wonder why I did what I did! I need you, not her, me. And I know if you don't get me away from here soon those people are going to find me, and I can't go back. I refuse to go back!

All of a sudden the woman's voice changed drastically.

I'm sorry. Please don't be angry with me. I love you and you know it. I just need you so much! You're all I have. You keep saying you are going to leave her and we are going to be together. But when? You have to know she doesn't love you like I do.

The woman began moaning and breathing heavily. Tyra's facial expression looked as if she had just bitten into a lemon "What the hell is she doing, masturbating?" And yes, that's exactly what she was doing.

Fuck me, baby, deeper, yes go deeper, yes, oh yesssss! she sang. Letting out a long sigh of relief, she hung up. For more information on this number press four. As Tyra sat there speechless, I pressed four and listened while the recording gave me the time and date of the call. Reaching across Tyra for the phone bill, I waved my hand back and forth in front of her, because she looked as if she was in a daze.

"Oh-my-God!" Tyra said, in slow motion, "I don't believe what I just heard. Who the hell was that! Sollie, something is not right! What was wrong with her? I'm sorry we even checked his messages."

"Well, I'm not!" I was determined to find out who the crazy bitch was. I began looking down the list of numbers from his phone bill. "You know he loves a freak!"

"Sollie, that girl was beyond a freak. She sounded psychotic! Did you hear how quickly her voice changed?"

My cell rang and I asked Tyra to answer it. I was too busy trying to find a number that matched the day and time of the phone call.

"Yes Mea!" Tyra said. "What!" Tyra blurted slamming her hand down on the table. "Mea said that Dino was murdered." She handed me the phone.

"What! Get the hell out of here. He was working for Ahmaun. As a matter of fact, Ahmaun just said the other day he found out that

113

Dino was stealing from him." My eyes widened. I looked at Tyra. "He couldn't have."

Mea said the article on Murder Ink said he was killed execution style in broad daylight. They said he was on the corner with some other guys. And next thing you know, Dino was on the ground dead with a gunshot wound in the middle of his forehead, and they never saw anyone. I hung up from Mea and walked over to the sink in total shock.

I stared at the wall as chills ran through my body. "So if they never saw anyone, who the hell killed him, a sniper?"

Oh my God, could Ahmaun have something to do with Dino's murder. "You know what, Tyra, forget this shit!" I said walking over to the table and ripping up the phone bill. "I don't care who the freak was. I just want him gone." I was terrified. The thought of Ahmaun playing a role in Dino's murder was a bit too much for me to handle.

"Are you sure?" Tyra asked.

"I'm positive!" I said mounting the phone back on the wall.

"Good! Now let's go upstairs and pack his things."

"Tyra, I will, but now is not the time. I was still going to make that bastard pay for all the dirt he has done to me."

I went upstairs and dressed. When I came back down, Tyra was sitting in the living room watching TV.

Ahmaun came in, vaguely spoke to Tyra, and she vaguely spoke back. He asked me to come upstairs; the sight of him made me sick to my stomach. I followed him up the stairs and into the bedroom. Folding my arms and leaning against the bedroom door, I asked him, "What's up?"

"I bought a new cell, got my same number, and my same pass code. I don't know what the hell was going on this morning. Anyway, check this out," he said taking a few items of clothes out the closet. "I'm going out of town for a few days to take care of some business. So take this." He handed me two grand. "All right, Shorty, I'm out!" As he leaned over to kiss me, I turned my head away. "I love you, nigga! And cheer up. I told you, she means nothing," he said as he headed down the stairs.

Tyra and I eventually left my house; I rode with her to run a few errands. Around four, Tyra dropped me off and I called my mother to see if she wanted to go to Tyra's with me for dinner, and she said yes. I called Tyra and reminded her of the promise she made not to play matchmaker. She laughed and said she promised. I laid my white linen wide-leg pants and a soft shimmer gold halter top out on the bed, took my shower, got dressed, and headed over to my mother's. And of course, I was paranoid thinking about the car that was following me. When I pulled up at my mother's, she was sitting out front on the bench, in front of the water garden, wearing a beautiful African print dress. Her hair was wrapped with the same print of the dress, and her locks sprouted out the opening at the top. I smiled as she so elegantly walked over to my car, carrying a wine bag with a bottle of sparkling cider inside of it. As she got in the car, I told her that she looked like an African queen.

I loved my mother, but now was not a good time for her million and one questions. Trying to drive, shift, answer her, and look out for the car was nerve-wracking. And I was relieved once again making it safely to Tyra's.

"Oh, Tyra's front is so beautiful," my mother exclaimed as we pulled into the driveway. "So did Tyra say what's she serving for dinner?"

"No, Mom, she just said that she was cooking my favorite." I chuckled thinking the way I love to eat that could be a number of things. But unfortunately, with all this mess going on I really didn't have an appetite.

"I'm so glad you two have remained as close as you have. That's a true blessing to have someone that you can truly call your friend."

When Tyra opened it she was so happy to see us both. Now, understandably, she would be happy to see my mother because she has not seen her in a while, but me, on the other hand, she had just seen earlier that day.

Terry came walking into the living room smiling and drying his hand on the black apron he had on. He said that Tyra has been running around like a maniac. I knew it, I thought, looking at Tyra smiling at me with that look. "Tyra please no match making. I'm not playing!"

"I didn't do anything," she said beginning to laugh. "We pinky swore, remember." She turned the TV on for my mother and offered her something to drink.

With dinner almost done, Tyra and I set the table and then joined my mother and Terry in the living room. Tyra looked at her watch constantly, and one time even walked over to peep out the window. Terry looked over at me and shook his head because we both knew what she was up to. A few minutes later the doorbell rang. Excitedly, Tyra jumped up from the couch and raced over to the door stumbling in the process. "All right Tyra, now that's ridiculous," Terry said frowning at his wife's behavior.

She looked back at us and smiled, tilting her head with a look of innocence. "I'm not doing anything," she said opening the door with a huge smile on her face.

"Hey, Tyra," B. said leaning over and kissing her. B. walked into the house alone, and Tyra's smile quickly disappeared.

"B., where is Lamar?" she asked curiously.

B. said that his brother flew back to Atlanta this morning. He found an apartment yesterday, so he's gone back to finish the rest of his packing. And he should be back permanently in about a week.

Tyra was so disappointed, looking over at Terry and me and rolling her eyes. We both laughed. We all headed into the dining room to eat dinner. As much as I loved stuffed lobster, I picked over all of it. I sat there and listened to B. discuss his business proposition, and by the looks on Terry and Tyra's faces they were going to invest. "Sollie, are you okay? You barely touched your food," my mother said looking at my half-eaten plate. I told her I was fine. I reached around and took my pocketbook off the arm of the chair and sat it in my lap, reached inside, and pulled out that hideous looking earring and stared it. Just as B. went to take a sip of his Heineken he looked at me.

"Sollie, where did you find that? Remi has been looking everywhere for it."

Slowly raising my head and leaning closer to him, to make sure I had heard him correctly, I tilted my head and asked in slow motion, "What-did-you-say?"

"I said where did you find it? Remi has been looking everywhere for it."

And for one quick second my heart stopped beating or at least it felt like it did. I looked over at Tyra and watched as she laid her fork on her plate, and lowered her head.

"Sollie! Where did you find it?"

"I'm sorry B.," I said quickly shaking my head from side to side, trying to come out of the shock that the words he spoke had put me in. My mouth opened but nothing would come out. My heart began racing, palms began to sweat and I literally became nauseated. Tyra quickly intervened.

"Sollie, didn't you find it the day of the cookout?"

"No, she just lost it yesterday. Was she at your house yesterday? She didn't mention that she saw you," B. said with a curious look on his face. "It doesn't matter anyway. I hate those earrings."

"I saw her at the mall yesterday. She lost it then. I didn't see it lying there until she walked away," I said hoping he bought the bogus story.

"Oh, yeah," B. exclaimed. "She did mention that she was at the mall,"

My mother continued eating and Terry looked at Tyra and me strangely, knowing that by the look on his wife's face something was wrong.

B. was right; she did lose it yesterday, but not at the mall. When she was in my fucking car! And she is obviously the one he was arguing with on the phone before he left the house. Grabbing my stomach tightly I slowly stood up from the table. And just as I did, my knees buckled, and I felt as if I was going to fall back into the seat. Holding on to the edge of the table and feeling the tears well up in the corner of my eyes, I realized I had to get out of there before one teardrop fell. I excused myself and quickly walked up the black iron spiral stairs to the bathroom. I rushed inside and fell up against the brass towel holder. "No, no, no, no!" I chanted, shaking my head from side to side, and slowly slid down the ceramic-tile wall. Bending down on my knees, I wrapped my arms around me tightly, rocking back and forth, trying to stop the unbearable pain. I wanted to scream but I couldn't. Still on bent knees, I reached my hand up and snatched the towel off the holder. Placing it up to my mouth, burying my face inside of it, I cried one of those cries where it sounds as if you were laughing.

"Sollie, Sollie!" Tyra called out in a whisper, lightly tapping on the bathroom door. She came inside. "Shit!" she said rushing over to where I was. Kneeling down behind me and wrapping her arms around me, she gently laid her face against mine as we both rocked back and forth in a rhythmic motion.

"I have to get out of here. I can't breathe! I can't breathe, Tyra," I muttered through the towel. Tyra stood up and walked over to the white linen cabinet and took out a wash cloth and wet it with cold water. She walked back over to me and wiped my tears as I cried out, "Why!?"

"I don't know why, Sollie," she answered, laying the washcloth on the side of the Jacuzzi, she turned and extended her hand out to me. With tears still streaming down my face, I reached out and took her hand. We walked into her bedroom and sat down on the king-sized bed, resting my head on Tyra's shoulder. Terry came upstairs and into the room and asked if everything was okay. Tyra smiled warmly and said, "No, but it will be."

What I was feeling didn't feel anything like all the other times he has hurt me. Even catching him in bed with someone else didn't feel like this! It felt as if a part of me had died.

As my heart tried to make excuses, my mind wouldn't allow it; there were none to make. It's funny how when things come out, all of the signs that I should have recognized began to appear in my head. "I have to go," I said standing up and walking over to the mirror. I took a tissue from the box and wiped my eyes. Through the mirror, I watched Tyra angrily walk into her closet and grab her small overnight bag that she always kept packed, in case there was an emergency. I turned to her. "Where are you going?"

"Where do you think? Come on," she said walking over to her bedroom door.

When we got downstairs, my mother, Terry, and B. were sitting in the living room watching a movie. Terry and B. were sitting there eating pretzels and drinking beer, and my mother was eating a bowl of grapes, and sipping her sparkling cider, falling out laughing at the movie. Trying to hide the pain from them, I walked over to the window and stared outside.

"What were you two doing?" my mother asked.

"We were just talking," Tyra answered. I turned slightly lowering my head asking my mother if she was ready.

"Baby, we just sat down to watch the movie."

Still not giving her direct eye contact, I said, "I know Mom, but I don't feel well."

"Sollie, go ahead, I will make sure your mom gets home safely," B. said.

"Mrs. Marie, are you going to be okay? I was going to ride with Sollie," Tyra said looking over at Terry.

"What are you two up to?" my mother asked suspiciously looking at us both.

"Nothing, I think Tyra's cooking made me sick." Everyone laughed and Tyra and I tried to utter a laugh. I walked over to the door and just as I turned the doorknob, I looked back at B.

"B., listen, don't tell Remi I found her earring. I'm going to surprise her with a new pair, because you're right they are ugly." B. Laughed and said okay.

"Where is Remi anyway?" Tyra asked standing behind me at the door.

"She's home. She's not feeling well. She thinks she has a stomach virus, and she cut her finger really badly the other day while she was cooking."

Once outside, Tyra angrily reached in her pocketbook for her cell.

"What's her number?"

"No, Tyra, I'm going to handle this myself."

"What are you going to do?" Tyra asked taking the car keys out of my hand.

"I don't know yet, but she'll regret the day she crossed me."

I got in the passenger seat and took a deep breath and laid my head back on the head rest. I turned to Tyra, and said, "Once again you were right."

"Yeah," Tyra shrugged shaking her head and frowning. "Yeah, but this time I wish to God I was wrong."

Chapter Twelve

T he drive to my house was quiet. So many thoughts and questions were running through my head: how long, when, where, did anyone else know about it. Tyra pulled up in front of the house. We went inside. And the first thing I noticed was the picture of Ahmaun and me. "You bitch!" I yelled picking up the picture and throwing it against the wall and shattering the glass frame. A few minutes later, the doorbell rang, And guess who it was? That nosey Mrs. Johnson saying she heard a loud noise. I assured her that everything was okay and she left. I guess it was good that she came over because watching her stand there with her wig on backward made me laugh.

Tyra called and told Terry what was going on and that she would be staying with me tonight and of course he understood.

We sat there talking for the rest of the evening. Tyra continued to tell me that everything was going to be okay, but I didn't see how. Does a pain like this ever go away? I wondered. And if so when?

We both headed upstairs to bed. I woke up around seven, Tyra was in the shower and I laid there hurting, thinking that this couldn't be happening. I curled up in a fetal position and cried. Tyra got dressed and pleaded with me to get up and eat something. But I refused. I didn't have an appetite to eat anything. I sat up and clutched my pillow tightly. She went down to the kitchen and opened a can of chicken noodle soup and brought it to my room, along with my pocketbook, telling me my cell was ringing. Who is calling this early,

I thought, reaching inside my purse for the cell and looking at the missed call. It was Ahmaun. And just as I laid the cell on the bed, it rang again, and I knew it was him calling back.

I had to get myself together because there was no way I wanted him to know that I found out about him and Remi. I cleared my throat and answered.

"Don't answer it!" Tyra blurted sitting the bowl of soup down. Waving my hand at her and covering the mouthpiece, I whispered that "I have to."

"Hello," I said trying to sound as I normal as I could.

"What's up, baby?" And when I heard his voice, the tears began to come again.

"Hi, Ahmaun."

"Shorty, what's wrong? Why do you sound like that?" he asked.

"I'm catching a cold. Are you in Atlanta?"

"Yeah, yeah I'm in the A. Baby look, I had to leave my car parked at my mother's. I caught a cab to the airport so I may need you to come and scoop me up. I'll call you and let you know for sure. Hope you feel better. Get some rest, and I'll holla at you later, I love . . ."

I hung up before he could even finish telling that lie. They played me, and now they were both going to pay dearly; I was now a mad black woman. And Ahmaun and Remi were going to feel my wrath.

I got up and went and took a shower. Standing there under the hot running water with my head back and my eyes closed, the water was soothing as it ran through my hair and down my face. And for a second, I had forgotten about them both! But only for a second, until I remembered what B. had said yesterday.

Oh God! I reached down and turned off the shower, got out, grabbed my towel, and quickly wrapped it around me.

"Tyra, Tyra," I called storming into the bedroom, grabbing my head and leaning against the bedroom door slightly chuckling and feeling like the biggest fool there ever was. Tyra looked at me and asked, "What's wrong?"

Stomping my foot on the floor, I said, "Remi was the one who slashed his tires! Remember B. said she cut her finger cooking? That slut! She ain't shit, and she's stupid for real. How the hell do you fuck with a baler and have nothing to show for it! Broke bitch, the way that nigga getting paid and her stupid ass walking around catching hacks and shit." Squinting my eyes, "It's on! Pay back was truly going to be a bitch!" I snatched the towel from around my body, and got dressed; I grabbed my suitcase and began to pack.

"Tyra, look, I love you," I said, beginning to pack a few clothes in my suitcase, "and I really appreciate you being here for me. But I have to get out of here. It feels like I'm going crazy."

"Sollie, where are you going?"

"I don't know, but I'll be okay. I just need to go."

"Okay, I'm going with you."

"Please, Tyra, I really need to be alone."

We left the house. I had to be driving about eighty miles an hour on my way taking Tyra home, and I didn't care if I ran into a tree. But when Tyra yelled for me to slow the hell down, I did, although I felt as if I wanted to die. I pulled into Tyra's driveway and she practically begged me to come inside. I told her I would call her later, although knowing I had no intentions on calling her or anyone else for that matter. I said good-bye and left.

I jumped straight on 295 S and headed for the Drake Plaza Hotel. I turned on the radio and damn it, that song from back in the day was playing, Secret Lovers. That song made my heart ache even more. I pressed the button for another station and then heard, You're My Little Secret. I turned the radio off and pulled into the parking lot of the hotel. The hotel was gorgeous, I thought as I entered the glass-stained revolving door feeling as if I had just walked into an enchanted garden. I stood there for a second and stared at the tall beautiful trees that surrounded a large water garden that extended from one end of the hotel lobby to the other. Two beautiful beams painted with green vines stood on each side of the garden, and fresh colorful flower petals floated inside the flowing water. The soft sounds of live jazz played from the restaurant and piano bar that sat off from the lobby.

It was so peaceful, thinking that I was right where I needed to be. The clerk greeted me warmly. I pulled out my wallet and handed the clerk my credit card, remembering that I told my mother I would use it only for emergencies. And this was definitely an emergency. As the clerk waited for my credit card approval, she raised her head, smiled, and then stared into my swollen eyes with a look of pity on her face, as if she knew exactly what I was feeling. She handed me my receipt and the key. I told her thanks, and walked over to the elevator.

Once on my floor I walked down the long corridor to my room. The suite was beautiful; the off-white living room set, glass coffee table, and end tables were all trimmed in gold. The carpet was so plush that even with tennis shoes on, my feet sunk down into it. I walked over to the other side and stood there staring at the spotless Italian wood dinette set; the wood was so shiny it looked wet. Over in the corner was a bar that I had free access to and was stocked with top-shelf liquors and wines. I quickly peeped in the kitchen that I unfortunately wouldn't be using, and then made my way back over to the other side of the suite to check out the bathroom, and it was beautiful as well: four steps surrounded the brown marble Jacuzzi. *I was definitely going to relax in there,* I thought. Only one thing about the bathroom that I didn't like: mirrors were everywhere, even on the ceiling, and feeling like the biggest dummy in the world, I couldn't stand the sight of myself.

I grabbed my luggage and walked back into bedroom suite. Sitting down on the bed, I buried my head into the palm of my hand and wondered how they could have done this to me. My phone began to ring and it was Tyra. I didn't answer. After the ringing stopped I turned it off, stretched out across the bed, and cried out for God to take the pain away, I stayed in the bed all day, flicking through the channels. I awoke around six in the morning, looking around, forgetting where I was, and then I remembered; and just that quickly the pain was back. I understood what the song, *Good Morning Heartache* meant. I tried to open my eyes but they were so swollen I couldn't open them fully; I could only imagine how they looked. I climbed out of bed and walked into the bathroom and stood there looking down at the ceramic floor, still ashamed to look at myself. I took a deep breath and slowly raised my head, and I didn't even recognize the person I saw; my eyes were so swollen and red. Angrily, I began hitting the mirror. I hate you Ahmaun, I hate you! I sat down on the steps of the Jacuzzi and cried.

Come on Sollie get it together I told myself. Just as I turned my phone on it rang. And it was Tyra. I wasn't going to answer it, but I did.

"Yes Tyra."

"Sollie where are you? I have been trying to call you all night!"

"Tyra, I'm sorry. I just didn't feel like talking."

"You sound terrible. Where are you?"

"I stayed at the hotel last night."

"What hotel, Sollie? What the hell is the name?" she asked.

"I'm at the Drake Plaza Hotel. You know the one where my mother had her retirement party."

"Sollie, those rooms are almost seven hundred dollars a night! What's your suite number?"

"712. But please don't come here. Honestly, I'm fine."

"Okay, I'm glad to hear you're fine. Today is a new day and . . ."

"So what and what the hell does that mean? Because I'm sure feeling what I felt yesterday," I said angrily.

"Listen, I'm going to drop the kids off at my parent's house, and I'll be there. Have you eaten anything?"

"No, I'm not hungry."

"Sollie, you have to eat something. What about some soup?"

"No thanks. Look, Tyra, I have to go," I said hanging up the phone.

After talking to Tyra, I took a long hot bath and climbed back in the bed and jut as I was about to call Tyra and plead with her not to come she knocked on the door.

"One second, Tyra," I said walking to the door. When I opened the door, Tyra looked at me as if she didn't know me.

"Oh Sollie," she said, with her eyes beginning to water up, "look at you! Sollie, come on, don't do this to yourself," she said hugging me.

And when she did, I felt comfort in her arms.

"It hurts, Tyra. It hurts so much!"

"I know it does, Sollie. You may not believe this now but the pain will eventually go away," Tyra said, taking me by my hand. We walked back to the bedroom suite and sat on the edge of the bed. I laid my head on her shoulders and whispered, "I will never ever love again."

"Yes, you will. You'll see, when it's time, and God's ready, he will send you the man he has, just for you. And you know what else, Sollie. Don't misunderstand me. I am in no way implying that any of this is your fault, but just think about it. Eleven years with that boy, and all he has caused you is constant pain, the cheating, lying, the disease, thankfully it was curable, catching him in bed with another women, and now this! God showed you time after time that he was not for you but yet you continued to ignore what God was showing you. Sollie, what I am trying to say is that anything detrimental to us, God will remove it, anything! Yet we try to hold on to it, thinking we need it or hoping we can change it, and make it what it's not! And everything we think we need ends up being exactly what we don't! And when we continue trying to keep what God is trying to remove, eventually it ends in chaos, and that's what you are in right now, a chaotic situation. I'm not acting like I am so holy. But I do have a understanding of how God moves in our lives, and I know that everything happens for a reason, and I hope you can find some kind of peace in knowing that the last eleven years, sweetie, was your plan, and not God's. Start listening and being obedient. When God says move, you move! I know you're angry, and you want revenge, but last night I prayed for you and asked God to give you the strength to let it go. I have no idea what you are planning for him or her, but it's not worth it, they're not worth it."

I took a deep breath "Tyra I heard everything she just said to me. And since we were on the subject of God, as He is my witness, those two pay are going to pay. I am relentless. And from the depths of my soul I'm going to go to any extreme to make it happen."

"Oh Lord," Tyra said shaking her head knowing I meant every word. "Come on," she said, walking over and reaching into my suitcase, pulling out a pair of jeans and a shirt. "Get dressed."

"Get dressed for what?"

"Sollie, just get dressed. Sitting in this suite all day is not going to make you feel better. You need to get out and get some fresh air."

"Look Tyra, I don't plan on sitting in here all day. I have to go home and get some more clothes. I have decided to stay here for the weekend."

"Sollie! That is going to cost you a fortune!"

"I have the credit card my mother gave me, and I also have some cash. I'm good. And Tyra, I really appreciate you being here for me, but I really want to be alone." I lay back across the bed.

"I am not going anywhere, unless you plan on physically throwing me out. And you know you can't beat me!" We both began to laugh, and she walked over and stretched out right beside me.

Lying on our backs and looking straight up at the ceiling, I looked over at Tyra and smiled. Truthfully, I was glad she was there with me.

"Hey Tyra, remember when we were little and Duce would make us fight each other, and that one time when you had me on the ground he bent over and squeezed my breast? We jumped up and whipped his ass. We forgot all about our fight." I chuckled, reminiscing about that moment.

"Sent him home crying, didn't we?" Tyra said laughing. "How about when we took my parents' liquor, and went up in my room, and he got drunk, climbed under the bed talking about he couldn't breathe, and started screaming?"

"Yeah, and your parents came running up the steps and caught us. That was funny. We were all grounded for a month behind that."

We both laughed and it really felt good, even though after the laughter the pain came right back. We lay there watching TV and I dozed off for a few hours. Tyra ordered me some soup and woke me up when it arrived, and I did manage to eat some of it.

"Tyra, you want me to feel better, right?"

"Yes, I do," she said looking at me strangely. "I know that look, Sollie. What are you thinking? Don't say going to the mall."

"No, well, yes, sort of. Let's ride up to Barneys."

Rising up from the bed Tyra blurted, "I know I didn't hear you right."

"No, you heard me correctly, Barneys of New York!" I repeated louder.

"Sollie, come on now. First of all, look at the time we don't live in New Jersey we live in Maryland, just in case you forgot. It's a four-hour drive. Hell, let's catch a flight to LA and hit Rodeo Drive while we're at it!" she said, still looking at me as if I had lost my mind.

"You're right, Tyra."

"And Sollie, you have been doing so good. You have not shopped in three days, although that's not a long time but for you it's great considering you shop every day. And besides, shopping is not going to take the pain away."

"Then what is?" I asked once again laying my head on her shoulder.

"Time Sollie, time."

We eventually left the hotel. The whole time riding to my house, I stared out the window; contemplating on how I was going to make them two pay. Just as Tyra turned the corner of my block, we saw an old man driving a gray Cadillac slowly up my street with Remi slouched down in the passenger seat.

"What is she doing?" Tyra asked.

"She's looking for Ahmaun," I said with certainty. "She obviously doesn't know he's out of town."

Tyra parked her car a few doors down from my house and we watched from a distance as the Cadillac circled the block again and then left. *Something more is going on with them two,* I thought. My mind shifted back to that day he left the house so angry after talking to her, and the blank look he had on his face when he returned. What could she have possibly said to him? I then thought about her attitude at the mall and how cocky she was. Something else was going on with this whole situation, but what?

Chapter Thirteen

T yra and I got out of the car and walked up the street to my house; as soon as I unlocked the door and went inside, we were both overwhelmed by a sour-smelling odor. I walked into the kitchen to make sure that there was no trash in the trashcan, and it wasn't. I had no idea what the smell was and the way I was feeling I really didn't care. I just wanted to grab a few things and get back to the hotel. I walked up the stairs to my bedroom and sat down on the side of the bed and began checking my messages. Most of them were from Tyra, one was from my mother, and the other three were from Jodi, telling me that she and LeLe were beefing again. I called my mother and tried to convince her that everything was okay, and when that didn't work I told her that I would talk to her about it later. Truth be told, I really wanted to go over to her house, curl up in her arms, and cry.

I got up and began packing a few more things. Tyra yelled up the steps telling me that noisy Mrs. Johnson was at my front door. *What does she want?* I thought walking down the steps.

"Hi Mrs. Johnson, how are you?"

"Hi Sollie," she said standing there wearing a torn housecoat with safety pins attached to the ripped pocket, and her wig was once again on backward. Mrs. Johnson was a small-built thin woman, but she seemed to look much thinner. "Sollie, I think water may have gotten in your basement. Yesterday my washer over flowed and water went everywhere. I looked for your car last night to tell you, but I didn't see it out front. Did you stay out all night?"

I didn't even answer her question. I told her thanks and that I would go down and check. As I went to close the door she reached her hand out and stopped me.

"I called the plumber," she continued. "I can't imagine where they could be. I called hours ago. If there is any damage, be sure to let me know, and I'll take care of it." She stood looking at me sadly. And I knew why. She wanted me to invite her inside.

I told her that I would let her know if there was any damage to my basement, not that she could afford to pay for anything if it was. She got on my nerves, always signifying, did I stay out last night? None of her business, I thought.

"Okay Sollie, I'm going to go now." With a sad face she turned and walked away.

And then it came to me to ask her about the other night when she said she heard arguing over here, even though I got butterflies just thinking about the answer that she was going to give. I was certain she would just be confirming what I already knew. I called Mrs. Johnsons and asked her if I could talk with her for a second. The lady turned back around so fast. "Certainly," she said anxiously pushing by me, and into the house.

"Oh, Sollie, the house is still so very beautiful." She walked over to the end table and picked up a picture of me when I was around ten. "This is around the age you were the last time I was in this house," she slowly rubbed her fingers along the front of the picture. "I remember that day as if it were yesterday. You had fallen off the bike, and split your head wide open. Your mother wasn't at home so Mr. Johnson and I rushed you to the hospital." Sitting the picture back down, she walked over and sat on the couch.

"Would you like a soda or something, Mrs. Johnson?"

"No thanks. I don't drink soda, but I will take a cup of tea if you have any."

Tyra got up to make her a cup of tea.

"One teaspoon of sugar please, dear. Where in the devil is that plumber?" she said looking at her watch.

I told Mrs. Johnson that I would leave the door open so if the plumber came she would be able to see him. Sitting down on the couch next to her I asked about the night when she said she heard arguing. And exactly whom did she see.

"I don't know her name, but let's see. She is built nice, light-skinned complexion, and oh yeah," she said snapping her finger, "she got that old funny color in her hair, that pink stuff. I don't know why girls wear that mess. It's just not becoming! Oh thank you dear." Mrs. Johnson said taking her tea from Tyra. "She's always over here, I thought she moved in." She blowing the steam from off her tea and sipping it. "The other night they were so loud I started to knock on your door and make sure everything was okay, but I didn't see your car, and that boyfriend of yours is so mean, he scares me sometimes." She looked toward the door and noticed the plumber coming up her steps. "Ooh, I have to go. He's here." She took a quick sip of her tea and sat it back down on the saucer and handed it to me. "Thanks for the tea, pretty girls. You two are so sweat. Maybe we can do this again sometimes, and I'll even bake some of my delicious homemade sugar cookies." She stood up and left.

"How could they do this to me? And in my house! But you know what Tyra? I shouldn't be surprised his father did the same thing to his mother. "I have to find out what else is going on before I can make a move, but how?" We looked at each other and at the exact same time we both said "Karen!" I ran up the stairs and grabbed my pocketbook, ran back down, and we headed out the door to go and search for Karen, praying that she would be hanging out somewhere down Popular Grove.

"Sollie, do you think she's going to talk?" Tyra asked.

"I hope so, Tyra. Like the old saying goes money talks, and bullshit walks." I reached into my wallet and pulled out a crisp one-hundred-dollar bill. We drove slowly through Popular Grove looking on each corner for Karen. After riding around for what seemed like hours, Karen was nowhere to be found. I asked a few guys who were

132

hanging around the corner if they have seen her. One guy said he saw her earlier that morning giving a nigga some head in the alley, but he had not seen her since. As we were leaving the area, I asked Tyra to stop at the store so I could get a Tylenol, and when I went inside, guess who the old Korean man had pinned up in the corner? Karen.

"You go to jail, you thief!" the Korean man yelled angrily shaking a wooden bat at Karen. The man's wife stood behind the counter pacing back and forth throwing her hands in the air speaking their language in an angry manner. Karen tried to pull away from the man's tight grasp around her arm, but she couldn't. He looked over his shoulder at his wife. "Call the police," he yelled. And when Karen heard the word police, she reached in her pocket and pulled out an Alka-Seltzer, ready to make her famous move.

"Don't try that with me!" the Korean man yelled, slapping the Alka-Seltzer out of her hand. Just as the woman went to pick up the phone to call the police, I intervened.

"How much does she owe you?" I asked pulling out my wallet. The Korean man turned and looked, and Karen's eyes got wide. I opened my wallet and she looked at her husband and he gestured for her to hang the phone up. Finally, releasing Karen's arm, he walked over to me, still pointing the wooden bat at Karen. His wife rushed from behind the counter and over to the door, spreading her arms out, and blocking it, just in case Karen tried to make a run for it. Karen stood there looking at me.

The Korean man held up three fingers. "She owes me three dolla. She come in here and steal all time, all time!"

"You're a fuckin lie!" Karen blurted.

"You see, you see, she trashy, she trashy girl. She got trashy mouth all time, I see her in alley, suck dick, all time!"

"I'll never suck yours, you flat face, chinky-eyed mothafucka!"

I held my hand up and told Karen to just shut up. I handed the man a ten-dollar bill. He handed it to his wife, and she rushed over behind the counter to the register to get my change. As the woman went to hand me the change I told her to keep it. A wide smile appeared on her face.

"Thank you, thank you," she said gratefully nodding her head. "You nice lady, you look nice too." Karen finally eased her way out the corner.

"Ah, ah, you wait right there," the man said making his way over to the counter, and his wife handed him a Polaroid camera. He turned to Karen and told her to stand up against the wall. He picked up the bottle of 20/20 that she tried to steal and handed it to her. I stood back and watched while Karen held the bottle of cheap liquor up to her chest and just as the man pressed the green button and the camera flashed she put her middle finger up and smiled. She slammed the 20/20 on the counter. "Bitches!" she yelled and hauled ass out the store.

"Karen, Karen!" I called, quickly walking out behind her. Karen stopped and turned.

"What!" Karen snapped.

"I need to talk to you for a minute."

"What you got to talk to me about. If it's about those shrimps, I'll pay you back when I get my food stamps."

"Look, Karen, it's not about the shrimp. Please, just get inside the car." I leaned over and opened the back door.

Karen hesitated at first, and then she slowly walked over to the car. Just before she got inside, Tyra reached in the backseat, grabbed a towel, and quickly placed it on the seat where Karen was getting ready to sit. Karen looked at Tyra and rolled her eyes.

"What's up? What y'all prissy asses want with me?" she asked shutting the car door.

Tyra rolled all four windows down to mask Karen's horrible odor. "Karen, check this out. I have been hearing some things about Remi. I know you and her are cool, but . . ."

"Oh, hell no, I ain't telling you shit. That's why you being all nice, Remi is my girl, I fucks wit her, what I look like talking about her? Fuck dat. Y'all ain't getting shit out me, I'm what you call a real friend and..."

Just as she went to continue, I held up the one-hundred-dollar bill. Her eyes almost popped out her head. "What you wanna know?" she asked anxiously reaching for the money. Tyra quickly put the child safety lock on just in case she tried to jump out.

I handed Karen the money. "I want to know everything." Karen puckered her ashy lips and kissed the hundred-dollar bill, folded it, and slid it into her back pocket.

"Ima get high as Georgia pine tree tonight!" She clapped. "Okay, okay, first of all," she said smacking her teeth, "she hates your guts, and she's fucking your man, and has been for a minute, you heard me?!

I found that out the night of your party. After you had me put out!" Karen said rolling her eyes at me. And then she continued. "I was standing out front and she came bursting out the doors talking about she couldn't breathe and shit, and that she needed something to calm her nerves. I asked her if she wanted a little hit, and she said no. So I asked what was wrong and that's when she spilled her guts and told me everything! I was lost for words. I couldn't believe that shit."

"You say they been seeing other for a minute, what's a minute?" I asked.

"Well she told me since she came out of treatment, the first time."

I looked at Tyra, and shook my head, knowing that's when Remi asked if she could stay with me.

"So anyway back to the night of your party." Karen continued. "She said that she questioned Ahmaun about buying you that Benz and he went off on her ass and that's the night that he cut that ass loose! She even went over to your house a few days later to talk with him. They got into a big argument and he threw her out! And that's why she fucked Tavon in your basement to get back at him. She was so depressed, walking around moping and shit. Girl, what that nigga got a gold dick?" Karen asked falling out laughing.

My stomach started turning as I began remembering the night of my party, and how I did notice the two standing in the corner of the club talking.

"Mhhh, I tried to tell her that all he wanted was that fat ass, but she wouldn't listen to me. She thought that fat ass was going to keep a nigga still. And do you know all she got from him was a wet ass, and a cell phone. And that was so he could reach her. I told her she was crazy. That nigga gettin money like he is and her dumb ass wasn't getting any of it. Oh yeah, and that boy she wit now, what his name is?" Karen asked snapping her fingers, trying to remember. "B. yeah, yeah that's it. That dumb nigga must be whipped for sure. She has been using him since they got together, and peep this, she even got the dummy to apply for a ten-thousand-dollar loan. She lied and told him she needed it to pay for her treatment at the recovery center she had just left and he believed her. Where the hell he thinks she was at the Betty Ford clinic? Mmhh, he needs to be worked, believing some bullshit like that!"

"So what is she going to do with the money?"

"Dahhhh, what do you think? She just told him that so she could get the paper. And once she gets it, that's when she's going to roll out on him. Oh yeah, another thing, Ahmaun came down here the other day and scooped her up, with your Benz! And the way he was looking, I could tell he was pissed. For what, I don't know. She got in your whip and they were gone for a few. When he dropped her back off, I asked her what was going on. All she said was that she finally had him. But you know what, I know I be burning people and doing my little dirt and shit, but ain't no way I be grinning in your face like she has been and be sleeping with your man. One time I asked her how she could do it. Girl, can you believe, she said it turned her on. That bitch is dangerous. You heard me?"

I took a deep breath, but I didn't cry. Sadly I told Karen thanks. Tyra unlocked the door. As Karen got out the car I asked her when she was going to get herself together.

"One day, but not today!" she shouted, and ran across the street.

Tyra sat there staring into traffic with a remote look on her face. "I'm a wife and a mother and I have no business fighting, and I know what I said to you earlier. But I'm going to whip her ass myself." She said as she pulled out the parking space. I didn't respond. I just sat there quietly. Although I did still wonder, what she could have told Ahmaun to have him so upset. A thought came into my mind, and I quickly brushed it off. *Couldn't be,* I thought. We pulled in front of my house and went inside.

"Sollie, say something," Tyra said coming in the door behind me.

"Tyra, there's really nothing to say. It is what it is." I shrugged.

We eventually went downstairs to see what damage if any was done, and there was. The cream carpet was badly stained from the water. I opened the windows to let the carpet air out and used the wet vac to get the water up. Just as we headed up the stairs, I walked by the wooden shelf and noticed my camcorder. "How did this get down here? Oh shit, this has been here since the cookout when I fell down the steps." Tyra and I both began to laugh, remembering that moment. "I know the battery has to be dead."

Once upstairs, Tyra put the camcorder on the charger. I headed back up to my room, packed a few more things, and stood there staring at my bed thinking about them two, wondering if they actually had sex on it. I didn't know for sure, but I wasn't taking any chances.

I gathered my things and got out of there. Before Tyra drove me back to the hotel, I stopped at the mattress store and purchased a box spring and mattress that would be delivered on Monday. Tyra tried to get me to hang out with her longer, but I really wasn't in the mood.

She dropped me off at the hotel and left. Soon as I walked into the large suite, I went straight into the bathroom and filled the Jacuzzi with hot steaming water, poured me a glass of wine, got into the Jacuzzi and relaxed.

Afterward I stretched out across the bed, and called room service and ordered lobster, steak, steamed shrimps, crab cakes, pasta salad, fried calamari, mashed potatoes, steam vegetables, and rice pilaf. And for dessert, I ordered a whole red velvet cake. And wouldn't you know, when it arrived, I didn't touch any of it. Instead I drank two bottles of wine, and that did nothing but make me feel worse then I already did.

My phone rang and it was Ahmaun. I didn't answer it, because alcohol made me say things I ended up regretting, and there was no way I was going to mess this plan up. I did however listen to the message.

Hey Shorty, what's up with you? I miss you, and I'll see you soon, I know your little ass is probably at the mall, holla at a nigga when you get a chance. Oh yeah, I am going to need you to pick me up on Wednesday. Love you nigga peace!

Yeah right! I thought, drunkenly tossing the phone on the bed. Only thing he loved was his money that was soon to be mine. I reached over on the nightstand and picked up the bottle of wine and turned it upside down and watched as one single drop fell into my glass. I started to open another bottle but I fell asleep.

The next morning I took a long hot shower, and I was horny as hell; I wanted someone to make love to me badly, but I knew that wasn't happening. I couldn't see myself sleeping with another guy. I have never been with anyone but Ahmaun.

I called Tyra and we talked for almost two hours as she continued to try and get me to come out for a little air, but I refused. All I wanted to do was lie in the king-sized bed and watch repeats of Insecure all day. I heard a knock on the door. I told Tyra I would call her back.

Room service came inside and noticed that I hadn't touched the food that I had ordered, and offered me a hotel gift card that I could use during my stay or at a later date. I decided to get Tyra's kids and my niece and nephew and have the slumber party that I had promised them. I called my brother to see if I could pick the kids up, and he said yes and so did Tyra. I hoped that spending time with all of them would make me feel better. I got dressed and headed in town.

Chapter Fourteen

A ll the kids were there, and we had a wonderful time. We ate, danced, watched movies, and played games, and by the time twelve o'clock hit, they were all tucked in their sleeping bags, knocked out. The next morning, we all got dressed, and I took the kids out to breakfast. And then we went to the zoo, and ended the day at their favorite restaurant, McDonald's. By the time I dropped off my niece and nephew, I was beat. Salique came to the door and yelled for me to come inside for a little while, but I told him that I had something to do and that I would talk to him later. Truth was I didn't want him seeing my eyes that were still swollen. I pulled off and headed over to Tyra's. I pulled up in the driveway. Little Terry got out before I could come around to the other side. He opened the back door and helped Trinity out of her seatbelt and even carried her overnight bag. Trinity jumped out the car and excitedly ran up to the front door peeping through the window and giggling. I walked up and asked Trinity what she was laughing at and she pointed at her mother and father standing in the living room slow dancing. Trinity stood on her toes and rang the doorbell and as soon as Tyra opened the door the kids excitedly ran inside showing them the souvenirs that they had gotten from the zoo.

Damn! I was doing good all day, I thought, feeling the tears welling up in my eyes again, hearing The Weekend *"I'll die for you"* playing. I began feeling the pain once again. I sat my bag on the couch and quickly headed upstairs to the bathroom to get myself together. Leaning up against the bathroom door still hearing the music playing downstairs, I began to cry uncontrollably. *Come on, Sollie, get it together,* I thought. I walked over to the sink and snatching a paper towel off the holder and wiped my eyes. Just as I was walking out the bathroom, Terry was coming up the stairs. He stopped and hugged me and said that everything was going to be okay.

"I just want the pain to go away. It hurts so bad Terry." I said as I laid my head on his chest.

"Look at this way, Sollie. This is probably a blessing in disguise. You were too good for that dick-head anyway!" I began to laugh.

"Why are you laughing?" he asked.

"You're starting to talk like your white colleagues at the law firm."

"Okay, okay, you got jokes, right? How's this, fuck dat clown!" he said mugging.

"Thanks Terry for making me laugh."

I went back down the stairs and straight to the bar and poured me a glass of Merlot, and sat down on the couch next to Tyra.

"Kids, give Auntie Sollie a hug and tell her thank you, and go upstairs, and tell your dad to run your bath water," Tyra said.

"I'm first," Little Terry said running toward the stairs.

"No, you're not. I'm first," Trinity said, trying to get in front of him. "Thanks Auntie Sollie," they both said running up the steps.

"Stop running!" Tyra yelled.

"You know what, Tyra?" I said watching Trinity run up the steps. "All day I watched the kids, especially the girls, and I know they have a very long time to become young women, but I pray that they will one day meet a good man, and they will never have to endure this pain that I'm in. They are princesses. And thank God the boys have great fathers who can teach them how to be a man, and how to treat women."

"You're right, Sollie, I look at Trinity all the time and think the same thing."

"Well, she has a good start by seeing you and Terry, and the loving relationship you two have. She's seeing firsthand what love really is. It's a blessing having two parents who really do love one another."

After making that statement, I tried to shake a feeling that had come over me. I hadn't thought about my father in years. And wherever it came from, I wanted it to go back. Thinking about him made me feel very uncomfortable.

During the ride to the hotel, I couldn't get my father off my mind.

As I walked into my hotel room my phone rang and it was Jodi, and I figured I might as well answer it. She's just going to keep calling.

"Yes, Jodi!"

"Sollie, where the fuck you been?"

"Nowhere Jodi. What's up?"

"I left you a few messages. Did you get them?"

"Yeah, I did. About you and LeLe beefing again?"

"Yeah, man, I am sick of her shit! And I am tired of her accusing me of fucking around! So since I am being accused of it, fuck it, why not do it! And another thing she's pissed because I won't let her use the dildo on me. I do, I don't get done. You feel me?"

"Come on now, Jodi, I really don't need to hear you and LeLe sex life right now."

"I know Sollie, but I don't have anyone else to talk to or anyone I can be real with."

"Jodi, I really can't give you much advice on your situation, but I will say this, if you're not comfortable with letting LeLe use a dildo on you, then just don't. Are you still there?" I asked hearing silence on the other end of the phone.

"Yeah yeah I'm still here." Jodi said in a low tone. Hearing the sadness in her voice I knew it was time to find out what else was going on with my friend.

"Jodi, check this out," I said turning the TV volume down. "Did you, or did you not, just say that I was the only person you could talk to and be real with?"

"Yeah, I did."

"And how long have we been friends?"

"Since we were eleven."

"Okay, so would it be safe to say I know you well?"

"Better than anybody." she said in a whisper.

"Do you trust me, Jodi?"

She cleared her throat. "You know I do." She said now crying.

I was now talking to the lost little girl. Although I knew that some doms didn't go for being penetrated, but something in my spirit told me that there was a lot more as to why Jodi wasn't having it.

"Jodi what happen to you, when you were younger, who hurt you Jodi?"

Jodi didn't respond for about sixty seconds. As she went to speak, I could hear her voice crack; she cleared her throat took a deep breath and then spoke.

"I was raped by my mother's boyfriend when I was twelve," she said as she began to cry. "Sollie it hurt so fucking bad, the nigga split me from one end to the other, and my mother walked in and caught him and did nothing, just shut the door and went down stairs. After he was done, I laid in bed crying and bleeding, and she did absolutely nothing, she even stayed with the nigga!"

Hearing that felt like someone was stabbing me in my heart all over again. I wanted so badly to hold her. *I knew it was more,* I thought, as Jodi cried, and so did I.

"So that's why you are so angry with your mother, not just because of the fact that she hasn't accepted your lifestyle?"

Crying uncontrollably, Jodi said, "Yeah, it is. But Sollie, she has never even mentioned it since it has happened. I was a fucking little girl." She cried gasping to catch her breath. "She didn't even take me to the hospital. She didn't call the police, nothing. She ain't do shit except tell me I probably enticed him. Fuck her! How the hell do you allow something like that to happen to your child and do absolutely

142

nothing, fuck her and fuck LeLe too." She yelled. "No mother fucker, woman or man will ever put anything, anything inside me again! I have to go. I'll holla at you later."

I dialed her number repeatedly praying that she would answer, but she didn't. I kept getting her voice mail so I left a message.

Jodi, I'm so sorry. I always felt that it was more but I had no idea it was that serious. Please call me back so that we can talk. I love you.

Chapter Fifteen

I   sat back on the bed, feeling so sorry for Jodi, I swear there were so many emotions going through my mind, and the more I tried to control my thoughts they became worse, and for some reason I began thinking of my past. I lay around all day, and when night came, I tried to sleep, but I couldn't.

The morning finally came and the warmth of the sun made its way through the tall trees outside the balcony and into my room. Just as I opened my eyes, I had a vision of my father. It was as if he was standing right there. Startled, I jumped up. What was going on with me? I reached for my phone to see if Jodi had called, but she hadn't. I headed into the bathroom and another long hot bath.

As I was getting dressed, I still couldn't stop thinking about my father. But why? I packed my things. I was about to leave the room when I stopped and turned, looked at the beautiful suite wishing I could have stayed there forever.

Now standing at the desk, waiting for the clerk to hand me my credit card, I noticed a fine-ass white man coming out of an office. As he walked in my direction, I slightly turned my head and looked the other way.

"Hello," he said standing next to me, sitting his black briefcase on the counter, and putting an envelope inside of it.

I turned to face him and tried to put a smile on my face. I said, "Hello," and refocused my attention back on the clerk. I could feel him staring as he walked away. Impatiently, I tapped my feet, waiting for the slow-moving clerk to hand me my credit card. And as soon as she did, I headed out the large revolving glass doors. I stopped and breathed deeply, taking in the fresh Sunday-morning air. As I walked past the huge water fountain out front, I noticed the man that was just inside the lobby tossing a coin into the fountain.

"Excuse me, miss."

I stopped and turned to him and said, "Yes."

"Did you enjoy your stay?"

"Yes, I did. Thank you for asking," I said beginning to walk away.

"You're very beautiful."

God, I am so sick of hearing that, because I sure don't feel beautiful. I turned back around to face him and said, thank you, lowering my head wondering if he noticed my swollen red eyes.

"May I ask your name?" he asked extending his hand to me.

"Sollie," I replied, still looking at how fine he was. Tall, slim with broad shoulders, his hair was close cut like Justin Timberlake's, and his tan was glowing as if he had been kissed by the sun. Sharply dressed, he could have easily been one of those dudes walking down the runway modeling Sean John. I shook his hand and he said that his name was Mason, and I couldn't help but notice the silver Rolex on his wrist. *What are they paying hotel managers these days?* I thought to myself.

"Nice to meet you Mason."

"Listen, Sollie," he said smiling and glancing down at my ring finger, "I don't see a ring. Even though I know these days that doesn't mean anything, if you are not involved, I would really love to take you out." He reached inside his suit jacket pocket and pulled out a business card and handed it to me. Just as I took the card, I noticed a black stretch limousine pulling up in front of the hotel. The limousine driver got out, walked around to the passenger door, smiled and tipped his hat to me, and gave Mason thumbs up. Mason nodded his head to the driver and told him that he would be right with him. "Sollie, it was a pleasure meeting you, and I hope to hear from you very soon."

"Nice meeting you as well." I dropped the card inside my pocketbook. As I began to walk to my car, I turned and watched the bellmen roll out a luggage cart and place Mason's Louis Vuitton suitcases inside the trunk of the Limousine. I wondered what it would be like to date a white man, and if he could possibly be capable of doing what Ahmaun had done. But one thing I did know, a cheater is a cheater regardless of his color. I sat in my car and looked back at the limousine and watched as the driver opened the door and Mason got inside. *Who is he?* I wondered, taking the card out of my purse that I never even bothered to look at. Mason Drake, Owner. Get—the—hell—out—of—here. Owner! I said looking up and watching the limousine pull off. Fuck him too! I ripped the card and threw it out the window and pulled off thinking Tyra would have had a fit if she knew what I had just done.

As soon as I pulled in front of my door, there was Mrs. Johnson, asking if there was any damage done to the basement. I told her no. I lied because I knew she didn't have any money to pay for it. As I headed into the house, she said how much fun she had sitting with Tyra and me yesterday. I guess she was trying to give me a hint. *Not today lady!* I thought shutting my front door.

I went up to my bedroom and began to unpack my things. I guess I'll be sleeping on the couch tonight. There was no way I was sleeping in that bed.

Tyra called and said she was coming over later to bring me some homemade soup that she had made, although I didn't want anything to eat. But of course she insisted. I put on my pajamas, turned off all the lights in the house, and curled up on the living room couch. I turned on Lifetime, and ironically, it just happened to be Betrayal Sunday.

Later, Tyra came over and opened all the windows and the blinds to let some fresh air and light into the house, fussing because I was lying in the dark. We were sitting there talking when she noticed the camcorder still plugged into the outlet.

146

"Sollie, this should be charged by now. What's on here anyway?" Tyra asked unplugging the camcorder.

"My party and the cookout from the other day, I think. I don't know. Hook it up if you want."

"You don't want to finish watching the movie?"

"No, I have had enough of that depressing shit."

My cell phone began to ring, and I prayed that it wasn't you know who! But it was, and I didn't answer it. Tyra hooked up the camera and we watched my birthday party and then the cookout, watching Duce's crazy-ass grin all on that lady like a mad man. Then everything turned upside down when I fell down the basement stairs.

Then the part where Duce was recording me stretched out on the floor came on, and next we saw nothing but the pool table.

"His simple tail never turned the camera off."

Tyra got up and walked over to the TV. "I'll just rewind it back to the part when you fell," she said looking back at me laughing. Just as she went to rewind the tape what showed up next put Tyra and me in a state of complete shock! The camcorder had recorded Remi and Joe fucking on my pool table. Tyra almost jumped into the television screen. I slowly rose from the couch. We couldn't believe what we were seeing. We watched with our mouth hanging open in disbelief. Everything was on there, everything!

That freak, Remi, was doing things I never even thought about doing, and the way she talked about B. and me was terrible. After the tape ended, Tyra turned and looked at me, and we were both speechless. Snatching the blanket from off me, I stood and stared at Tyra with a very devious look on my face.

"Tyra, let's have a party, and guess who will be the guest of honor?"

Her eyes widened "You're not," Tyra said.

"Watch me! Plan one is happening tonight, Remi is going down!"

Most people knew she was a freak but tonight everyone was going to see it on a seventy-inch flat screen, compliments of Ms. Sollie Carr.

147

Tyra was concerned about B. and so was I. But right now my main concern was one thing—getting her back! I just hope that B. would find it in his heart to forgive me.

"First, we need to call your friend at the phone company, and tell her to disconnect Ahmaun's number. That way when this goes down tonight, Remi won't be able to contact him or leave a message, because I cannot risk Ahmaun finding out that I know." Tyra called her, and thank God this was her weekend to work. We gave her his cell number. She then told us to give her about thirty minutes and his number would be disconnected.

I gave Tyra some money, and she went to the market and bought all kinds of snacks for tonight. I didn't need to buy drinks. There was still plenty of beer and liquor left from the cookout.

I called everyone, even people that I hadn't talked to in a while. I told them all that I was having a get-together this evening, and every last one of them said that they would be there. Jodi finally answered the phone. I tried to talk to her about what she had told me, but she didn't want to talk about it; I respected that, and left it alone. She did, however, say that she was coming this evening. But I wonder if I may have made a mistake by inviting her, because when she finds out what Remi has done, she will tear another hole in Remi's ass. And then I had to deal with simple Duce.

"What the hell kind of get-together are you having on a fucking Sunday, and at seven o'clock in the evening for that matter. I'll pass!" Duce said sarcastically.

"Duce, please come. I promise it will be worth your while."

"Look girl, I'm getting ready to get some ass!" he whispered. "Can you top that? Can—you—top—that—hooker?"

"Duce . . ."

"Nah, Nah, answer the question!"

"Yeah, I can!" *What the hell am I doing,* I thought, realizing I was begging. "You know what, Duce, screw you, and stay your black ass home! I'm not going to be kissing your ass," I said ending the call.

Just as I was going up the steps, my cell rang. I chuckled thinking it was Duce, but as I looked at the screen, it read Ahmaun.

148

I thought she was going to have his number disconnected. This evening was not going to happen unless his phone was disconnected. There was no way I was going to risk Remi calling him, because he was next. My plan for his ass was already coming together in my mind. And I must admit, it was a little extreme. But it had to be done this way, 'cause one thing was for sure. That no good bastard sure wasn't going to just hand me half a million dollars, so I had to take it! And that's just what I planned on doing—taking it!

I called Tyra to find out why his phone was still on. She called her friend and she said for us to check it in about five minutes. I sat back down on the couch holding the phone with my fingers crossed. Five minutes had passed; nervously dialed his number. Yes! I thought hearing the recording say that the number was no longer in service. I ran up the steps to change and continued trying to rationalize with myself that what I was doing was okay and that B. was going to be just fine.

Just as I came down the steps, Tyra was coming through the front door. I helped with the bags and began setting everything out on the dining room table. After we were done, it was time to call the guest of honor. I walked into the kitchen and reached for the phone and began dialing and just before pressing the last number I realized I couldn't do it and hung up. I looked at Tyra. "I can't do this to B."

"Okay, then don't, let's just go over there and slap the hell out of her!" Tyra said.

I took a deep breath "God, forgive me," I said, picking the phone back up and dialing B.'s house phone. "Yes?" Remi answered, still with that same cockiness in her tone. And just hearing the arrogance in her in her voice, all the reservations that I may have had about this evening were gone. I swallowed hard, and said, "Hello"

"Yes?" she replied again.

"Hi Remi, check this out. I'm going to get straight to the point. I have no idea what's been going on with us lately, but I don't like it. I'm having a little get-together at the house this evening and I would like you and B. to come over. And maybe you and I could talk and clear the air."

"I appreciate the invitation, but I'm really not feeling well."

I covered the mouthpiece and said, "Damn! Now what was I going to do?" Tyra leaned over and whispered in my ear to yell Ahmaun's name out as if he was upstairs and I did.

"Ahmaun is there?" Remi asked with desperation in her tone.

"Yeah he is, why?"

"I was down the way earlier, and I thought I heard someone say he was out of town."

"Well, no, he's upstairs in the shower."

"Sollie, I changed my mind, will be over," Remi said urgently.

"Good, I'll see you two when you get here."

Tyra looked at me and smiled. A few minutes later the phone rang. I looked at the caller ID and it was B. asking me what was going on. He said Remi was running around the apartment like she was crazy searching for something to wear. I told B. I would talk to him this evening when he got here. The guilt was hitting me harder and harder. *I can't do this,* I thought again. Just as I went to tell B. the truth, I heard Remi in the background yelling at him asking, "Why the hell aren't you getting ready!"

Oh hell no, I thought, quickly changing my mind again. Who the hell does that girl think she is?

I told B. that I would talk to him when he got here. Just as I hung up, the doorbell rang and it was Duce. As pissed as I was with him for acting so stupid earlier, I must admit since we were kids he always came when Tyra and I called.

"Get in here stupid!" I laughed as I opened the front door.

"Shut up, wench! Can't you see I'm waiting on my date?" he said, looking at Sis Betty getting out of her car.

"Why are you on the porch, and she's still trying to get of the car?"

"Look, what's the motherfuckin business?" Duce asked pushing by me as he walked into the house.

I walked out onto the porch and met the woman as she tirelessly walked up the steps almost tripping as she peeped over at Mrs. Johnson's house making sure she wasn't looking out the window. One thing I know, if you have to creep doing anything, you obviously had no business doing it.

I walked her into the living room offering her something to drink. She said she would like a beer so I headed into the kitchen to get it.

"Why did you bring that church lady with you?" I said trying to whisper and getting a beer out the refrigerator. "Duce, please, just tell that lady to come back later and pick you up. She really does not need to see this."

Throwing his arms in the air, he said, "See what? What the hell is going on?! And check this out, Shorty. If it's some nasty shit, believe me, it ain't nothing she hasn't seen or done. That woman is freak in disguise, I'm telling you shorty, Sister Betty sucks the hell out of a brother's you-know-what! Girl, when she takes them dentures out, it's on. Shit!" He shivered, falling out laughing and raising his hand in the air for Tyra to give him five. We both just stood there shaking our heads and watched as he walked into the living room.

Within the hour the house was packed. Duce even had to go down in the basement to get some more chairs. The music was playing, and the drinks was flowing. Realizing that chips and dips were not going to be enough, I ordered five pizzas, and a tray of Buffalo wings. The doorbell rang, and I began to feel butterflies in my stomach, knowing who it was. I looked at Tyra. "Are you okay?" she asked rubbing me on my back. I was fine. There was just one person on my mind—B. *Oh well,* I thought walking over to the door. Lights, camera, action!

Chapter Sixteen

T   he guilt hit me harder as opened the door. B. was standing there smiling as usual. He walked inside and hugged and kissed me. As he moved to the side, I was now eye to eye with the bitch that had betrayed me. I wanted to slap her up and down right then and there. I uttered the word "Hello," and then reached around her and shut the front door. She turned and looked at me strangely, noticing my attitude was not one of a person who wanted to make amends.

I offered B. a beer as the nervousness I was feeling took over my vocal cords. I was so nervous, you would have thought I was the guilty one, and I guess in a sense, I was, for what I was about to do to B. Remi slowly walked into the living room and said hello to everyone. She sat down and looked at Tyra who hadn't yet stopped mugging her. Gripping her bag tightly, and I guess, feeling the tension that was in the air, she stood up, walked back over to the front door, and told B. that she wasn't feeling well, and that she was ready to leave.

"What do you mean?" B. asked with his mouth full of pizza. "We just got here, and the way you were running around the apartment getting dressed I thought you wanted to come over here and chill with your home-girl."

Tilting my head to the side, I said, "That's right Remi. I am your home-girl, right?" And with the look on my face she really knew something was up.

"B.," Remi snapped, "I said I'm ready to go."

"Oh, hell no!" Tyra blurted, jumping up from her seat and walking toward Remi angrily, asking her, "Why are you talking to him like that?"

"Ah shit, fight, fight, fight, fight! Tear that ass up Tyra!" Duce yelled, whip—dat—ass! He said rocking back and forth, while Sister Betty sat there with a terrified look on her face.

"Man, hold up," B. said sitting his beer down on the table. "Nobody's doing any fighting!" Tyra stood there in front of Remi ready to do just what Duce said. And I knew if I was going to go through with my plans, I had to intervene.

"Listen, everyone. Let's calm down and enjoy the evening. Ahmaun is on his way back with some more drinks," I lied. I turned and looked at Remi, although she still looked a little skeptical. I guess, hearing those words she agreed to stay. B. frowned and shook his head at Duce's asinine behavior.

"Slim you really need to grow up." B said.

"Yeah, okay, and you need to wise up, sim!"

B. shrugged his shoulders. "And what is that supposed to mean?" B. questioned.

Duce was about to tell B. that Remi had sex with Tavon the other day, but I stopped him.

B. shook his head and said that he was going to the bathroom. "Come on, Shorty, sit down," Duce said, moving over on the couch, hesitantly Remi walked over and sat next to Duce. "You see what being clean does freak, I mean shorty? You got your ass back! Gaining weight and shit, your face is glowing, and to top it off, you got the dumbest nigga in the world," Duce laughed.

When B. came back downstairs, I asked him to come into the kitchen.

"B., you know I love you, right?" I said taking him by his hand.

"Oh, no doubt, why would you ask me that?"

"B., I know all about the loan Remi asked you to apply for. Just please tell me that you haven't given it to her yet, please." B. looked at me strangely.

"How did you know about the loan? And as a matter of fact I gave it to her yesterday."

"Shit! B., where is the check? Please tell me she hasn't cashed it."

"Nah, it was too late when I gave it to her. The banks were closed, so she's going to the bank in the morning, why, what's going on?"

I shook my head. "B. where is the check?"

"In her purse, she's not letting it out of her sight. Sollie, what is going on?"

"B., when this evening is over I just hope you can find it in your heart to forgive me. And know that I never meant to hurt you, never!"

"Hurt me?" he asked, looking at me strangely.

I grabbed him by his hand. "Come on, I'm going to show you right now." B. followed me back into the living room with a look of curiosity on his face. He walked over and sat down next to Remi and put his arms around her.

Duce shook his head and whispered in Remi ear. "See what I mean, dunb!"

I asked everyone to come inside the living room and told them that we were going to watch a video. Tyra then pressed the play button on the remote.

"Man, shit, this is the video from the cookout," Duce said disappointedly. Everyone began to laugh as they watched Duce and Sister Betty dance. I looked over at Remi and right then she knew what was going down. She jumped up again.

"I have to go!" she said rushing over to the door, and before I could say a word, Tyra jumped up and blocked her.

"Girl, sit down. You're not going anywhere," Tyra snapped.

"Tyra, what the hell is up with y'all tonight?!" B. asked.

I walked over and stood next to Tyra, refusing to let Remi go past, as B. went to ask again. His attention was quickly taken off us when he heard a very familiar voice on the video. "I'm sorry B. This is what I was talking about earlier." Remi stared at me with a look that would kill.

"Hurry up, Tavon!"

"Shorty, I'm coming. What the fuck is wrong with you? What, that nigga ain't hittin it right? Can't be, the way you acting."

"Sollie is going to whip your ass!" Tavon said, as his jeans dropped down around his ankle. Remi rushed back over to him after getting a towel out of the hamper and laid it across the pool table.

"Fuck Sollie!"

"Fuck Sollie?" I thought that was your girl. You know what, Shorty, you got everybody thinking you changed and you still the same old Remi, love to fuck, and out here trying to get yours, looking out for only you.

"So what?! You got to look out for yourself, ain't nobody going to look out for you. And yeah, you're right. I'm still a bitch! But until I get this loot from dumb-ass I have to play it cool. But after I get mine, fuck all of them, especially, Sollie! And little does she know she's in for a very big surprise!"

"What does that mean? Then again I don't even want to know. Turnover. You still like it in the ass?" Tavon asked turning Remi around and bending her over and entering her asshole.

"Now that's what I'm talking about!" Remi moaned with pleasure.

After digging in her ass for a few minutes, Remi excitedly turned around and got down on her knees, grabbed his dick, spit on it, wrapped her hand around it, and sucked it like a champ.

"Damn, Shorty, let me at least wipe it off!"

"Mh, mh," she muttered.

"Shit! girl!" Tavon said as his head fell back with pleasure.

After she finished, she wiped her mouth. She stood up and tried to kiss him.

"Hell no! I ain't doing no kissing," Tavon said turning his face away.

"Why not? It's your dick!"

"Yeah, and that was your ass it just came out of!"

He pushed her back down on the pool table to finish what they had started.

"This pussy wide as hell. Can you even feel it? You talking about the boy B.'s dick is little. Somebody else has to be hitting this ass. Who else you fucking?"

"Wouldn't you love to know?" she asked deviously smiling, rising up to kiss him.

"Check this out. You was trying to go, I was trying to go, so we here! All that other bullshit, I'm not with. Shit! I'm getting ready to cum he said breathing heavier. You still swallow?" he asked while quickly snatching off the condom.

"No wait!" Remi said loudly. "I haven't cum yet."

"I can't wait!"

Tavon said looking over at the steps. "I think someone is coming." He grabbed Remi's arm pulling her up from the pool table, held her head back, and released every drop in her mouth.

Tyra pressed the stop button. And needless to say, everyone in the room was speechless and for the first time ever, so was Duce. I gently touched B. on his arm and my heart cried out for forgiveness as I watched a tear roll down his face. "B., I'm sorry. Please forgive me."

"You are going to pay for this!" Remi snapped.

Tyra went to respond, but I quickly interrupted her.

"Check this out whore! Number one, you can fuck who you want, but you crossed the line when you decided to smile in my face and at the same time fuck Ahmaun." Everyone's eyes got bigger. "That's right I know! And for real you're lucky I'm not whipping your ass right now. What did I ever do to you?" Remi just stood there staring at me as if she wanted to spit in my face. Jodi jumped up and tried to get to Remi, and thank God Duce grabbed her in time.

"Bitch, you have lost your mind!" Mea yelled, who also got up and tried to get to Remi, when one of her boyfriends grabbed her. "Get off me!" Mea screamed trying get out of his firm hold.

B. looked at Remi in pure disgust and asked, "What the hell is wrong with you? How could you do this to Sollie and me? don't you know I loved you."

"Sollie, you didn't have to do this," she cried out. "You could have come to me like a woman."

"A woman." Tyra said walking over to her. "I don't believe you just said that out of your mouth. Tramp! You obviously don't know the definition of a woman!"

"You are sick!" B. said, "And don't you dare make this about Sollie. I don't blame her one bit. I would have put you out there too. Everyone warned me. What kind of person are you? Sollie has done nothing but look out for you, and this is how you repay her. God help you!" I told B. about the lie she told to get the money and how she had planned on leaving as soon as she got it. "Oh yeah, well guess what," he said snatching Remi pocketbook out of her hand reaching into her wallet and pulling out the ten-thousand-dollar check. Unfolding the check he held it up to her. "You want it, you got it!" B. ripped the check up and threw it right in Remi face. Remi looked down on the floor and stared at the bits of paper. When she raised her head, the look that was on her face was priceless. Duce was still trying to calm Mea and Jodi down, and everyone else still couldn't believe what they had just witnessed. B. sadly walked into the kitchen, and went out back on the deck.

"That ten grand you lied so hard for, I could get that in a day! You obviously wanted to play the game, but unfortunately, you didn't know how! Because if I got down like you, I would have something to show for it not just a wet ass and a cell! And look at you. Ain't got shit, but what I gave you!" I chuckled and then told Remi to get the fuck out my house!

"B," she cried out, attempting to walk around me. Tyra walked over and stood in front of her stopping her from going any further.

"Are you deaf or something? Where the hell do you think you're going?" Tyra asked.

"Move," Remi snapped, trying to go around Tyra, "I need to talk to B."

"You really have a lot of nerve. B. doesn't want to talk to you and I think Sollie told you to get out. You think this is a game?!"

"You don't have anything to do with this!" Remi yelled.

157

"What—did—you—say," Tyra asked in slow motion, moving closer to Remi. "This is my best friend, my best friend! Something you obviously don't know the meaning of. And on the contrary of what you may think, I have everything to do with it! And you stand here smugly acting as if someone has done something to you. For real, Remi, you need to leave because you're about a minute away from me slapping the shit out of you!" Tyra said putting her finger in Remi's face. "And you know what? Your minute is up!"

Before I could grab Tyra, she slapped Remi so hard, she fell into the wall. Remi grabbed her face, shaking her head from side to side, and trying to come out of the daze Tyra had just put her in. I grabbed Tyra. Duce yelled for one of our friends to come and get Jodi, and just as they did, Duce came running from out the kitchen. "Just roll out freak!" Duce said as he grabbed Remi's arm and pulled her toward the front door, "Before I let my girls whip your freak-ass for real."

Tyra stood there definitely wanting some more. Tyra wasn't a joke once she became angry. And being the wife of a big-time lawyer didn't mean anything! As prissy and cute as she may be, didn't mean anything and the upper class neighborhood where she lived now had nothing to do with where she grew up; the hood would always be a part of her. B. ran inside after hearing all the commotion, and watched as Duce pushed Remi out the front door.

"Bitches," Remi yelled, holding the side of her face, "I hate all of y'all! And Sollie! I do have something you don't!"

"What could that possible be, Remi? I have money, jewelry, clothes, a Benz, and sadly for you, his heart! You just got the dick. All you were was a side-chic! What could you possibly have that I don't?!"

Chapter Seventeen

"H   is baby!"

"What!" B. said as he and I both stood there in total shock.

"Aw go head freak, with your nasty ass!" Duce said. "Didn't you say you didn't have anywhere to go? Yes you do! Go find the baby's father." He slammed the door in Remi's face.

For the next hour and a half everyone talked about what had happened, and I was sick of being asked if I was okay. I went out on the deck and talked with B. and begged for his forgiveness, but he wasn't even angry with me. Duce came out and angrily asked where Ahmaun punk-ass was. And I begged Duce to let me handle Ahmaun. I didn't want him doing or having anything done to Duce. And I assured him that I was going to take care of Ahmaun myself.

My good friend Kane called from the police station and wanted to know what was going on. He said Remi had just left there and had taken out a warrant for Tyra's arrest. I told him what happened and he said that he would make sure that the warrant doesn't get processed.

I asked B. if Remi was really pregnant and he said that she had been complaining of nausea lately and how if she was pregnant it wasn't his, he said him and Remi used protection.

"Are you two okay?" Tyra asked walking out on the deck.

"She all right, she's a soldier!" Duce said rubbing my back, giving me a hug, pulling Tyra toward him, "I love y'all." Duce kissed us both on the cheek and said he had to go, but not before asking if he could have the tape of Remi. He said Sister Betty really enjoyed it. I told him no.

Movie night was over, and everyone was gone. I went upstairs and prepared myself to start my new job. I was going to use what happened as an excuse not to start, but no more excuses. I looked through the suits hanging in my closet, trying to find what I was going to wear on my first day at work. I then remembered the suit that I had found in Ahmaun's trunk, wondering who he could have bought it for, 'cause Remi definitely wasn't out the couture mob. I went in the guest room, set the alarm clock, and lay in the bed wondering if Remi was really pregnant, and if she was, the way she was out there, Ahmaun needed to be in line with the rest of them getting a DNA. But whether the child was his or not still didn't change the fact that he had slept with her.

I then thought about Kane and thank God, Kane said he was going to make sure the warrant wasn't processed. I could see Tyra now sitting in a cell down Central Booking. That's it! Kane could help me, but would he? That was my friend and he looks out for me, but would he go that far. And then I wondered if Ahmaun would remember him from my party. I doubt it. Ahmaun was so smoked up the night of my party. And Kane was lying low. I'll call Kane tomorrow and talk with him. Hopefully, he won't think I've lost my mind.

Before I knew it my alarm was going off, and my cell was ringing.

"Hello," I answered half asleep.

"Chop! Chop! Get your ass up!" Duce yelled into the phone making me laugh, "nah, Shorty, for real. I just called to check on you."

"I'm good. Why are you up so early? I asked.

"Yo! I'm telling you all the lady wants to do is fuck! Give a nigga a break," he exclaimed.

"Oh, well, you wanted the old head, so you got her."

"Whatever man, have a good day at work. Love you and I holla at you later."

I got out of bed with a big smile on my face. It was time to start handling my business. No more crying, whining, or feeling sorry for myself. It was time to level up! I walked over to the radio and popped in Mary J and blasted the cut Just Fine, and jumped in the shower. I then danced around the room as I got dressed, wiggling my hips into my black Gucci pants, slid on my shoes, put on my white shirt that sprouted ruffles down the front of it and slipped into the jacket. I turned off the radio, snatched my black leather briefcase off the doorknob, and when I stepped out the front door, I was back! I was definitely a hottie, ready to start my new job, loving my new attitude, and looking forward to becoming half a million dollars richer in just two days.

Mrs. Johnson was out front watering her flowers and just as she lifted up she had a very painful look on her face. Placing her hands on her back, she said, "Oh Sollie, you look so nice. Was everything okay last night? I heard some commotion."

"Everything was fine, Mrs. Johnson," I said, walking off the porch. I walked around the Benz to make sure that Remi didn't come back last night and slash the tires or even key my car.

Driving and singing along with Sam Cook *Too Good at Good byes*, to the top of my lungs, my perked-up attitude quickly became dim as I sang each lyric. While tapping the wheel and impatiently waiting for the light to change, a brother pulled up next to me and I stared at him with such hatred, rolled my eyes, and continued to sing. When the light changed, I sped off. I noticed him trying to catch up with me. Don't change, don't change I said looking at the yellow light, but it did.

God, what does he want?! And no you cannot have my number, I thought.

"Hello," the very handsome, clean-cut intelligent-looking brother said.

"Yes," I responded sarcastically.

Dawn Barber

"May I ask you a question?"

I nodded my head yes.

"Why did you look at me like that back there?"

I wanted to say because men ain't shit, but I didn't.

"Obviously, because I wanted to." I snapped, thinking who the hell is he to question me as to why I looked at him like I did.

"Well, from the lyrics of your music, and the look you gave me, it's obvious someone has hurt you. You're too beautiful to let that beauty turn into anger. And for the record, I'm one of the good guys. You have a beautiful day, sister," he said.

Damn! I thought he was trying to holler. I felt like Jodi fuck men! I turned the music back up, flipped down the sun-visor, and looked at myself in the mirror; and he was right. After taking a good look, I saw the anger that he was speaking of, and I hated Ahmaun and Remi for causing it.

I arrived at work and walked inside the building. Walking over to the receptionist, I told her who I was. She told me to have a seat, and she would let my boss know that I was there. I nervously sat down in the seat and thought this is it, the beginning of my independence. George came through the double doors, walked over to me smiling, and firmly shook my hand. "You look great!" the middle-aged bald white man said. "I really want to apologize again for having to delay your start date, but I'm very pleased you're here. I know you're going to be a great asset to this company."

He offered me doughnuts and coffee, then took me around to meet the others. After meeting them, he showed me my work area; the cubicle was small, but cozy. I sat at the desk, and turned on my computer. Although I was familiar with their database, he still assigned one of my coworkers to work with me throughout the day.

"Hi, I'm Elizabeth," the perky thirty-something freckle-faced red-head said.

She was really skinny and very tall; she had to be about six feet two. I chuckled because she reminded me of "Olive Oyl."

Extending her hand to me, she said, "You're very pretty, and I love your suit, and your shoes are gorgeous. What is that fragrance

162

you're wearing? Do you live nearby? Do you have Indian in you? Your skin is flawless. You look so young. How old are you, if you don't mind me asking?"

Take a breather bitch, I thought. I looked at her like she was crazy. She then started talking badly about all the other employees; telling me all their business. Another worker walked by my cubicle that I hadn't met yet and introduced herself to me. As she walked away she looked at Elizabeth, and then at me, and shook her head, as if to give me some kind of warning.

"Listen, Sollie," Elizabeth said sliding closer. "Watch her," she whispered talking about Clair who just introduced herself to me, "and watch him," she pointed over at Jim. "And oh my god, that bitch right there," she said pointing over to Ms. Susie, the little old lady across the room.

This lady is nuts, I thought. I wasn't even there an hour yet, and she was already telling me who to watch! My mother didn't raise no dummy. I knew the one I was going to watch would be her ass. And as soon as Ms. Susie walked by us, Elizabeth told her that was a lovely shirt she was wearing.

Ain't that something! She just finished talking about the lady. Ms. Susie must be down with her too. She didn't even say thank you. She just looked at me and smiled, and told me if I needed her help I should feel free to ask.

Elizabeth said that she would be right back and when she returned she brought a stack of invoices with her that needed to be entered into the system, and they were dated back two weeks. She showed me how to do one of them. And just as I went to do another, George came over, looking very angry.

"Elizabeth!" George said angrily standing at the entrance of my cubicle. He walked inside and reached over picking up the invoices and looking at the dates. "These invoices should have been done!" he said holding almost a hundred invoices. "I need to see you in my office, now!"

"Sollie, I'll be right back. We can finish the rest when I return," she said, nervously following George to his office.

"Good!" the guy, Jim, said who sat right across from me.

I noticed Ms. Susie walking over to my cubicle. "Are you okay, sweetheart?" she asked, looking over at the invoices, and shaking her head. "If she stays out of everyone else's business, she would be able to get her own work done. It's just not right. And now she's trying to push them off on you."

Ms. Susie seemed to be very sweet and I couldn't believe Elizabeth called her a bitch. I had no idea what was going on in George's office but Elizabeth was in there a very long time, long enough for me to have finished entering most of the invoices in the system.

Elizabeth finally returned, and her face was red as an apple. George came out behind her.

"Sollie, what happened to all those invoices? Did someone help you?" he asked.

"Actually, no, I entered them in the system on my own."

"No way! All of those?!" he said with disbelief, flipping through the stack of maybe forty. He turned to Elizabeth. "I don't think Sollie will be needing you, and remember what we discussed. Great job, Sollie!" he said giving me a thumbs-up. He quickly walked away but not before giving Elizabeth a very stern look. Elizabeth lowered her head and muttered, "Asshole," and walked back to her cubicle.

I spun around to see what Jim was doing, and he was sitting at his cubicle looking over at her and laughing; he seemed very happy that Elizabeth had obviously been reprimanded.

Before I knew it, it was lunchtime. But I still didn't have an appetite. I went and sat outside at the picnic table, and watched the beautiful view of the lake. And that loneliness that I never wanted to feel again was staring me back in my face. But I was determined to go through whatever pain I had to endure to get that bastard out of my system!

I called and talked to Tyra before I went back inside. She sounded really worn out, and said she had been lifting and purging files all morning at work. After talking with her, I headed back inside. When I got back to my desk I noticed there was another pile of invoices sitting there. I didn't mind. The work kept me busy. And before I knew it, it was four thirty. As I was gathering my things to leave, George walked inside my cubicle and asked if I would be able to stay until six, to help out with the heavy workload. I told him yes. I called Tyra.

"Hey Tyra, are you still at work?"

"Actually, I'm just finishing up. Girl, my back is killing me! Why, what's up?"

"I'm working over, and the mattress company is coming today at six thirty and I may not be home in time."

"Whatttttt, you're working overtime?!" she teased. "I am so proud of you. No problem. I'll pick the kids up from my parents' house, and then we will come straight to your house. Wait, let me make sure I still have your house key on my ring. Okay, I have it."

"Are you going to stay until I get off?"

"Yeah, I can. The kids will love to see you."

"Thanks, Tyra. Love ya!"

Chapter Eighteen

I t was six, and I was ready to go. As I was leaving the building my cell rang. "Out of area" appeared, and I knew it was Ahmaun. *Not now!* I thought. I jumped in the car and headed home. While driving, I thought about the plan and wondered if I could possibly get away with it.

When I pulled in front of the house, I smiled proudly; and I must admit, it felt really good knowing I had just worked a nine-to-five. Soon as I walked through the door, Tyra said that someone had been calling the house phone like crazy. When I looked at the caller ID, it said "out of area." I knew it had to be him, and I wondered if he had talked to Remi. I went to call him but forgot I had his cell turned off. He'll call back.

"Hi cutie-pies," I said, hugging little Terry and Trinity as they came in from out back.

"Aunt Sollie, can we have some ice cream?" Trinity asked.

"No, you may not. You haven't eaten dinner yet!" Tyra said.

"Awwww Mom," Trinity said frowning.

"Well, guess what, we can fix that. How about chicken fingers and french fries?"

166

"Heyyyyy working girl," Duce said coming through the front door and walking straight to the refrigerator to get a beer, "how was work, Shorty?"

"It was fine."

"Where's Sis Betty?" Tyra asked.

"I know where she ain't! And where she ain't going to be," Duce said, frowning. "I didn't know they were here, heyyy nephew and niece," Duce said hugging Trinity and giving little Terry five. Reaching into his pocket, he handed them a dollar each. "Take this and don't spend it all in one place."

"Cheap-ass!" Tyra whispered.

Duce and I went into the living-room, Tyra went up stairs to get the Tylenol. She said her back was really hurting. Jodi and LeLe came over. Jodi was still pissed from last night, and of course, Duce started to go in on Jodi. But I quickly shut it down, after what Jodi had revealed to me, she definitely didn't need to hear his smart mouth.

Tyra walked in on Jodi telling Duce that he was a dog, and that all of his womanizing was going to catch up with him.

"Excuse me." Tyra said walking into the living room. "First of all, my son is not allowed to horror movies. And you know that, little Terry." She said standing there with her hands on her hips giving him that motherly stare. "Go in the kitchen with your sister." She said looking to make sure he was in there. "And secondly I don't appreciate y'all talking that negative talk about men around my son. If that's how you feel, fine! But have that discussion when he's not around, or any child for that matter!"

"What was wrong with our conversation?" Jodi asked.

"What was wrong?! What was right?! You should see the women with their sons coming into social services. Five, six, and seven-year-old little boys already with the pants hanging off their tails, looking like baby thugs, and the women sit there talking about their fathers, boyfriends, and what they did, who they did it with, and how men are such dogs. That may be how they feel, but these kids don't need to hear that. What are they going to start thinking about themselves and the same for little girls, what are they going to grow up thinking about men, if all they're hearing is negativity? Y'all may think these kids don't be listening, but they do. Little Terry may have been watching that movie, but I guarantee if I asked him to repeat everything you two said, he could. All I am saying is children are what they hear and as adults we need to watch what we are saying around them."

The mattress set was finally delivered and eventually everyone had left. Still feeling very guilty, I decided to call B. His voice mail came on so I left him a message.

Hey B., just calling to see how you're doing, and to apologize again. Love you.

I looked at my watch to see if I had time to get to the mall, because along with my new mattress and box spring, I needed new sheets.

I grabbed my purse and headed out the door. I was flying up Rt.1 when the next thing I saw was blue lights flashing behind me. I slowly pulled off the side of the road. "Shit," I said reaching over and opening the glove compartment to get my registration card.

"License and registration please, ma'am," a voice said that I recognized.

"Kane," I said looking up at him laughing.

"Sollie, why the hell are you speeding?" Kane asked.

I told Kane I was trying to get to the mall before they closed. I also told him that I needed his help, and if we could meet up tomorrow after work. He agreed and told me to slow my little ass down.

I looked at my watch and realized I had twenty minutes before the mall closed. And by the time I finally got there, I had about ten minutes to shop. I grabbed my sheets and as I was walking ass the shoe department Jimmy Choo called my name.

On the way home, I called Tyra to see if she was able to meet with Kane and me. She said yes and tried to get me to tell her what I had planned, but I told her I would tell her tomorrow.

I finally got home, took a shower, and went down into the kitchen and made a big bowl of ice cream. I curled up on the couch and watched more repeats of Insecure, and if they showed Danielle black fine necked ass again, I was going to scream. They were off the hook, and the sex scenes were hot. Sitting there horny as hell my phone rang, and it read "Out of Area." I cleared my throat and answered.

"Hello."

"Baby, I'm sorry! I swear, I'm sorry," Ahmaun said trying to sound as if he was crying.

Got damit He knows! Who in the hell told him? Well, I guess anybody could have told him the way people run their mouths. I was so concerned with getting Remi back, I never even thought about him finding out from someone else; this messes up everything. I knew at that moment I had to act my ass off in order for this nigger to believe me.

"Remi, Remi!" I yelled. "How could you do this to me, how, and she is supposed to be pregnant!"

"Sollie, please chill out, Shorty! Fuck that girl, and that baby ain't mine. Shorty, I'm sorry."

"It's over! I'm done. This is the last time you will ever hurt me again. When you get back in town, I want you to get your things and want you out of my house and out of my life! I will never forgive you for this."

For the next half an hour we went back and forth. He continued crying and begging me to forgive him, and I knew if I was going to go through with my plan I had to start right now, while at the same time praying that I wasn't moving too fast with this whole thing. What if Kane says no? Fuck it, I have to do this right now.

"What was that?" I said with fear in my voice.

"What was what? What's wrong?!" he asked.

I told Ahmaun that two houses in the block had been broken into, and I was really scared because they haven't caught the burglar yet. It was all bullshit, just all a part of the plan. He begged me to stay at my mother's until he returned.

"Ahmaun, are you even listening to me? When you return, you won't be staying here. It's over!"

169

"Look, Sollie, I ain't trying to hear that shit! It ain't never going to be over. Fuck that bitch, fuck all of them whores. Look, Shorty, just take thirty thousand of that money and go nuts, buy whatever you want. Make sure all the doors are locked, and I'll see you soon." And he hung up.

Take thirty thousand!? Yeah, right, come Wednesday, I was going to take all of it. I turned off the TV and went upstairs to go to bed.

I was beginning to get used to tossing and turning. Around four in the morning, I was finally able to fall asleep, and seven thirty came quick. I got up, took my shower, got dressed, and headed to work.

"Good morning, Sollie," Elizabeth said walking past my cubicle straight over to hers and quickly began working.

"Good morning," I said. I looked over at Jim wondering why Elizabeth was in such a hurry to get started working. Jim held up his index finger gesturing for me to wait a second.

"Hey Sollie, how's it going? You look nice," he said sipping his coffee. "She's working now, isn't she? Yesterday when George called her in the office, I heard he told her she has one more time to screw up and she'll be canned! All she does is sit on her ass, and talk about everyone. She's a real piece of work, I swear."

Jim praised me on being so proficient and asked if I could show him later the method I was using to enter the invoices into the system so quickly. And I told him that I would. "Thanks," he said as he walked back to his desk. The phone on my desk began to ring, and the ID read in-house call.

"Hello, this is Sollie."

"Sollie its Liz."

"Yes, Elizabeth, what's up?"

"What was that asshole talking about?" she said whispering.

"Elizabeth I have work to do." I said ending the call.

I dialed George's extension to see if he needed me to work over again tonight. Thank God he said no because I really didn't want to cancel my meeting with Kane and Tyra. I only had one more day to make this thing happen.

After work I drove straight home, got a large green trash bag and headed up the stairs. 25, 10, 12, 10, 8, and 9. *Now that's what I'm talking about,* I thought as the large door to the safe opened, and butterflies lined my stomach at the sight of all that money. I sat there for a second and stared, again wondering if I could possibly get away with this. And then stack-by-stack, I began placing the money inside the green trash bag until the safe was completely empty. Shit! I thought struggling to pick up the heavy bag. I dragged the bag over to the top of the stairs and down the steps; as heavy as it was there was no way I could have carried it. Finally, at the front door, I peeped outside to make sure no one was around and dragged the bag out the front door, down the steps, and over to the car. Just as I pressed the unlock button to the trunk, there comes that nosey, Mrs. Johnson.

"Sollie, let me help you," she said coming down her front steps and over to my car.

"Mrs. Johnson, no thank you. I have it, really."

"No, I'll help!" she insisted, reaching down and grabbing the bag. I raised the trunk. "One, two, three" she counted, just before we lifted the heavy bag.

"My Lord, Sollie, what's in there? A dead body?!" she asked tirelessly placing her hand on her back once again looking as if she was in pain.

It's not a dead body lady, but it's damn sure a whole lot of a dead president! I silently thought.

"Actually, it's some old things that I'm giving away." I chuckled, thinking if she saw how much money was inside the bag, she would probably have a heart attack, knowing she's never seen that much money in her lifetime. "Thanks for your help, Mrs. Johnson." I shut the trunk and rushed back in house. Looking at the time, I realized that I needed to hurry up so I could meet Kane and Tyra.

I ran back upstairs, and picked up the safe with no problem. It wasn't as heavy as it looked. I carried it down the stairs and got another trash bag and put the safe inside of it. I looked out the door and noticed Mrs. Johnson walking down her front steps with a flowered hat on her head, carrying her black Bible and happily humming a church hymn. Tonight was Tuesday and she was on her way to the Bible class. I put the safe inside the car.

I drove around the corner to some apartments and backed up to the large dumpster, and tossed it into the dumpster. Oh well, Ahmaun, you should have never crossed me the way you did.

When I got to the restaurant, I walked inside and spotted Kane sitting at the bar, drinking a beer. I made my way over to where he was without him noticing me, I stood behind him, and reached around and covered his eyes. "This is a stick up!" I said with a very heavy voice. We both laughed.

"Hey sexy," he smiled. Looking me up and down, feeling the material of my suit, he said, "Shorty, you stay fly, don't you? Come on, let's get a table. You drinking?"

"Yeah, why not? Let me have a Mai Tai," I told the bartender. As we headed over to our table, Tyra came walking in looking as if she was in pain.

"What's wrong? Is your back still hurting?"

"Terry must have put it down last night!" Kane said laughing.

"Whatever Kane," Tyra said playfully hitting him on his arm, "They have me purging all those old files, and entering them in the new system. I work out every day so it's no way I should be feeling like this. I am wondering if I may have pulled a muscle or something."

"Do you want to go to the hospital when we leave here?"

"No, I am going to wait and see how I feel in the morning. If it's not any better, I'll call my doctor and make an appointment."

"So you're still volunteering at social service?" Kane asked.

"Yes, I am," Tyra said proudly.

"Time sure flies, Tyra. You hurting like that you need to be on payroll. Do you enjoy it? I guess that's a stupid question. You have been there all these years."

"Yeah, actually I love it," Tyra said with a painful look on her face.

The waitress came in took our order. While we ate dinner, I explained the whole plan, and thank God, Kane agreed to help me.

Although Tyra was a little reluctant at first, she eventually agreed. Kane did have one concern though, that Ahmaun may recognize him from the party. I told him it's possible, but I doubt it. He was really smoked up that night.

"I heard the boy is getting paid," Kane said. "But he's going down real soon."

"Good!" I said happy as hell, "Because that's the only way I'll get him out of my life. Kane, that reminds me, what happened with the boy, Dino?" I asked taking a bite of my buffalo wing.

"Dino, Dino, oh yeah the boy who was knocked off down Popular Grove. I spoke to the detective that's assigned to that case the other day, and he said they have no leads whatsoever." Kane sipped his beer.

"Is it true what they said?"

"What do you mean?" he asked curiously.

"The way they say he was killed."

"What, execution style? Oh yeah, whoever killed him definitely had skills. Somebody that knew what they were doing, and has obviously done it before! They left no traces whatsoever. All right pretty ladies, I have to go." Kane quickly finished his beer. "Sollie, no more Mai Tais, and Tyra, hope your back feels better," he said kissing us both.

"Thanks, Kane."

"No problem, anything for my girl. I'll see you tomorrow. Y'all be safe."

Tyra and I finished our food, and we left. Tyra went home to rest and I drove to the storage and rented a space to put the money inside, figuring the money could stay there until things calmed down, because after tomorrow it was going to be a mess! I had taken Ahmaun's one true love: his money!

Chapter Nineteen

B   ack at the house, I was getting my clothes together for work, and the phone rang. It was him.

"Hello."

"Shorty you all right?"

"What is it Ahmaun?!"

"Come on, baby, don't sweat that shit! That baby ain't mines!"

"Ahmaun, you are missing the whole point. It doesn't matter if the child is yours or not. You know what Ahmaun I'm not going through this again, your ignorant and you need to accept that it is over."

"Look, Sollie, I said I'm sorry. And I ain't going to keep apologizing, like my man said you know who number one is, so he doesn't even know why you're trippin!"

"Ahmaun, fuck you and your man." *Why did I let him take me there? As angry as I am, I don't want to give him any idea that I'm that angry to steal from him.* "Ahmaun, I don't want to argue anymore. We can be friends, but we can never be any more than that," I said trying to calm my tone.

"Yeah, whatever. Are you picking me up tomorrow?"

"Yeah. What time does your flight arrive?"

"Five. Did you go shopping?"

"No, I didn't."

"See, Shorty that's what I talking about. I told you to take thirty thousand and go do your thing and you didn't even touch the money. You're different from them other whores. Nigga just hang in there with me. Love you!"

I'm not as different as you think! I thought.

Ahmaun really thought what he did was forgivable. I guess with all the other things he did and I still stayed, why should he believe I was serious this time; and truth be told, a part of me still wanted to be with him. Now that's some crazy shit! *What is wrong with me,* I thought.

Six thirty came fast. I got up, did my normal routine, and left for work. As I walked into my cubicle, I noticed my desk was full of invoices, and for the first time I made several errors on them. I was so nervous about this evening, I was unable to focus. I called Tyra to see how she was feeling. She said she and Terry were just leaving her doctor's office, and she did pull a muscle in her back. She said the doctor had placed her on light duty for a few days. I asked if she was up to going through with the plan, and she said yes, although she still tried to talk me out of it. But that wasn't happening.

I sat there tapping the pen on the desk, staring at the clock. Time seemed to be moving slowly. Nervously, playing with my Rolex, remembering the day Ahmaun had bought the "His and Her" watches.

Four O'clock was here. I gathered my things and left. As I drove down 295 S and veered off on the exit that read BWI Airport, my heart began beating faster. Calm down Sollie, I told myself. As I drove closer to the airport, I was able to see the colorful Air Jamaica plane take off and wished that I were on it.

Just as I was pulled into the arriving-flights lane, he was walking out the door, I hit the horn to get his attention and angrily stared at him as he walked over to the car, smiling as if everything was okay. The sight of him made me sick. I rolled my eyes and purposely laid my cell on the dashboard.

"What's up, Shorty?" he asked throwing his bag in the backseat. He got inside the car and leaned over to hug me. Angrily, I pushed him away, and told him not touch me. I honestly wanted to spit in his face. "You look like you lost weight. I got your favorite." he said holding up the bag of food.

"No, thank you. I don't have an appetite, and if you had just gone through what I have you would have lost weight too!"

"Sollie, don't start that shit. I said I'm sorry. What the hell else do you want me to say! Shorty, for real, I thought you were stronger than this, letting this bullshit get to you."

I didn't respond, but I did wonder how a person could be so ignorant.

"I see you got the Benz looking real good," he said looking around inside the car. "Sollie, take me downtown to the phone spot so I can see what the hell is wrong with my cell."

I looked at my watch and knew it was time. I got out the car and walked around to the trunk, opened it, and pretended that I was looking for something.

Ring, ring, I thought. And it did. I yelled for Ahmaun to answer it, and disappointedly listened as he told the person on the other end that they had the wrong number.

Wrong number? What is Tyra doing! She should have called two minutes ago. God, I hope she didn't change her mind, I thought, looking at my watch.

"Sollie, come on!" Ahmaun yelled to me out the window.

"I'm coming. I'm trying to find my CD case!" I yelled back.

"Just come on! I told you I needed to get downtown, before the phone spot closes, and your CD case is right here."

Finally, the phone rang again. *Please be Tyra, please!* I thought.

"Yeah!" he answered rudely. "Sollie, come and get this. It's some security company," he said, putting Kanye West CD on.

"Security Company?" I said curiously, getting inside the car, and taking the cell out of his hand.

Holding the phone up to my ear, I quickly changed my facial expression as if I had suddenly become worried. I hung up and told Ahmaun the bullshit story. "I hope everything is okay. If it's not one thing it's another. The police are on the way, and the security company said they already notified Tyra."

"What the fuck they call Tyra for?"

"Because I have her down just in case they are unable to reach me. I took a deep breath and slowly pulled off.

Chapter Twenty

A   hmaun didn't say one word. But I could tell by the look on his face that there was only one thing on his mind; His money. When I turned the corner, two police cars were parked out front. *What is Kane doing?* I thought to myself. *Why would he bring another police with him?* I got out the car and looked over at the police, and he slightly nodded his head to me. I then realized he must have been cool. I guess he was there to make everything seem more real. Ahmaun followed behind me and didn't even look in the police's direction. I looked over at Mrs. Johnson standing on the porch trying to peep over into my house to see what was going on. I spoke to her and quickly made my way inside, ready to make my acting debut!

Scene One!

"Tyra, what happened?!" I asked.

"Are you Ms. Carr?" Kane asked, while standing there holding a pen and a fake police report.

"Yes, I am, officer. What happened?" I asked looking around. I watched Tyra stare at Ahmaun with such hate. Ahmaun looked at Kane, offering him a simple nod of the head. He then walked over to the stairs and leaned up against the banister. I looked at Ahmaun, wondering if he remembered Kane. I didn't think he did.

"Ms. Carr, your backdoor shows signs of forced entry. I did a walk-through to make sure the assailant wasn't still inside your home. However, you need to do the same to check and see if anything has been taken."

"Oh my God! Are you saying someone broke into my house?" I asked serious as hell. Just as Kane went to speak, I notice Mrs. Johnson walking up my front steps. If she messes this up, I swear . . . I quickly walked over to the door. "Mrs. Johnson, I am really busy right now, I will have to talk with you later. Someone has broken into my house," I said trying to pull the door shut and just as I did she stuck her big black orthopedic shoe in between the door and the frame, stopping me from shutting it.

"No wait! You know, I saw someone running down the alley!"

Oh my god, now if this shit ain't something; she nosey, and she's a liar! I looked over at Tyra and she did everything in her power not to laugh and so did Kane. This was downright ridiculous. I looked at Ahmaun and I could tell that he wanted to go upstairs so bad to check on that safe. Ahmaun walked into the kitchen and looked at the broken lock on the door. Kane played it off and asked Mrs. Johnson to come inside and tell us exactly what she had seen. He reached into his top pocket and pulled out a small pad.

"He had on dark color jeans, white sneakers, and what you call that thing a . . . ah, ah ah, yeah, a puddy."

I put my hand on my forehead and turned slightly away. *Unbelievable. Fucking unbelievable,* I thought.

"No, ma'am, I think you may be referring to a hoody," Kane said smiling, again, trying not to laugh.

"That's right, officer, a hoody. Please forgive me. This old mind is fading away on me. It was black."

"Did you happen to see his face?" he asked, pretending to write something on the small pad he was holding.

Ahmaun quickly returned, hoping Mrs. Johnson could give a description. If this lady lies and makes up a description, I won't be any more good, I stood there with my arms folded waiting for her answer.

"No, I am sorry, officer. My eyesight isn't that good anymore. You know my doctor said I have a bad case of glaucoma."

Enough with it, lady! I stood there thinking. Kane went along with the program and took a little more information from Mrs. Johnson.

"Ms. Carr, this is yours," he said handing me the fake police report. "Please make a list of anything that may have been stolen, and here is my card." He looked at Mrs. Johnson and told her thanks for her help. I opened the door for her and she left.

"Thank you, officer," I said still trying to keep a straight look on my face. Kane wasn't out the door completely before Ahmaun ran up the steps. I went behind him, looking back at Tyra as she stood there watching.

Scene Two

"Shit! It's gone! Sollie please tell me you moved the safe, please," he said walking back and forth, with his hands resting on the back of his head.

"They took the safe?" I asked with a shocked look on my face. Ahmaun sat on the edge of the bed, shaking his head in disbelief. I walked over to my dresser.

"Ahmaun, they took all my jewelry!"

He jumped up from the bed and walked over to the dresser and angrily slapped a stack of papers on the floor. "Let me find out who the fuck took my shit!" I grabbed the phone and looked at the card Kane had just given me acting as if I was going to dial the number.

"Who are you calling?"

"I'm calling 911 and ask them to send the officer back!"

"Sollie, hang the fucking phone up. You can't tell them someone stole that kind of money. They will ask all kinds of questions, and they are already on my heels. I know who took my shit!" And when he said that my heart fluttered.

"Who Ahmaun?" I asked nervously waiting for him to respond.

"One of those clown-ass nigga's you be having over here, that's who! Let me find out for sure. Whoever took it is going to get a hot one right in their fuckin head!"

180

When he said that, I felt nauseated, knowing that's how Dino was killed. And I knew then Ahmaun had something to do with his death, and for a minute I didn't want to continue with this stage play anymore. I just wanted him out of my life. I went to the bathroom and splashed cold water on my face. Snatching a paper towel off the holder and patting my face dry, I leaned against the wall wondering what the hell had I gotten myself into. I turned and looked into the mirror, ran my fingers through my hair, and took a deep breath realizing I had come too far to quit now. I headed back into the bedroom.

"Ahmaun, did you mention to anyone the money was here?"

"Hell no! I don't talk to them nigga's like that. Are you crazy? The game is sold, not told! And why the hell are you so calm?" he asked looking at me incredulously.

Make it good Sollie, make—it—good!

I walked over to him and folded my arms and with a very calm tone, I said, "Let me tell you one thing. All the crying I just did, the loss of appetite and sleepless nights, after finding out about you and Remi, I promised myself nothing, or no one would ever take me there again. And don't you ever attempt to imply that I had something to do with this!" He just looked at me and sat back down on the bed.

Tyra yelled up the steps that she was going to the hardware store to get new locks for the back door.

"Why is she still here?" he asked mugging.

"Because that's my friend, that's why she is still here! And I am sorry about your money. You don't want me to call the police back, and I told you we were over. So why the hell are you still here?!"

"I ain't going nowhere. I want my fuckin money!" he yelled.

"Well, what do you want me to do? I wish you had your money, and I wish I had my jewelry! I'm going downstairs to see if anything else was taken." About fifteen minutes later, I heard a horn blow. I quickly sat down on the couch and put my head down as if I was worried. Ahmaun came running down the steps.

"I have to go take care of something," he said as he stormed out the door. I didn't even bother to look and see who was picking him up. I just wanted his sorry-ass gone.

About a half an hour later Tyra returned.

"Is he still here?" Tyra asked as she came in the door.

I smiled brightly "No, he's not!"

"I must say you deserve an Oscar for that one."

Tyra didn't just buy new locks for the back door she brought locks for the front as well. After we were done, I poured each of us a glass of wine, and we sat on the couch and toasted. But I didn't feel at all like I thought I would.

"I thought this so-called revenge would make me feel better, but I feel worse. Even after all he has done to me."

"Sollie, you can always give it back. Tonight, you stepped out of who you are. And yes, I helped you so I'm just as guilty, and I don't feel good about that. But you know, I will do anything for my girl."

Tyra and I talked for about an hour and she left. I wondered where Ahmaun could have been and if he was with Remi. Around two in the morning, my phone rang and it was him, demanding me to open the door. He wanted to know why his key wasn't working.

"Ahmaun, it's over!"

"Ain't shit over! And I want my fuckin money!"

Ahmaun continued yelling for me to open the door, and although I wasn't, I told him I was going to call the police.

"The police? You going call the police on me! I can't believe what you just said. It's cool. I'm out, but trust and believe if I don't get my money, somebody is going to die!"

I got out of bed to walk over to the window, pulled the curtain back, and watched as he got in his car and sped off.

A week had gone by and Ahmaun called my phone and rang my doorbell night and day. And I was a complete wreck, staying over at Tyra's and my mother's house for hours each day after work. I finally decided to call Salique, but I only told him half the story. And that was all he needed to hear. Salique and Duce were at my house, morning and night. They were like my own personal bodyguards; they even went with me to take Ahmaun's things to his mother's house.

I pawned all the jewelry Ahmaun had given me over the years, all except the Rolex and my ring. The owner of the pawn shop was a little skeptical at first until I was able to convince him that all the jewelry was stolen. I walked out of there with ten thousand dollars and I put it right with the other money I had stashed.

Work kept me busy, but I have to admit even with Salique and Duce protecting me, I was still terrified. But most of all, my conscience was eating me alive about the money I had stolen. And watching Elizabeth skip over to my work area didn't make it any better. She pulled up a chair and flopped down in it.

"Hey, Sollie girl, did you hear about Ms. Susie?"

"Elizabeth!" I snapped. "My name is not Sollie girl."

"God, Sollie I was just joking. Don't bite my head off for Pete's sake."

Lady will you get away from me! I thought to myself, looking at the screen and noticing it was Ahmaun calling again. I picked up my cell and placed it on vibrate mode and sat the phone inside my desk draw.

Refocusing on Elizabeth, I said, "No, I haven't heard anything."

"Well, you know the old bag has custody of her five grandchildren, because their mom is strung out on that crack—a—lack—a—lack!" she said slapping her leg and falling out laughing. "Anyway, one of her grandchildren has been diagnosed with some form of leukemia, and if they don't begin treatment soon the little brat may die." She leaned over and looked down toward George's office making sure he wasn't coming.

I felt so bad hearing that. "Okay, so why don't they begin treatment?"

"The insurance she has won't cover the extensive treatment she needs, so I'm going to take up a collection on Friday for her. Wow! Sollie, someone sure wants to talk with you," Elizabeth said hearing my phone vibrate again. "Who is it, your honey bun, sugar plum, or your chewing gum?" she said slapping her leg and once again falling out laughing, this time even crying as if what she just said was so funny.

"Elizabeth, what is wrong with you? It wasn't that funny. As a matter of fact it wasn't funny at all. Look, I need to get back to my work."

"Sollie, I'm sorry I don't know why I'm being so silly. It must be the coffee."

Hearing her desk-phone ring, she jumped up and skipped her flighty ass down to her cubicle. I looked over at Ms. Susie, and she did look very worried. *That's terrible. I sure hope everything works out for her,* I thought. I continued to work when all of a sudden a feeling of anger came over me.

Don't be angry at him. If you're going to be angry at anyone, be angry with yourself, my conscience reminded me. After letting that thought sink in, it was truly correct. I chose to stay in that unhealthy relationship, but why? Why would anyone want to stay with someone like him? Was it the money, sex, jewelry, what was it? One thing I knew. I needed some answers.

"Everyone listen up, I have some terrific news." George said standing in the middle of the floor. "I just finished the monthly report and we have met our monthly quota in record time, and because of that I'm letting everyone off early with pay. Great job, you guys, great job!" he said giving thumbs up, "But I will see you bright early in the morning."

It was only eleven thirty. What was I going to do? I was afraid to go home. *Go shopping,* the irresponsible side of me said, but I didn't. Shopping was the furthest thing from my mind. I called Tyra and to see what she was up to.

"Hey Tyra, are you at work?"

"Yea, girl, and you should see my desk, full of these old records that need to go in the system. Why what's up?"

"My boss is letting us off early. I thought we could hook up, and go hangout."

I BE DAMN

"I wish I could, Sollie, but I can't. Are you going to call Salique or Duce to meet you at the house?"

"No, I'm just going to go home and pray that Ahmaun doesn't come around." Turning off my computer, I leaned back in my chair, took a deep breath, and said, "I don't know what is wrong with me."

"What do you mean?"

"I think you were right; maybe I really need to talk to someone. I need answers. I was thinking about taking your advice and going to see a therapist. Tyra be honest with me, do you think I'm crazy for wanting to talk to a shrink?"

"No, I do not! It's nothing wrong with that, Sollie, if that's what you feel you need to do. That's the first thing people think if someone sees a therapist, and it's not true. I think you're crazy if you know you need help and refuse to seek it. I say go for it! And you know I'm here for you."

"Thanks Tyra call me when you get off."

I left work and the whole ride home I thought about what Tyra had said. I stopped at the post office and picked up my bank statement from my PO box and closed it out. Driving home, I slowly turned onto my block and prayed that Ahmaun was not sitting in front of my door. I hated the fact that I had to live in fear. I parked the car and hurried into the house, picked up the mail that was on the floor, and looked through it. It was just a few bills. Normally I would take them to my mother or have Ahmaun pay them, but no more. I wrote out checks for each of them and laid them on the table for me to mail tomorrow. I lay on the couch looking at my cell and proceeded to check my messages.

Twenty-seven new messages.

By the time I listened to the last message, I was terrified—I heard Ahmaun say that he was going to kill me! What was I going to do? I threw the cell on the couch and began pacing the living room floor, nervously rubbing my hands together and crying. I was thinking how that's all you hear on the news—men who have killed their wives or girlfriends. And what made it worse is I knew that he was capable of doing it.

185

Forget it, I thought, I'm just going to stay with him, because there was no way I would ever get rid of him. He'll change, I reasoned with myself, picking up my cell to call him. And just as I did, it rang, and it was Tyra.

"Hello," I said, trying to stop crying.

"What's wrong?!" Tyra asked with concern. I told her about the messages Ahmaun had left and she went off. I also told her that I was going to get back with him and she really went off. "Sollie, right now you are talking out of fear. You need to call the police and let them know that he has made threats against your life. That boy is crazy and you should not take his threats lightly! But getting back with him is not an option. Just give him his money and that car back! Have you found someone to talk to yet?"

"No, I am not calling anyone. Forget I even mentioned it. I'll be fine."

"I'm not forgetting anything. Listen, Terry always talks about the therapist that his law firm uses for some of their cases. He says she's really good. I'm going to call him and get her number. Is your mother still paying your health insurance?"

"Yeah but . . ."

"Sollie, let me call Terry and get the number. I'll call you back in a minute. Sollie, I love you and don't worry, everything is going to be fine."

I sat back down on the couch and fell asleep, and was awakened by the phone. It was him, and I decided to answer it.

"Hello."

"Hello! Hello!" he said sounding surprised that I answered the phone. "Why haven't you been answering the phone or the door?"

"What do you want, Ahmaun?"

"You know what the hell I want. I want my money!"

"Ahmaun, where are you?" I asked knowing I was getting ready to make the worst mistake of my life.

"I'm out front your house!" I walked over to the door, and there he was laid back in the seat of his Infinity. Are you going to let me in?"

"Yeah, Ahmaun." Everything Tyra had just said went out the door when I opened it to let him inside. As he walked in the house, I wondered if this was going to be my last day on this earth. He stood directly in front of me and raised his hand and gently ran his fingers through my hair and then placed the palm of his hand on the side of my face. "Why you doing this shit? You took my clothes to my mom's, got your locks changed, and cut me off just like that. I love you, nigga. For the last eleven years, I loved you! And all this bullshit over Remi and those other hoe's, fuck them! I keep telling you, I love you! You're number one.my Baby, I'm sorry I be hurting you, just please give me one more chance, I promise, I'm going to change. I promise I am." He pulled me closer to him and hugged me tightly. "Damn, girl I miss the hell out of you!"

I couldn't believe I had actually let Ahmaun inside my house. I was doing so good, staying away from him. I went to speak and he placed his finger on my lips.

"Shhhhhh, Sollie listen, I know I said a few things that were out of order and I apologize. I would never hurt you! And I know you would never take anything from me, but when I find out who did take, they're dead! But check this out," he said pulling out his cell and scrolling down showing me a picture of a six-bedroom colonial home in Harford County. "Say the word and it's yours! And this is yours too." He reached into his pocket and pulled out a small black velvet box and opened it, and inside was the five-karat teardrop diamond ring that he had promised me.

"Ahmaun, I can't," I said backing up, and pushing his hand away.

"Yes, you can." He reached for my hand and slid the rock on my finger.

He turned around and shut the front door, took me by my hand and led me over to the couch. Ahmaun began to kiss me and at first I hesitated, but not for long. I began kissing him back. I knew I was a fool, but truthfully I wanted him badly even after knowing that he had been with Remi. He laid me back on the couch and slowly began unbuttoning my shirt. "Damn!" he said opening my shirt fully, and staring at my breast.

What are you doing, Sollie? I silently asked myself.

My pussy ached as he began sucking my breast, gliding his tongue down my chest, and licking me all around the diamond that pierced my navel. I reached down and began loosening his belt. He stood up and I watched as he unzipped his jeans and they fell to the floor. He reached out for my hand.

Sollie, don't do this! He slept with your friend.

He turned me around and began licking me all over my back, while unzipping my skirt.

"Damn, you wet as hell," he said fingering me. "Can I hit it from the back?"

"Yeah, you can." I reached around, grabbing his ass, and pulling him closer. I might have been stupid but I wasn't crazy. I told him to wait and walked up the stairs to get a condom from the drawer. Just as I returned Ahmaun was coming up the stairs.

"I want it right here," he said opening the condom and putting it on. "Turn around," he said. I turned around, bent over gripping the banister as he entered me with such force. With one hand on my shoulder and the other around my waist, he fucked me like never before. And just as we both came, all kinds of emotions ran through my mind. But after those three minutes of pleasure, I was literally sick to my stomach. Out of breath and resting his head on my back, I told him to move. He backed away, and walked back down the steps. I went into the bathroom, leaned over the porcelain toilet, and vomited. I turned on the shower and climbed inside and scrubbed my body like never before, crying and feeling worthless. Why did I fuck him?

Just as Ahmaun came inside the bathroom, I grabbed the shower curtain and covered my wet body.

"What are you covering up for? That's mine," he said with certainty, walking over to the sink and washing up. "That shit was the good! Wasn't it, Shorty?"

I didn't respond. Still covered up with the shower curtain, I reached for the towel and wrapped it tightly around my body. I went into the bedroom, sat on the edge of the bed, and cried.

Ahmaun came into the bedroom and said that he had to make a run and that he would be back later to pick me up so that we could go and look at the house. Never even noticing my tears, he reached into his pocket and pulled out a stack of money. He counted out three thousand dollars and laid it next to me on the bed. He asked me to get him a key made, kissed me good-bye, and left. I walked over to my dresser and opened up my jewelry box. I slid the five-karat ring off my finger and laid it inside. After getting myself together, I headed back down the stairs. And just as I walked past the mirror, I stopped and stared. I wiped the falling tear from my face. I was so disappointed with myself. I looked up to God and vowed with mind, body, and soul that Ahmaun would never, ever touch me again.

Chapter Twenty-One

A   lthough it was only three-thirty in the afternoon, I poured a glass of wine, turned on the television, and curled up on the couch. I flipped through the channels trying to find something to watch on television. My cell rang and I saw it was B. But I didn't answer. I came across a show talking to people about their past and then they showed a clip of Oprah, saying that she has no regrets about the pains of her past, because she knows that it is her past that has made her the woman that she is today. I thought if I was going through all of this to become a better woman. I wondered as I flipped through the channels.

I came across a show with a woman on there, who was a millionaire, and she started out with just five thousand dollars. Now that's what's up! I got that and a whole lot more. Anyway, the woman surprised another woman with a large monetary donation toward her non-profit organization. The woman was in tears and so was I and immediately I thought of Ms. Susie, and how I could help her with her grandchild's medical treatment. Tyra called and I told her that Ahmaun had just left, and needless to say she was upset that I even let him in the house. I told Tyra everything that was said between him and me, but as close as Tyra and I was I couldn't bring myself to tell her that I had slept with him. She gave me the therapist's number and made me promise that I would call her.

After contemplating to call for more than an hour, I finally called. The shrink was very calm-mannered and soft-spoken. She asked me all kinds of questions in reference to me, my relationship with Ahmaun, and my family. I began to cry, and I apologized. She told me not to apologize, and that it was okay to feel everything that I was feeling. Just as we hung up, Tyra called.

"Hey," I answered sadly, wiping my eyes.

"Did you call?"

"Yes, I did, mother."

"Good, I am glad, and yes, I am your mother," Tyra said laughing. "But seriously, I was also calling to see if you wanted to come over to the house later this week, B.'s coming over again. We're going to celebrate. Terry and I decided to back his business, and you know his brother is here permanently."

"That's why you want me to come, wench!" I said laughing. "I doubt it, Tyra. I think I'm going to hang out with my mother and Aunt Bessie on Saturday. I really haven't spent a lot of time with either of them lately." Although disappointed, Tyra understood.

After talking with Tyra, I walked into the kitchen and looked out the window and noticed Mrs. Johnson sitting on her back porch reading the Bible. I thought about going out and talking with her, but I knew she would talk me to death.

That night Ahmaun called and rang my doorbell like crazy and wanted to know what kind of games I was playing. Little did he know, I said it so many times before, but this time I was done!

The next morning, I called Salique and Duce and told them not to come to the house and convinced them both that I was going to be fine, although I did decide to leave an hour early for work just in case Ahmaun came by.

On my way to work I stopped at the storage lot and took out some money from my stash. I arrived at work, and just as I sat down in my chair and turned on my PC that simple Elizabeth came skipping her flat-ass down the aisle, heading over to my cubicle, carrying a bright yellow envelope in one hand and a bag of popped popcorn and the other. I quickly grabbed my invoices and began to work.

"Good morning, Sollie."

"Good morning, Elizabeth."

"Listen Sollie, I'm going to be off the next few days, so I am taking up a collection today. I really don't want to, truthfully. I can't stand the old bitch!" she said looking over at Ms. Susie.

I stopped typing and asked, "Then why are you doing it?" She looked around, leaned closer to me, and whispered.

"Why else to get in good with George. He's really been on my ass lately, so I figured if I do this he will lay off my ass a little, and it won't be so flat! Get it?" She said falling back in the chair and laughing. "Do you want to give your donation now?" she asked holding up the bright yellow envelope.

"No, I'll give my donation to Ms. Susie personally."

Elizabeth tilted her head. "Suit yourself." Hearing her desk phone ring, she jumped up and happily skipped down the aisle to her cubicle.

I called George's extension, and asked if I could speak with him. He said yes and just as I was walking past Elizabeth's cubicle I heard her on the phone.

"Hey Hun, listen I slipped a twenty out from the money I collected so far for the old bag! So it's a go. We will be eating pizza tonight babes!"

That bitch! I thought as I headed into George's office. Just as I entered the office, I looked back and noticed Elizabeth walking over and collecting money from another employee.

"Hi, Sollie, is there a problem?" George asked as I entered his office.

"No, everything is fine, but would you call Ms. Susie in here with us?"

"Sure," he said with a curious look on his face as he dialed her extension. A few minutes later, Ms. Susie sadly walked into the room.

"Hi George, Hi Sollie," the little lady said sweetly.

I turned to her and pulled the chair closer to me and gestured for her to have a seat. "Ms. Susie, I was told about your grandchild's condition. Elizabeth asked me for a donation, but I told her I would

192

give it to you personally. I know medical treatment for your grandchild is very expensive, but I hope this will be of some help to you and your family," I said handing her an envelope. I looked over at George and smiled.

"Sollie, that is so thoughtful of you," she said taking the envelope. She looked down at it and saw the amount written on the front and almost fell out of her chair. George came from around his desk, placed his hand on her shoulder, and asked if she was okay.

"George! George!" she said, now holding her chest.

George's eyes widened. "Susie, what is it?" Still holding her chest she held the envelope up to George and muttered, "Ten thousand dollars." His eyes widened. He went back to his seat and stared at me as if I was some sort of an angel, shaking his head in disbelief, while Ms. Susie began to cry. She reached out for my hand. "Thank you, thank you, Sollie, so much. This is going to help my granddaughter tremendously!"

George told Susie that he had planned on donating as well, and after this act of kindness he was going to match what I gave her dollar for dollar.

It had become so emotional in his office, and the feeling of giving was so overwhelming, I had never felt anything like it. Ms. Susie finally got herself together and went back to her desk. As I was leaving out behind her, George asked me to come back.

"Sollie, I don't presume to know your financial status, and frankly, it's none of my business. But to give such an enormous amount of money to someone you barely even know, has touched my heart, and I want to assure you that you will be blessed! That was very, very thoughtful of you."

I walked out of his office door everyone stood and began to clap. I smiled, thinking, word had traveled fast.

Hearing all the clapping, Elizabeth came skipping from the other side with her bag of popcorn and her hand, and crumbs all around her mouth to see what all the commotion was about. But what she didn't see was George standing in his office door.

"What the fuck is going on over here?" she blurted.

"Elizabeth!" George snapped, scaring the hell out of her. She jumped and her popcorn went flying in the air. George was appalled at the language. "I need to see you in my office, now!" Nervously wiping the crumbs from her mouth, she followed George into his office. "Have a seat. I will not have you using such profanity in this building, and what exactly are you doing anyway?" he asked.

"Sir, I feel so bad for Ms. Susie and her poor little granddaughter that out of the kindness of my heart I decided to take up a collection to help with her granddaughter's medical treatment. And although things are tight with me, I'm going to chip in with twenty bucks," she said, pulling the twenty-dollar bill from her pocket that she had taken from the envelope earlier. "Everyone has donated except Sollie," she snarled deviously. "She seems to have a chip on her shoulder this morning. I asked her to donate and she outright refused."

George sat there quietly in his chair with his hands folded across his stomach and listened; he then stood. "You know, Elizabeth, I am so fed up with you. For you to come in here and tell that bold-faced lie on Sollie is quite frankly inexcusable. Your poor work performance, talking about your coworkers, and pushing your work off on others is no longer acceptable. And to say that Sollie refused to donate, I find simply appalling! For your information, Sollie just gave Susie a ten-thousand-dollar cash donation!" Elizabeth lowered her head and was speechless. "You put in for two days off correct?" George asked with a very serious face. Elizabeth slightly raised her head and said, "Yes, sir."

Getting up from his desk he walked over to the steel file cabinet. "I tell you what," he said removing her employee file from the cabinet and walking back over to his desk. "You're off indefinitely! As of this moment, you are no longer an employee of this company."

Elizabeth jumped up from her seat and screamed, "You can't do that!"

"It's already done. Please, clean your desk out and leave this building immediately!" He hit his button and asked his secretary to send security to escort her out the building.

Everyone watched as Elizabeth cleaned out her desk and placed those ugly-ass wicker scarecrows she collected in the cardboard box that security had given her. Everyone stood outside their cubicle watching and whispering as Elizabeth prepared to take her walk of shame. I walked over to Jim's cubicle and told him about the money that she had taken. Waiting outside of his cubicle with arms folded and tapping his feet, Jim stood there patiently waiting for Elizabeth to walk by. Once packed, she slowly walked down the aisle carrying her box of belongings, and Jim and I both noticed the yellow envelope full of money sticking out the box. She walked by Jim's cubicle with the dumbest look on her face.

"No pizza tonight! I think this belongs to Ms. Susie," Jim said snatching the yellow envelope form out the box.

"Asshole!" she snapped.

"That may be true, but I'm an asshole with a job!" Jim said laughing. He leaned up against his cubicle and sarcastically began to clap, as everyone joined him.

That was so funny. I sat down to finish my work, and I couldn't stop laughing. My phone rang and it was Duce telling me Ahmaun got knocked off! I was so happy I didn't know what to do. Everyone began calling asking me if I had heard about it. The ride home from work was so relaxing and it was a pleasure to turn into my block and not have to worry about him possibly sitting out front my door. That night I slept like a baby. There were so many stories as to why he was arrested. Someone even said he slapped Remi. I didn't know. And guess what, I didn't care.

The weekend finally came. I went to my mother's and made dinner for her and my aunt. I listened as Aunt Bessie continued to tell me how proud she was of me for still working. At the same time she was chewing and sucking on those bar-b-que ribs like a mad woman, making my mother very angry. She hates how Aunt Bessie eats.

After Aunt Bessie finished eating her ribs, she praised me on how delicious they were. One by one she stuck each finger in her mouth licking off the homemade Bar-B-Cue sauce.

My mother angrily rolled her eyes in pure disgust at Aunt Bessie's eating-etiquette. "Bessie please! Do you have to eat like that!" my mother asked loudly, which was definitely not her style to raise her voice.

Aunt Bessie wiped her mouth and then licked her lips, taking her tongue to each corner of her mouth to get any sauce that may have been there. "Listen!" she said quenching her eyes at my mother, "I eat how I want to eat! I don't have to eat all proper, for what?" Her eyebrows met. "Hand me a beer, Sollie baby." She threw her napkin on top of her finished ribs.

I sat the beer on the table and walked over to the cabinet to get her a glass. But it was too late. She took that beer, popped the top, and took that beer straight to the head, nonstop; my mother was pissed. "Like I said, baby, you need to hurry and get your restaurant," she said sitting the beer can down and reaching on her plate grabbing a spare rib-bone eating the small pieces of meat that were left on it. "Your food is delicious! And that potato salad was out of this world! And what the devil kinda season did you put in those greens?"

"Everything was really delicious, Sollie," my mother said smiling and picking up the dirty plates. Just as she reached for Aunt Bessie's plate, Aunt Bessie pulled it away and told my mother that she wanted to suck on the bones a little more. My mother once again rolled her eyes. "Any way, Sollie, I respect you for wanting to accomplish opening the restaurant on your own, but remember that I will open it for you, all you have to do is say the word."

"Oh, let the child be, Marie! You already done spoiled her enough. Let her see if she can do it on her own. If she needs your help, then you help her! The good Lord say, you take one step and he'll take two!" Aunt Bessie said as she downed the rest of her beer, let out a long loud burp, and asked for another one. My mother jumped up from the table and stormed into the living room.

"So are you still with that Amonk boy?" Aunt Bessie asked.

"Aunt Bessie, his name is Ahmaun, and no, I am not," I said smiling and feeling finally free of him.

"Good for you baby, good for you. You get yourself a good man like my Kirkwood, bless his soul. Well, baby," Aunt Bessie said raring back in the chair looking stuffed and satisfied, "I have to go. I'm going home now and rest my heart."

On the way back from dropping Aunt Bessie off, I asked my mother again about my childhood, maybe things that I had forgotten.. I needed to know why I was person I was. And she still says it was normal.

I stayed at my mother's all evening. Salique and his family came over and we played a few games of Monopoly. We hadn't done that in a while and it really felt good hanging out with them. As I drove home, I called Tyra to see what B.'s reaction was to their decision on backing his business. I know he was delighted!

"Hey, Tyra."

"Hey girl, what's up?" she said not sounding like herself.

"How did B. take the good news?"

"Actually, I had to cancel it. Terry had to go to the office unexpectedly."

"You sound weird. Are you okay? And where are the kids?"

"The kids are at my parents' house, and I have something on my mind. I'll be fine."

"Do you want me to come over?"

"No, really, I'm okay. It's probably just..."

Tyra stopped talking.

"What were you about to say, it's probably just what?" I asked

"Forget I said that. I was just talking out aloud. I'm fine, seriously. I'll call you tomorrow. Maybe we can have lunch or something."

"Okay, but call me later if you need to talk."

What is wrong, I thought to myself, worried; Tyra is always happy and cheerful and the way she sounded just now was really strange. I thought about calling her back, but decided to wait until tomorrow. Hopefully, she will feel better and tell me what's going on. Instead of going home, I decided to go to Club Rumors and have a drink and celebrate that bastard being out of my life.

Chapter Twenty-Two

A   s I pulled up in front of the club, I noticed that there weren't many cars, which was a good thing. I walked inside snapping my fingers to the music and rocked my way over to the bar. Looking around for someone to take my order, just as I sat down at the bar I heard some commotion. I looked over at the entrance of the club and saw Karen yelling at the bouncer to let her inside. He grabbed Karen by her arms and pushed her out the door. And I shook my head in disbelief as I watched Karen turn around, pull her pants down, bend over and tell the bouncer to kiss her ass. She then ran down the street.

"What's up, Sollie?" Sam, the bartender, said coming from out the back of the bar.

"Nothing much Sam, may I please have a Mai Tai."

"You're looking good as usual. Girl, you dangerous!" he said smiling. "I heard about movie night at your crib," he laughed. "I wish you would have called me. I would have loved to see that. As a matter of fact, Remi just left. I think she was over there begging B. for some money. You know she's back on that shit" He topped my drink with a cherry and fresh slice of pineapple and a colorful umbrella. "And if it's true about her being pregnant, I sure feel sorry for that kid."

"Is B. still here?" I asked trying to change the subject. Ahmaun and I were over, but the thought of them two being together and that she might be carrying his child, still hurt me.

"Yeah right, where's he going? You know this is his second home. He's over there shooting a game of pool."

"How much do I owe you Sam?"

"You good, it's on the house." he said.

I told him thanks and headed over to where the guys were playing pool. "Hi B.!" I said excitedly.

"Hey baby, how have you been?" he said hugging me. "I called you earlier this week."

"I know, B. Sorry for not getting back to you. It's been a little rough lately. But it's getting better," I said smiling.

"I understand. That girl just left. You know she's back out there."

"Yeah, I heard. B., is she really pregnant?" I asked as I began swaying to *This Is Why I love you*".

"Sollie, I don't know. She lies so much." As B. was talking, he saw one of his pool partners staring at me. What you staring at?" B. asked, "Don't even think about it. She is off limits!"

"To who?"

I heard a voice say from behind me, and I watched as B. began to smile. I turned around and thought I was going to pass out. As I stood there staring into this man's eyes, for some reason, his eyes seemed to have looked right through me. I felt butterflies. This must be what Tyra often spoke about when she met Terry, and come to think of it, she still says she gets them at just the thought of him. I broke the stare and bashfully turned away. My heart was beating faster, and my body felt light as a feather. B. was still smiling from ear to ear as he finally introduced me to his brother, Lamar. Tyra wasn't lying when she said he was fine. He stood there neatly dressed, with a crisp white Ralph Lauren button-down shirt, a pair of neatly fitting jeans, and a pair of brown Prada shoes. From his style of dress, he was obviously a clothes lover like me. His fresh shape-up outlined his close cut twisted bush; his mustache was neatly trimmed; his complexion was dark; his skin was flawless. And all of the above made this man absolutely beautiful.

"So this is the famous Sollie?" he said extending his hand, smiling, as I turned back to face him. His beautiful smile revealed the hidden dimples on both sides of his cheek, and at that very moment his smile was etched in my heart forever.

I was lost for words. I tried to get it together so that I could speak. *This was crazy,* I thought. What the hell was going on with me? Lamar looked at me strangely and asked, "Are you okay?"

"I'm sorry—I'mmmmm um sorry—I mean, I'm fine," I repeated, feeling like a confused, giddy, teenage girl, when she meets her first love. I took another deep breath and tried it again. "It's very nice to finally meet you, Lamar," I said nervously shaking his hand, almost dropping my Mai Tai.

"B. said you were pretty. He could not have been more wrong. He should have said gorgeous!" he said staring at me, seeming to go where no one had ever gone before.

What the hell was I feeling? It was a conspiracy. It had to be! Just in this short encounter, something much, much more was going on, as if our souls had spoken to one another. Lamar smiled again and asked if I was sure I was okay. I said I was fine and walked over and sat my unfinished drink on the counter, and then told Lamar I had to go. Never saying a word, he just smiled at me with a look of peace and confirmation on his face as if he knew something I didn't.

"Sollie, why are you leaving?" B. asked.

"Yes, why are you leaving?" Lamar asked.

"Sollie! Sollie!" Mea called as she and one of her many boyfriends walked over to where we were. "Hey girl, what's up?"

I looked at my watch and asked Mea what she was doing off this early on a Saturday. She's usually in the shop at least until one, two in the morning.

"Girl, the water pipes burst, and I didn't have any hot water. So I had to cancel all my appointments. And can you believe my clients didn't care. They still wanted their hair done!" she said, at the same time using her peripheral vision to look at Lamar. "Hey B.," Mea said, while pulling me closer to her. "First of all, how have you been? And secondly who is that fine-ass-brother—right there! Mhhh girl, damn!"

"That's B.'s brother. He just moved here from Atlanta," I said laughing at her.

"Girl, is he married? How old is he? Look at him looking like a black stallion! I bet he's well hung," she said staring at Lamar.

"Mea let my arm go, with your crazy ass. I don't know anything of what you just asked, and guess what, I don't care! Now, I have to go."

"Sollie, don't leave. Come on and chill with us. We haven't hung out in a while," she whined.

I looked over and saw Lamar walking over to us.

"How are you doing? I'm Lamar," he said extending his hand out to Mea.

"Hi Lamar. It's very nice to meet you," Mea said turning his hand over looking for a ring.

No, she didn't just do that! I thought

"Sollie, are you sure you don't want to stay a while?" Lamar asked.

"No, I am going to . . ."

"She's going to stay!" Mea said jumping in and cutting me off.

"Cool. How about we get that booth over there?"

Picking up my drink from the counter, we all went and sat down with the exception of B. He had started another game of pool. B. loved Club Rumors. I always tell him, if anyone was out to get him they would know where to find him.

"So, Lamar, I don't see a ring. Does that indicate you're single?" Mea asked, blushing at Lamar.

Stirring my liquor and thinking that Mea had lost her mind, I reached under the table and slapped her leg, warning her to stop it. Lamar smiled and said, "Yes, I'm single."

Before I knew it, two hours had passed. Mea and her boyfriend had gone up on the dance floor. I sat there nervously playing in my hair, folding and unfolding my napkin. I couldn't seem to keep my hands still.

"Sollie, would you like to dance?" Lamar asked

"No, thank you."

"May I ask you a question? Why is someone as gorgeous as you are, single?"

"I could ask you the same thing," I said swaying to *Make Tonight Beautiful* "It's obvious you like this song. Come on, dance with me." He stood up and held out his hand for me to take it. I hesitated at first. *What the hell,* I said to myself, as I took his hand and he led me to the dance floor. I looked over to where B. was, and he looked up just as he was about to take his shot, and smiled. Mea was about to die with her simple-self, tapping her friend on his back for him to look at Lamar and me.

I was unsure where to put my hand. I felt dumb with my arms just hanging on the side of me. I looked back over at Mea and watched as she demonstrated on her date were my hands were supposed to be. Lifting my arms, I nervously placed them around Lamar's waist, looking up at him and thinking he had to be about six feet two.

Come with me tonight, share my dreams, change my life…. I sang softly to the song

As we danced, I felt so secure and safe, something I never felt with Ahmaun. It seemed perfect. As a matter of fact, the whole day was perfect. A little to perfect if you asked me, and because of that I knew I had to get the hell out of there. I removed my hands from around his waist and backed away, and told him I really needed to leave. I thanked him for the drink and headed over to the booth to get my pocketbook.

"Sollie, wait!" Lamar said, following me. I dug through my purse in search of my car keys. "Let me walk you to your car."

"No thanks. I'll be fine. Lamar, it was really nice meeting you." I waved B. good-bye and headed out the door. Mea yelled out my name, and I acted as if I didn't hear her.

"Sollie, I am walking you to your car. It's dark outside, and it's also dangerous."

Once outside, I stood there and breathed in the warm summer air. Lamar came out behind me and we began walking slowly down the street to my car, with him staring at me the whole time. A woman walked by us and said that we made a beautiful couple. I went to tell her we weren't a couple. And just as I did, Lamar put his finger up to his mouth and whispered, "Shhhhhhhh."

"Wow, this is a really nice car," he proclaimed. I hit the unlock button. And Lamar reached over and opened the door for me.

"Sollie, if I give you my number will you call?"

"Lamar, I really don't think that's a good idea. Did B. tell you about his ex and my ex?"

"He told me something about the girl he was seeing cheating on him with his good friend's boyfriend. Ah, wow, that was your boyfriend," he said putting his head down. He then looked at me. "Sollie, I didn't know. I'm sorry."

"So now you know. I am just getting out of a very bad, bad situation," I said throwing my pocketbook over into the passenger seat.

"So let me guess. You need time to yourself?"

"Exactly," I said staring at how fine he was.

"Sollie, listen, I respect that, as a matter of fact, I have been where you are, and I know that it's not a good place to be." He pulled out his business card. "Please, just take my number and call when you are ready, and only when you're ready. May I?"

I smiled and nodded my head yes. He then leaned closer and softly kissed me on my cheek. I said goodnight and got inside the car and smiled, as I gently rubbed my hand along my cheek.

Pulling off, I looked up in my rearview mirror at him and noticed him looking up to the sky, as if he was talking to someone. I then realized I was still rubbing my cheek. Oh hell no! I said pulling my hand away from my face. Call him, yeah right! So he can hurt me like Ahmaun. I don't think so. No one will ever hurt me like that again.

I pulled up in front of my house, turned off the engine, and sat there listening to the radio. I couldn't seem to get Lamar off my mind. I reached for his business card and remembered the warm feeling that

I had all over my body when we danced. And there went those butterflies with just the thought of him. I went to rip up the card as I had done with so many others. But for some reason, I couldn't. I put the card inside my wallet.

The morning came and the first person I thought about was Tyra, wondering if she was okay; and I couldn't wait to tell her about last night. I dialed her number. I told Tyra that I had finally met Lamar and although she sounded excited I could tell that whatever was bothering her yesterday was still on her mind today. I asked her what was wrong and again she said nothing, just that she had a terrible headache.

"Well, it sounds to me that he's interested in you, which I knew he would be. And obviously, he is very respectful of your feelings."

"But I not calling him, I can't!" I said.

"Sollie, will you calm down. It's not that serious. He only gave you his phone number. It's not like he proposed or anything. Like he said, call him when you are ready."

After talking with Tyra, I lay there thinking about Lamar. Truthfully, I wanted to call him, but I didn't dare. I often heard people say you don't jump out of one relationship and into another; take time for yourself. Right now all I wanted was to do me, start my therapy sessions that I really wasn't looking forward to, but hopefully I could get some answers. I went downstairs and began doing my chores, which should have been done yesterday. My cell rang, I started to not to answer it because I didn't recognize the number. "Who is this?" I wondered as I pressed the answer key. I said hello and with the noise in the background I realized it was Ahmaun calling from the jail. The inmates were loud, and I could barely hear a thing.

"Ahmaun!" I said yelling into the phone.

"Yeah, why the fuck you ain't been answering your phone, Sollie?" I went to speak and he cut me off. "Check this out. When I come home, I want my ring, car, and that five hundred grand you stole from me. Yeah, that's right, cause all that burglary shit was bullshit." I went to speak again, and he cut me off again.

"For real, save that shit. I'll be on the black top before you know it. And I will be coming for what's mine!" He hung up.

Damn! Why did I answer the phone, and how was he calling? He obviously had a cell phone inside the jail. God, please don't let him make bail, please!

Finally, finishing my cleaning, I took a shower, and got dressed to go to the market. As I was leaving out of my bedroom, I stopped and walked back over to my dresser. I removed the five-karat diamond from the jewelry box and stared at it. I could have easily taken it back to the jewelry store and got the money, but I wasn't pressed. I took the ring to his mother and asked her to make sure Ahmaun got it. And she was very happy to hear that I had finally left her son alone. As I was driving to the market, I knew that sooner or later I was going to have to give this cute little Benz up too. But that was it. Although my conscious was still eating me alive that money was mine; I was keeping every dime of it! Ahmaun talked that shit, but he really didn't know if I had the money or not. And if I was still letting him hit, he wouldn't even be worried about that money. He wanted to fuck! So he got fucked!

Sitting at the red light, I couldn't believe what I was seeing again. On the other side of the street, Karen and her filthy baby daddy Clyde had blocked the traffic a mile long as they struggled to carry a refrigerator across the street. Motorists angrily blew their horns for them to get out of the way. I just shook my head and watched as they both struggled to lift the refrigerator up on the curb. And after they did, Karen turned and gave each driver the finger as they passed.

I pulled into the parking lot of the market, and it was empty. That's just how I liked it. I was so glad to finally have my appetite back; and looking down inside my cart, it showed. I was determined to gain back the few pounds that I had lost, not that I needed to. What I really needed was to join somebody's gym.

As I continued strolling down the aisle, I heard someone call my name and thought to myself, it couldn't be. Was he following me? I turned around and it was Lamar looking fine as ever in his black Nike sweat suit, and a fresh pair of black-and-white Air Jordon.

"Hi Lamar, what are you doing here?" I asked blushing, and then thinking that was a very stupid question to ask.

"I needed to come and pick up some things. A brother cabinets are bare. And besides, this is the times I come; early in the morning, or late at night. I hate when markets are crowded."

I stood there realizing that this had to be a setup! Who in the world told him I felt the same way? Tyra I bet.

While Lamar continued to talk, I stood there peeping down into his cart. Looking at the items inside, it was certain he was a healthy eater. We said good-bye and once again he leaned over and kissed me on my cheek. I blushed and walked away. Half way down the aisle, I turned back to look at him, and just as I did, he had turned to look at me. He waved and so did I, once again feeling like a giddy teenage girl.

As I got it up to the counter, the two clerks were standing there, whispering and watching something. I looked over and they were staring at Lamar as he was leaving out the door.

"Girl, now that's a fine brother! I know he's taken. Has to be," one of them exclaimed.

"If he comes in here again, I will find out. And if he is taken, so what!"

"Nah, girl, I don't want nothing, that belongs to someone else," said the first one as she began to ring my items up.

I paid the clerk and headed out the market, silently hoping that Lamar was in the parking lot waiting for me. But he wasn't. When I got home I put my groceries away, grabbed a spoon, my chunkey monkey ice cream, a bag of chips and headed into the living room. I laid across the couch and turned on the Lifetime channel and before I knew I had already watched three movies. Just as I began to watch another movie, B. called.

"Hey Sis, so what's up? What do you think about my big brother?"

"He's all right, I guess." I said chuckled.

"I already know you're digging him."

"You don't know anything. Nah, he's cool, but . . ."

"But nothing, Sollie, I know exactly what you're getting ready to say. Sollie, life is too short to go and climb under a rock, because another man hurt you! I am not saying get right into something, whether it's Lamar or someone else. Regardless of how bad your relationship with that clown was, you and he were together for a minute, and I don't expect you to get over him in a day. However, just get out there and do some things, experience some new shit, meet some new people. Remi hurt me real bad, and yeah, I shut down for a minute but that was all, a minute! Now, I'm hanging out again and having fun. And yes, I am meeting other females nothing serious believe me! I recognize that one of my problems was the feeling that I had to have a woman. But one good thing that came from all this mess is that I got the lesson. I now know that it's okay to be alone. And the next sister that walks by with a fat ass and a cute face, I'll dig just a little deeper to make sure that there is substance and morals behind the outer extremities. But Sollie, all the years I have known you, I have never seen that look on your face that I saw last night when you met Lamar, and guess what, I never seen that look on his face either. I may be speaking prematurely but it's something there. So please, baby girl, don't shut down. You have too much to offer. And stop saying you're done. Only thing you're done with is that clown. Look Sis, I have to get this other line. I'll talk to you later and please think about what I said. Love you."

I hung up from B. and smiled. He was right. Something was happening between Lamar and me.

Monday morning came fast. I lay there listening to the rain hit up against the window. All I wanted to do is roll my ass over, pull the sheets over my head, and go back to sleep, I thought, pressing the snooze button on the annoying alarm clock. I was really tired, and the thought crossed my mind to call out, but I didn't. I got up looking through my clothes, grabbed a pair of dress pants and a shirt, took a shower, got dressed, and headed downstairs to the kitchen. I opened a pop tart and a soda. Running back upstairs, I reached in the closet and pulled out the silver raincoat that Ahmaun had bought me, and suddenly became sad, even missing him for a brief moment. I remembered what B. had said yesterday, and he was right. I wasn't going to get over him in a day regardless of what he had done to me.

I opened the front door and it was pouring, and with the wind blowing the cold rain made it a very nasty Monday morning. I jumped into the car and headed off to work.

Damn, why didn't I leave earlier, I thought as I sat in the traffic that was backed up a mile long.

When I arrived at work everyone seemed to be very happy that Elizabeth was no longer employed there. Around lunchtime, I noticed the deli down the street coming in with several different lunch platters; they must have been having a luncheon or something. Since the rain had stopped, I decide to go outside and call Tyra. Hopefully, she was ready to talk about whatever it was that was bothering her. As I was leaving, George stopped me and said that he needed to see me. I hope he doesn't need me to stay over. I start my therapy sessions this evening.

"Hey George, what's up?"

"Hi Sollie, come with me please." he said as he walked toward the lunchroom and just as we walked through the doors all of the employees stood and began to clap.

"You all didn't have to do this," I said smiling, feeling very much appreciated.

"Yes, we did," George said shaking his head. "Ms. Susie just wanted to show you how grateful she is, and on behalf of all of us we would like to thank you again."

As the hours passed and getting off time came near, I tried to convince myself that I didn't need to see a shrink. All I needed to do was change my way of thinking. I gathered my things and headed out the door remembering the brief conversation the therapist and I had. And with all that crying I had done, it was evident that something more was going on with besides the break up with Ahmaun. I have no idea what, but something obviously needed to be addressed. So, here goes, I said, throwing my pocketbook onto the passenger seat. As I drove to my appointment, I called Tyra five times and didn't get an answer, and I knew then that something was definitely wrong. As soon as I finished with my appointment, I was going straight to her house.

I headed into the building, slowly walking down the long hallway that would eventually lead me to her office. "One twenty-eight," I mumbled standing in front of the door. I reached for the doorknob, took another deep breath, and entered.

I walked up to the front desk and signed my name. I took a seat and nervously played with my hands. I picked up the magazine that was lying on the table; f lipping through it, I tried to ignore that part of my mind that was telling me to get the hell out of there. Looking up at the desk, I wondered where was the receptionist was. Forget this, there isn't any wrong with me, ! I'm getting out of here. Laying down the magazine, I hurried to the door. And would you believe it, as soon as I reached out and turned the knob . . .

"Sollie Carr?" the receptionist called out.

Shit! I turned around. "Yes, I'm Sollie Carr."

"I apologize. We had an emergency in the back," she said warmly.

I slowly walked back over to her desk. She placed a stack of papers on the clipboard and handed it to me along with a pen and asked me to fill them out completely.

I sat down and began filling out the papers. They wanted to know my life's history. "Was my mother or father ever on drugs?" was one of the questions. They even wanted to know about Salique. I wondered what my brother had to do with anything. Once all the papers were filled out, I took them back over to the front desk. And she had disappeared again! As I stood there waiting for her to return, a middle-aged woman came in the door, looking as if she was totally out of it. She walked up, stood next to me, and said hello. She signed her name and went and took a seat.

The receptionist returned and told me that Dr. Parker would be with me shortly.

I sat there glancing at the woman that had just sign in, I wondered what was wrong with her; she seemed to be so sad. The woman reached into her purse and pulled out a book titled It's Okay To

Mourn, and then I realized she had obviously lost someone close to her. As she began reading, she started crying. I brought her the box of tissue that was sitting on the table next to my chair.

"Thank you, sweetie," she said sadly taking a tissue from the box and wiping her tired red eyes. "It's so hard. Everyone says it will get better, but it hasn't," she cried even more.

I didn't want to come right out and ask her who she had lost, but I did sit down in the chair next to her. "I just don't understand why it happened. Parents are not supposed to bury their children."

I now knew the reason she was crying. I felt so bad for her. It must be devastating to a parent, to lose a child.

"How old are you, sweetie?" she asked warmly.

"I am twenty-nine." I replied.

"That's how old my son was when he was killed, as if he'll get another life tomorrow. It has to stop, these senseless killings. I don't understand what do they get out of taking another's life? Do they stop and think about the victim or the devastation it causes the family? Or are they just so cold that they don't care? And the sad part about it, not only does the victim's family suffer, the other family suffers as well. Because, eventually, the person will be caught, or somewhere down the line the same will probably happen to them. Don't they know that life is so very precious? They say he was selling drugs, and maybe, he was. But he didn't deserve to be shot down like an animal. But you know what, honey?" she said placing her hand on top of mine, "That's all that life brings you—death or jail and it's just not worth it." Anger suddenly filled her eyes. "And I don't care what that detective says. They don't have any leads. That's a bunch of bull. And what are the blue lights for if they can't help solve a crime? Exactly where my son was gunned down a blue light camera was posted directly across the street! But one thing I know—my son's death will not become a cold case! I am determined to prove that boy had someone kill my son."

"You know who did it?" I asked curiously.

"I sure do!" she said with her eyebrows raised. "He called my house the day before my son was killed, fussing and cursing at him about some money of his that my son had supposedly taken. He told my son he would be taken care of, and the next day Dino was dead!"

Oh my God. I thought

"I told the police I know who killed my son. They say they needed more proof than just hearsay. They act as if they don't care. Just another murder to add to the growing murder rate in Baltimore City! But I'll be damned if Ahmaun gets away with this one. That boy is a snake in the grass. He has done so much to so many people and always seems to walk away scot-free! And I heard he gets someone else to do all his dirty work, which makes him in my book a coward! This is my son right here," she said, handing me a key chain with a picture of Dino on it. I silently read the words.

RIP Dino. A coward dies several deaths, but a soldier dies only once. I handed the key chain back to her. She was able to utter a smile as she ran her finger along the picture of her deceased son.

"It's something. Back in my day your picture was on one thing, the obituary. Nowadays these folks have them on shirts, hats, anything. Baby, I'm so sorry. I'm sitting here talking your pretty little head off"

"No, you're fine," I said. Although I was terrified, I knew he had something to do with his murder. God please, please, don't let him make bail.

Chapter Twenty-Three

T he therapist finally called my name carrying in her hand a folder. I gently touched the woman's arm, and told her that I hope she finds closure in her son's death. I grabbed my pocketbook out the chair and walked over to the shrink standing there waiting.

"Hello Sollie, I'm Dr. Parker. I can finally put a face to the voice," she said shaking my hand. "Come with me."

As we were walking down the hall, she turned to me and smiled. "I love your pants. House of Dereon, right?"

I smiled and said "yes." Dr. Parker was sharp! I thought she would look like a shrink, but she didn't. She looked more like a high-paid lawyer. She was very petite, wearing a black editor's suit, white shirt and a red tie that hung loosely from the collar. Her hair was blonde and cut into a short pixie cut that fit her small thin face perfectly, and a pair of black framed glasses sat on top of her head.

As we entered her office, I immediately looked for the long black couch I was supposed to lay on; but there was none. Instead there was a beautiful red leather sofa trimmed in chrome, sitting up against the bright yellow wall. A tall wood bookcase sat in one corner. And in the other corner were two large palm trees. She smiled and told me to have a seat. I sat down and stared at her many degrees that outlined the bay window that gave me a perfect view of the city skylight. I nervously watched as she walked behind her Italian brown wood desk and sat her petite body in a large swivel leather brown chair. Her office was nice, and it definitely complemented her style. She offered me something to drink. I told her, "No, thank you."

I couldn't help but think about the conversation I had with Dino's mother, the role Ahmaun played in his death, and who he could have possibly gotten to do something like that.

"Are you okay?" Dr. Parker asked pulling out a small tape recorder and placing it in front of her. "You seem to be a bit nervous. Take some deep breaths and relax. And don't worry, Sollie. What you're feeling is perfectly normal." She opened my folder and began reading over the papers. "Sollie, would you mind if I recorded our session?"

"No, not really, but may I ask you why you are recording it?"

"I'm recording our session today, as well as future sessions to refer back to when necessary, and also to keep up with your progress. I can assure you that all information that's going to be recorded will remain strictly confidential. However, if you're uncomfortable with me recording the sessions, I won't. It's totally up to you."

"I guess it's fine," I said looking at my nails, noticing I was in desperate need of a manicure.

"So let's begin," she said pressing the record button. She stated my name, the date, and the time and said that I was aware that the session was being recorded. "So tell me a little about yourself."

After telling Dr. Parker about me, she didn't say much. She just listened and did a lot of writing. She then asked about my childhood, wanting to know if it was a happy childhood.

"Yeah, it was," I said smiling thinking about all the fun Duce, Tyra, Jodi, and I had growing up.

"Why are you smiling?" she asked.

"I was just thinking about my friends that I grew up with."

"Are you still in contact with them?"

"Yes, I am, and we're all still very close."

"That's a good thing. Okay, please continue." She reached over and pulled out a peppermint from the crystal candy jar, and then offered me one.

"It's nothing more to tell." I shrugged

Dr. Parker looked down at my folder and asked me to tell her about your brother Salique.

"Did I pronounce his name correctly?"

"Yes, you pronounced it right."

"You two have very odd names. They're very beautiful. Tell me about Salique" She smiled.

And once again I wondered what my brother had to do with me.

"Well, he is ten years older than I am. So growing up we really didn't spend a lot of time together. But he always protected me. He's a good brother."

"What's the relationship between you two now?"

"We are very close and to this day he still protects me."

"Protect you how?" she asked with a curious look on her face. "I mean, does he protect you because that's what big brothers do, or is there someone or something in particular that he protects you from?"

See, now she's being nosey! "Why did you ask that?" I guess seeing the expression on my face; she gave a very quick response.

"Sollie, I didn't mean to offend you. It was just a question, and you don't have to answer it if you don't want to. But I will say it's obvious that something is going on in your life, because of your response. And I really want you to feel comfortable discussing anything with me. I am not here to judge you, only to help you. And you may feel that a lot of my questions are irrelevant to your therapy. But I ask these questions so that I may get a better understanding of you and your life."

"I apologize." I told Dr. Parker about Ahmaun. I even told her what happened with him and Remi.

The more I explained my relationship with Ahmaun to Dr. Parker, I felt like a real idiot. Although Dr. Parker said earlier that she wasn't here to judge me, I just couldn't help but think that she had to have had some type of opinion of me for staying in a relationship with someone for so long.

"Why did you choose to remain in such an unhealthy relationship, Sollie?"

And with that question she hit a painful memory, one that for years I had tried to forget. "I can't do this," I said. I lowered my head and my eyes fill up with tears. I reached for tissue and wiped them, beginning to feel vulnerable like I once did as a child. Jodi wasn't the only one with a little girl inside, crying out.

"You can't do what, Sollie?" Dr. Parker asked with concern.

"This!" I snapped.

"Yes, you can. Take your time, and continue when you are ready."

"Why am I even here?" I asked.

Dr. Parker removed her glasses from her head and laid them on the desk. "You're here because you made a conscious choice to seek help, and I commend you for that. It's going to be all right, I promise."

I took a deep breath. "I stayed with him because I didn't want him to leave me, and I knew if he left I would feel the pain again of being left. And I guess also with him giving me anything I wanted, made it even harder to leave."

"When you say 'anything,' can you be more specific?"

"Money, jewelry, clothes, expensive furniture. I even had the option of not working if I didn't want to. Dr. Parker, I know without a doubt that Ahmaun loved me although he cheated."

She tilted her head slightly to the side, looking as if she wasn't fully understanding. "Why do say that, Sollie?"

"What man is going to give a woman so much if he doesn't love her? He even bought me a Mercedes Benz!"

"Okay," she said continuing to write in her notes. "Did you ever take Ahmaun up on his offer not to work?"

"Sometimes, I would get a job and leave after a few weeks because I knew I didn't have to worry about money."

"I see here you are employed. How long have you been with your current employer?"

"Only two months." I chuckled.

"Two months is a good thing. It's a start."

"You know what Dr. Parker," I said sitting back in the chair feeling a little more at ease, "Even if Ahmaun wasn't in my life I still didn't have to work. My mother would have taken care of me, but I'm really trying to grow up and become a responsible adult."

"Is it safe to say that you are spoiled?" she asked smiling.

"Yeah, it is," I chuckled.

"Okay, Sollie, our time is up. You did very well and again let me commend you for finding the courage to remove yourself from an unhealthy relationship, and making the decision to seek help. I'll see you in one week. The receptionist will schedule your appointment."

On the way out, memories of my childhood began running through my mind. Why were those memories coming back? I thought they were gone.

Once in the car I turned my phone on and checked to see if I had any messages. Jodi, Duce, B. Mea and Tyra had called. I listened to Tyra message first.

Hi Sollie, I know you have been calling, and I am sorry I haven't been answering. And yes, you are right. Something is going on. I have to leave for a few days to clear my head. The kids are going to be with my parents, and I'll call you as soon as I get back. Love you. Oh yeah, and please call Lamar, because I know you haven't.

What is wrong! I didn't even listen to the other messages. I called Tyra's cell and house number and didn't get an answer. I dialed Terry's office.

"Whistleburger, Turner, and Palmer Law offices, how may I direct your call?" the receptionist said. The receptionist said that was Terry was unavailable. I left my name and number and told her to have him call me as soon as possible.

I dialed Tyra's number again and still no answer. I prayed that everything was okay with their marriage. Could Ahmaun have been right, when he said Terry cheats also? No, I didn't even believe that.

Terry and Tyra loved each other to much. I wonder if the kids are all right. All kinds of thoughts ran through my head. My phone rang and I saw that it was Terry's job number. I quickly answered.

"Terry! Where is Tyra?"

"Well, hello to you too," Terry said in a calm manner.

"I'm sorry Terry, hello. Now can you please tell me what is going on? Are you, Tyra, and the kids okay?" I asked desperately needing some answers.

"Sollie calm down. Everyone is fine. Tyra went to stay with her aunt in Philly for a few days; she said she was beginning to feel stressed out. I am going to pick the kids up this evening, and I'll take them back to her parents in the morning. She'll be back in a few days, so stop worrying. She's fine. As a matter of fact, I am going to see our travel agent tomorrow and surprise her with a trip to Africa. You know she always wanted to go there. I guess with the kids and volunteering at social services it has taken its toll on her. So how have you been, everything going all right with you?"

"Yeah, Terry, everything is fine. I have to go. I will talk with you later. Kiss the kids for me."

Bull! Maybe that's what she told him, and maybe, he believed it, but not me. I have known that girl the majority of my life, and though it's not impossible to get stressed out, Tyra is nowhere near stressed. Something else was going on, stressed out, yeah right. I dialed her cell again and still she didn't answer.

Fine! I said tossing the phone on the passenger seat. I don't know if I was angry because she wasn't answering or because she felt she couldn't talk to me. I backed out of the parking lot and headed home.

What the hell is she doing now! I thought looking at Karen standing in front of The Cheesecake Factory. Wearing a pair of huge black glasses, holding a mug in one hand and a blind man's stick in the other, she was begging people for money as they walked by. And they were actually giving it to her. That bitch!

I got home, flopped down on the couch, took my shoes off that were killing my poor feet, walked straight to my wine rack, opened a bottle of Merlot, and sat down at the dining room table. Everything and everybody ran through my mind. I felt like screaming. I reached into my purse, pulled out Lamar's number, and contemplated whether or not I should call him. No! I ripped the card up, grabbed my purse, and headed to where I had no business going—the mall. But not before calling to check my credit card balance. I had almost six thousand dollars, and I was going to spend every last dime of it. My cell began ringing.

"Yes, Mea!" I said.

"Excuse me! What is your problem?"

"I'm sorry, Mea. I have a lot on my mind."

"Listen. Fat Cat is down here with some real cute pieces. I know you would love."

"Mea, I am on my way to the mall now!"

"Sollie, stop down here first. I'm telling you he has some really cute shit!"

"Okay, I'm on my way."

As I drove to Mea's shop, I wanted to turn around and go home. I was doing so good not spending money. But hell, I was stressed! Although I would have rather been lying in my bed with someone and relieving some of the stress I was under, I knew that wasn't happening. So this was the next best thing to make me feel good.

"Hey Sollie," everyone said as I walked into the salon.

A few of the broads sitting in the waiting area began whispering, and I knew just what they were whispering about—that shit with Remi and Ahmaun. I started to say something, but realized it wasn't worth it. And besides, if I leaned on everybody that ran his or her mouth about that whole situation, I probably wouldn't have a voice. To hell with them. People are going to be people.

"What's wrong, boo?! Are you okay?" Mea asked while curling her client's hair.

"I'm fine. I just have a lot on my mind. That's all."

"Do you want to talk about? I'll be done in about twenty minutes," she said, at the same time burning her client's scalp. "Oh! Girl, I'm sorry," she said to her client who was pissed. Mea looked up at me and smirked, and told me that Fat Cat was in the back.

I walked to the back where he was and as soon as he saw me he smiled broadly, because he knew I spent money. Also I wasn't one of those chic's who tried to talk him down on his prices, like the broad he was dealing with was doing.

"Melissa, come on, now you're killing me!" he exclaimed.

"No, you come on, five hundred dollars. Shit! I can get this for half that price," she replied.

"Yea, maybe you can, but ain't real. I got the real shit! Ain't no knockoffs over here baby!" Fat Cat said folding up a pair of Gucci pants.

"Hey Sollie, how have you been, girl. I heard about that shit with Remi and Ahmaun. That's some fucked up shit! Bitches ain't shit! Smile in your face and be fucking with your man! That's just why I don't fuck with them! But like I tell everybody, you got yours and more!" she said giving me five.

"Sollie, tell this girl this shit is real! You know what's up, and I'm feeling those pants you have on."

"Yeah, it's real. Actually what he is charging you is a good price. If you don't want it, I'll take it."

"No, I want it," she said taking the designer bag out of my hand. "But Fat Cat, can I give you half now and the other half next week when I get paid."

"Girl, you killing me! You still owe me a hundred from last month. Yeah, you thought I forgot. I ain't forget. And stop trying to play me! I keep telling you, I'm too old of a cat to get fucked by a kitten. Give me half, but Melissa, I want my money, all of it, next week!"

"Check this out, Sollie. This is hot right here," Fat Cat said, handing me a Valentino Garavani purse. By the time I was done, I had spent a little over three thousand dollars, and guess what, I still felt like terrible! Fat Cat on the other hand was happy as hell! I walked back out into the salon, said good-bye to everyone, and Mea followed me out to the car.

"Girl, this a bad car! I should have copped this, instead of the Lex."

"Yeah, it is, but I am getting ready to give it back."

"Why?!"

"I just don't want it. I'm going to get the BMW out of my mother's garage and start driving that again. And to think I was going to give Remi that car."

"How about that! And girl, I saw her the other day, that girl looks a damn mess, anyway fuck Remi! back to you. Will you please, tell me what is wrong?" Mea said rubbing my back.

"I just feel crazy. My nails are a mess and you know that's not me. My hair, my face is beginning to break out," I said looking in the window of my car. "And I don't know why I just bought all this shit knowing I don't need it. Mea I have to go. I don't feel well!"

Mea looked at me and placed her hand on her hip. "I guess you don't. You just stood here and beat yourself up! Come on now, Sollie, get it together. This is really not like you. And whatever happened with that fine-ass, Lamar?"

"Nothing happened, and nothing is going to happen!"

"See, that's what your problem is. You need a man! You ain't going through anything that some good dick won't cure."

"Mea, please, do you think about anything else?"

"No." She laughed. "And let me give you a word of advice."

My eyes rolled back in my head, because I knew what was coming "What Mea?"

"The quickest way to get over a man, is with another man. See you've only been with one guy, so you wouldn't know that dicks come a dime- a –dozen. All sizes and colors, shapes and forms. Yasssss, honey yasssssss, so get yourself together and call that brother and after call another and another. Fuck Ahmaun

I shook my head. "Listen I have to go. I'll call you later."

"Sollie come on why don't you just stay, I'm on my last head, we can go out, have drink and talk." Mea said

I hugged Mea and left. I would have loved to talk ad get some of this shit off my mind. Mea was cool, but she wasn't Tyra

Chapter Twenty-Four

O   ne week had passed and still no word from her. By now Terry was getting worried himself. He didn't say it, but when I went to visit him and the kids, it was all on his face. My concern for her was slowly turning into anger at the fact that she had not even called me and said anything. And every time we called her aunt's house we didn't get an answer. But each day she was gone I called her phone and left the message "I love you."

My life was beginning to get pretty boring. All I did was work and come home, and I dreaded my therapy appointment today. I tried to reschedule but Dr. Parker was booked for the whole week. My phone rang and as much as I loved Duce, I really didn't feel like him right now. But I answered anyway.

"Hey shorty!"

"What is it, Duce?!"

"Ain't no what it is Duce," he said. "I called you a week ago. Mea said that you seemed a little depressed. I know it can't be over that punk-ass nigga?"

"Duce why was he arrested, was it about Dino?"

"Nah, they say he had a warrant out on him for an FTA, but between me and you, I did hear that he had something to do with it.

And whoever did it, was real smooth with it. That's fucked up though, killed that boy for taking a couple stacks from him.

What the hell would he do to me if he knew for sure I had his five hundred thousand?

"I heard he went up for a second bail hearing, and they denied him again. I think he goes to court soon. If that punk does get out, I hope you don't plan on fucking with him again."

"No, it's really over this time!"

"And where the hell has Tyra been?"

I made up a quick lie and told Duce that her job sent her out of town on business.

"So what's good with you?" he asked.

"Nothing much. I was trying to get out of an appointment I have."

"What kind of appointment?"

"None of your business!"

"Awwww shit! Please don't tell me you're pregnant."

"It's none of your business. I tell you, everyone and their mother would know!"

"Yeah, right, you know I don't run my mouth about nothing concerning you or Tyra!"

"I know, I'm sorry, Duce. And you're right." I took a deep breath and told Duce that I have been seeing a therapist. I felt slightly ashamed.

"I knew you were crazy," he said yelling in the phone, "ever since you fell off those monkey bars!" Then he paused. "Nah Shorty seriously, do what you need to do. Shit, I probably need to see one myself."

"You're going through it aren't you?" I asked.

"Yeah I am, Jodi told you that he made parole?" Duce asked

"Yeah she did." I said sadly, feeling his pain.

"It's cool, as long as he stays his distance."

"But Duce, that's your brother."

"Sollie that nigga stop being my brother the day he did what he did. Look, I have to go but you handle your business. And call me if you need me. Love you, Shorty. I'll holla at you later."

After talking with Duce, I decided to keep my appointment. I got myself together and headed over to see the shrink.

Now at the Dr's office I thought I might run into Dino's mother, but I didn't. I still felt a little nervous, but not like my first visit. I sat there flipping through a magazine, until I was called to the back.

"How have you been, Sollie?" she asked seeming to be concerned.

"I have been fine, and yourself?" I said sitting down.

"I've been great!" she said smiling and offering me something to drink. She placed the recorder on her desk and pressed record. "Tell me a little about your parents."

There really wasn't much to say about my mother. As far as I was concerned, she was and still is the greatest mother in the world. I jokingly told Dr. Parker that my mother took full responsibility for me being as spoiled as I am.

My father was a good father as well. He and my mother divorced when I was four, and he has since been married three times and those marriages have all ended in divorce.

But he was good to me. I couldn't wait for school to let out for the summer. I would go and visit him, and I really looked forward to those visits because I knew that all I would be doing was shopping. He would always give me his credit card and let me go do my own thing,

"Sollie, do you and your father have a relationship now?"

"No, and come to think of it we really didn't have one then."

"What do you mean?"

"I mean, when I was growing up, we weren't close like Tyra and her father were. I really admired the relationship Tyra had with her dad, and I secretly longed to have the same with my father. I remember when I would go out with Tyra and her father, he would always hold both of our hands. And the protection that I felt from this huge masculine hand holding mine, always comforted me. And I looked for that same protection from my father but I never got it. He was so into wives that he really never spent one-on-one time with me. All we would do was shop, and go to nice restaurants. I remember hearing my mother fussing at him one day. During one of my visits, she had found out that I had gone out shopping by myself each day of the two weeks that I had been there, and I remember her telling him that he needed to spend quality time with me."

"Sollie, what steps are you now taking to become more independent?" she asked flipping her notepad over and beginning to write on a new page.

"Leaving Ahmaun was my biggest step, and as far as I'm concerned my greatest accomplishment yet. Also staying employed, paying my own bills, and saving my money, although I slipped up when I went to my girlfriend's beauty shop and spent unnecessarily all because I was stressed out."

"Well, we slip up sometimes. The next time you feel the urge to go on a shopping spree, replace that by doing something else that interests you. But it sounds like you're on the right track to gaining your independence! Sollie, in our last session I questioned you about your relationship with Ahmaun and why you felt you had to stay in an unhealthy relationship. And your response was you didn't want to feel the pain of being left."

I knew it. I knew she was going to go back to that. This is why I didn't want to come. I don't want to talk about this!

"Are you okay, Sollie?" she asked looking at me as I nervously began to play with my nails. "Would you like to take a break?"

"No, but can I ask why you are going back to that question? We discussed it last week."

"I know we did, Sollie, but if it's okay with you I would like to discuss it further," she said writing something in her notes, and asked the question that I tried so hard to avoid. "Sollie, who was it that left you?"

She thinks she so slick!

"Why are you doing this?" I asked, lowering my head. Dr. Parker took a tissue from the box and reached over and handed it to me.

"Sollie, I am trying to help you," she said softly. "Who was it that left you?" she asked in slow motion.

224

As the painful memories resurfaced, crying, I raised my head and said, "My grandmother. My grandmother left me."

"You said she left. Where did she go?"

"She died!" I snapped, now crying out of control. "Why did you have to know that! What does that have to do with anything, Dr. Parker?" I felt as if I was thirteen all over again. "I can't do this! It hurts to bad. I have to get out of here!" I stood up from the couch and walked over to the door.

"Sollie, please don't leave. You are doing such a good job!" she said getting out of her chair and walking over to me. "I'm sure this is painful for you but this is a process you are going to have to go through in order for the healing to begin. Please understand that you may feel that all these emotions are new but they have always been there. They were suppressed. And now that they have resurfaced, and if you want to get better, you have to deal with them!"

I stood there crying, feeling the pain that was so familiar to me. "But why, why did they come back?"

"Sollie, you have just gotten out of a very unhealthy relationship and a very bad breakup. Finding out that Ahmaun was sleeping with someone you thought was your friend may have triggered all these painful emotions from earlier losses in your life. This is what you are now experiencing, but running from them is definitely not the answer, no matter how painful they are. Now please, come and sit back down so we can continue."

I reluctantly walked back over and sat down on the couch.

"Would you like to tell me about her?"

"She was everything to me." I smiled warmly. "I can remember sitting in the kitchen watching her make chicken and dumplings, and the radio would be playing and she would whistle each note perfectly. I remember her beautiful black thick hair. I remember sanding at the bathroom door, watching her put on her make-up. She was so beautiful."

As I talked about Nana, her face slowly began to appear in my mind. I have many pictures of her, but after she died I refused to look at them. And over the years, I had even blocked out the mental picture of her, up until now. Just visioning her beautiful face felt as if she was alive once again.

"Sollie, when your grandmother died, how did you feel?"

"I felt abandoned, hurt, angry, lost. The pain of losing her and not having her in my life was for a long time unbearable." Until, I met him.

"Sollie, you said you were thirteen at the time of your grandmother's death, correct?"

"Yes."

Dr. Parker asked me to finish telling her about my memories of Nana, and I did. She continued writing her notes. She then asked me to tell her about the fondest memory I had of her. Well, I guess that would be when we would make root beer floats and sit out on the porch in the swing chair and eat them. The doctor then gave me a task for tonight and said that she wanted me to make a root beer float, and to think about all the happy times that Nana and I shared together. My hour with Dr. Parker was up, and as I was leaving, I told her about Lamar and asked her if it would be okay to call him?

"Sollie, I don't see where that would be a problem. You are a beautiful young woman, and you should be out there enjoying your life. However, keep it simple, no expectations. And I think you should also make your intentions very clear to him. With you just getting out of a relationship and the other issue that you have going on right now, in my opinion, I feel it is way too soon to start anything serious. But a phone call, maybe, even a simple dinner or a movie would be fine?"

"Okay, but I'm still not sure if I'm going to even call him. But believe me Dr. Parker, I know that a relationship is not what I need. My main focus is getting through whatever is going on with me."

"Good for you, and Sollie, relax. You're going to be just fine. I'll see you next week."

Chapter Twenty-Five

O nce inside the car I called Tyra hoping she would answer, but she didn't. I left my usual message and headed straight to the market to get the ingredients for the root beer float. But I made a quick detour to get a much needed manicure.

The nail shop was crowded. I laughed as I watched one of the customers cuss out the Korean lady, for unevenly arching her eyebrows. They finally called me back and the short little Korean tried her best to get me to add tips to my nails.

"You need tip!" the Korean lady exclaimed, looking at my nails. "You want eyebrow arched?"

"I don't need tips. The length of my nails is just fine. And yes, I do want my eyebrows arched!"

"Tip make prettttty! You get gel on tips." she said shaking her head in a yes motion.

"Tip make too thin," I said marking the Korean lady, which she didn't like; and I didn't care. They get on my nerves always trying to get you to spend more money.

My nails were finally finished, and I sat there and dried them for about two minutes. But the excitement of making a root beer float wouldn't allow me to let them dry completely. I drove across the street to the market and picked up a gallon of vanilla ice cream and a large root beer soda, and excitedly headed home to do what Dr. Parker suggested. And wouldn't you know it, guess who was sitting out front of my house—Ahmaun! Duce said he heard he was going to court but I didn't think it was anytime soon. Oh my God! What if he brings up that money, I started to pull off but he wouldn't have done anything but follow me. Realizing eventually I had to face him, but not alone, I thought reaching in my purse. I called Salique. He answered on the first ring. I told him what was up, and he said he was on his way. Ahmaun got out of his car and walked over to the Benz. I rolled the window down just enough to hear what he had to say.

"Get out the car, Sollie!"

"No, I'm not!"

Ahmaun noticed me holding my cell. "What you going to call the police on a nigga? You thought a nigga was down for good. Shorty, you know I get out of whatever. Money talk and the bullshit walk! Get out the fuckin car, Sollie!" He pulled the handle of the door but it was locked. "Treating a nigga like he ain't shit and you around here pushing the Benz that I bought you! What, you fuckin with somebody else, is that it?"

I sat there praying that Salique would come around the corner. It had come to the point where I was actually scared for my life knowing what he was capable of doing. Finally Salique came speeding around the corner. Not even parking his car, he stopped in the middle of the street, jumped out and rushed over to my car.

"Get out the car, Sollie!" Salique said with a very serious look on his face. I unlocked the door, he opened it and helped me out the car. "You don't have to run and hide from anyone, because no one, no one is going to do anything to you that can't be done to them!" He turned and looked Ahmaun.

Ahmaun knew Salique was serious, and he also knew despite his mild-mannered demeanor he was not to be played with. "Ahmaun, what's up man?"

"Ain't nothing. I'm just trying to holla at your sister that's all."

"I understand that, but I believe she said she doesn't want to talk to you. So what part aren't you understanding? Look, check this out,"

Salique said bypassing all the bullshit, "I'm going to make this real simple. I don't like you! I have never liked you. It's something about your spirit that has never sat well with me from day one! And I think I demonstrated how I felt a few years ago an if deemed necessary, Ill venture there again. Now my sister has told you several times that she does not want to see you, but yet you choose not to respect her wishes, and I'm not having that. So for the last time stay away from my sister or this whole situation is going to get uglier than it already is!" Ahmaun tried to respond but Salique would not let him.

"Nah, nah, slim, I don't need to hear anything. Just bounce!"

Ahmaun looked at me with a look of embarrassment and malice. He was such a coward, just like Dino's mother said. Instead of his father running around and screwing everything, he should have been teaching his son how to be a man, or at least how to fight. He walked away looking dumb as ever, jumped in his Infinity, and sped off. Salique parked his car and helped me carry my bags into the house.

Salique smiled when I told him what I was making. He said he remembered when Nana would make them for him. He declined a root beer float, but did ask me to make him a vegetable smoothie. And I did. We sat and talked for a little while longer, and he left reminding me to call him immediately if Ahmaun came back, which I doubted he would. With Salique stepping to him, that would keep him away for a while. But I knew for him to stay away indefinitely, I had to give him what was his. But guess what? I wasn't.

It must be true what they say; how the smell of things triggers memories, because just the smell of the root beer float took me right back to a time in my life when everything was perfect. And for once, anger didn't follow the thoughts of my grandmother, just sheer happiness as I reminisced about the good times she and I had shared together. I went into my closet and pulled out the old torn photo album, and cried as I flipped through it. But this time they were tears of happiness.

I wanted to call my mother, but I wasn't ready to tell her about me seeing a shrink just yet. And besides, this was something I had to do alone, and not with my mother holding my hand every step of the way. The rest of the evening, I lay around. I eventually took my shower, and got my clothes ready for work. I lay across my bed and thought about Lamar, and what Dr. Parker had said. Finally, getting up the nerve, I called B. to get his number. "Nothing serious, just friends," I muttered as I dialed Lamar's number. My stomach filled with butterflies just hearing his voice.

"Hi, Lamar, how have you been?" I said waiting for response. *Maybe he doesn't want to talk, maybe he has company. Just moved here, and has met somebody already. Men!* I thought. "Well obviously I caught you at the wrong time, I..."

"Sollie, I apologize, I was just a little shocked to that you called, do you know that this has been the longest three weeks of my life. And I'm good, how are you?"

I smiled, taking a deep sigh of relief. "I have been fine, so what were you doing?" I asked.

"I just finished going over some blueprints for the construction site I am overseeing. I'm really glad you called. I'm sorry. I said that already, didn't I?"

We both began to laugh.

"So are you learning Baltimore?"

"Yeah right," Lamar said laughing, "I know how to get to work, the market, and B.'s apartment and his second home."

"And let me guess, that would be Club Rumors."

"You guessed right. That boy loves that club!"

"Have you been there lately?"

"We hung out the other night and shot a few rounds of pool. Do you play?"

"Not really. I just play for fun. I mean, I don't be calling pockets or anything. Actually I have a pool table in my basement."

"That's cool. Hopefully one day we can play a game, just for fun."

I answered his questions, and he answered mine, and before we knew it, it was three thirty in the morning.

"Sollie, I'm sorry. I completely lost track of time and we both have to get up and go to work."

"It's fine, Lamar. I was enjoying our conversation."

It was so nice talking to a brother with dreams and aspirations and every other word out of his mouth wasn't a curse word.

"Do you think we could finish this conversation over dinner on Saturday? And again only if you are ready."

Nothing serious, I silently thought while lying there and twirling my hair around my finger, feeling very much like a teenager once again. And I said yes.

"Cool, now you told me your favorite food is soul-food. Do you have a favorite restaurant?"

"But you said your favorite food was Jamaican food. Since you're new in town, we can go to a Jamaican restaurant, although I would really like some pig feet and hog maws."

"Sollie, please don't tell me you eat that mess!" I laughed, and then told him I was just joking. He sounded very relieved. After talking a little while longer we both said goodnight.

Wow, good conversation, he listens, he's funny, and he seems very interested in my goals for the future. God, I need to talk to Tyra! I reached over and turned my night-light out.

The next morning I woke up and immediately began to smile thinking about the day I had yesterday. I couldn't wait to make another root beer float, and I couldn't wait to talk to Lamar again.

Chapter Twenty-Six

T   he week ahead, Lamar and I talked everyday for hours. I couldn't believe all the things he and I had in common. The weekend finally came and Saturday evening I was so nervous. After all, this was my very first date ever, outside of Ahmaun; I must have changed twenty times before I found the perfect outfit to wear. As I was getting dressed, my cell rang; it was Duce.

"Hello."

"Hey Shorty, what's the business?" Duce said yelling in the phone.

"Duce, why are you so loud! What is it?"

"I just left Mea's shop. She told me you are going on a date. I know she's lying, right?"

"No, she's not. I am going on a date!" Trying to put lotion on and hold the phone wasn't working; I placed the phone on speaker and tossed it on the bed.

"With who!" he asked with demand in his voice.

"Why? You don't know him," I said loudly.

"So what?! I want to know who. What, you got yourself another baler? 'Cause you know you like that cash!"

"Actually, he works every day."

"That's good to know. You could have at least let me meet the brother! You know, check him out. Make sure he good peoples."

"Whatever, Duce, I have to go. Love you. I'll call you tomorrow."

"Love you too Shorty. Be safe."

I slipped into a shimmer gold-color lace bra and panty set, and wore my chocolate Christian Dior suit. Damn! I said looking in the mirror at myself, running my hand through my roller wrap until it fell just right. The jacket to the suit had three buttons on it, and I left all but one unbuttoned, showing off just a little of my six pack. My cell rang again..

"What is it Mea?"

"What you doing? Are you dressed yet? What are you wearing? Did your hair fall just right? Did you wrap it back up like I told you to? I know you looking all cute and shit!"

"Take a breath, bitch!" I said frustrated.

"What the hell is your problem?" Mea asked.

" I'm trying to put these shoes on!" I said, struggling to buckle the thin strap. "Jimmy Choo, twelve hundred dollar shoes. This is ridiculous! Jimmy should come over and buckle them for me." Mea began to laugh. "What the hell are you laughing at? And you need to stop running your mouth so much, telling Duce I had a date!"

"Girl, calm down. It is not that serious!"

"Forget this!" I said pulling off the shoe, and hurling it across the bedroom. "They will be going back tomorrow. Mea, I will call you back. I'm going to call Lamar and cancel. I don't have any business going out with him anyway!" I said flopping down on the bed frustrated.

"Girl, you better not!" Mea snapped. "Don't start that again. Go out and enjoy yourself, and besides, you said he's picking you up at eight. It's seven forty-five now. Go ahead and finish getting ready, and call me when you get home. I don't care what time it is. I want to know all the details. Have fun. Bye."

I took a deep breath. And then hopped across the room and retrieved the shoe, walked back over to the bed, and sat back down. *Finally!* I thought. Buckle the strap.

233

The doorbell rang. I looked over at the clock, and it was seven fifty-five. My heart was racing as I walked down the stairs to the front door, peeping out the peephole; I excitedly, but nervously, turned and leaned up against the front door, and smiled. I turned and opened the door. Wow! We were both lost for words at just the sight of one another. All the anxiety that I had built up this week of just talking to Lamar on the phone was worth it. My heart fluttered as I stood there staring into his eyes.

"Hi Sollie," he said showing the smile that my mind remembered, and my heart wouldn't allow me to forget.

"You're beautiful!" he exclaimed staring at me shaking his head.

The only response I gave was one that I thought was most appropriate. "And so are you." Lamar then handed me one single red rose. He was neatly dressed, wearing a pair of dark brown linen pants, and a white linen shirt.

Mrs. Johnson came out of her door just as we were leaving off my porch.

"Oh, Sollie, you two look so nice," she exclaimed, staring at Lamar wondering who he was. I told her thanks. Lamar said hello to her and she excitedly spoke back. I walked over toward the white Audi that was parked in front of my house. *Now that's what's up!* I thought to myself.

"Sollie, this isn't my truck. My car is parked over there," he said laughing at how my facial expression quickly changed. We walked over to the 2001 Honda Accord. Lamar walked around to my side and proceeded to open the door for me.

I laughed to myself about that Audi. It's all good. That's exactly what I am trying to get away from—basing everything on materialistic shit.

"So finish telling me about your restaurant that you're going to open."

"Lamar, right now I am just talking, although it is what I hope to do in the future."

"Okay, that's cool, but don't say hope. Say that's what you are going to do. Start speaking your dreams into existence!"

"Okay, the grand opening will be in one month!" I said laughing.

"Now that's what I'm talking about. And guess what. You're saying that being funny, but it may just happen."

Yes it is going to happen, as long as I have that five hundred thousand.

We arrived at the restaurant. The smell of oxtail, jerk and curry chicken, and other Jamaican foods filled the air. The colorful green, red, and yellow walls of the restaurant had a huge painted mural of Nelson Mandela; the voice of Bob Marley, No Woman No Cry, blasted from the loudspeakers. A tall, thin very dark-skinned Rasta, wearing a pair of black slacks and a white T-shirt with a peace symbol on it walked over to us. And I'm assuming his hair was in locks because the black Rasta hat he wore sat up very high.

"Welcome, Mon to Jamaican paradise," He said smiling broadly. He then looked at me and placed his hand on his heart. He nodded his head and warmly said, "Peace. Will you be dining in tonight, Mon?" We both said yes, he grabbed two menus and asked us to follow him. Lamar walked and rocked his way to our table. "You like the music, I see, Mon?" the waiter asked rocking to it as well. He seated us, handed us our menus, and took our drink orders.

"Sollie, I'm definitely feeling this restaurant. I mean, the atmosphere, the pictures of my man, Mandela, the music, it's really cool. I'm glad you brought me here."

"It is nice," I said, looking around and noticing an older couple, a few tables down from us, staring.

The waiter returned with a glass of wine for me, and a red snap beer for Lamar. "Let's toast," he said holding his beer in the air. We toasted to a new friendship although our friendship didn't seem new; it was like we had known each other forever.

We both ordered oxtail, cabbage, black beans, and rice with a side of coco bread. The evening was perfect, as Lamar and I continued to do what seemed to come natural to us, which was talk.

As we were eating, Lamar talked a lot about his family down in Atlanta, how close they all are, and how his grandmother raised him and B. after their parents was killed in a car accident. He said he and his grandmother were so close that when his job offered him a promotion and he found out he had to relocate, he declined at first because he didn't want to leave her. But she convinced him that she would be okay.

I began thinking about Nana and smiled; something that I would not have done a week ago. I looked up and noticed again the couple staring. I refocused on Lamar and tried to ignore them, but I couldn't help but wonder why they were staring at us.

"When my grandmother meets you, she's going to love you."

"How do you know we're going to meet?" I asked blushing.

He smiled. "I just know. Sollie, you know the last two times I saw you, I can tell you love clothes. That's a really nice suit you're wearing."

"Thank you, I love to shop. But that's something I am trying to work on. I'm now realizing that there's more to life than shopping."

I looked back over at the couple that was staring and watched as they paid for their meal, and I curiously looked as they began to walk toward our table. I sat my wine glass down, and wondered what they wanted.

"Hello, I apologize for interrupting you," the middle-aged woman said with beautiful gray locks hanging down her back. A gentleman stood next to her with his arms around her waist. He leaned over and shook Lamar's hand and said hello to me. "But I had to come over and say this. You two are simply gorgeous together."

Awwww lady, please. I thought

"You two have something very, very special. It speaks to others, and it's a very beautiful thing."

"But miss, we have known each other only for a short time!" I exclaimed wondering what in the hell she was talking about.

"And in a short time you two have found what most search for in a lifetime," she said with such wisdom and certainty. "When you have something special it shows. My husband and I noticed it the moment you two entered the restaurant. Bless you both." She smiled warmly and they walked away.

"That was something," I said looking at Lamar.

"Yeah, it was," he said with his eyes piercing right through me as if he believed everything the woman had just said to us.

Lamar asked if I was ready to go home, and I wanted to ask him if he was crazy. I was enjoying him and this evening too much. We finally left the restaurant and walked down by the water and sat on a bench. Other couples were walking by and holding hands, and I remember wanting that at one time. And being with Lamar tonight has made me want it again

"So are you tired yet?" Lamar asked

"No, I'm not. I wish this night could go on forever." *Why did I say that!* I thought. *Nothing serious, just friends I repeated to myself.*

Lamar smiled, and then looked out at the beautiful water and said, "So do I, Sollie." And then he asked if I felt like dancing.

"Yeah, that's cool, come on."

I jumped up from the bench and pulled Lamar by the hand, and we walked two blocks to the club.

The club looked like an old, empty warehouse. It was wall to wall people inside, everyone standing around drinking, talking, and enjoying themselves. "Do you want a drink?" he yelled, trying to talk over the loud music. I told Lamar yes. He took me by my hand and we attempted to make it through the crowd, the line for the bar was long. So we decide to hit the dance floor and before we knew it the lights in the club came on. I couldn't believe that we stayed on the dance floor all night.

"Sollie, you got a little bit of skills, don't you?" Lamar said as we walked to his car.

"Yeah, I can do a little something," I said pushing my sweated out hair out of my face. My hair was ruined! But I didn't care. I obviously needed this night out. As we drove to my house, I looked over at Lamar and told him, "thank you."

"For what?" he asked with a curious look on his face.

"For this evening, it was amazing."

Once back at the house, I prayed Ahmaun wouldn't be sitting out front of my house; and although he wasn't, I had an eerie feeling that he was somewhere around.

"Are you okay, Sollie?"

"I am fine." I shrugged, feeling very uneasy, as a matter of fact, the same way I felt that morning when the car was following me. I looked at Lamar and wondered what he would think of me if I told him I was seeing a therapist. Here goes. "Lamar, I was really apprehensive about going out with you, but I'm glad that I did, but I think there is something you should know. I have a lot of things going on right now, and because of that I'm seeing a therapist to help me sort through this mess of my life."

"May I ask why you are seeing a therapist?"

"The situation with ex, the way I spend money recklessly, and some issues I had from my past have resurfaced and now I have to deal with them as well. I am just a mess right now."

"Don't say that, Sollie. It may seem that way, but things will get better for you. And seeing a therapist is a good thing. B. and I had to go to counseling after the death of our parents, and I honestly believe if my grandmother had not gotten us in therapy, he and I both would probably be dead or locked up. We were both so angry, but the therapist showed us positive outlets to direct our anger toward. And if you ever need to talk I'm here for you. So do what you need to do. Take your time. It's a process. And the shopping issue you're having will pass too. If you were doing it to fill a void, I can almost guarantee your therapist will get to the bottom of it. Maybe one day we can get together, and I'll give you some information on investing, profit sharing, and other good resource's for saving money. I like nice things too but I am also very conscious of the way I spend money. Try this the next time you want to go out on a shopping spree: envision your restaurant and think that the money you are getting ready to spend could be going toward it. I'm glad you felt comfortable enough to share that with me, and if you wanted to scare me away, unfortunately it didn't work." He smiled.

"So I am going to see you again?"

"I would love to see you again. Is tomorrow too soon? Well, actually today," he said glancing at his watch.

I blushed and said, "Today would be fine." I wasn't sure of what I was doing. All I knew is that it felt right, so it must have been, realizing that being with Ahmaun for the last eleven years, I never, ever felt like this.

"What do you want to do?" Lamar asked.

"Anything you want. It really doesn't matter."

Just as long as I was with you I thought. And I quickly reminded myself to take it slow.

He got out of his car, came around to my side, and opened the door for me. He then started laughing as we walked to my front. I turned and asked, "What's so funny?"

"Your feet hurt, don't they? I see you limping. Sollie, I really enjoyed myself tonight. Thank you," he said as he leaned over and kissed me on my cheek. He then balled a fist. I did the same and smiled as we touched fist. "I'll see you tomorrow."

I told Lamar to call me when he got home. Before shutting the door I looked up and down the street. I still had that feeling as if someone was watching me. Pulling the screen door shut, and locking it, I stood there and watched until Lamar pulled off. I shut the door, stretched out my arms and smiled, thinking about the night I had. I headed up the steps to the bedroom, sat on the bed, and took those damn shoes off. My cell rang. *This can't be Lamar that fast,* I thought as I reached inside my purse to get my cell. Unknown caller displayed on the screen.

"Hello, Hello, Hello! Is anyone there?"

"Dumb bitch!" someone yelled into the phone.

"Your Mother!" I yelled back in hung up.

Who was that? I couldn't make out the voice. The phone rang again.

"Hello!" I snapped.

"What's wrong?" Lamar asked.

"I'm sorry, Lamar. Someone was just playing on my phone."

"Are you okay?"

"Yeah, I'm fine. I know it was someone that bastard is dealing with!"

239

"Did they say anything?"

"Yeah, they called me a dumb bitch!"

"Well, they obviously had the wrong number," Lamar said trying to make light of the situation. "Look, Sollie, I'm going to the gym in the morning. Would you like to go?"

"The Gym! I don't know, Lamar. I really don't do gyms." I said wiggling out of my pants, noticing again how my hips were spreading. "But I guess I need to start."

Chapter Twenty-Seven

S   ix forty-five came quick. Lamar was picking me up at seven thirty. I had just got dressed when my cell rang, it was Lamar telling me he was out front and that B. was with him.

I ran into the kitchen and grabbed an apple, a bottle of water, two pop tarts, two sodas, and headed out the door. I handed Lamar the apple and the bottle of water.

"Thanks," he said biting into the apple.

"I don't want no apple!" B. said.

"B., how long have I known you? Here," I said handing him a pop tart and a soda.

"Now that's what's up!" he said smiling.

"How can you two put that junk in your bodies?" Lamar asked.

"Go head man, and drive. Let Sollie and me do us!"

"So B. What's been up?" I asked.

"Nothing much sis. I heard you went on a date last night with someone. Who is he?"

Lamar looked in his rearview mirror at his brother.

"Maybe you will meet him one day," I said playing along with B. "But I am telling you now, don't get jealous. He's finer than you are." Lamar laughed; B. didn't find it to funny. Just as we pulled into the gym parking lot, my cell rang. Seeing that it was Mea, I smiled, because I knew just what her nosey ass wanted. I told Lamar and B. to go on and that I would meet them inside. They got out of the car.

"Yes slut!" I answered.

"Sollie, I told you to call me after your date last night," Mea said sounding half asleep. "What happened, and don't leave out nothing. I want to know everything!"

"Everything Mea, are you sure, I did some freaky shit?"

"Yes, girl I'm sure, what did you do?!" She asked anxiously.

"I fucked him, and sucked his humongous dick, I even sucked his balls!"

Mea screamed with delight so loud into the phone, I held it away from my ear, as I laughed at her crazy-ass. "You sucked his dick and his balls? he loved it didn't, I told you honey men love their balls to be sucked, he went nuts didn't he?" She yelled. "So tell me, Can he fuck? I know he can."

"Girl yes!" I chuckled.

"Oh my God!" she screamed again, and then began singing. "Sollie, finally got some new dickkkkkkk."

"Syk! I was just joking."

"You bitch! Why are you playing like that?" Mea said disappointedly.

I told Mea I would call her back later with the details of our date, and she was disappointed to hear that nothing happened. She was happy to hear that Lamar and I were at the gym together.

I got out the car and walked into the gym. It was crowded and I saw firsthand just how serious people were about working out. Lamar was standing by the vending machine holding a bottle of water in his hand. As I walked over to him, he handed it to me. I asked Lamar where B. was. He frowned and then pointed over to a group of females that B. was talking with.

"That's probably why he came here, 'cause he's definitely not trying to work out," Lamar said looking at B. He took me by the hand, and we headed to the back and began the grueling workout.

We did everything from pushups, scrunches, walking the treadmill, and weight lifts. Lamar laughed the whole time as he held my ankles, and I struggled to raise myself up. I was so out of shape, it was ridiculous.

"Lamar, why did I agree to this," I whined as we headed out the front door. "I am so sore. I can only imagine how I am going to feel tomorrow."

"Sollie, stop whining," B. said. "I feel fine."

"I guess you do. You didn't do anything!" Lamar blurted. "Sollie, it's normal for you to feel this way. You used muscles you have not used in a while. It will pass. Do you have some alcohol at home?"

I told him yeah and he suggested for me to go home and soak in a hot tub of water. "Hopefully, you will feel better by this evening," he said looking at me smiling.

"What's happening this evening?" B. asked as his eyes widened with curiosity.

"None of your business," I responded jokingly.

"Seriously, what's up? Y'all hanging out later?" We told B. yes and he asked if he could hang out with us. We both said no in unison.

Lamar dropped me off, and I did just what he suggested. After I stretched out across the bed, totally necked enjoying the warm summer breeze that blew through the window. Laying there smiling thinking about seeing Lamar again. Two dates in a row! I could count on my ten fingers how many times in the last eleven years Ahmaun and me had gone out on a date.

The alarm went off. I I had enough time to soak my body again in a hot tub of water.

As I slid into the warm bathwater, I laid back and closed my eyes, and memories of Ahmaun began invading my mind. When were they going to stop? I wondered as I tried to refocus my thoughts on something else.

That half an hour in the tub and those two Tylenol that I had taken had my aching body feeling much better. I threw on a pair of jeans and searched through my T-shirts. I decided to wear the T-shirt that I had made with a picture of Tyra and me on the front of it when we were little girls. It's so cute, I thought, holding it up and looking at it. We were hugging each other and our hair was braided with a million beads hanging from the braids, we looked like a fake-ass Venus and Serena. I quickly threw my hair back in a ponytail. Lamar had arrived and although I had seen Lamar earlier, it was like seeing him for the first time.

He smiled, standing there with a red Rising Star T-shirt on, ripped jeans and Tom Ford sliders.

"Do you feel any better?" he asked.

"I'm still sore but between the Tylenols and two alcohol baths I'm feeling a lot better."

"So you are going back with me, right?" Lamar asked smiling.

"Yeah right!" I replied.

"Come on, Sollie, once your body has gotten used to it, you'll begin to enjoy it. It will become second nature. And you know you will be turning thirty next year so you have to start taking better care of yourself. Your and B.'s eating habits definitely are not good."

"So what are you saying, I'm old?"

"No, I'm not. Twenty-nine is not old. I'm thirty-two. But we aren't getting any younger either. Just think about it. With you getting older you know you can lose that six-pack that you wear so well." Lamar pointed down to my stomach. That statement scared the hell out of me.

"Hi Sollie. Hello, young man," Mrs. Johnson said smiling at us both as we were leaving the porch. I went on an introduced Lamar to her. He walked over to her porch and shook her hand.

"Very nice to meet you, Mrs. Johnson." She was smiling from ear to ear.

"Nice to meet you too, dear," she said looking at me as if to say he was much better than Ahmaun.

"She seems nice," Lamar said opening my door.

"Yeah, nice and nosey!"

"Don't say that, Sollie. You will probably be the same way if God allows you to live that long." Lamar smiled at Mrs. Johnson and waved as he pulled off. "Does she have a husband or any children?"

"No, her husband died about three years ago, and she doesn't have any children. As a matter of fact, I don't think she has any family members."

"That's sad. She's probably lonely. Do you ever go over there and talk with her?"

"No!" I answered looking at Lamar like he was crazy. "If she's on the porch, I'll talk to her."

"Sollie, we are young, and we get lonely sometimes so you can imagine she does being in that house alone with no one. I'm not trying to tell you what to do, but sometimes if you're not busy why don't you go over there and spend some time with her? She would probably like that. No husband, kids, or family. That has to be rough."

"You know what? I never even thought about that. She just gets on my nerves being so nosey, but, you're probably right. She probably is lonely. One of the sisters from her church used to visit her often but after she met a friend of mine she hasn't been back to see her since. Okay, let's make a deal."

"What kind of deal?" Lamar asked curiously.

"When or if I decide to go over there, you will go with me."

"Deal!" he said.

We decided to go to the movies; while Lamar was getting the tickets popcorn, I ran to the dollar store and bought my candy, I refused to pay five dollars for a box of raisin nets! After the movie we left and headed down to my favorite seafood restaurant. We ordered steamed corn, a dozen of crabs, and two dozens of mussels.

While we were eating our crabs, I watched as the little kids played at the table next to us and asked Lamar if he wanted kids.

"Definitely!" he exclaimed.

"How many do you want?" I asked as I poured us another cup of beer.

"However many God blesses me with. That's what they are, blessings, you know. And you know what I love to see?" Lamar said, laying the crab he had just opened down on the table. And just that quickly, I saw passion in his eyes. I then realized it wasn't him who was about to speak, it was his spirit. "I think the most beautiful thing in the world is a woman carrying a child. How beautiful and awesome is that to have life growing inside you." He had such a peaceful look on his face.

While riding back home, Lamar and I sang along to different songs that came on the radio. And to my surprise, he could really sing.

The next morning, I didn't hurt as bad as I thought I would. After getting dressed for work, I headed down into the kitchen and reached for a pop tart and a soda. Just as I went to put the pop tart into the toaster, I thought about what Lamar had said about my eating habits. I grabbed a banana and bottled water. I walked over to the window and peeped out the curtain and then headed out the front door, suspiciously looking around. I still had that uneasy feeling that I was being watched. I jumped into my car and pulled off.

All day at work I was distracted, smiling to myself thinking about the weekend and how much fun I had. "Tyra, Tyra, Tyra!" I said throwing my pen on the desk in disgust, thinking about how much I had to tell her.

Just as I was leaving for lunch, Lamar called, and asked if we could have lunch together. I happily said yes and gave him the address to my job. I sat outside at the picnic table and waited for him to come.

He arrived; we sat there eating our shrimp salad sandwiches, and fed the birds as they walked up on the grass.

"I hope the mayonnaise doesn't upset their stomachs," I said just being silly, but Lamar thought it was so funny.

Miss Susie walked out, I introduced her to Lamar, when she went back inside I told him what I had done for her.

"Sollie, that was really nice. But do you have ten thousand dollars to just give away like that?"

"Not really." I said. I told him about the show I had watched and how the woman on there had paid it forward. Remembering that day as if it was yesterday, and the state of mind I was in, I was a mess! I quivered at the thought; and I never wanted to be in that miserable space again.

246

"Well, it's obvious you aren't as reckless with money as you think you are."

We finished our lunch and Lamar left. I went back inside the building and over to my cubicle, flopped down in my chair, and happily spun around in it. Just as I began my work, B. called.

"Hey sis."

"Hey B. What's up?"

"Listen, I know you probably don't care, but Remi was pregnant, but not anymore. They say some girl beat her really bad, and caused her to miscarry."

I rose up in my chair "What! Who was the girl?" I asked.

"No one knows. They said she came out of nowhere, walked up to Remi, and beat her down! She's still in the hospital. I was thinking about going to see her."

"Whatever! I'm sorry B. but I don't feel sympathy for her one bit. What goes around comes around. When was this supposed to have happened?" B. said it happened Saturday, and I remember that's the night I thought it was Remi playing on my phone. B. and I talked a little longer and then we hung up.

Four thirty came and I hauled my ass out the door. I pulled in front of my door once again looking to see if Ahmaun was anywhere around. I was so tired of living in fear, even though I knew Salique and others had my back. But I also knew how Ahmaun got down, and as far as I'm concerned he was probably behind Remi getting her ass whipped.

I thought about Lamar and wondered if he had eaten yet, and decided to call him and see if he wanted to come over and have dinner with me.

Lamar said yes, and I ran through the house like a mad woman, thinking to myself, this getting to know someone is exciting, new, and fun! I put on a sundress. *Just friends, Sollie,* that irritating voice of reason said. *Tell it to my pussy that was about to explode!*

I lit the grill, took out two steaks, two potatoes, and dumped the bag of fresh salad in a bowl. Thank God for microwaves, I thought, putting the potatoes inside of it. I put the steaks on the grill and decided we would eat dinner out on the deck. I set the table. The doorbell rang.

He's here, I silently sang. I hurried over to the door, took a deep breath, and opened it. We were both smiling as if we hadn't seen each other all day. And there were my friends again, quivering around in my stomach. I love this feeling! I wanted to scream. He came inside and handed me a bottle of wine. We then went out onto the deck. We didn't do a whole lot of talking this time. We were too busy staring at one another. Truth is, I wanted him badly; and the way he stared at me I could tell he felt the same. Dinner was finally ready and Lamar loved the steaks although, I think, he was exaggerating a little. He claimed that it was the best steak he had ever eaten.

After we ate, we went into the living room. I sat down Indian style on the floor and looked through my rack of CDs and Lamar joined me. We sat there on the floor drinking our wine and listening to Al Green and ironically How Do You Mend A Broken Heart was both of our favorite song.

I decided to tell him about the money.

"Lamar, I feel that I can trust you, and I really need your opinion on something that my conscience has been eating me alive about."

"I'm listening," he said with a very curious look on his face.

I told Lamar the whole story, and not once did he interrupt me. "I guess you don't think I am such a great person now, do you?" I lowered my head out of shame.

Lamar stood up and sat his wine glass on the table, he then took my glass and helped me up from the floor. We walked over to the couch and sat down.

Chapter Twenty-Eight

"L   isten, first of all, I do still think you're a great person. Sollie, you were betrayed, and badly hurt, and sometimes out of sheer anger we do things based on how we are feeling at that moment. We want to hurt them like they hurt us. We want revenge, but that's not your call. God said revenge is mine. You may be spoiled and love to spend money, but one thing I am pretty good at is being a good judge of character and like you said we haven't known each other for long. However, one thing I do know is that you're not a thief. You don't have to do anything to pay him back, that's automatic. It's called karma. You keeping that money doesn't make you any better than him. You asked my opinion, and my opinion is to give the clown back his money. I know it's hard but you have to let all that mess go and forgive them both, because as long as you keep holding on to the anger both of them is still in a sense controlling you. Give him that money, and you continue working on your life. Is that how you were going to open your restaurant?" Lamar said smiling.

"Yeah, it was. I was serious, wasn't I?" We both began to laugh.

"Don't worry. What comes easy is not worth having. Just wait when the day finally comes, and the feeling you are going to get from knowing all the hard work you put into obtaining your restaurant. Because if you had opened it with that money you would have felt the same thing you're feeling now, guilt. Okay, call the clown," Lamar said reaching for his wine glass. "And tell him to come and get his money!"

I agreed, and I told Lamar the money was in storage. He stood and asked, "Okay, can't we go and get it?"

"We!"

"Yes we. You can't think I am going to let you go through this by yourself? Nah, that's not happening."

"Are you sure, Lamar?"

"Positive!"

I called the storage company to make sure they were open. They were. We left and headed over there to get the five hundred thousand dollars. As we drove, I questioned myself as to what in the hell I was doing, realizing that once again Ahmaun was getting away with hurting me like he did. I wanted to tell Lamar to turn the car around and take me back home, but I didn't, because I knew that everything he and Tyra said was true. All I wanted was for this to be over, and I prayed that when I gave Ahmaun his money back that it would be. As we pulled up to my storage area, Lamar got out of the car and stood there next to me while I opened the lock. L   Lamar walked over to the bag, bent down, and untied the knot. He opened and looked inside. "Wow!" he said looking at the money and then me. "Okay, call him and find out where you can meet him."

I nervously dialed Ahmaun's number.

"What the fuck you want!" he answered.

He hasn't changed a bit, I thought.

"Listen Ahmaun, I need to see you."

"Oh, now you are trying to see a nigga, calling your punk-ass brother, like I was trying to hurt you or something. He better stay the fuck out my face. Nigga lucky I ain't have his ass put to sleep!"

"Ahmaun, don't threaten my brother!" I snapped. "You know what, forget it, forget it!" I hung up the cell.

"What happened?" Lamar asked.

"He makes me sick!" I said putting my cell back into my purse. "I'm not giving him anything back!"

"Let him say what he wants. Call him back," Lamar said.

Before I could respond my cell rang.

"I'm on my way. I'll be there in a few minutes," he said.

"I'm not home, Ahmaun!"

"Look! What the fuck is going on! What you playing games or something?" he yelled.

"Will you just meet me at the McDonald's on Franklin Street?"

"McDonald's! What, I can't come to your crib now? Oh yeah, you on some bullshit, all these years and you going to carry a nigga like this, you got dat! I'm on my way!" He hung up.

"Lamar, take me to my car, and I will call you as soon as I'm done. He can be dangerous and I don't want you involved in this."

"Sollie, I am not letting you meet him by yourself. If it makes you feel any better, I will stay in the car, but you're not going alone. That's definitely out the question."

Lamar picked up the heavy bag and placed it inside his trunk, and we pulled off. When we pulled up in McDonald's parking lot, Ahmaun was standing outside of his car and talking on his cell.

"There he is," I said with those unwanted butterflies quickly forming in the pit of my stomach. I asked Lamar to pop his trunk.

"Are you going to be able to lift it? I can carry it over to him," he said.

I told Lamar I would try. We walked back to the trunk, and just as I tried to lift the bag I dropped it back down. Lamar reached inside and took out the bag and shut the trunk and we both walked over to where Ahmaun was standing. Ahmaun slowly moved the cell away from his ear and gritted on Lamar as he placed the large bag next to his car. Lamar never even speaking to him, looked at me, and told me he would be right over there. He walked a few feet away and stood and watched.

"Ahmaun, that's your money," I said pointing to the bag on the ground. Ahmaun was so busy trying to see who Lamar was, he wasn't paying me or what I said any attention. "Ahmaun!" I said louder, "Here is your money."

"You—mother—fucka! I knew that burglary was bullshit!" He bent down and reached inside the bag, digging his hand around inside of it. "It better all be here! That's fucked up!" he said looking at me with disbelief. "You crossed me like this, like this, and all over a bitch!" he yelled. I looked back at Lamar and he was slowly making his way back over to us. "I should whip your fuckin ass." Ahmaun said moving closer to my face. Onlookers stared as they got out of their car.

As I went to walk away Ahmaun grabbed my arm, snatching me toward him, pointing to Lamar angrily asking who he was. I tried to get out of the firm grip Ahmaun had on my arm. But I couldn't.

"Boy, let her arm go! And back up out her face!" Lamar snapped.

"Boy! Boy! Who the fuck you calling, boy, I'm a grown-ass man, nigga."

"Yeah okay," Lamar said with a smirk on his face knowing Ahmaun was just what he called him.

"Who the fuck is you anyway, nigga? What you fuckin this nigga?" he asked looking at me, and then finally released my arm.

"Sollie, let's go," Lamar said taking me by my hand. Just as we walked away, I turned and watched Ahmaun put the money inside his trunk and then quickly ran over to us.

"He has the money. Why doesn't he just leave?" I said.

Ahmaun's followed us; yelling and cursing causing a crowd of onlookers to gather closer. I noticed the manager come out the door and rushed back inside, probably to call the police. Ahmaun ran around from behind us, jumped in my face. "You ain't any different from the rest of these bitches, bitch!"

I was in total shock. He had never called me a bitch before, but I wasn't the only one in shock so was he. Before I knew it, Lamar had hit Ahmaun dead in his mouth! He hit him so hard, he fell to the ground. I couldn't believe it, and neither could Ahmaun. Blood was everywhere; he jumped up from the ground, holding his mouth and ran over to his car.

Pulling Lamar by the hand, I told him to come on, because Ahmaun probably had a gun in the car. Ahmaun ran over to his car and reached down under the front seat, but I guess hearing the police sirens coming from a distance he knew he had to get out of there. He jumped inside the car, and yelled, "You're a dead man!" and then sped off leaving a trail of black burning rubber in the parking lot.

"Lamar, this is why I didn't want you involved," I said getting into his car crying.

"Sollie, calm down," Lamar said grabbing my hand that was now shaking uncontrollably.

"I can't calm down!" I yelled. "Suppose Ahmaun . . ." Lamar didn't even let me finish.

"Sollie, I am really not concerned about him. My only concern is you, and you need to calm down. You are going to make yourself sick! Listen, I'm a man! And there was no way I was going to stand there and let him disrespect you the way he did! And I'll just have to deal with whatever he decides to bring."

"Lamar, you don't understand. You have no idea what he is capable of. Believe me when I tell you he is going to retaliate someway, somehow, I assure you, he is going to retaliate!"

Chapter Twenty-Nine

W   e pulled up in front of my house, and I thought for sure, Ahmaun was going to be there waiting. Thank God he wasn't.

Once in the house, I walked back and forth constantly looking out the window for any sign of him. My cell began to ring and I prayed it wasn't him. It was Salique, just calling to check on me. There was no use telling him I was fine; he heard the nervousness in my voice. I told Salique what happened and he was not happy about me taking the money. But he was happy to hear that I didn't have to face Ahmaun alone. Being nosey, he asked if Lamar was my new boyfriend. I told him no.

"Well, whoever the cat is, he's my type of brother!" He asked to speak with Lamar and thanked him for looking out for me. Lamar told Salique there was no thanks needed. He only did what a man was supposed to do.

I finally sat down on the couch, and tried to calm down. We finished the bottle of wine and played some more CDs, but I knew that Ahmaun was coming back for us both.

Lamar offered to stay with me, suggesting that he could sleep on the couch, I told him no, and that I would be fine.

When I hugged him goodbye, he felt so good, too good! So I quickly let go. He leaned over and kissed me on my cheek and reminded once again to call him if I needed him.

I watched him until he pulled off. I wanted to call Ahmaun and try and talk things out, but I knew he wasn't trying to hear anything I had to say. I put my nightclothes on and climbed into the bed. The phone rang and it was Lamar letting me know that he had gotten home safely. I tossed and turned half the night. I was finally able to doze off and was awakened by the phone.

"Hello," I said half asleep.

"You dumb-ass bitch, you –will- pay! You're next! God, this is what I have waited for!" a woman's voice said, and then she hung up.

"Hello! Hello!" I looked at the phone, and it read unavailable. That was the person that called the other night, I said, remembering the voice.

Unable to fall back asleep, I sat flipping through the channels for the rest of the night, terrified.

It was only six in the morning, but I didn't care. I had to get out of the house; I took my shower, got dressed and left. I reached into my purse to answer my phone, praying that it was that woman. I had to find out who she was, but it was Lamar calling to see if I was okay. I told him about the threatening phone call, and he said Ahmaun was probably just trying to scare me. I told him it worked! I couldn't shake those bone-chilling words she spoke: You're next!

I arrived at work and the stress that I was under obviously showed on my face, as everyone constantly asked if I was okay. I told George that I wasn't feeling well and asked if I could leave early. He said yes.

As I was leaving, I stopped and sat down at the picnic table as the word's "You're next" ran through my mind. Next for what? Maybe that was the person that bet Remi ass. Lamar called while I was sitting there and asked if I wanted to go to dinner later and I told him yes. He said that he would meet me at my house when he got off. I left my job and decided to drive over to the mall. Walking inside, I noticed I didn't feel that urge to shop as I once did. I sat in front of the fountain. Sitting there, I thought about everything, but mostly Tyra, as the thought of her brought tears to my eyes. I missed my best friend and I so desperately needed her; and I knew that she needed me too. Noticing the time, I decided to head home. When I turned the corner, Lamar was sitting in front of my house waiting for me, looking fine as ever even in his work clothes. I walked over to his car.

"You look worried. Stop worrying. Believe me, I got you," he said getting out the car grabbing my hand as we walked toward the house.

Mrs. Johnson was out on her front struggling to rap her water hose around the hook.

"Do you need some help?" Lamar asked, walking over to her fence. You would have thought he offered her money looking at the smile that came across her face.

"Yes, young man, if you don't mind."

"These hands are so sore, old Arthritis has taken over," she exclaimed while rubbing her hands together. "Are you okay, Sollie? You don't look well."

"I'm fine, Mrs. Johnson."

"Sollie, how about some tea?"

What the hell! Was she in the car the other night when Lamar and I were talking? Lamar looked up at me and smiled.

"Sure Mrs. Johnson, but just one cup. I have something to do this evening."

"Oh goody!" she said excitedly. She smiled and asked Lamar if he would join us. Lamar looked at me and smiled.

Once in her house, I was surprised at its condition. The rose-colored wall paper was faded and dry rotted, and the living room set was old and torn, with a piece of brick underneath of it holding it up where the leg had broken. A black La-Z-Boy sat in the corner with a red throw-blanket lying across the arm of the chair; that's where Mr. Johnson sat. I always remembered seeing him sitting there looking out the window.

I continued to look around at the old worn furniture. It was sad to see only a small thirteen-inch TV with missing knobs sitting on the stand, and to make matters worse she had pair of pliers lying next to it. I guess she used that to turn the channels. The coffee-table leg was broken too, and a brick was holding that up as well. A vase sat in the middle of the broken coffee table with fresh roses inside of it that had obviously come from the rose bush in her backyard. I always wondered what she did with those flowers she picked every morning. Her dining room was gloomy, and the old wooden dinette set was scratched up badly. There was missing glass from the china closet's door. The furniture may have been old and the house torn down a little, but it was neat and clean, without a speck of dust anywhere.

"Have a seat you two, and make yourself comfortable."

Mrs. Johnson went into the kitchen; Lamar leaned over to me and whispered, "See how things work? We spoke this into existence."

"Yeah, I do. I guess that stuff really does work huh?" I said whispering back to him. "Okay, now let's say we see ourselves leaving out the door. See if we can speak that into existence." I rolled my eyes.

"Not funny Sollie. We made a deal. Remember?"

Mrs. Johnson brought our tea and some homemade sugar cookies. We all sat there looking right simple. I wanted to get in the house, change, and get the hell away from here.

She began asking Lamar a million questions, and telling him how he reminded her of her late husband.

"How long were you two married?" Lamar asked.

"Fifty-three years," Mrs. Johnson said proudly.

"Mrs. Johnson, you were pretty!" I said looking at their wedding picture hanging on the wall.

"I'm still pretty." she said smiling.

"Mrs. Johnson, Sollie told me you are here alone, and if you ever need anything done in your home just let me know, I'll be happy to help." Lamar said as he reached into his wallet and pulled out a business card.

"Oh! Thank you so much. You're such a nice young man. Do you know anything about electricity?" she quickly asked.

Well, I be damn this lady is unbelievable. She sure didn't waste any time, I thought to myself.

"I know a little something. Where's the problem?"

"Come with me, Lamar. I'll show you."

She showed him the problems, that and about five other. "Sollie, I hope you don't mind," she said as they walked toward the basement.

"She doesn't mind at all," Lamar said looking at me and smiling.

Lamar and Mrs. Johnson headed down into the basement. I sat my cup of tea on the saucer and walked over to the front door.

"Is someone at the door dear?" Mrs. Johnson asked as she walked back into the living room.

"No, I was just looking, that's all."

"I was so happy to see Salique the other day . . ."

Heard it all before, lady, I thought, not even looking at her because I knew she was ready to strike up another conversation. Next thing I knew Lamar was bringing a ladder out of the basement and began to screw light bulbs in the ceiling fan.

"Sollie, your friend is such a nice young man. I hope you don't mind me saying this, but he's ten times better than that other boy. He was mean!" she whispered. "I told you I think he put his middle finger up at me one night."

"All right, Mrs. Johnson, I'm all done," Lamar said looking at me with a strange look on his face as if he was upset about something.

"Here, let me give you something." She turned away and unpinned the few dollars she had pinned to her bra and peeled off two one-dollar bills and handed them to Lamar.

I couldn't believe it, nosey and tight!

"No thanks, Mrs. Johnson, you don't owe me anything."

"Are you sure?"

"Positive. And you have my number. Call if you need me."

"Ohhhh! Bless you, bless you both!" she exclaimed walking us to her front door.

We left and Lamar still had a strange look on his face. "Are you okay?" I asked as we walked up the steps to go into my house.

"Sollie, did I hear Mrs. Johnson correctly when she said that clown put his finger up to her?" Lamar asked with a very serious look on his face.

"Yes, Lamar, you did."

"Did he really do that?"

I shook my head yes.

"That punk. I should have whipped his ass for real!"

"Do you want a washcloth so you can wipe off?" I asked quickly trying to change the subject.

"No, I'm going to go home and take a shower. I just wanted to see you first and make sure you were okay."

"I'm fine," I said although I wasn't. I was a nervous wreck! I sadly sat my purse on the couch. I really didn't want him to leave.

Lamar saw the look on my face, and asked me if I wanted to come with him. I snatched my purse off the couch and headed out the door.

"I'll take that as a yes," Lamar said laughing, and following me out the door. I jumped in his car and he drove over to his place.

His apartment was nice and the deep burgundy painted walls gave the place a very masculine feel to it. And the beautiful statues and pictures he had on the wall all represented family. I sat down on the black soft leather couch and picked up the statue of the pregnant woman.

"Sollie, this represents my wife carrying our child. See, these pieces are what I pray to have in my future so I surround myself with them."

He explained the whole concept to me about how your thoughts are very powerful. Pretty much where the mind goes, the tail follows; and I made a promise to try and start speaking and thinking more positive.

Lamar offered me a beer and I accepted. He told me to make myself comfortable and that he wouldn't be long. I walked over to his stereo and looked through the hundred of CDs, put on The Weekend. Just as I sat down, he was coming out of his room, wearing nothing but a white towel wrapped around his waist. *Lord, have mercy,* I thought taking a sip of beer. And then it started, that part of my mind that had no morals whatsoever!

Go get that dick, girl!

259

I can't, I just met him.

So what does that mean? You haven't had none in four months! You know you want that dick.

I slowly sat the beer on the table and contemplated the thoughts, *I can't!* I picked my beer back up, and crossed my legs trying to calm my throbbing pussy down.

Oh, stop acting like a child. If you're scared, say you're scared.

I ran my fingers through my hair, and yes, I was horny as hell. I had even begun envisioning myself riding him. But sleeping with Lamar or any other man was not on my agenda. My agenda consisted of one thing and that was to continue working on myself.

"Sollie, are you okay?"

"I'm fine," I said almost dropping the beer.

"You were in deep thought, weren't you?" he asked standing in front of me, now fully dressed and smelling wonderful. "Why are you looking like that?"

I told him it was nothing. He walked into the kitchen, grabbed a beer out of the refrigerator, came back, and sat on the couch next to me asking where I wanted to go and eat. I told him I really didn't have an appetite so we decided to just chill. Later, Lamar headed back into the kitchen to fix himself a snack.

B. called very upset, after hearing from Salique what had happened the other night with Ahmaun. We both assured him that we were fine. After hanging up from B., Lamar went back into the kitchen, and I followed so that I could see what kind of snack he was making. Whatever it was, it smelled terrible. "Lamar, we have been doing a lot of talking lately," I said, as I stood at the entrance of the kitchen with my hand slightly covering my nose. "And I know that there is more about you that I will find out but is there something important you want to tell me?" I asked as I stood there and watched him stir up that stinky tuna fish and oodles of noodles which in the cut they call "hook up." Lamar looked at me curiously, and then looked at his food.

"Nah, nah, Sollie, I have never been incarcerated." He laughed. "But my cousin was. He put me down with this. Try some!" he said walking over to me putting a fork full in my face.

I told Lamar, "No, thank you,"

We watched the movie *Set it Off.* Seeing all that money I started thinking about the big mistake I made by giving that boy his money back.

"What are you thinking about?" Lamar asked while scraping the last bit of food from the bowl.

"That money, I shouldn't have given him anything. I'll never get my restaurant."

"Sollie, I told you anything that comes easy is not worth having. If owning a restaurant is really what your heart desires, trust me, you'll get it!"

"But Lamar, I'm broke! I mean, I make okay money at my job, and I have money in the bank. But a half-a-million gone. I'll never have that much money at one time again."

"Sollie, everything is done, and everything happened in the order in which it was supposed to. There is no need for should, coulda, wouldas. What you do is, start from now. As a matter of fact, right now!"

Lamar went back into his bedroom, and came out with a folder filled with very informative information on investing money.

For the next hour and a half, Lamar showed me all about investing my money, everything from 401K to buying stocks. He asked if my parents taught me about saving when I was younger.

"Nope not at all, my mother was too busy going to school to earn her doctorate degree, and my father was too busy buying for his ex-wives and me, trying to keep us all happy. When I graduated from high school, his present to me was a credit card with a five-thousand-dollar limit." Lamar's eyes got wide with disbelief and even wider when I told him I spent the whole amount on clothes, in one day.

"Wow!" Lamar said shaking his head. "You know, Sollie, I have much respect for your parents and their educational achievements, but you see it starts from home. These things that I'm showing you now should have been shown to you years earlier. But when I'm done with you, watch and see how your money will begin to grow. And believe me our kids . . ."

My eyes became wider and my eyebrows arched. "Our kids!" I said interrupting Lamar.

Lamar stared at me. "I have to be honest in how I'm feeling. You're going to be my wife," he said with such certainty. "So, yeah, as I was about to say, our kids will be taught early."

My mind told me to get the hell out of there, but my heart said something totally different. I looked over at the statue of the pregnant women and thought what if . . .

Come on, Sollie, fuck him and keep it movin! Don't believe that garbage. Y'all kids, his wife, picket fence, Yeah right. He's just like the rest of the bowwows! All the good men have left the building! I quickly changed the subject.

"Lamar, even though Mrs. Johnson gets under my skin, I feel sorry for her having to watch that little broken up thirteen-inch TV." He looked at me and smiled because he knew I was purposely changing the subject and then he said let's go. I asked where we were going and he said to Wal-Mart. Once there, I followed Lamar back to the electronics section, and although I knew he was a nice guy, I really knew it now, as I watched him pick out a forty-inch flat screen TV for Mrs. Johnson. Once at the register, I tried to give him half but he refused to take it. And that negative part of my mind went to talk again and I quickly responded. Shut the hell up! Lamar was definitely one of the good guys.

Driving to Mrs. Johnson's house, I began getting nervous, and Lamar knew it. He placed his hand on mine and said, "Stop worrying." As we turned the corner, we noticed Mrs. Johnson's lights were out. So we figured we would give her the TV tomorrow. Lamar parked the car. I got out and walked over to the house to unlock the door. Just as Lamar was carrying the TV up the front steps, our attention was taken by the noise of screeching tires coming from a car speeding around the corner. It then came to a screeching stop right in front of my house. Lamar sat the TV down on the porch and walked over to the door where I was standing and shielded me.

"Oh—my—God!" I said pulling him by his arm to come inside, noticing it was the same car that was following me that morning. The person driving rolled the window down just enough for her words to be heard and her face not to be seen.

"You better watch your back bitch. I told you you're next!"

Lamar pulled away from me, and just as he walked over to the steps, she sped off.

"Sollie, I'm not quick to get the police involved, however, I think you need to call them."

"Lamar, I know I need to, but this person is obviously someone Ahmaun knows, and by him knowing that I set him up, going to the police may put my friend, who's a police and the one that helped me with the plan job in jeopardy." Lamar picked up the TV and brought it inside the house. I walked over to the window and looked out of it wondering who in the hell that woman was, and why was she so angry with me. And once again "you're next" resonated in my mind.

"Sollie, listen, please know that I have the utmost respect for you and I don't want you to take this the wrong way, but I can't stand seeing you like this," he said looking into my eyes that were filled with fear. "Why don't you stay at my apartment?"

"Lamar, I can't stay at your place."

"Why not? Sollie, I have a two-bedroom. You can stay in the guest room. I'm not suggesting that we sleep in the same bed, although I wouldn't mind. Nah, nah, I am just joking. So what do you think?"

I lowered my head contemplating the offer. "Yes, I would love to stay at your place." I hugged him tightly and silently said thank you, not to Lamar, but to God, because I knew at that very moment he was God-sent. And yes, I was going to be his wife.

Chapter Thirty

A fter I finished packing I transferred my house phone to my cell. I suggested to Lamar that we give Mrs. Johnson the TV tonight. Because until I find out who this chick was, I would not be returning anytime soon. Lamar carried the TV over to Mrs. Johnson. Just as I went to ring her bell, she opened the front door.

"Hi Mrs. Johnson. Why are you still awake?"

"I fell asleep in La-Z-Boy. But I heard some yelling, and woke up." she said staring at the box Lamar was carrying. "What's that?" she asked.

"Just a little something Sollie and I bought you," Lamar said while carrying the TV inside her house. Mrs. Johnson just stood there in disbelief while Lamar took the TV out the box.

"Oh you sweethearts," she said beginning to cry. "No one has ever bought me anything, besides Henry, and it's so fancy."

She reached in her housecoat pocket and pulled out a handkerchief and wiped her eyes. Lamar sat the TV up and programmed all the channels. I told Mrs. Johnson that I would be gone for a while, and you would have thought she was losing her best friend. She reached out for Lamar's hand and told him to take care of me. She hugged us both and we left. As we walked down her front steps, I turned back and she was standing in the door sadly waving

264

good-bye. I got in my car and pulled up on the side of Lamar and told him that I was going to stop at the market to pick up a few things.

While at the market I ended up buying one hundred and fifty dollars worth of food. Well, actually Lamar bought it. He insisted on paying for it. We left the market and headed to his apartment.

Once we put the food away, Lamar showed me the guest room where I would be sleeping. Inside the room was a beautiful lightwood bedroom set with a king-sized bed, a computer, TV, stereo, and a desk. Unlocking the sliding doors, I stepped out into the balcony closed my eyes and breathed a sigh of relief.

Lamar knocked on the bedroom door just as I was putting my things away and asked if I wanted him to run me some bath water. I told him yes.

I sat down on the bed and asked myself what I was doing here. Although I was completely comfortable with Lamar, I knew that eventually I was going to have to face this mess. Maybe once I gave Ahmaun the Benz back, he would leave me alone. But who was that woman? Finally, getting undressed, I put my robe on and headed to the bathroom. As I walked by Lamar's room, he was lying cross the bed reading a book. Lamar had placed several candles all around in the bathroom. I pinned my hair up and climbed inside the tub of hot water.   After my bath I put on my nightclothes and wrapped up tightly in my robe. When I walked into the kitchen Lamar looked at me and began laughing.

"Sollie, why do you have your robe wrapped so tight? Loosen up, get comfortable. I hope you are hungry."

I loosened the robe and sat down at the wooden breakfast bar. "What are you cooking?" Still laughing, he said, "Shrimp Alfredo, salad, and garlic bread." He dipped a large wooden spoon into the Alfredo sauce and brought it over to me, and I tasted it. "I'm impressed. Fine, sexy, intelligent, and can cook. What else could a girl ask for?"

"Great minds think alike. I feel the same about you."

While we were eating, I told Lamar that I was going to do what I should have done a long time ago, and that was to give Ahmaun his car back. Hopefully, Mea would follow me over to his mother's to drop it off. Lamar said that he would come home for lunch. I suggested we go out to eat but he quickly reminded me about saving money and with us just going to the market I could make lunch. And I agreed.

After eating I did the dishes, and we opened a bottle of wine. We talked and listened to some of his old-school CDs. I was so comfortable and so relaxed more than I had been in a very long time. I called my mother and told her that I would be getting my car out of her garage, and needless to say she was thrilled. And she was very happy to know that Ahmaun was finally out of my life, and then she went on and on about how proud she was of me. After answering what seemed like a hundred questions, I said goodnight. I called out for Lamar; he said he was in the guest room. When I walked into the room, Lamar had just finished hanging up pink floral curtains.

"Lamar, why did you change the curtains?"

"My grandmother gave me those along with some other things," he said smiling. "I told her they were too feminine for me. Anyway, they came in handy and besides, they make the room look much better than those plain white blinds. I just want to make you feel as comfortable as possible."

"Okay, I'm going in my room. Call me if you need anything, and I will see you in the morning." He leaned over and kissed me on my cheek. I climbed in the bed, curled up under the sheets, and I was out!

The next morning Lamar knocked on the door, and asked if he could come in. I said yes, and quickly pulled the blanket over my face.

"Sollie, why is your faced covered?"

"I don't want you to see me. I look a mess!"

"You're gorgeous. You could never look a mess. I wanted to give you this," Lamar said, laying a key on the nightstand. He saw the look on my face and smiled and said, "Don't even say it. You need a key to get in and out. Are you hungry?"

"Yeah a little."

I showered and slipped on a sweat suit, and then called George to let him know I wouldn't be in today. He told me to enjoy the day off. Lamar made pancakes, turkey bacon, and eggs. We ate breakfast and he headed off to work.

As he was leaving, he turned and told me that he was glad.

God, am I moving too fast, I thought picking over my eggs, but we are not sleeping together. We're just friends. We haven't even kissed yet. What harm is it causing? But one thing I knew, being with Lamar felt as natural as breathing.

I went back into the bedroom and lay back down. I was mentally drained. I laid there for about an hour. I called Tyra although I knew she wasn't going to answer. I left her a message telling her that I loved and missed her. I called Mea to see if she would follow me over to drop the car off at Ahmaun's mother's house, and although she said yes, I had to listen to her tell me how crazy I was for giving it back.

While waiting for Mea's slow ass to come, I went outside and cleaned the car out. As I walked away I turned and stared at the Benz remembering the day he had given it to me, and silently hoping that I was giving back the one last connection between us.

Mea finally came. We drove over to Ahmaun's mother's house. I turned the corner slowly and prayed that neither of them were home, and thank God they weren't. I pulled up, signed his name on the back of the title, reached into the glove compartment to retrieve the registration and removed the tags. I looked over at Mea sitting there looking at me as if I was crazy. I ran up the porch steps and put the key and paperwork inside the mailbox. Thank God it was finally over! I jumped inside Mea's car and told her, "Let's go." Even though Mea didn't know the whole story as to why I was staying with Lamar, she was just happy to hear I was there. She asked me if the dick was good, and I told her I wouldn't know.

Mea's facial expression changed drastically. She pulled over and parked. "Mea, why are you parking?" She reached inside her purse and pulled out a Newport and lit it, reached over and turned the volume down on the radio, pushed the hair out of her eye, and took a long drag off her cigarette. "Sollie, you mean to tell me you haven't fucked him yet?"

"No, I have not!" I snapped.

"And you are sleeping in another room. Girl, that shit is crazy, as fine as that brother is, ain't no way!" she said sucking her teeth and taking another drag. "Girllllll I be riding that dick 24-7! Fine ass brother like that!"

"Well, guess what, Mea? There are other things besides sex, although I will admit the thought has come across my mind. But that's all it is, a thought, although when and if it happens I want it to be right! Now, will you take me to the MVA" I turned and looked out the window.

"So, Sollie!"

"Oh my God, Mea, what!"

"Just one more question." Mea said curiously. "Has he even tried to hit?"

"No, he has not!"

Mea threw her hands in the air and frowned. "Child, that nigga gay!" she said turning the volume up on her radio and plucking her cigarette out the window.

"Whatever. Why can't it be that he's a gentleman?"

"Yeah okay, I know his type all too well. Fine as hell and on the down low!" she said pulling off.

I shook my head and turned and looked back out the window trying to ignore her. We pulled up in front of the MVA and it was packed as always. Thank God I was just dropping off the tags and registration. When I was done, Mea took me to my mother's house to get my car out of the garage. She asked if I wanted her to wait and I told her no. I had enough of her mouth.

My mother wasn't home. I went into the house and down in the basement which led out to the garage. I stood there with a smile of relief as I stared at the white 745 BMW. I got inside and turned the ignition. It hesitated at first and then it started. I decided to go get some maintenance work done on it. since it had been sitting such a long time, and drove to the dealership. It really felt funny being back in this car, but I knew I had done the right thing.

After getting the car washed and an oil change I headed to Lamar's place.

Inside, I dropped the keys on the table and flopped down on the couch. "It's over, it's finally over," although something in my spirit told me it wasn't. Ahmaun was going to retaliate, but when, and how? Lamar called and said that he was on his way and asked if I could reheat him up the left over's from last night.

Just as I finished, he walked through the door with a huge smile on his face that was very refreshing. The only time Ahmaun smiled was when he was getting some ass or counting his money.

"Is it okay to say I missed you?" he asked sitting down at the breakfast bar.

"It's fine because I missed you too," I said blushing.

"I saw the car out front. It's really nice. So everything went okay?"

"Yeah, everything went fine." I sat down at the breakfast bar and stared at him and asked if we were moving too fast.

"Sollie, listen to me. We are friends. Check this out." He reached over and held my hand. "I won't dare sit here and say that I am not physically attracted to you because I am. What man wouldn't be? But if we were to sleep together now, all it would be is physical, and I want to get to know Sollie first! If I don't like what's inside of you, the intimacy won't last long. I don't care how good the sex may be. And eventually that will end if that's the only thing our relationship is based on. I'm more interested in getting to know your inner self than I'm in knowing you on a physical level. So, no, I don't think your being here is considered moving too fast."

After he ate, Lamar decided to take the rest of the day off and we drove into the city to go and chill out at Druid Hill Park. While sitting at the light, Lamar told me to look. I looked over and it was Karen, running out the store with a pack of raw chicken in her hand. And the Korean lady ran behind her carrying a bat and then angrily called her an ugly black bitch! When Karen heard those words, she stopped and

269

turned. "I may be black, and I may even be a bitch, but one thing, I ain't is ugly." She gave the lady the flip and hauled ass up the street. Lamar shook his head and then laughed at the stories I told about Karen.

We stayed at the park for most of the afternoon walking and talking, and then sitting on a bench directly in front of the reservoir. I could have stayed there all day with him, but unfortunately, I had another therapy appointment. We left the park and drove back to his place.

As I drove to my appointment, I didn't feel as nervous as I did the first few times, which was a good thing. I pulled into the parking garage and headed inside. I looked through the stacks of magazines on the table next to me and picked up the one with a beautiful picture of our first lady, Michelle Obama. Dr. Parker came out and called me to the back.

"Classy lady, isn't she? You can have it if you like."

"Thank you," I said as I followed her into her office.

"So, Sollie, how's it going?" she asked as she sat down in her chair.

"It's going good," I said smiling thinking about Lamar.

"Would you like to tell me what has you smiling so brightly?" she asked.

I told her no, although I wanted to tell her, but she probably would have said that this thing with Lamar was moving entirely too fast.

"Okay, let's get started," she said sitting her recorder on her desk and pressing the record button. "Sollie, did you do what I suggested?"

I told her yes. She then asked how it made me feel. I told Dr. Parker that making the root beer float allowed me to remember all the good times that my grandmother and I had shared, and that for once I didn't feel the anger that I had toward her. Dr. Parker asked me to share with her a little more about Nana, and I did. And the one thing that stood out in my mind was the last day that I saw my grandmother alive. I remembered it so clearly. My mother and I had gone to the hospital to see her. The doctor came inside of her room and asked my mother to step out in the hall. Without them knowing, I stood behind the door and listened as the doctor told my mother that Nana had taken a turn for the worse. And after hearing that, I ran over to her bed, laid my head on her chest, and begged her not to leave me. She gently stroked the side of my face and said she would never leave me and that she would always be in my heart.

Dr. Parker reached over and handed me a tissue.

"Sollie, tell me about your grandmother's funeral?"

"It's really nothing to tell. I had become so upset they had to take me out of the church." I said as the tears began to flow even more.

"What are you feeling now Sollie?" Dr. Parker asked.

"Pain, Dr. Parker please tell me what does this have to do with now?"

"More than you know, Sollie." She smiled warmly, saying it as if she knew something that I didn't. I continued, and before I knew it, my hour was up.

"Sollie, you did great. I have another task for you. When you get home, I want you to write a letter to your grandmother telling her all the emotions that you have experienced since her death. And then I want you to tell her how grateful you are for having her in your life and thank her for all the wonderful memories she left you with."

"Dr. Parker, I don't understand. What is writing a letter going to do? I came here because I needed help with myself, and now you are telling me to write a letter to my deceased grandmother! Why?"

"Sollie, trust me. You may not understand now, but you will. A lot of what you are experiencing is mostly because of your past. Writing the letter is going to allow you to release all these painful emotions that you have carried around for all these years. And most importantly, Sollie, I want you to tell your grandmother good-bye."

"I can't!"

"Yes, you can, and you must if you want to heal. You have to say good-bye so that you can put closure to her death and when the painful memories surface, let them. Don't shut them out. Honor each and every one of them. Sollie, you did wonderful today and as I told you before. You are going to be just fine."

I grabbed my purse and headed out of her office, still not understanding why I had to say good-bye to my grandmother. Once outside, I was ready to call the police thinking someone had stolen my Benz, but then remembered I no longer had it. I got in my car and headed for Lamar's.

When I walked into the apartment, Lamar was sitting in the living room going over some blue prints. He asked how my session went, and I told him that I decided that I wasn't returning to therapy.

"Why not?" he asked rolling up his blueprints.

"Because Lamar, she is asking me all kinds of questions about my grandmother and I don't understand why. What does her death have to do with anything, and now she wants me to write a letter telling my grandmother how I have felt since she died. That was sixteen years ago! And she even wants me to say good-bye to her, talking about putting closure to her death! I just don't understand," I said getting up and going into the kitchen. I opened the refrigerator and went to reach for a soda. Changing my mind, I grabbed a bottle of water. "I have so many emotions going on inside me. I'm just not certain about anything anymore." I continued, as I walked back into the living room, and sat next to Lamar on the couch. "I already have too much on my plate. Ahmaun, the chick that's threatening my life, Tyra, it's all really too much. I am not going back." Lamar moved over closer to me and put his arms around me.

"Sollie, listen, I am quite sure it's hard dealing with all these feelings, but you know a lot of times it's the past that holds the key to the present, and future. And what you said about the letter she wants you to write, I think it's a good idea. Just try it, and see how you feel. Are you hungry?"

"No, I am fine. I just want to take a hot bath, write this letter, and get it over with," I said as I walked down the hall to the room. After taking my bath, I went into the room. There was a notepad along with a pencil that Lamar had laid on the dresser for me. I walked over to the stereo and put in Avant CD and listened to "Sailing." I then changed into my nightclothes. Back over at the desk, I sat down and hesitantly picked up the notepad and pencil.

Chapter Thirty-One

A t first I didn't know what to write, but as I followed my heart, words came pouring out onto the paper, and so did the tears. By the time I was done, both sides of the paper were full, leaving me only one line to write. *"Until we see each other again, good-bye, and I love you."* I walked over to the bed and curled up into a fetal position and cried just as I did when I was a child.

"Sollie! Are you okay?" Lamar asked knocking on the door.

"Come in," I said sitting up on the bed, and wiping my eyes.

Lamar sat next to me on the bed and hugged me tightly.

"I loved her so much, Lamar."

"I know you did. Grandmothers are the best. You had a lot to say to her, didn't you?" Lamar looked at the paper. "Are you done?"

"Yeah, I am. Dr. Parker said to tear it up, burn it, and do whatever I wanted to do with it, just as long as I wrote it. Well, I wrote it." I said understanding why she insisted that I write the letter. I felt as if I had cleansed my soul. Lamar went to get a match and I burned the letter. As we both watched the flames of the burning letter go out inside the small steel trashcan, he asked me how I felt. I told Lamar that I felt like a weight had been lifted off me.

"I know you're sorry you met me. You have a nut case for a friend" I said laughing.

"No, I don't. I have a beautiful friend with a few issues that's strong enough to deal with them."

That morning Lamar took me to work, and picked me up. I missed Mrs. Johnson so we decided to stop over for just a few seconds to check on her. She was so happy to see us both. She told us that she had seen Ahmaun riding through the block several times. I went next door and grabbed a few more of my things, wondering why he was still coming around. He has everything! And then it came to me, yeah he has everything but me!

Each day Lamar and me were becoming more and more close, and I finally realized that I had to stop running and hiding. I had to face this mess like the woman that I was so desperately trying to become. And most importantly, I was becoming dependent on Lamar, like I was with Ahmaun. Although the situation was different, I was still in a sense depending on a man.

That evening while Lamar and I were sitting in the living room watching TV, I told him exactly how I was feeling and that it was time for me to go back home. He didn't like it, but he respected my decision.

I headed into the guest room and packed my things preparing to leave tomorrow. The next morning, I sat up in the bed and looked around the room and sadly nodded my head yes, it was time for me to go. I took a shower, got dressed, and carried my luggage out into the living room and sat them next to the door. When I walked into the kitchen, Lamar was cooking breakfast. He turned and tried to utter a smile and said good morning.

I could tell that he was upset because I was leaving. Good morning, I said, sitting down at the table. Lamar made our plates.

After picking over his food, he pushed his half-eaten plate away. Lamar looked at me and said that he didn't want me to go.

"But Lamar, I have to stop running from this."

"Okay fine, let me stay at your house!" he said looking at me with a very serious face.

"Lamar, I can't keep depending on men. What's going to happen when you leave?"

"Sollie, get that out of your head, and please don't ever say anything like that to me again. I am here for the duration! Unless you feel differently, I'm not going anywhere!"

"Lamar, just let me see how things go, but I thank you for being so concerned. And to answer your question that you indirectly asked, I feel the same way you do, and I'm not going anywhere either!"

Lamar helped me carry my luggage to the car. When we were done, he hugged me tightly and then without warning, he lifted my head that was resting on his chest and kissed me like I had never been kissed before. I started to pull away but my heart wouldn't let me. I put my hand behind his head pulling him closer to me, and I surrendered to everything I was feeling. I knew at that moment that I was falling in love with him. I stared as he walked away.

I walked away and got in the car looking at him from my rearview mirror as he stood and watched me drive down the street. This wasn't supposed to be happening, I said, banging my hands on the steering wheel, almost running into the back of the car in front of me. I wanted to turn around and go back but I couldn't. I continued driving, and by the time I made it to work, I was an emotional mess! Once in the building I quickly walked to the bathroom. Turning on the faucet and splashing cold water on my face, I was able to get to my cubicle without anyone seeing me. I looked over and noticed Ms. Susie wasn't at her desk, and her computer wasn't on, which was unusual. I was told that the thirty-three years she has been employed at the company she has never been late or missed a day. And wouldn't you know it, a few minutes later Jim walked over to my cubicle and told me that Ms. Susie's granddaughter had fallen into a coma.

Although I didn't know the little girl, the fact still remained that she was an innocent child facing a terrible illness! I couldn't take it anymore. Everything had finally taken its toll on me. I also, at that moment, realized as important as I thought money was, it wasn't saving that little girl's life. I was a mess. Broke, angry, confused, and to top it off, I was falling in love at a very bad time in my life. All I wanted at that moment was what money couldn't buy me, and that was peace within myself. I would give anything for peace.

I needed to talk to someone. I wanted to call my mother, but didn't want to worry her. I called Dr. Parker and prayed that she could fit me in, and that I wouldn't have to wait for a whole week to see her again. Thank God, Dr. Parker said that she would be able to see me.

I went into George's office and told him that I had an appointment and asked if I could leave early. By the look on his face, I could tell he wasn't too happy about me asking to leave early again, but he said okay. Just as I got back to my cubicle, my cell rang. Looking at it and seeing "Out of Area," I jumped up and made my way to the lunchroom for some privacy. Because this time I was going to get a dialogue started with this bitch!

"Hello!" I snapped.

"Oh, what you tough now?" the woman on the other end asked.

"Bitch, I been tough, but you aren't hanging around long enough to see how tough I am. bitch !"

"Yeah okay," she said sarcastically laughing, "You need to know one thing. When I see you, I'm going to show you how tough you really are. And the only reason I haven't stepped to you yet is because I was told not to! But please trust and believe we will meet! And when we do, you're dead, you dumbass bitch!"

"Check this out, coward!"

"Coward, coward!" she yelled interrupting me. "Do you know who the fuck I am?"

"Yeah, I do! Who's putting you up to this, Ahmaun?" And with that question came silence, only confirming what I had just asked.

"You bitch!" she screamed. "We will meet and I am going to be your worst fucking nightmare!" She hung up before I could respond.

I stormed out of the lunchroom, gathered my things and left. Driving to Dr. Parker's office, I was determined to get some answers. Once there, I signed in and had a seat and waited for her to call me back.

My mind kept going back to the phone call, wondering if I should notify the police, or at least call Kane to get his opinion. Dr. Parker came out and called me to the back with a look of concern on her face.

I jumped up and rushed over to her. "Dr. Parker thanks for seeing me. I really need to find out what is going on with me,"

"Sollie, please have a seat. Would you like some water?" She asked as we walked into her office.

"No! I don't want any water. All I want to know is what the hell is going on? I have so many emotions and none of this started until I began this stupid therapy! And if that's not enough, someone is threatening my life."

"Sollie, please, calm down. Let's discuss this. First, what is this about someone threatening your life?"

I told her about the phone calls although I couldn't tell her the whole story. She also suggested that I notify the authorities.

"Dr. Parker, I appreciate your concern, but I will deal with that later. Right now I need to find out why I am feeling like this!"

"Sollie, this is highly unusual for me to be diagnosing your condition after only a few sessions, but I will give you my feedback as to what I feel the problem is. However, I wish you would wait a few more sessions for me to discuss your prognosis. You are doing so well. Did you write the letter to your grandmother?"

"Yes, yes, yes, I wrote the letter." Dr. Parker stared. "You know what, forget it. Don't tell me anything. I am going back to the old Sollie, the one that I was comfortable with. Forget trying to change and becoming responsible, the job, not shopping, indulging in food, and most of all forget Lamar! I am getting back with Ahmaun! I don't deserve a guy like Lamar anyway! It's comfortable with Ahmaun." I stood up and snatched my purse off the couch, and once again got ready to walk out. I walked over to the door, turned the knob, deep inside praying for Dr. Parker to stop me as she had done before, but she didn't. She let me walk out of her office in tears. I looked back at her to see what her reaction was, and she showed none at all. She just sat there holding her pen in one hand and her coffee mug in the other.

As I walked down the hall, it seemed like a mile away to the waiting room. And at what felt like the lowest moment in my life, I heard the voice of the person that has been right by my side through all of this, encouraging me every step of the way. "Hang in there," I heard Lamar's voice say. And hearing that gave me the strength to turn around and go back. As I walked back down the hall, I noticed her standing at her office door, as if she knew I would be returning. I went in without saying a word and sat in the red couch that now seemed to welcome me. Dr. Parker sat back down.

"Are you ready to continue?" she asked warmly.

"How did you know I was coming back?"

"Most of my patients do."

"You mean, I am not the only one who has walked out?"

"No, you're not, Sollie, and I doubt that you'll be the last. Sollie, from all the information I have gotten from you it is clear to me that because of the break up, you went into depression. And as I mentioned in an earlier session, the break up triggered painful memories that had been suppressed, and the fact that you stopped doing the things that allowed you to keep those feelings suppressed such as shopping, spending money excessively and eating gave those feelings the opportunity to resurface. Now try and understand what I am about to explain to you, and feel free to stop me at any time if what I am saying becomes confusing."

After talking with Dr. Parker for well over two hours, I now had a better understanding of who I was and why. What really amazed me was when she said by my father not supplying me with a nurturing and emotional relationship, it had played a very pivotal role in the woman that I had become. I had no idea how important it was for the father to be actively and emotional involved in his daughter's life, never knowing that a father can teach a daughter what a mother cannot. I realized that my father had supplied me with everything that wasn't important, and none of what was, never teaching or showing me qualities that I should have looked for in a man. And that's exactly why I attracted a carbon copy of my father.

I also finally realized and understood that Nana's death left me with a painful void and a feeling of abandonment. And that's why I stayed and accepted all that he had done because I didn't want to feel that feeling of abandonment again.

I felt so much better, as all that Dr. Parker had said to me began to make sense. I thought about Nana and how I would always keep her memory alive. I thought about my father and how up until now I realized that him taking care of me financially didn't make him a good dad, realizing as a young girl I needed so much more than he gave. And I was finally able to admit that I was angry with my father for not being what I needed him to be most to me, a dad. She also made it clear to me that there are millions of women that has grown up without a father in their lives and still grew up to be well-grounded women. Some women are affected by not growing up with a father and some are not.

Dr. Parker said I needed to contact him and tell him exactly how I felt and that I also needed to forgive him. I was kind of skeptical at first, but then decided that I was going to do whatever needs to be done to get my life back on track. As I left her office, I felt happier than I had felt in a very long while. Sitting inside my car, I began crying tears of happiness, because I really thought for a moment I was losing my mind. I wiped my eyes and called Lamar.

"Hi, Lamar."

"Hi, Sollie, how are you doing?"

"Everything is actually a lot better. I left work early to come and see my therapist."

"But I thought you didn't have another session with her until next week."

"I didn't, but after I left you I became so overwhelmed with everything that has been going on, I called to see if she could see me today and she said yes. And Lamar I am so glad she did. This time she explained to me in detail some of what I was going through and why. Although it's still sinking in, it makes complete sense. I know I still have a lot of work to do, and I am willing to do it."

"I am glad to hear that, and you know I am here for you."

"Yeah, I do. I felt your presence earlier, even though that kiss this morning complicated matters a little more."

"Do you feel that I'm a complication?"

"No, and I am sorry if my choice of words offended you. Truthfully, Lamar, I feel you are a blessing. I just don't want us to move too fast, and I think that's what we're doing. I am beginning to feel something for you I have never felt before, and I hope that it's not because I am vulnerable right now."

"Sollie, I heard and respect everything you said, but please hold that thought. The concrete-mixer driver just pulled up, and I need to direct him. Oh, damn, it's a woman driving, now that's what's up! Can we continue this conversation later?"

"Yeah, we can. Call me when you get off. And thanks."

"For what?"

"For being here."

"Sollie, there's no thanks needed. I'll call you when I get off."

My mind still seemed to be racing with everything Dr. Parker had said. I drove back to work. I decided to take a few days off just to regroup, hoping George didn't think I was crazy. When I arrived to work, I immediately went to George's office.

"Hi Sollie, you're back. I didn't think you would be returning today. Did everything go well with your appointment?"

"Yes, everything went fine," I said sitting down. "George, I have been seeing a therapist because of some personal issues I'm having, and I have a few things that I need to sort out. I was hoping that I could take some time off. I know I have called out recently and also left work early the last few days, but I really need to deal with these issues. If you rather I resign I will understand." George just sat there and listened to me. I had no idea what his response was going to be.

"Sollie, your resigning is out of the question. Take all the time you need to sort through whatever it is you are going through, and return when you are ready. Your position is safe!"

As I walked outside and decided to go over and just sit for a minute and re-group. I began to think about my father, and what I would say when I called him. I decided not to wait.

Hesitantly, pulling out my cell phone I strolled down until I got to his name and stared at his number wondering if I should do this, and how it would be a lot easier to write a letter and mail it to him. But that would have been too easy. I dialed the number while a part of me hoped it had changed, or at least get his answering machine. I swallowed hard when I heard his voice.

"Hello," he said sounding a lot older than he did when I talked to him almost four years ago.

"Hi, Daddy."

"Sollie! Is this you?" he actually sounded happy to hear from me.

"Yes, it's me. How have you been?"

"I have been well. And yourself?"

"I have been okay."

"Is there something wrong? Do you need anything?"

"No, I don't need anything, but I will tell you what I did need. I needed you!" I said getting straight to the point. "Daddy, I'm currently in therapy. It was told to me by my therapist that I remained in a very unhealthy relationship partially due to the relationship that you and I didn't have. I don't know if you remember, but I tried to build a relationship with you and for some reason you didn't want it. Whenever I would call to talk, your first question was always 'what did I need?' And I see that things haven't changed. What I really needed was a dad!"

"Sollie, I didn't have a dad," he said interrupting me.

I shook my head. "You know what Daddy I don't mean to be disrespectful, but I will not accept that and I don't believe a man with your intelligence would even attempt to try and justify your actions because of someone else's. That reason alone should have made you want to be a better father. So you knew what it felt like not having a father and yet you chose to follow in your father's footsteps instead of saying you weren't going to be like him. Instead of breaking the cycle, you chose to continue it!"

"Sollie," he said sounding as if he was about to break down. He took a deep breath. "Please, let me say something. I'm sorry! I'm so sorry that you feel as hurt as you do, but the truth is I didn't know how to be a father. And yes, I did think buying and giving you everything you wanted was all I needed to do. Back then, Sollie, I myself was in so much pain, wife after wife after wife. I was trying to find someone, anyone, to make me happy. For years I tried to use me not having a father for an excuse, and if you would not have interrupted me a few seconds ago, I would have used it again. You're right, and again I'm so sorry for the pain I have caused you as a child and obviously as an adult."

I was stunned. Because when he spoke, I could actually feel his pain and honesty. And I knew that his apology was sincere, and he had finally owned up to his mistake. "Can you find it in your heart to forgive me?"

I paused for a minute took a deep breath. "Yes daddy, I forgive you."

"Sollie, do you know, for years I have dreaded this conversation that I knew one day we were going to have, but I'm so glad we did. I also had to seek therapy and during my sessions my therapist suggested that I call you and that was two years ago. I couldn't. I just couldn't face or admit my wrong doings, and this is something, you're calling me and facing your stuff head on. I admire that! You're obviously a strong woman like your mother. You mentioned therapy. Are you really okay?"

"Yes, I'm getting better, and after talking with you I feel much better."

"Sollie I would really like it if we could start over. You or I cannot change the past but I hope this conversation we have had will be a start to building a relationship with you."

Just as he said that, my other line beeped, and my eyes widened when I saw that it was Tyra.

"Daddy, please hold on for one minute. I have to take this call." I switched lines. "Tyra where have you been, are you okay, what is going on?!"

"Sollie, I'm sorry, I really need to see you," Tyra said sadly.

"Hold on. Let me tell my father I'll have to call him back."

"Your father!" she said sounding shocked.

"Yes, my father," I smiled.

I switched over and told my father I would call him back. He apologized and thanked me again for calling him. I gave him my cell number, and told him that the house number was still the same and that I would talk to him later and my heart smiled when I heard the words I love you come out of his mouth. I quickly switched back over to Tyra.

"Tyra! Okay, what is going on?"

"Are you at work?"

"No, I was just leaving."

"Can you come by the social service building?"

"I'm on my way!"

What now? God please let everything be okay, please, I said walking quickly to my car. I jumped inside and sped off. I arrived and couldn't get in the building fast enough. Now standing at the receptionist desk I asked to see Tyra Palmer.

When Tyra walked through the huge wooden double doors, I didn't even recognize her. She had lost so much weight, her eyes were red and swollen, and she looked tired as if she hadn't slept in days. I stood up slowly staring in total disbelief. My eyes welled up with tears as we walked toward one another and hugged each other tightly. I missed her so much.

"Tyra, please tell me what is wrong?"

"Come on," she said wiping her eyes. "I'll tell you everything." Tyra said pulling by my hand through the doors. We went up to Tyra's office. She told me to wait and that she would be right back. I walked around the office looking at all the pictures of her, Terry, and the kids and hoped that whatever was going on had nothing to do with them. I walked over to her bookshelf and smiled as I looked at the picture of Tyra and me.

She also had several plaques and certificates of recognition for her years of volunteer work. I noticed a mystery book sitting on her desk. She loves those kinds of books. I think I'll recommend to her that she should follow her dream and go on to college and get her degree in criminology, because I sure was, I had decided to get my degree in business management. But knowing Tyra, she will say she's fine and her life is complete, being a wife, and stay-at-home mom, and volunteering here. Tyra came back into the office and shut the door.

She sat in her chair and began to cry.

"Are the kids okay? is it Terry? Please, don't tell me he is cheating." I walked around to the chair she was sitting in, and put my arms around her.

"Sollie, the kids are fine and no, Terry is not cheating." She said reaching for a tissue from the tissue box. She then got up and walked over to the window and stared.

"Then, Tyra, what is it!" I followed her and placed my hand gently on her back. She took a deep breath, turned, and faced me.

"Remember I told you my supervisor asked me to purge the old records, because we are starting a new computer system? All the files are going to be able to be accessed from the computer."

"Yeah, that's when you pulled a muscle in your back, right? Is something wrong with your back?"

"No, Sollie," she said sadly shaking her head.

"Then Tyra what is it?" I snapped, becoming very inpatient with her. "I'm sorry, I'm sorry, go on. I'm listening." Tyra turned and looked back out the window, took another deep breath, and continued.

"The files were our adoption files containing personal information on children who were adopted through the department of social service."

Uncertain and not understanding where this was going, I stood there quietly and continued to listen.

"One of the charts had my father's name on it, Albert Jones, and the child's mother's name."

"Okay, how do you know it's your father? There could be a million Albert Jones in this state."

Tyra turned back to face me, "But not with the same birth date, year, social security number, and the address to where I grew up at. Sollie, social service is one of the places where a person who has been adopted can come once they have reached a certain age to find out information on their biological parents if they want to locate them."

"Okay, I'm aware of that, so what does all this mean?"

"Remember when we were younger; I would always come to your house crying because my parents would argue?"

"Yeah, I do."

"I would always hear my mother say she would never accept the child. I didn't understand what she meant then. But ever since finding out this information, all that I keep hearing in my mind is her saying those words."

"Okay, so what are you saying? You may have a half sister or brother? I think you need to go to your parents and confront them."

"Sollie, you don't understand!" she said shaking her head.

"Tyra, I am trying to."

"The child I'm speaking about biological mother's name was Louise Baker. We lived in the 2600 block, and she lived in the 2800 block. She died while giving birth and the father, who was my father, gave up all rights to the child, who was eventually adopted a year later."

By this time I could barely understand what Tyra was saying. She had become so emotional she could barely catch her breath. I told her to wait. I walked over to the office-size refrigerator and reached for a bottle of water. Tyra went and sat down in her chair and then curled over holding her stomach and rocking back and forth.

"I feel sick, Sollie," she said gagging as if she was about to vomit.

"Come on, drink this, and I'm taking you to the hospital."

"No, I am not going to the hospital!" she said still holding her stomach.

"Okay, let's go to your parents' house so you can talk with them."

Tyra jumped up and cried out "No! You don't understand!"

"Yes, I do! Your father cheated, got the woman on the next block pregnant. She died giving birth to the child. Your father gave up all parental rights, the child was adopted and you have a half brother or sister out here somewhere. So why don't I understand?"

"Sollie, no!" she cried, flopping down in the chair, bending over grabbing her stomach again. She raised her head up and continued. "Before this child was adopted, he had my father's last name. Once the adoption took place, the adoptive parents gave the child their last name," she said screaming like she was completely losing it.

"The last name is Palmer! Sollie, Palmer!"

My eyes widened, right before watering up with tears "Tyra, please, no, don't say it," I cried out, "please don't say it!" I said shaking my head backing away from her.

"My best friend, my soul-mate, the father of my kids, my husband, is my half brother!" She cried out. She was so distraught and at that moment so was I. Tyra fell to the floor and I quickly went over to her sat down on the floor next to her. I had no idea what to say, so I didn't say anything. Minutes passed and I noticed she was beginning to calm down. I helped her up to the chair. And all she kept asking was what she was going to do.

"Tyra, maybe it's a mix up." Even though I knew it wasn't, not with dates names and social security numbers matching.

"Sollie, I wish it was a mix up. I tried to tell myself that over and over again, but everything is right here in black and white," she said picking up the brown envelope and throwing it against the wall. "How do I tell Terry something like this?"

"Okay, let's go to the source and get some answers. Talk to Terry's mother and your parents. Does Terry even know he's adopted?"

"No, he doesn't," Tyra answered sadly. "Everything was going so great. He flew to LA this morning to purchase a building. He's opening a law firm in LA."

"Are y'all moving?"

"No, the firm is doing so well, they're expanding to the west coast." She took another deep breath and said that she would talk to her parents and his adoptive mother, and when Terry returned from his trip she would tell him everything.

Tyra gathered all the information she had. She said she made copies and put the originals back in the files.

"Sollie, I'm sorry for leaving like that. I just had to get away, and I missed you like crazy. And I got every 'I love you' message that you left," she said trying to utter a smile. Tyra quenched her swollen eyes and stared at me curiously. "But there's something different about you. What have you been doing? Are you still seeing the therapist?"

"Yes, I am, Tyra. You wouldn't believe all the stuff that's been going on in my life, but that can wait. Right now my main concern is you. Are you going home?"

"Yeah, I was going to my parents to pick the kids up, I miss them both so much, but I may see if they can stay the night. I don't want them to see me looking like this. I really need to go home and try to do something with myself."

I told Tyra I was going with her to her house, but she said she really needed to be alone. We walked out of the building and I walked her to her car.

"I love you, Sollie."

"I love you too, and call me if you need me for anything." I hugged her and she began to cry again.

"I guess now I know why both of my babies have learning disabilities. It's not fair, Sollie. It's just not fair!"

"Tyra, please let me go with you to your house. You really should not be alone!"

"I'll call you later, I promise." Tyra jumped into her car and sped off.

Once again when you find out something, things start to make sense. That's why Terry and Tyra look so much alike. I always thought because they had been together for so long. Damn! It's always something I thought reaching for my cell and saw that it was Lamar calling. "Hello."

"Hey Sollie, are you busy?"

"No, why, what's up?"

"You sound strange. Are you sure you're okay?"

"I'm fine. Just some things going on with Tyra."

"She's back?" Lamar asked. "Is everything okay with her?"

"Not really. Hopefully everything will work out okay. What's up?"

"Actually, I am getting ready to leave for work, and I was hoping we could finish our conversation from earlier."

"Lamar, disregard what I said earlier, although I do still think we should take it slow. But I'm open to whatever may come of our friendship. Life is so short, and I am going to stop being afraid of loving, and being loved. Are you still there?" I asked hearing silence on the other end.

"Yeah, Sollie, I'm here. I'm just really glad to hear that you feel that way. So are you on your way home or did you decide to come back to the apartment?"

"No," I said chuckling. "I'm going home. I told you I have to stop running."

"Is it okay if I come over?"

"Of course, have you eaten yet?"

"I had lunch. Do you want me to stop and pick something up?"

"Yeah, how about pizza?"

"Pizza it is. I'm on my way. I am going to stop home first. My phone is going dead. You know what, that's okay. It can wait. I'm going to be with the only person I want to hear from anyway."

We hung up and I drove home thinking about Tyra and what she was going to do. She and Terry are like the perfect couple. I began thinking about when they met and how Terry always said that it was like his and Tyra's souls were connected. Why don't people tell about these children that are born under these circumstances; it's probably a whole lot of half brothers and sisters that don't even know it. I pulled up to my house and just as I went to call and check on Tyra my attention was taken when Mrs. Johnson stormed out her front door, down the steps, and over to my car.

"Sollie," Mrs. Johnson said out of breath.

"Mrs. Johnson, calm down." I got out of the car and asked her what was wrong.

"That crazy boy has been riding back and forth through here. He even parked and sat in his car for about an hour and just stared at your house, looking as if he was on another planet or something."

I told her thank you. I quickly ran up on my porch, thinking about what Mrs. Johnson had just said. Ahmaun was either smoked up or high off E pills and if he was, I knew I had to get the hell away from here. Once in the house, I nervously dialed Lamar's cell.

"Lamar!"

"Hey, you changed your mind about the pizza?"

"No, I was calling you to tell you not to come over here. I will meet you at your place. Mrs. Johnson said she saw Ahmaun riding through the block. Lamar, are you there? Lamar!" I said calling his name again. What the hell happened? I looked at the phone and it read "lost call." "Shit!" I said stomping my feet. I forgot he said his battery was going dead.

I had to get out of here in case he comes back. I tried to call Lamar again and his answering machine picked right up. I couldn't leave. Lamar was on his way! I'll go over to Mrs. Johnson's until he comes. I rushed to the door and got the shock of my life: Ahmaun was standing there.

Chapter Thirty-Two

H e pushed his way inside. From the blank look on his face, I knew all too well, he was definitely high off E pills, which meant all hell was about to break loose!

"Where the fuck you going, over that nigga house?" he said pushing me back into the house. "You know that nigga fucked up when he put his hands on me!" He shoved me up against the wall. "Where your bitch-ass boyfriend, Sollie?"

"He's not my boyfriend. We're just friends," I said terrified slightly turning my head from the stale smell of alcohol that was on his breath. Ahmaun was definitely losing it. He never drank alcohol.

"Oh, you fuckin that nigga! Nigga taking up for you and shit, but he fucked up when he decided to step to me! And I found out who he is. He's the boy B.'s brother. He moved here from Georgia." He grabbed my arm.

"Ahmaun, you're hurting me!" I said trying to pull away.

"I'm hurting you! I'm hurting you! All that shit I did for you, gave you whatever the fuck you wanted, eleven years, and you going to just say fuck a nigga just like that, and carry me like you did. I told you before I will kill your fuckin ass before I see you with another motherfucker. You forgot I said you was mine? And this is mine!" He reached around and gripped my ass.

Before I knew it, Lamar ran in the door, through the pizza on the floor. Ahmaun reached down in his dip for his gun and pulled it out.

"Lamar, he has a gun!" I yelled.

Lamar grabbed Ahmaun, and threw him up against the wall. The impact caused him to drop the gun. Lamar grabbed him up in his collar and threw him on the floor and beat the living hell out of him. With every blow splatters of blood hit the wall. I started to call 911 but obviously Mrs. Johnson beat me to it. I heard the police sirens coming from a distance. I tried to get past them to get the gun, but I couldn't.

"Lamar, please stop!" I yelled as he continued to whip Ahmaun's ass.

Ahmaun tirelessly tried to reach for the gun, but with the blows Lamar was landing on his face he was unable to grab it.

"Hurry, hurry! They're inside," I heard Mrs. Johnson yell to the police.

"Police!" They yelled as all three of them burst through the door.

The officers ran inside, with their guns drawn, demanding for Lamar to back away from Ahmaum. Lamar rose and put his hand in the air, and the officer grabbed him pushed him up against the wall, as the officer was about to place the cuffs on Lamar. I yelled "Not him!" And pointed over to Ahmaun, but it was too late. With all the attention focused on Lamar, Ahmaun was able to get up and grab his gun. He stood up in a daze and aimed the forty-two right at Lamar.

"Drop your weapon!" The officer yelled to him, now pointing his weapon at Ahmaun.

But Ahmaun didn't listen. Next thing I knew shots rang out. Lamar pulled me in his direction, throwing me onto the steps. Ahmaun burst out the front door, jumped in his car, and sped off. The third officer proceeded to follow Ahmaun at the same time calling for backup and repeating, "Officers, down."

"Sollie, come on," Lamar said helping me up off the steps. "Don't look," he said taking me into the kitchen away from the site of the wounded officers. I sat down in the chair and Lamar rushed back into the living room and stayed with the two injured officers until the paramedics arrived. The sound of one of them trying to talk and gasp for air was killing me.

I was in complete shock. In a matter of minutes my house had become a crime scene, foxtrot, a million police officers and news reporters were at my home; all my friends were there as well. Word had traveled fast around the city. Along with everything else that was going on, it didn't help matters. Hearing my mother out front, upset, and repeating how she knew this would eventually be the outcome of my relationship with Ahmaun.

The detectives led Lamar and me outside, and the sight of the yellow crime scene tape that surrounded my porch made my stomach turn. Some other law officials rushed by us and hurried into my house, never saying a word to me. I also noticed every neighbor in the block standing on their porch staring, cell phones and their hand videotaping the whole scene. Everyone ran up to me asking if I was okay, and looking at Lamar wondering who he was. The detective opened the backdoor of the blue four-door Continental as Lamar and I climbed inside.

"Where are you taking her?" my mother asked hysterically.

The nasty detective didn't respond to her question. He just walked around to the driver's side and got in the car. I felt ashamed as I looked at her and said that they were taking us downtown for further questioning. Everyone hurried to their cars and proceeded to follow us to the station.

As we pulled off, I turned and looked at poor Mrs. Johnson standing on her porch, looking as if she didn't know what to do. I watched as Salique went over to her front and comforted her.

While sitting in the back of the detective's car, I laid my head on Lamar, and kept repeating I was sorry. All I could think about was the condition of the two officers, and couldn't get the vision out of my head as one of them lay in my living room with a gunshot wound to his head.

After being questioned for what seemed like forever, we were finally released. When we walked out into the lobby, everyone was there waiting for us, even Tyra. And for the first time ever, Duce and

Jodi was sitting there quietly together. My mother ran over to me and hugged me.

I introduced my mother to Lamar. Salique came over and gave him a brotherly handshake, and hugged and thanked him once again for looking out for me.

"You do have a lot to tell me," Tyra whispered in my ear and shaking Lamar's hand.

"Hey Sollie," Kane said sadly getting off the elevator.

"Hey Kane."

"Are you okay?"

"Kane, please tell me they caught him, please!"

"Not yet, but we will. Every police in the state is looking for him."

"Kane, how are the officers doing that were injured?" By the look on his face I knew it was bad news.

"One is in critical condition, and the other died during surgery."

"No, Kane, please don't say that, please." I felt so bad for the officer and his family. All he was doing was trying to protect us.

I wasn't allowed back in my house until I was given the okay from detectives. Lamar asked if I wanted to go to his apartment, but I really needed to be with my mother and he understood.

Everyone went back to my mother's with me, but I begged Tyra to go home. She had her own stuff going on. We all sat quietly in the living room and with every noise I heard, I jumped, wondering if it could have been Ahmaun.

Once everyone left, my mother ran me a bath. After I was done, I got straight in the bed, and needless to say I tossed and turned all night. That morning I jumped up and grabbed the remote flipping through the channels hoping that the news stations were reporting that Ahmaun had been captured, and I watched as they flashed his picture on every news station there was. The story had even made world news! But he still hadn't been caught. I tried to call Kane, but I didn't get an answer. Reaching for my purse, I retrieved the card that the detective had given me last night. I picked up the phone and called.

"Detective Holloway, this is Sollie Carr. How are you?"

293

"I'm fine," he said.

"I was just wondering have you all had any leads as to where he may be?"

"We have been getting tips all night, and they are being followed up on as we speak. Is there anything else that you can tell us that you may have forgotten to mention last night? Any family members, friends, his hangouts, anything!"

"No, I have told you all I know. Wait! Detective Holloway."

"Yes, Ms. Carr."

"He did live in Atlanta when he was younger with his aunt, and he still has friends there that he visits often."

"Do you know the aunt's name?"

"I'm sorry, I don't, and she is no longer living. His mother could probably give you more information. One more thing, will it be okay to go to my house and get some things? I'm going to be staying with my mother for a while."

"I know that CSI has to go to the home again today. Let me contact that department. It shouldn't be a problem. And you have my card. I'm available 24-7, if there's anything else you can remember. Oh you mentioned you will be staying at your mother's. What's her address and telephone number?" I gave the detective my mother's information.

My mother came into my room and tried to get me to eat something but I couldn't eat a thing. The detective called back and said that it was okay for me to go to my house and pick up some things. I took a shower and waited for Lamar to pick up my mother and me. The drive over to the house seemed very long for some reason, and none of us said a word.

When we pulled up, I sat there for a minute just staring at the house and realizing how your life can change in a minute. Mrs. Johnson came over to the car, hugged Lamar and me as we got out. I thanked her for calling the police. I guess her nosiness had finally paid off.

As we walked in the house, everything from yesterday came right back to me. I stopped and stared at the blood-stained carpet. I quickly went upstairs, grabbed some clothes and other items. As I was leaving, I stopped at the door and thought of all the fun times I had growing up in this house, all the parties, laughter, and memories that I would cherish forever. But I knew that I would never ever come back or live here again!

My mother sat inside the car, while Lamar and I went over to Mrs. Johnson. I told her that I would be staying with my mother. I felt bad as she stood there once again looking as if she had lost her best friends.

Once back at my mother's, I was able to talk Lamar into going home and getting some rest. I went back into the living room and smiled at my mother waiting for her to give me her opinion of the man that I was falling in love with.

"Sollie, he seems like a really nice young man and he's gorgeous!" she said.

"Yeah, I think he's pretty cute. Mommy, I just want them to catch Ahmaun, and I feel so bad for those officers' family, especially, the one that died." She wrapped her arms around me, and didn't speak. She just held me tightly and there was nothing I needed more than to be comforted in the arms of my mother.

Every news station was still reporting the incident, and several news reporter's had even come to my mother's house trying to get a statement.

I checked my messages. George, Jodi, Duce, even Dr. Parker was on the phone making sure I was all right, and then a voice that I recognized so well.

Now, bitch, I hope your life falls apart like mine! Remi blurted.

Later that evening, Lamar came back over and I listened as my mother asked him a million and one questions about himself and his family. Interrupting her, I told my mother that I wasn't going back to that house. She asked if I was sure, and I told her that I was positive. She said that she would call her realtor and put the house on the market to be sold.

Lamar stayed a little while longer and then left. He said he was going to go and meet B. at Club Rumors. I begged him to be careful.

As soon as Lamar left, I headed straight for the stairs, and was startled when Salique came through the door. Salique walked up the stairs and hugged me. My mother told him that all I have been doing was staying cooped up in the room, and the only time I came down was when Lamar came over.

"Oh yeah." Salique smiled. "He's cool, Sollie. I really like the brother. Sollie, listen staying upstairs in the room is not going to make you feel any better. Come on and chill down here with me for a while. Let's play a game of monopoly or something."

"No, I don't want to chill with you and I do not want to play monopoly. I'm going back to bed," I said becoming very agitated.

"Oh my god! Who is that?" I asked hearing the doorbell ring. "I'm not here Mommy!" I said trying to hurry up the steps.

When I heard Kane's voice, I immediately turned around and headed back down the stairs. Telling him again how sorry I was about the officer that was killed.

"Sollie, listen, it's always painful when we lose one of our own, but when we took that oath we knew that we were putting our lives on the line every day. When we leave our homes it's no guarantee that we will be returning, and Julian died doing what he loved to do. And when we catch that boy, and believe me he's going to get caught, he'll pay. I do have some good news. The other officer that was injured condition has been raised to stable."

When Kane left I went upstairs and called to check on Tyra.

"Sollie, I've made up my mind. I am not talking to my parents or Terry's mother."

"But Tyra, you have to tell Terry."

"No, I don't. I am not going to destroy my family! And besides, it's probably a mix up like you said."

"Tyra, come on. Now you said it yourself, you checked and rechecked! I can only imagine what you must be feeling, but you can't live your life knowing that your husband is your half brother!"

"I have made up my mind, and that's settled." She hung up. I tried to call her back but she wouldn't answer the phone.

A week had gone by, and I only went to Lamar's apartment and my mother's. And there was still no sign of Ahmaun. It was like he had dropped off the face of the earth and he was now labeled as public enemy number one! The officer's funeral was aired on television and I watched the whole ceremony. He was only thirty-two years.

A month had passed; I continued my therapy sessions and my mother went with me on a few of my sessions and so did my father, which was great. It allowed him and me to really open the lines of communication.

Lamar and I even joined church. It seemed as if my life was finally getting back on the right track, with the exception of Ahmaun still being on the run. Lamar made sure Mrs. Johnson didn't need or want anything. He even brought her a new living room set. I had no idea that we would become so attached to her like we did. She would often tell us that we were the children she never had.

One evening we went there, and I decided to tell her that I wouldn't be coming back to my house. Lamar and I assured her that we would be in her life forever.

"Sollie and Lamar, as you both know, I don't have any family, and I have to go in the hospital to have some tests taken."

"What kind of tests? Are you all right?"

"Oh, I am fine baby, don't you worry."

I knew that wasn't true. Lamar and I had already noticed a few weeks ago that she was losing a lot weight.

"They say I might have cancer and if it's okay with you two I'd like to give them your names and numbers, just in case of an emergency. I'll be gone for two days." She reached into her beautiful green-flowered housecoat that I had bought for her and handed each of us a set of keys. "Can you come and water the flowers and the plants for me while I'm away and keep an eye on the house? Oh don't look like that, I aint studdin them doctors." She said to us both, as we listened with sad faces. "I'm going to be just fine, you'll see, just fine. Now would you two like to join me for dinner?" We both said yes.

297

Mrs. Johnson said that she was going to catch mobility transportation to the hospital, but Lamar said that he would carry her.

I sat there eating and thought how mean I was to Mrs. Johnson at one time, and if it wasn't for Lamar, I wouldn't be sitting here now. I leaned over and kissed him on his cheek. He smiled and asked what that was for and I told him for teaching me humanity, and he reminded me, that he didn't teach me anything. And that I showed humanity the day I gave Miss. Susie that money for her granddaughter medical treatment.

"You two make such a lovely couple. Are you still courting or have you made it official?"

"We're just friends, Mrs. Johnson."

"Well, don't wait too long when God sends you that person that fits! You run with it. Life's too short for a whole lot of waiting and waiting for what you already know in your heart to be true. Life is too short!" she repeated as she poured herself another cup of tea. We finished our dinner and left.

That morning, Lamar picked me up and we headed over to Mrs. Johnson's house. She was standing at the door waiting, holding her overnight bag in one hand, and her black Bible in the other. She was quiet the whole ride there, and appeared to be nervous, although I think Lamar and I were as nervous as she was. When we got there, she registered and we later found out she wasn't fine, and that she knew she had cancer. She was there to have surgery. Lamar eventually went to work, but I stayed. I watched her lying there helpless with so many tubes hooked up to her.

Chapter Thirty-Three

I   walked over to her bed and gently stoked her gray strands of wisdom. I picked up her Bible and began reading to her a scripture that she had highlighted. "The Lord is my shepherd, and I shall not want . . ." She began to mumble something and slowly tried to open her eyes. When she saw me, all she could do was smile.

"You still here!" she muttered.

They eventually moved Mrs. Johnson in a room and she slept most of the day, Lamar came with a huge bundle of flowers for her, and a single rose for me, and we sat there with her until visiting hours were over.

When we got back to my mother's, she was talking on the phone with her realtor. She asked me if I was certain about the house. I told her yes, and she said the sale sign was going up in a few weeks. She asked Lamar would help her and Salique clean the house out and of course he said yes.

The next morning Lamar took me to see Mrs. Johnson. He left to go and meet my mother and Salique at the house. Mrs. Johnson was doing fine, but the doctor said he wanted to keep her another day just for observation.

When Lamar picked me up from the hospital, we stopped at the market so that I could get Mrs. Johnson some things, I thought, she might need when she came home. I also went to Wal-Mart and bought her several more housecoats. We took the things back to her house and straightened up a little and headed back to my mother's. As we were going in the door, my phone rang, and it was Tyra.

"Sollie," Tyra said crying, "I can't do this anymore. I just can't!"

"What happened, Tyra?"

"I don't know. I can't even make love to Terry. I tried but then stopped. He's my half brother, for God's sake! Now he's all upset thinking something is wrong, and that's not fair to him. I have to tell him, but first I have to go and see my parents. Will you go with me?" I told Tyra yes. She said that she would pick me up in an hour.

I told Lamar that I had to make a run with Tyra. He said he was going to go meet B. As he was leaving, my mother asked if he would join us for dinner later, and that she was making her famous Lasagna that I had told him about. Lamar happily said yes.

Tyra pulled up and blew the horn. As I was leaving the house, I looked up and asked God to be with us and couldn't help but notice how gloomy and dark the clouds were. Silently we drove over to her parents' house. We pulled in front of their house and parked. We headed inside.

Just like when we were kids, they were both sitting in the living room, Mr. Jones in his La-Z-Boy smoking his pipe, Mrs. Jones sitting in the corner of the couch knitting.

"Hi, Mr. and Mrs. Jones."

"Hi Sollie, how have you been?" Mrs. Jones asked getting up and hugging me. "How is your mother and brother doing? And how have you been with all this mess that's going on? Have they caught him yet?"

Mrs. Jones still asked a lot of questions, I thought, as I tried to answer them all.

"How you been, Sollie? Good to see you," Mr. Jones said taking a long puff off his pipe and blowing the thick smoke in the air.

"Tyra, where are my babies?"

"They're home with the babysitter."

"Is Terry still working?"

"Yes," Tyra answered.

"That reminds me, I need to call my boy," Mr. Jones said proudly sticking his chest out and grabbing hold to his suspender strap, taking another puff off his pipe. "I bought us two tickets to the Oriole game." Tyra looked as if she wanted to vomit.

He's definitely your boy! I thought. All these years and now that the truth is out and Terry does in fact look like Mr. Jones.

"Mommy and Daddy, I need to talk to you," Tyra said. And I swear by the look on her mother's face, after all these years she knew that the Pandora's Box had been opened. She looked over at Tyra's father with a look that could kill. She laid the blanket that she was knitting down next to her, stood up, and began pacing the floor. Within seconds she began sweating uncontrollably. She reached for a tissue and nervously patted the sweat from her brow. Mr. Jones just sat watching the baseball game, paying none of us any mind.

"Mommy, will you please sit down!"

"Why baby? I don't need to sit, just go on and tell me what we need to talk about. Come on now what is it?" Mrs. Jones asked still pacing the floor.

"Mommy! Would you please just sit down?!" Tyra yelled, finally getting the attention of her father.

"Tyra, what is wrong with you? Don't talk to your mother that way!" Mr. Jones said sitting up in his La-Z-Boy.

I asked everyone to calm down. I took Mrs. Jones by her hand and led her back over to the couch, then told Tyra to come sit down next to me.

"No, Sollie, I'm fine right where I am!" Tyra said leaning against the living room wall angrily staring at her father.

Mrs. Jones sat down next to me, still wiping her forehead, and placing her hand on her leg that was shaking uncontrollably. Tyra breathed deeply as she tried to prepare herself to ask the question whose answer, she knew, might change her and her family's life forever. She took her attention straight to her father and told him she needed the truth.

"Now wait a minute, young lady. Have I ever lied to you before?" he said.

"No," she snapped, "But you haven't exactly been truthful with me either. Did you father a child outside of you and Mommy's marriage?" Mr. Jones dropped his head.

"Oh Lord, I knew it, I knew it!" Mrs. Jones cried out, falling back on the couch.

"Helen! Helen! Are you okay?" Mr. Jones yelled as he got up and ran over to his wife.

He went to help her up and she screamed, "Get away from me. Don't touch me!" He backed away from her and looked at Tyra, and after staring at her for a short moment he finally said yes.

"Baby, I'm sorry! We wanted to tell you."

"You wanted to tell me, you wanted to tell me! Well, goddamn it, you should have told me! Do you know what you have done! Do you know what your little secret has done to my life?!" she screamed.

Her father just looked at her with a confused look on his face. Poor Mrs. Jones, she sat there never taking the stare of hatred off her husband.

"Tyra, calm down," her father said, "it's going to be okay. I'm sorry, baby. I had no idea that you would be so upset from this. Come sit down. I'll tell you everything, come on . . ."

"Do you know who your son is? Do you have any idea as to what you have done? Your son, your son, your boy is my husband!" she yelled.

Stunned, with his mouth hanging wide-open and speechless, he said, "What—are—you—saying?" Mrs. Jones asked as she slowly lifted her head up and turned in the direction of Tyra, "Your husband." She repeated with her eyes quenched. She slowly stood up from the couch.

"That's right! Terry is Daddy's son!"

Mrs. Jones passed out right there in the middle of the living room floor. Mr. Jones sat his pipe in the ashtray, and ran over to his wife, yelling for us to call 911.

"Helen! Helen!" Mr. Jones yelled. She began coming around, Mr. Jones picked her up from the floor and laid her on the couch. By the time 911 arrived, she was fully awake. Her blood pressure had risen, but she refused to go to the hospital.

"Tyra, what in God's name are you talking about?" Mr. Jones asked, once the paramedics left.

"Why didn't you two tell me?" Tyra cried out. "My life is ruined. she said. "Everything is right here in black and white." She tossed the adoption information onto the coffee table. Mr. Jones walked over, picked up the folder and quickly browsed through the papers. He laid the folder back down, and with a look of shame and guilt, he closed his eyes, and dropped his head.

"Tyra, I'm so sorry, baby," Mrs. Jones said, turning to her husband and giving him a stare as only a mother could after someone has hurt her child. "I told you it would come out! Now look what your secret has done to my child!"

He walked over to the bar, lined up three shot glasses, and filled each of them with Old Grand-Dad, and stood there and drank each one straight down. "My son!" he mumbled, as he poured his fourth shot.

"Come on, Sollie!" Tyra said snatching her pocketbook from off the couch.

"Tyra wait, please don't leave," Mrs. Jones said begging and pulling her daughter by her arm.

"Honey, please don't go. We need to talk about this," Mr. Jones said with his eyes filling up with tears.

"Oh now you want to talk! You should have done that years ago and maybe we wouldn't be here now, talk, yeah right, there is nothing else to talk about." Tyra walked out the door.

"No-no-no!" Mrs. Jones yelled out, stomping her feet on the floor. "Baby, please come back!"

I turned and hugged Mrs. Jones and said good-bye to Mr. Jones. Tyra never looked back. As I was leaving out the door, I watched as Mrs. Jones walked over to where her husband was standing and angrily slapped his fifth shot of liquor out of his hands.

"All these years and I knew that it would one day come out. You hurt me so badly when you had a child by that tramp up the street, and even though you gave up all parental rights, we both said that we would tell Tyra when she graduated high school. And when that time came you didn't, using her accident as an excuse. God, why did I listen to you? Let it go Helen, you said, she doesn't need to know, it's over with, and now, because of your inability to be a man, and your lack of integrity, my child's life is ruined! Albert, I stopped loving you years ago. I only stayed because I wanted our daughter to have two parents in the home, and as wonderful a woman she turned out to be I thought I had made the right decision, and then for her to marry and start a family with a man every mother wants for her daughter was even better, but it's over." She threw her hands in the air. "I don't see how this mess can be worked out, but one thing I do know. I want you out of this house. This marriage is over!"

"Helen, please listen to me!"

"It's over!" Mrs. Jones yelled. She stood there staring at Mr. Jones with such hatred. She walked away and slowly turned back to face him. "Albert, it's funny how the child I said I would never accept I came to adore! Pack your things, and get the hell out of this house!"

Chapter Thirty-Four

I   quietly shut the door, and ran out to the car and told Tyra that I was driving; she was in no condition to drive. We headed over to Terry's mother's house. We visited Terry's mother, and yes, although we knew it, everything was true, and needless to say Terry's mother was in shock as well finding out that those two were half siblings. She gave Tyra a large envelope containing all the adoption information on Terry. She asked to go with Tyra while she told him, but Tyra told her no.

As we were leaving out the house the wind began gusting and I noticed the clouds becoming even darker. The weatherman had said Maryland was going to get parts of hurricane that was down South.

I drove Tyra home and asked if she wanted me to go inside and wait with her until Terry came. She said no; she wanted to tell him alone. I pulled up in front of her house, reached over and hugged her tightly, and told her that I loved her.

Carrying the envelope that Terry's mother had given her, she slowly got out the car and headed into the house, and I thought that walk up the walkway had to be the longest walk of her life!

Lamar called just as I was pulling off and said that he and B. we're going to shoot another game of pool and then he would be on his way. Now back at my mother's house she was in the kitchen cooking. Sitting at the table, I placed my hand on my forehead, thinking to myself, what next? And then I thought about Ahmaun wondering where in the hell he could be hiding all this time.

"So Lamar is on his way? I really like him Sollie."

"I really like him too. I'm just afraid of being hurt again."

"Awwww baby," she said hugging me, "Hurt is unpredictable, but we can't run from love out of fear of being hurt. Don't be afraid to open your heart and love. True love is one of the most beautiful things we are blessed to have on this journey, and I believe in my spirit that you and Lamar are going to be just fine. Do you remember the first thing I said when you brought Ahmaun to the house?"

"Yes, I do," I said laughing.

"What did I say?"

"He wasn't out the door five minutes and you said you didn't like him."

"Now that you're older, do you understand why I said that?"

"Yes, Mom, I do. And I wish I had listened."

"It's okay, baby, you live and you learn," she said gently rubbing my back.

"Do you like Lamar?" I asked smiling.

"Yes, I do very very much! Mothers know. You have got yourself a good guy! And everything is going to be fine. Don't be afraid to love, Sollie. Love is a blessing, and you have been blessed!"

When Lamar arrived, we all sat down and ate. I excused myself to go and call Tyra, but I didn't get an answer. I wondered if she was telling Terry. I went back to join them and just stared at Lamar and couldn't help but think how badly I wanted to make love to him and that I was ready to take our relationship to another level. Lamar asked if I wanted to go to the movies, at first I said no and then I changed my mind. Like Lamar and my mother said I would lose my mind constantly living in fear.

"You two have fun and be careful. You know that storm is passing through here," my mother said walking us to the door.

"My mother really likes you."

"I like her too, and I really, really like her daughter," he said leaning over and kissing me.

Soon as we pulled off, the rain started, and it poured. We could barely see the lines in the street. Lamar suggested we skip the movies and just spend the evening at his place.

By the time we pulled up to Lamar's apartment, it was raining so hard we had to sit for a minute, hoping it would slack up a little but it didn't. Lamar jumped out, ran over to my side, opened the door, and put his sweat-suit jacket over the top of my head. We jetted toward his door, and while we were running in the building, Lamar slipped and fell. I laughed so hard, my stomach was hurting. We made it into his apartment, both drenched! "Are you okay?" I asked still laughing.

"Oh, it's funny, right," he said laughing along with me. He walked over to me and ran his fingers through my hair, and said he was fine.

"Yes, you are!" He looked so sexy standing there with the water running down his beautiful smooth dark skin. We were interrupted by my cell phone, which was probably a good thing 'cause I was ready to make love to him right where we were standing. I grabbed the phone praying it was Tyra, but it wasn't. It was my mother.

She told us to turn on the news and that they had spotted Ahmaun. I was so happy. It was finally over. Until the news reporter said it had been a case of mistaken identity. "I can't take this anymore!" I yelled.

"Baby, look," Lamar said lifting my head up and looking me in my teary eyes, "I am not going to ever let Ahmaun or anyone else ever hurt you again, ever! They will have to come through me. Sollie, earlier I said that I really, really liked you, but that wasn't exactly the truth. The truth is, Sollie Carr, I'm in love with you." I pushed Lamar's hand away from my face and walked over to the window.

"Lamar, don't say that to me. Please don't say that to me." Lamar walked over and put his arms around me.

"Why not? It's the truth."

"I don't know what the truth is any more. Ahmaun, Mr. and Mrs. Jones, Mrs. Palmer all of them lied every last one of them. I want to believe you but . . ." He turned me around to face him.

"I am not a liar, Sollie. And all those other people you just mentioned, I don't have anything to do with them. All I know is that

I'm in love with you. Remember what I told you the night we met? I knew from that moment I saw you that you were the one, and when you pulled off I looked up to the sky . . ."

"I remember you doing that," I said softly. "What were you doing?"

"I was telling God, 'thank you,' because that was the night that he sent me my future wife. I love you!" He turned me around to face him and softly kissed me on my forehead. I laid my head on his chest, took a deep breath, and whispered, "Lamar, I love you too."

I said that to one other person a thousand times and it never felt like this. We must have held each other for at least ten minutes, still soaked and wet from the rain.

"Baby, come on, let me get you some dry clothes before you catch a cold, and me too for that matter."

Lamar took me by my hand. I stopped and looked at my phone, ready to call Tyra, but changed my mind and laid it back on the table, figuring she would call me if she needed me.

"You changed your mind?" Lamar asked watching me lay the phone down.

"Yeah, as a matter of fact, I'm cutting my ringer off. I need a break from this phone anyway."

"Yeah so do I." Lamar said turning his cell off as well.

Of course, he went into the bathroom, and I knew exactly what he was doing. When he came into his room, I was sitting on the bed. He handed me a pair of white silk drawstring pajamas with a matching shirt.

I grabbed a washcloth and towel from the linen closet and headed for the bathroom.

I knew it. Candles were all lit around the bathroom. The water was so hot and relaxing. I am not going to think about anyone or anything. I must have stayed in there an hour before Lamar knocked on the door and asked if I was okay. He asked if I wanted the bag I had left in the guest room. I had forgotten about it. I told him yes. I got out the tub and dried off, and looked through the Victoria's Secret bag forgetting all about the things I had brought—my favorite lotion and body spray along with three pairs of sexy panties with the bras to match.

I put a chocolate-colored laced bra-and-panty set on. I then put Lamar's pajamas on covering up the beautiful lingerie looking at myself in the mirror. I wondered if this was going to be the night that we finally made love.

"Lamar, I am done!" I said yelling down the hall.

"Okay, I was trying to call B. but I think the storm knocked the phone lines out."

"Use your cell," I replied.

"Nah, it wasn't important. I can holla at him tomorrow." When he came down the hall, I was standing there and he stopped and stared at me. "You're beautiful," he said taking my hand and turning me to face the mirror on the wall.

"What are you doing?" I asked laughing.

"Just making sure what everyone else has told us is true," he said standing directly behind me with his arms around my waist.

"And what is that?"

"That we make a beautiful couple. And they were right. We are going to have some good-looking kid's baby," he said staring in the mirror and kissing me on my cheek. "Baby, why don't you pick out a movie, I'm going to go jump and the shower."

I went into the kitchen and took some cheese, crackers, and grapes, and placed them on a tray, grabbed a bottle of wine, dimmed the lights in the living room, put on a CD, and waited for Lamar to join me. I picked up my cell, ready to turn it back on and call Tyra, but I laid it down remembering what I said earlier. I walked over to the window and the rain was coming down even heavier.

"No popcorn and beer?" Lamar asked walking over to me with a long black cotton robe on.

God, I want him, I thought.

"Even with the rain, it's a beautiful night," he said resting his head on mine.

"Yes, it is." I took a deep breath, knowing that tonight was the night.

"So what are we going to watch?" Lamar asked, still holding me.

"A love story," I replied.

"Baby, for real, I'm engaging in a love story of my own." He turned me around to face him, and kissed me softly. I pulled him close to me; his lips were so soft and his tongue was warm as it entered my mouth. I was so nervous I began to back away.

Chapter Thirty-Five

Tyra and Terry's house

T　he babysitter had already put the kids to bed. Tyra walked her to the door and then nervously sat down on the couch waiting for Terry to arrive, as she listened to her jazz CD that always seemed to calm her down. But this time it didn't, and she had no idea how she was going to tell her husband that he was her half brother. She prayed, and prayed, as she got up and began pacing the floor. The door opened. Terry walked in soaking wet from the storm.

"Hey where is your car?" Terry asked while sitting his briefcase down and dancing over to Tyra, giving her a kiss.

"Sollie has my car." Tyra said sadly.

"Where are my babies?"

"They're asleep. Terry, we have to talk," she said in a low tone, while wiping her eyes.

"I know, baby, and we will. Look at you, all stressed out. Baby, I know I have been working crazy hours at the firm, and then my recent trip out of town, and I know with me being gone so much lately may be the 'cause of our recent problems in the bedroom. But the good news is that today we finalized the purchase of the building in LA, and we will be interviewing attorneys as early as next month, and after that, baby, our lives will be back to normal, I promise. Baby, don't you know this is all I have dreamed of for our family. Damn! I love you." He took Tyra by the hand and happily turned her around. ""Baby, pour us a glass of wine. Let's celebrate! I'm going to get out of these wet clothes and then we will talk," Terry said grabbing his briefcase and headed up the swivel stairs. Tyra stood shaking her head as she sadly stared at him.

"Oh baby! I forgot," he said walking back down the stairs and sat his briefcase on the coffee table and opened it, pulled out an envelope, and asked Tyra to close her eyes.

"Terry, please, we need to talk!"

"You're such a drag," he said smiling, and opening the envelope himself. Inside were four tickets to Africa. "I, you, and the kids are out of here!"

Tyra began to cry.

"Terry, please stop! And listen to me," she said crying.

"What's wrong?" he asked as wiped her tears.

"Come on, Terry, sit down," she said taking him by his hand and leading him to the couch.

Lamar's Apartment

"Sollie, we don't have to do this if you aren't ready." Lamar said kissing me on my forehead and then my lips.

I looked him in his eyes. "I'm ready. I just only wish that you were my first and not Ahmaun."

"But guess what? I got the best of you."

"I don't understand." I said.

"I got your heart and soul." He smiled.

"And that you do."

Lamar took my hand and led me to his bedroom. I sat down on the bed. Lamar walked over and put a CD on.

Tyra, Terry, Sollie, and Lamar

Tyra walked over and turned the music off.

Lamar told me how beautiful I was as he unbuttoned the white silk pajama top.

Tyra told Terry how much she loved him as she loosened the wet tie from his collar.

Lamar began to lick every part of my body.

Tyra told Terry everything. Terry eyes widened, he couldn't believe it.

My eyes widened when I saw the size of Lamar's man-hood.

Terry grabbed Tyra's hand and yelled out "No!"

Lamar asked me if I was ready? I softly whispered yes.

Terry grabbed Tyra's wine glass and threw it against the wall.

I grabbed Lamar and pulled him closer wanting him badly.

Terry cried as he held Tyra tightly.

Lamar moaned as he began giving me what we both had longed for.

"Baby, you feel so good. You're so warm," Lamar whispered.

"I don't feel good." Terry said grabbing his car keys from off the end table.

"Terry where are you going? It's a terrible storm out there!" Tyra screamed as Terry ran out the door into the rainy night distraught from what the love of his life just told him.

"Tyra," yelled out Terry.

I softly whispered, "Lamar."

Terry sped off heading for his mother's house.

Lamar and I were heading for ecstasy.

Terry cried in disbelief.

A tear fell from my eyes never knowing how making love really felt. Lamar and I were going nonstop, and so was Terry, as he drove through the red light. Terry heard a loud horn. Lamar and I heard the beautiful voice of Beyonce singing 1+1.

Terry looked to his left.

Lamar and I looked at each other.

"Sollie, say you will stay with me forever?" Lamar asked. "Damn baby" he moaned, while kissing me softly.

The emotions were so strong, but Terry was so weak, while Lamar and I laid there in each other's arms.

Terry lay in the rain, twenty feet from his mangled Jaguar, after it was hit by a tractor trailer. Lamar, Terry, and I had just gone to heaven. The only difference being that Lamar and I came back!

After making love Lamar and me laid there in each other's arms in complete silence. The evening was perfect.

After taking a shower, we went into the living room, wrapped up in a blanket on the couch, and ended up watching Love Jones, until we both dozed off, and were awakened by someone banging on the door. Lamar jumped up, and of course, I freaked out.

"Who is it!?" Lamar asked half asleep.

"Man, its B.!" he said sounding out of breath. Lamar opened the door.

"B., what's wrong?" I asked getting up from the couch.

"Why the hell do you two have your phones off, and what's wrong with your home phone man?" B. asked angrily as he leaned against the doorway, trying to catch his breath.

"The storm knocked the lines out, man! What is wrong with you?"

"Sollie, Sollie," he said holding his head, "There has been a terrible accident!"

"An accident? What kind of accident?! B.,what kind of accident!" I yelled. But he couldn't speak.

"B.!" Lamar yelled, "What happened?!"

"Terry was killed tonight!"

"Terry was killed! No!" I screamed. "What happened? Where is Tyra? Where is she?"

"She's at the hospital, Sollie."

I was a mess as Lamar drove as fast as he could to the hospital. When we arrived, everyone was there sitting in the family room. I walked straight over to my mother and asked what happened, and where Tyra was.

"Sollie, we don't have all the details yet, but the police said Terry ran a red light and his car was hit by a tractor trailer."

I looked around noticing all of his colleagues sitting there. "Where is she?"

"Baby, Tyra was so hysterical, she had to be sedated."

The nurse allowed me to go back to the room where Tyra was. Her parents and Terry's mother was in the room with her. Mrs. Jones sat next to the bed rubbing Tyra's hand. Mr. Jones stood over in the corner, just staring straight at the wall. I sat down next to when I noticed Tyra coming to. She looked around, and when she realized where she was and why, she began to cry. I hugged her tightly.

"He's gone, Sollie," she cried, "he's gone!" She stared at the three of them with such hurt and anger.

"No one, no one will ever know what led up to my husband's death!" Terry's mother went to say something and Tyra quickly interrupted her. "My husband was a well-respected man and attorney, and it will remain that way. I will not have anyone whispering anything about him! You all shouldn't have a problem with this. After all, this little secret was kept for thirty years. Each one of us and this room will take this to our graves. Pandora's box is once again closed!"

Terry's mother and Tyra's mother stood wiping their tears, and poor Mr. Jones looked as if he wanted to die. We eventually left the hospital, and needless to say, Tyra walked out of there in somewhat of a zombie state. I went to my mother's, packed my suitcase, and stayed with Tyra and the kids. The next day I didn't go with Lamar to pick up Mrs. Johnson from the hospital, but he said she was very happy with the things I had bought for her. She had a nurse come in for two hours a day, so between the nurse and Lamar she was fine. I stayed at Tyra's helping her finalize Terry's funeral. The kids stayed with her mother for the first two days. When they came home, Trinity ran and hugged me. While little Terry walked over and sat in the chair and just stared at the wall. I tried to talk to him but he wouldn't respond. Tyra said after everything was over she was going to get him counseling.

"Aunt Sollie," Trinity said smiling. "Guess what?"

"What Trinity?" I asked, picking her up and holding her tiny body in my arms.

"Mommy said my daddy's in heaven with the angels!" she said smiling, with her two ponytails going in different directions. I smiled and told her that is exactly where her father was, in heaven.

The day of the funeral arrived, and it was a very sad day. I still couldn't believe that we were burying Terry. A tear fell from my eyes as Tyra and the kids walked slowly down the swivel steps. Tyra wore an all-black suit with a wide-rimmed black hat. Little Terry wore a black suit with a light blue tie, and Trinity wore a white dress with a huge light blue satin bow around it, with light blue ribbons in her hair, both holding their mother's hand. I myself wore a sharp black double-breasted pin-striped suit. And guess what? It didn't come from Nordstrom or even Lord and Taylor's, I got it from Target. We headed out the door, and we all walked slowly to the limousine that was parked out front waiting. Trinity loved the limousine ride, although she didn't fully understand exactly what was going on. Little Terry still wasn't talking. He just stared out the window. As we rode past Frederick Douglass High School, Tyra began to cry. That was the school where she and Terry had met. When we arrived at the church, there was a long line of people waiting to enter the church. There wasn't a parking space in sight, just the one reserved for the limousine. We watched as the police directed traffic. It was so crowded. I wasn't a bit surprised. Terry was well-known and loved by everyone. The limo driver got out of his car and walked to the back and opened the door for us. I climbed out and helped the kids get out. I turned to see what Tyra was doing, and she was sitting there staring at nothing in particular. I climbed back inside and sat next to her and gently touched her arm.

"I can't do this, Sollie," Tyra said holding her stomach. "How do I bury my soul mate, and their father?" she asked as her eyes welled up with tears.

"With love."

Tyra looked at me, and raised her head. Placing her small black clutch under her arm, she climbed out the limo and held her hands out for little Terry and Trinity, and we walked over to the church entrance. I stood directly behind her. Once inside the chapel, Tyra took a deep breath bent down, and kissed her kids. We all proceeded to walk inside and the organist began to play, His eyes is on a sparrow. Everyone stood as we entered the church, and the walk to where Terry laid in the beautiful sky-blue casket seemed a mile away. The church was standing room only. As I was walking, I noticed all our friends were there and some that I hadn't seen since high school. I spotted Mrs. Johnson standing there with Lamar holding on to his arm, and looking very frail and thin. I even noticed that the mayor of the city was there.

"Daddy!" Trinity yelled out, snatching her hand away from Tyra, dropping her doll, and running up to the casket. "Daddy, Daddy!" she yelled, reaching her tiny hand up to touch her father's arm, and then looked up at her mother. "Mommy, you said Daddy was in heaven. He's not in heaven. He's right here sleeping."

"Wake him up, Mommy," she said staring at her mother. "I want him to see my new dress." Tyra didn't know what to say as the tears streamed from her eyes. Tyra's mother walked over and took Trinity by the hand and took her over to the front pew where she was sitting. Little Terry still hadn't said anything. He just stood there next to his mother. Tyra bent down, and kissed Terry on his lips.

"I'll love you forever," she said softly.

She took little Terry by his hand, and went and sat down. "See you buddy, I love you." I said kissing Terry on his forehead. Everyone spoke so highly of Terry, and Judge Minor even cried as he said his remarks. After Judge Minor spoke, I looked at Mr. Jones, and he had the look of a proud father on his face. The eulogy was given; it was time to say good-bye. Tyra slowly walked up to the casket and kissed her husband one last time. Just as she proceeded to pull the satin spread up over Terry's face, little Terry jumped up.

"Daddy, I need you!" he yelled as he ran over to his mother's side crying hysterically.

I walked over and took him back to the seat and was able calm him down. I asked him if he wanted to go out and get some air, he shook his head no. I then asked if he wanted to go back over to see his father, he said yes.

I walked him back over to the casket, Tyra bent down and wiped the tears from her son eye's and told him how much his father loved him and after a few seconds passed little Terry finally said the words that I wish I had been given the chance to say sixteen years ago: he said good-bye to his father, and then assisted Tyra as she pulled the satin cover over his father's body. We all walked back over to our seat and Trinity climbed into her mother's lap and cried.

Chapter Thirty-Six

T he funeral was over and there were so many cars in the recession line that we had to be escorted by the police. The burial went quickly, and afterward we went to the banquet hall where the repast was being held. Lamar and Mrs. Johnson ate and then he took her home. She said she was tired. He returned and stayed until everything was over.

The weeks that followed were rough for Tyra and the kids. I missed Lamar like crazy, but I was where I needed to be. Tyra and Terry already had money, and now even more with the two-million-dollar insurance policy Terry had left.

She did tell one other person about Terry being her half brother and that was the kid's pediatrician. And what was once a mystery to them as to why the kids had a learning disability no longer was.

"Tyra, I can stay longer."

"No Sollie, you have done enough. You have been with us a whole month, you need to get back to your life and that fine boyfriend of yours.

Tyra handed me an envelope, inside was a check for ten-thousand dollars, she said she was giving it to me for staying with her and helping her through this trying time, of course I didn't take. I told her what I did was what friends are supposed to do.

Lamar came just in time, because I really didn't feel like going back and forth with Tyra, 'cause there was no way I was taking that check. I set the check back on the table, gave everyone a hug good-bye, and left.

Lamar and I headed straight to Mrs. Johnson's house. As we pulled up, I stared at my old house looking at the large red sign reading "SOLD."

Mrs. Johnson was so happy to see me, and I was equally happy to see her. At that moment I realized just how much I had come to love her, but I couldn't help notice how much weight she had lost. I wondered if the cancer had returned.

"Mrs. Johnson, Lamar told me that you are refusing to go back to your doctor and you have lost a lot of weight in just a short period of time. Why don't you...

She raised her hand "No Sollie I'm not going back."

"But Mrs. Johnson I think you . . ."

"Listen, sweetness," she said interrupting me again, "When it's time, I'll be going to glory." She had a very peaceful look on her face.

I looked at Lamar, and he tried to smile but I knew he was sad, because we both knew Mrs. Johnson didn't have long.

A few of Mrs. Johnson's church members came and had prayer with her. But Sister Betty wasn't there, and the ones who were didn't really seem sincere. One of them had one eye shut and the other open during prayer, looking around at Mrs. Johnson's house.

After they all left, we stayed and watched TV. Mrs. Johnson began fading in and out, while mumbling something that neither of us could understand. She was so weak Lamar had to carry her up to her bedroom. I wiped her down and then rubbed lotion all over her thin body, put her nightgown on, tucked her in the bed, and read scriptures to her from the Bible until she fell off asleep. We left and drove over to my mother's to drop off my suitcase.

After talking with my mother, we left and headed over to Lamar's place and for the next hour and a half we showed each other just how much we missed one another.

"Baby, what are you doing to me?" Lamar asked rolling over trying to catch his breath.

"I put it on you, didn't I?"

"Did you?!" He smiled.

My smile quickly disappeared; I curled up in his arms. "

What are you thinking about?" he asked.

"Everything; Mrs. Johnson was right. Life is really short."

"Yeah, it is. That's why we shouldn't take anything for granted," he said pulling me closer and holding me tighter.

I got up to go take a shower and Lamar pulled me back down on the bed. "Sollie Carr, I love you!"

"I love you too!"

The next day Lamar called out from work and we spent the whole day together, and later that evening we stopped over at Salique house.

Salique told me I was glowing, and how good it was to finally see me happy. And yes Lamar had a lot to do with my happiness, but for once, I was finally happy with me. All the work I had done with Dr. Parker was worth all the pain I had to endure. I was even ready to return to work and stop being afraid, and besides, Ahmaun probably wasn't even in the state anymore. As we drove over to see Mrs. Johnson, I told Lamar that I was going back to work.

"Are you sure?" he asked.

"Yes, I'm sure. I am going to call George tomorrow and let him know, and you know I haven't been getting paid."

"Sollie, listen if you feel you're ready then that's cool, by all means go back. But if you are doing it because of the money, I have money and you know I got you, right?"

"Thanks, Lamar, but I'm ready."

Lamar making that same statement as Ahmaun once did, telling me he had my back took me to where I never wanted to be again, and that was depending on someone to take care of me, which made me know that I was growing. As we pulled up to Mrs. Johnson's house my cell rang. It was Mrs. Johnson's doctor saying that she was just brought in by ambulance. Lamar pulled off and drove to the hospital.

When we arrived, Mrs. Johnson was hooked up to so many machines. The doctor came in and introduced himself to Lamar and me and asked us to follow him to his office.

"Please have a seat," he said.

"I don't want to have a seat. Just tell me what's wrong."

"Mrs. Johnson's blood work just came back from the lab and the cancer has spread throughout her body. I'm sorry, but the most we can do now is keep her comfortable."

"What about chemo?" I asked.

"I don't recommend it at this stage of the cancer. And at her age, the chemo would have no positive effect. It would make her sicker then she is. However, you are her power of attorney and the decision is totally up to you."

I didn't want her suffering any more than she was, but I didn't want her to die either.

"Ms. Carr, take your time and think about what I just said. I have to check on my other patients and I'll return shortly. And again I'm very sorry."

"Lamar, what should we do?"

"Baby, she's eighty-eight years old. She has lived past what God gives us, three scores and ten. If the chemo is going to make her sicker, then I agree with the doctor, I wouldn't recommend it."

"Lamar, what is three scores and ten?" I asked not understanding what he had just said to me.

"I'll show you later. It's in the Bible." Lamar and I headed back inside the room and sat quietly. I stared at the wooden cross that hung on the wall over the top of her hospital bed and prayed that I was making the right decision. I looked over at the large clock that slowly ticked realizing that each second that passed Mrs. Johnson was getting closer and closer to death. The nurses and the techs were back and forth checking her vitals. Each time they left the room they all had that remote look on their faces; that look of knowing that she would soon be gone. When the doctor returned, we told him that we decided against the chemo. Sitting back by Mrs. Johnson's bedside, I lowered my head and said, "I can't do this!"

"Yes, you can, Sollie. We are all she has, and you are not doing it alone. I am right here with you."

We left the hospital and went back to Mrs. Johnson's house and made sure all the lights were turned off. The next day Lamar called out of work, and we went back to the hospital. When we got there we were shocked to see Mrs. Johnson sitting up and talking to the nurse.

"Hi, how are my two sweetie-pies doing?" she said smiling at us as we entered the room.

I leaned over and kissed her on the forehead. I walked over to the crystal vase that sat on the small wooden table next to her bed and put fresh flowers in it that I had picked from her rose garden last night, and sat her "get well" card next to it.

"How do you feel Mrs. Johnson?"

"Oh, I feel fine, baby, just fine. I dreamed about my Henry last night, and he was so happy to see me. I miss him so much," she said as she began humming and rocking her head side to side to an old hymn "When I see Jesus." She stopped and looked at us and asked bluntly, "When are you two getting married?"

"I don't know, Mrs. Johnson," I said smiling, but not understanding the drastic change in her from yesterday.

"Soon," Lamar said interrupting me. "So you hurry and get better so you can be at the wedding!" She smiled and reached out for our hands.

"You two take care of each other. She's your queen, and he's your king, and don't put stuff off. Life's too short! Seem like just yesterday Henry and I was your ages, and I thank God that he blessed us with fifty-three years of a beautiful marriage." A tear rolled down her face. "But promise me. Promise me, you will stick together." She squeezed our hands tighter and then began to cough uncontrollably.

Lamar reached for the pitcher of water and poured some into the cup, he gently lifted Mrs. Johnson's head so that she could take a sip. Just as he laid her head down, she said softly that she wasn't going home. And with the look in her eyes, I knew that what she said was true.

"Yes, you are. Look at you. You're doing better already"

"No baby not that home." She gently rubbed my hand.

"Listen to me. Go to my house. Then look in my bedroom inside the dresser next to the window in the third drawer under my panty hoses. You'll find a folder with all my funeral and burial arrangements already made. All you have to do is give the undertaker my insurance policy. And Sollie," she said beginning to lose her breath, "Put me away in all white."

"Mrs. Johnson, don't talk like that. You are going to be just fine!"

"It's okay. I lived a good life, sugar pie, a good life!" she said beginning to fade in and out.

"Mrs. Johnson!" I said shaking her hand. "Lamar, get the nurse!"

As Lamar went to leave the room, she slowly opened her eyes. Lamar walked back over to her bed and she smiled with a look of peace on her face, and softly whispered, "Henry," took three deep breaths and closed her eyes, and that was it. The woman that I had grown to have heartfelt love for, was gone.

Chapter Thirty-Seven

T   he nurse confirmed Mrs. Johnson's death. We did exactly what Mrs. Johnson asked, and the folder was where she said it would be. I notified the funeral home, called the few numbers she had in her phone book. It was hard to believe she had no family members, none at all. I went to the mall and bought Mrs. Johnson a beautiful white dress, and five days later we buried her. It was only a handful of people; the funeral was short and so was her obituary. I had very little information about her life; only what few church members could tell me. After the funeral, a church member gave me her number and said to call her if I needed help cleaning out Mrs. Johnson's house. I knew that her house was paid for, but there was nothing anywhere saying who the house goes to. I found the deed, but the only person's name on it was hers and Mr. Johnson's.

Lamar and I had no choice but to lock the house up and check on it periodically to see if any letters or anything might come telling us who the house goes to.

I went to work the following week, and it was a pleasure to be back. Ms. Susie's granddaughter was doing well, and everything seemed to be coming back together with the exception of Ahmaun still being out there somewhere.

I sat at my desk staring at the picture that Lamar and I had taken, and I thanked God for him once again. Later that day, he called and said that he wanted to take me to dinner. My workday was over, and I headed straight home to get ready for our date.

When I got to the house, I wondered where my mother was. I had talked to her earlier and she didn't mention that she was going anywhere. I called to check on Tyra, and she didn't answer. I headed up to my room, put on my Al Green CD, pulled out my sexy little black dress, took a quick shower, got dressed, and headed downstairs to get the door.

"You're beautiful!" Lamar said smiling, as I opened the door.

"Thank you, Mr. Lamar." I smiled. "So where are we going? I'm starving."

"Ocean Air," he replied.

On the way to dinner, we stopped at Mrs. Johnson's to see if there was any mail concerning the house, but there was nothing but bills.

When we arrived at the restaurant the waiter escorted us to our seats, and sat us in a very secluded area, away from the other people that were dining.

"Lamar, you know I'm nosey. Why did he sit us so far away from everyone else?"

"I wanted some privacy."

I then looked down and noticed one single red rose lying in front of me on the table. I smiled as I picked it up and smelled it.

"You told them to do this, didn't you?" I asked as I leaned over and kissed him.

The waiter took our wine order and returned with our two glasses of Merlot. He nodded his head to Lamar and walked away. What was that about, I said, getting ready to call him back. He didn't even ask if we wanted to order any appetizers. Just I went to call him, Lamar asked me to wait. He stood up from his chair and walked around to me, and wouldn't you know it, he got down on one knee. My eyes widened, and just that fast filled up with tears.

"Oh my god Lamar."

"Baby, I love you, and I want, no, I need you in my life. This last year you have been through a lot, and yes it was a struggle at times, but you came out the winner, and I'm so proud to have watched you grow. You are a beautiful, intelligent, strong black woman who I have had the pleasure of falling in love with. I had no idea when I moved to Baltimore that my one true gift was here waiting for me. It was totally unexpected, and yes, that's what you are to me, my gift, my blessing. And I welcome you with open arms to be in my life forever. I don't want another day, another minute of my life to go on without knowing that you will soon become Mrs. Lamar Lane. I love, cherish, and adore you. Sollie, please say you will spend the rest of your life with me." He reached in his pocket and pulled out a beautiful teardrop diamond ring. "Sollie Carr, will you marry me?"

"Yes, Lamar, yes, I will marry you." I said holding my hand out, and watched as he slid the beautiful ring on my finger and it fit perfectly. Before I knew it, all my family and friends came over to us.

"Y'all knew about this?" I asked, crying and hugging all of them.

And then B. walked in with their grandmother as a surprise to Lamar. He was so happy to see his grandmother, he cried. He walked over and hugged her tightly. Everyone stood there watching this beautiful eighty-four-year-old woman gracefully reach her hand out for me to come to her. Lamar introduced us, and she leaned over and kissed me.

"You're precious!" she said staring at me with her eyes filled with wisdom. "I have heard nothing but lovely things about you. Welcome, Sollie, to my family."

We moved to a larger table that Lamar had reserved, and the questions began.

"When are you two going to set a date?" my mother asked.

"Big or small?" B. asked.

"Big, of course!" my mother exclaimed.

"Have an evening wedding. They're so romantic." Mea said.

"Sollie, I know, I'm it," Jodi mugged.

"Yeah right! And whose side are you going to stand on, Mr. Man!" Duce gritted, while Tyra fell out laughing.

"All right, Dante!" my mother said, calling Duce by his real name, and warning him not to start it.

"All I know is, I don't believe in long engagements, so if it's all right with Lamar, I would like to start planning our wedding as soon as tomorrow."

"Tomorrow is not soon enough!" Lamar said kissing me.

We all sat and ate, and continued talking about the upcoming wedding. B. left to take their grandmother back to his place. She was leaving in the morning to fly back to Atlanta. I went over to Lamar's place, and we celebrated our engagement all night long.

The next morning, Lamar went to the airport with B. to see their grandmother off. I was so tired, but I made it to work. Everyone was so happy for me, especially, George. As I was leaving work for the day, my mother called and asked if I was coming straight home. I told her I was going to stop at the mall to pick up some wedding magazines and then I would be there. She said that she had stopped at the old house earlier to meet with the realtor and that there were several letters addressed to me and Lamar from a law firm.

I wondered what they could have been about, and why they would be addressed to Lamar; he never lived there. When I got to the house, Lamar and my mother were sitting in the kitchen talking. I kissed them both, and she handed me the letters. I asked Lamar why he didn't open them. He said he wanted to wait for me.

I began opening the letters and every one of them asked that Lamar and I both contact the office immediately. I dialed the number and placed the call on speakerphone mode while I made a sandwich.

"Good evening, Simon and Simon Law Offices, may I help you?" the woman said politely over the phone.

"Hi, my name is Sollie Carr. I have received several letters from your law firm to call immediately, and I have no idea as to why."

"Oh my! Please hold on a second. Mr. Simon has been trying to reach you!" I looked at Lamar and my mother still not understanding what this was all about.

"Hello, Ms. Carr. I'm attorney, Ray Simon. I have been trying to contact you for a little over a month. One number I have is no longer a working number, and the other has been changed."

"Yeah, I had my number changed. But can you please just tell me what this matter is concerning," I said, putting a heaping spoonful of mayo on my sandwich.

"Is it possible that you could come to my office? I would really like to get this matter resolved today."

"What matter?" I asked beginning to get very impatient.

"Oh gee! I apologize. I represent the estate of the late Mae Johnson."

I looked at Lamar and my mother and whispered, "Estate."

"Ms. Carr, you do know the whereabouts of a Mr. Lamar Lane?"

"Yes, I do. He's my fiancé. And he's sitting right here with me."

"Wonderful! I need Mr. Lane to accompany you."

Lamar looked at my mother in confusion and so did I, not understanding what was going on. We all headed for his office.

"Lamar, maybe, he has information on whom the house goes to. I sure hope he doesn't think we were trying to keep it. That's the only thing I can think of that he could want."

"Sollie, we will explain to him the circumstances behind it. We had no idea Mrs. Johnson had an attorney handling her business matters."

We pulled up to the huge building in the heart of downtown. We all went inside and stood there waiting for the elevator and had to ride fifteen flights up. Although elevators make me feel queasy, for some reason, that ride made me feel worse than normal.

"Hello, I'm Ray Simon. Nice to finally meet you," he said walking out into the waiting area and shaking all of our hands. "I know earlier I was talking a bit fast, and I apologize for that. I was on my way to meet some other colleagues at the golf course, but when the call came from you, Ms. Carr, I knew I needed to cancel. I really want to get this matter resolved, at any rate. Let's get started. Come with me." We followed him back to his office. "Please have a seat. Our office was notified about Mrs. Johnson's death through her insurance company. It was written in her policy for this office to receive the balance left after all of her funeral and burial costs were paid. Are you two still at this address?"

"No, we're not, and with so much going on, I never put in for a change of address," I said.

"Okay, you're here now, which is great! Let's get to the matter at hand," he said, scratching out the old address and flipping through the papers inside the brown folder. "Mrs. Johnson must have been very fond of you two. She left you and Mr. Lane her entire estate!"

"Mr. Simon, what are you talking about her house?" I asked.

"No, Ms. Carr, Mrs. Johnson had quite a bit more than her house." He chuckled. "I think it would be safe to say, Mrs. Mae Johnson was a millionaire!"

"What!" Lamar said.

"Mr. Simon, what exactly are you saying?"

"I am saying you two have inherited everything!" he said removing his glasses and laying them on his desk. "After sorting out everything from insurance policy, stocks, bonds, investment, and CD in which she and her late husband accumulated over the fifty-three years they were married made her a very wealthy woman!" He smiled warmly.

After all was said and done, Mrs. Johnson was in fact a millionaire, and that was not including the house that she left for us. We were all speechless.

"Sollie and Lamar, right before Mrs. Johnson became ill; she came to the office and changed her will, from who she initially had left everything to."

"Mr. Simon, is it possible you can tell me who that person was?"

He paused for a moment, I guess, knowing that it was confidential information

"Ooh, what the hell," he said, opening the folder. "The person that she had down originally was a Betty Brown."

"Betty Brown," I said, "ohhhh, Sister Betty."

"Do you know her, baby?" my mother asked.

"Yes, I do. She was one of her church members."

330

"Well, whoever she was, for some reason Mrs. Johnson had became very displeased with her. I didn't question her as to why she was changing her will, but when she was signing the papers she whispered something about her backsliding and that she was running around with the devil himself! And how Mr. Johnson would roll over in his grave if she got all the money they had saved all these years, and that she was leaving it to two well-deserving people, which was obviously you two."

I tried not to laugh, knowing the devil she was speaking of was Duce.

"Sollie and Lamar, it says a lot about you two for someone to leave you this much financial wealth. Please feel free to call my office if you have any questions regarding this matter. Congratulations and good luck to you both." He shook our hand, and handed us the folder.

"Well, baby, I was going to give you the money from the sale of the house, but I guess you don't need it now," my mother said hugging Lamar and me. "You two are truly blessed."

The next morning, we both called out from work and went to Mrs. Johnson's bank, and spoke with a financial analyst. And when we walked out of there, Lamar or I never had to work again if we chose not to.

"Lamar, are you okay?" I asked looking at the blank look on his face.

"Sollie, I just can't believe it. I don't know what to say."

"And all this time, I assumed Mrs. Johnson was broke. Why didn't she ever fix her house up and always wearing old torn clothes?"

"Never judge a book by its cover!" Lamar said still seeming to be in shock.

"Well, I guess I can finally open my restaurant."

As we stopped at the red light, I looked over and there was Remi looking a hot mess! I prayed she wouldn't spot me, but she did.

"Sollie, Sollie!" she said running over to the car. "Girl, you look good!" she said bending over and scratching her back. "How you doinnnnn?" she asked Lamar. "Girl, is this your new man? I heard he was fine, but goddamn, he fine as fuck!" she said stomping her feet and placing her hands on her hips. "Sollie, can you spare some change, just a little something so I can get me something to eat. I'll pay you back, I promise. I start my job next week!" She lied. "Oh girl! I know you heard somebody whipped my ass and made me lose my baby!" She scratched her arms, dancing to the music that was obviously playing in her head.

No, she didn't just mention that baby. I was heated. But at that very moment I thought about all the work I had done on myself and learning what forgiving does for your spirit. I forgave Remi.

"Remi, did they ever find out who did it?" I asked.

"Nah, girl, that motherfucker must have been a ghost or something. I didn't even see her coming! And I damn sure didn't see her leaving. You know she beat me unconscious!"

"How do you know it was a female?"

"Sollie, come on now, look at my face. All these fuckin scratches and shit, and look at this." She lifted her shirt. "Look how that bitch scratch my stomach up! It was like her main focus was my baby! Shit, I had to get thirteen stitches right here." She pointed to an ugly scar on her stomach. "The way she whip my ass, that bitch must have been some kind of animal!" She fell over laughing like something was funny. "Sollie, come on, hook a sister up," she asked, now doing the *Cha-Cha.*

I looked over at Lamar, and he had this look of sheer disbelief on his face as he looked at her scars. Before I could say anything, Lamar reached in his pocket and asked me if it was okay. I nodded my head yes, and he handed her a twenty-dollar bill.

"Oh my God. Thank you, brother! You is all right, goddamn you all right," she said clapping her hands together. "Y'all be safe." As she walked away she turned and called my name. "I'm sorry. I really am sorry for all that I did to you." Then she quickly ran across the street, almost getting hit by a car, and straight up the alley to catch the guy that had exactly what she needed. Lamar couldn't believe that Remi was B.'s ex-girlfriend.

"Lamar, I want the biggest, most expensive wedding ever!"

"Sollie, listen. Yes we do have money now, but we must spend and invest it wisely or it will get away from us. I want you to have the wedding of your dream and you're going to, but you don't have to spend a million dollars. So right now let's set a spending limit."

"Okay. Eighty thousand," I said jokingly. Lamar looked at me as if I was crazy.

"Twenty thousand," Lamar said smiling.

"Twenty!" I whined. "Forty thousand."

"Sollie, we still have to live after the wedding, and where going to invest it, just as Mr. and Mrs. Jonson did. We have to think of our future, and most importantly, our kids. We have got to start building for their future as well. And I guarantee, if we don't do the right thing with this money, it will get away from us."

"Okay, thirty- thousand, and that's my final offer!" We both began to laugh.

"Sollie, what would have been our limit if we never got this money?"

"I don't know. I guess with both of our income, maybe twenty thousand," I said, slowly coming back to reality, and realizing that Lamar was right.

"Now that's what I'm talking about. Twenty thousand it is."

"Okay, cool, but that doesn't include the cost of the wedding planner, and I know exactly who I want." I said.

"Okay so twenty thousand for the wedding, and whatever the wedding planner charges. And who is the wedding planner you're going to use?"

"Tyra's cousin, and she is excellent. I saw a few weddings she had done. I'll get in touch with her later." When we pulled up at my mother's house, Detective Holloway was pulling up at the same time.

"Hi Ms. Carr, how have you been?"

"I have been fine. Why are you here? Has Ahmaun been caught?"

"Unfortunately, he has not been apprehended. However, there has been a reporting that he was spotted on the west side of the city, with a woman."

"A woman." I replied. "You what I bet it's the person who was calling and threatening me.

"We have retrieved the surveillance camera from the area in which he was spotted and I would like you to come down to central and take a look at it to see if you recognize him or the woman."

Lamar, my mother, and me rode downtown with the detective. He took us to a room filled with all kinds of computerized equipment and monitors. We sat at the table and proceeded to watch the surveillance video although I could barely see anything. The video was really blurred. The detective hit a button and the picture cleared up just a little. All I could see was someone wearing a black hoody slouched down in the seat of a car, and almost fell out the chair when I recognized the car.

Chapter Thirty-Eight

"O   h my god, that's the car that was following me that day!"

"Yes it is!" Lamar said nodding his head.

The detective eyes widened "So you recognize this car?"

"Yes, I do!"

"Ms. Carr, do you recognize the woman?" he asked, pointing to the monitor at a woman getting in the car. She was wearing a long black trench coat but I couldn't see her face. She got in the car and kissed whoever it was inside.

"Right here, Ms. Carr," the detective said anxiously hitting the button once again. "Take a closer look. When they are pulling off, the person in the passenger seat turns his head slightly!" He hit another button and the screen zoomed in closer. And yes, it was Ahmaun!

"That's him! He is here in Baltimore. Where could he have been all this time?" I frantically asked.

"Ms. Carr, we really don't feel that he has been in Baltimore or the surrounding area. We feel that he just returned to the state."

"Calm down, baby," Lamar said. "They're going to catch him."

"No, they're not! All these months he has been on the run." I looked at the detective. "Where is this located?" I asked.

"It's at a gas station on W. North Avenue. Ms. Carr, we are going to place a twenty-four-hour cruiser at your home."

"No, you're not, because I won't be there! And Mommy, you're staying with Lamar and me, or over at Salique house."

"Who is Salique?" The detective sked.

"He's my brother."

"Sollie, that is out of the question. I am not leaving my house," my mother said.

"Ms. Carr, does Ahmaun know where your fiancé lives?"

"Knowing him, he probably does!"

"Sollie, I doubt that seriously. Only one who knows where I live is you and B. so there is no way he can know," Lamar said.

"Yeah, and Mea, the way she runs her mouth." I called Mea down the shop and she swore she never mentioned to anyone where Lamar lived.

"Ms. Carr, I think it would be safe if you stayed with your daughter, I assume that the suspect knows where your son lives.

"That's right, he does."

"This suspect is armed and, of course, very dangerous. Just know that we are truly doing everything in our power to apprehend him."

Back at my mother's, she packed a few things and called Salique to let him know exactly what was going on. We all left and headed over to Lamar's. I showed my mother where she would be sleeping. She calmly changed into something comfortable, pulled out her book, and put on a gospel cd.

I asked her, how she could be so calm.

"That's the God in me." She smiled warmly. "And we all are going to be fine." She said hugging and kissing me.

"Lamar, I can't get him, and that car, out my head." I said walking into the living room. "So I was right. He did know who was following me that day. And the phone calls and the women are all connected." I said.

"Sollie, I know you're afraid and you have every right to be, but try and stop worrying. Come on and sit down." Lamar said.

I suggested to Lamar that we postpone the wedding until he's caught.

I could tell he didn't like it, but we needed to do this. No one knew Ahmaun better than me, and he was going to do whatever he had to get Lamar and me back.

"Sollie, I'm agreeing to this, but I'm letting you know now, we are not going to put our lives and dreams on hold for that clown. Hell, they may never catch him! And then what?"

I could hear the song *No Weapons Formed Against Me* . . . playing in the guest room. A feeling of comfort and peace came over me. And I realized Lamar was right. I was not going to put our lives on hold for him.

I happily told Lamar that we weren't postponing anything.

A few minutes later B. knocked on the door. "Hey B." I said, greeting him with a hug.

I headed into the kitchen to make dinner.

My mother woke up from her nap and joined us in the living room.

"Oh yeah, about the wedding, I forgot to tell y'all I met this fine sister the other night, and during our conversation I mentioned the wedding to her. And she's actually a wedding planner." B. reached into his wallet and handed us her card. "The way she pushed up on me, I thought for sure she was trying to holla, but she later told me that she was married. B. said disappointingly. "Check her out, if you're interested."

"No, no, no! I already have a wedding planner."

"You do?" my mother asked.

"Yes, I do. Tyra's cousin. She's classy, has good taste, and besides, I know her work. I have seen a few weddings that she had done."

"Melanie Omar, Melanie Omar." Lamar repeated. "That name sounds familiar," Lamar said, looking at the card. "B., we went to high school with some Omar's. You remember those two crazy brothers? You know, man, Bobby and Michel Omar."

"Yeah, that's right. Those cats were treacherous! Remember, their whole family was crazy. Weren't they in the mob or something?"

"No they weren't, but they should have been. They were terrible. You only see how they carried it on television. The family was dangerous; the father, uncles, all of them. People used to say they were raised from kids to be hit men."

"Well, anyway, we don't need a wedding planner. I have one," I said taking the card from Lamar and walking into the kitchen, throwing the card on the kitchen table. As I began setting the table for dinner, I heard Lamar say, "Turn it up! Sollie! Come in here!" he yelled.

"What's wrong?" I asked running into the living room.

"Look! They caught him. Wait, wait, listen!"

Chapter Thirty-Nine

"W   e interrupt this program for breaking news to report," the news reporter said excitedly. *"Thirty-two-year-old Ahmaun Moore has just been apprehended by the U.S. Marshall's at the Baltimore/Washington International Thurgood Marshall Airport. Authorities say a tip lead them to the fugitive's arrest. The suspect has been on the run for several months. He's wanted for the alleged murder of Officer Jullian Smith and attempted murder of Officer Raymond Guy. Please tune in for the five o'clock news for more on this breaking story. Now back to your regular programming."*

"Thank you, Jesus!" my mother screamed. She opened her arms widely "It's over, it's finally over! I told you, baby, I told you everything would be all right. Now let's go get married in peace."

My mother started singing *Going to the Chapel* as she danced around the living room. My cell was ringing off the hook, and I was so busy talking on the phone, I burned the spaghetti. We all went out for dinner. And it was a pleasure not to be looking over my shoulders for once.

During dinner my mother convinced me to let her pay for my wedding gown. And I knew just what I wanted, a Vera Wang original.

"What are you two going to do with the money the lady left y'all?" B. asked.

"Well, a lot of it we are going to continue to invest. Sollie is going to finally be able to open her restaurant. We're going to buy a house, and we are going to turn Mrs. Johnson's house into an assisted living home for elderly people with no family. And then you know, we have to look out for Ms. Marie and Grandmother."

B. looked at us with a look as to say "What about me."

Lamar and I laughed and told B. "You know we got you."

"Well as for me, I'm fine. You and Sollie take that money and do just what you said, and besides, my bank account is a little fat also!" my mother said smiling.

B asked were we going to quit our jobs, and Lamar asked him was he crazy. I did asked Lamar how would he feel about me quitting my job and becoming a full time student, I wanted to get a degree in business management. He told me to go for it. And my mother was beyond happy. The next day I went to work and handed in my resignation. George wasn't pleased, but was happy to hear about my good fortune.

"Remember, I told you that you were going to be blessed, and you have been blessed with much, much more than you gave." He hugged me and wished me good luck in my future endeavors.

I left the job and headed to Lamar's place. As soon as I walked in the door, I stretched my ass across the couch. I smiled as Lamar walked through the door.

"Were you bored today?" he asked, leaning over and kissing me.

"Yeah, right, are you serious? I called some colleges and requested that they send me some information on the business courses they offer. When we return from our honeymoon, I'll go and visit a few of them."

"That's good. Are you excited?" Lamar asked.

"Very excited," I said, thinking of how great my life was.

We ate dinner and then left to go to my mother to meet with the wedding planner. When we got to her house, Tyra and Jasmine were sitting in the dining room talking with my mother, and I couldn't help but notice the sadness that still filled Tyra eyes.

Jasmine smiled as we walked in. "Tyra said you two were a beautiful couple, and you really are." She said.

Tyra seemed to perk up a little once we started talking about the details of the wedding.

"See this is why I wanted you as my wedding planner." I said looking at the table with samples of everything, from save the date invites to fabric samples.

"Okay first things first. It's always good to set a spending limit. Have you two set one?" Lamar quickly answered, yes. I looked at him and laughed.

"Jasmine, all my groomsmen reside in Georgia with the exception of Brother. Is that going to be a problem?" Lamar asked.

"Not at all. The company you have chosen has a store inside Lenox Mall. Once you have chosen your style of suits, I will call each of them, and they can go there and get fitted. But for now let's browse through the book just to get an idea of the style you want."

"Sollie, have you chosen your bridesmaid's yet?"

"Actually, I have."

"And of course, we know who your maid of honor is," Jasmine said, smiling at Tyra.

"No, actually, I was going to make Jodi the maid of honor," I said, trying to make Tyra laugh.

"Sollie, don't make me fight you!" Tyra said, managing to smile just a little.

"And Jasmine, you know me," I said, pulling out the bridal magazine I had bought, "I pick these dresses for the girls. I already e-mailed all of them a picture and they all loved the dresses. Also I took the liberty of calling the wedding boutique and making an a appointment for this Saturday. " I smiled.

"Well gees, do you even need me?" Jasmine laughed.

"I'm sorry and yes I need you, I'm just excited that's all." I said wrapping my arm around Lamar.

Tyra looked at us and smiled. "I'm so happy for you two," she said wiping her eyes.

I called all the girls and told them to meet me at Mother's house on Saturday."

The upcoming week was hectic. We had to meet with Rev. Martin, the videographer, the photographer, the manager, and the top chef at the Champagne Room who had all kinds of sample food for us to choose from.

My cell rang, and it was Jodi, probably calling to see why I didn't ask her to be in the wedding.

"Hello."

"What's up, nigga!"

"Heyyyyyy, Jodi."

"Where the hell you been?"

"Jodi, come on, now. I'm getting married or have you forgotten?"

"No, I haven't forgot. I just left Mea's shop and that's all everyone is talking about, Sollie's wedding. You weren't going to ask me to be in it? Mea said that you all go for the first fitting this weekend," Jodi said disappointedly.

"Jodi, look, you know you're my girl, but are you willing to put a dress on?"

"Hell no, I ain't puttin on no damn dress!"

"Exactly, that's why I didn't ask you. Listen, I have to go. I promise I will call you later."

"Is she upset?" Lamar asked.

"I guess. I would love to have Jodi in our wedding. We have been friends forever, but like she said she's not putting on a dress."

"Oh well, too bad," Tyra said rolling her eyes, "she will just miss out. That's all."

"Sollie, why don't we let her be an usher? We only have Duce so far. That way she can wear a tux and still be a part of the wedding."

"Girlllll, Duce is going to have a fit!" Tyra said smiling.

"Whatever! He will just have to get over it! Jasmine, I'm sorry, we're just talking, let me explain what is going on."

I explained the situation to Jasmine. She didn't exactly think we were crazy. She told us that she was gay also, and that statement quickly took the smile off Tyra's face, now knowing she has a gay cousin. I called Jodi back and asked her if she wanted to be an usher and she happily said yes.

"What did the little boy say?" Tyra asked. She then looked at Jasmine. "I'm sorry, Jasmine," Tyra said realizing she may have offended her cousin.

"Girl, please, that mess does not bother me. I think it bothers you more. You need to get over it and let people be who they are."

We all said good night to each other, and Lamar and I headed back to the apartment. We were so tired we ordered a pizza and dozed off on the couch, until we were awakened from the phone ringing. It was Jasmine telling us that she had to leave town on emergency. Her mother's house had been robbed, and she had been severely beaten. She said that she would be right over to return our deposit to us. I felt really bad hearing about her mother, and I prayed that she would be okay. But I must admit I was very disappointed that she wouldn't be able to finish the job.

"Let's elope!" I said hanging up the phone.

"Are you serious?"

"Yes, I am, very serious. We can go anywhere in the world we want."

"Okay, come here. Let me take you to paradise," he said, laughing and pulling me closer. "Baby, we can't elope our family would kill us!" He placed his soft lips on mine, just as I started to remove my jeans Jasmine knocked on the door.

"Lamar, the door!"

"Let her knock," he mumbled as he sucked my breast.

"Lamar, stop!" I said laughing, trying to pull away from him. "It's probably Jasmine."

"So what?"

"She has our deposit"

"Oh shit! Let her in." He laughed.

I quickly tried to fix my clothes and opened the door.

"Hi Jasmine."

"I'm sorry, did I disturb you?" Jasmine smiled, looking down at my jeans as I tried to zip them up. "Here you are, Sollie, and I'm so sorry about this. And also here is the number of a wedding planner. She is a very good friend of mine, and she does excellent work as well. I already called her and left a message, so she should be expecting your call. You guys be blessed." She rushed out the door.

You guys be blessed. I repeated angrily. I was pissed as I dialed the number on the card she had just given me. She must be mighty good to be able to come and take over where Jasmine left off. She answered the phone, and said, unfortunately, that she was booked. This was unbelievable. What was I going to do? Lamar was sitting there eating a cold slice of pizza. Guys have it so easy, no worries in the world! Pick out a tux, get their haircut, and just show up! I walked over to the closet and took out the yellow pages. "Two months before the wedding!" I said angrily flipping through the pages.

"See what I mean. It's always something," I said to Lamar.

"Baby, what about some of your other friends. Can't they plan a wedding?"

"Lamar, no. I want a professional wedding planner, a professional."

"What about the card B. gave you last week?"

"What about it? I don't know her, and I don't know what kind of work she does. I'm rich now. I'll hire Colin Cowie to be our wedding planner!" We both laughed, even though Lamar had no idea who he was. "Lamar, seriously, what are we going to do?"

"Sollie, call the lady and see what she is talking about. Just ask for some references, that's all."

I glanced up at Lamar and smirked. "I think I threw her card away."

"No, you didn't. It's still lying there on the kitchen table. Go ahead, baby. Call her."

I hesitantly walked in the kitchen and grabbed the card off the table, looking at how very tacky it looked. "Looks like somebody just threw it together," I said, reaching for the phone and dialing the number. She answered on the first ring.

"Hi, I'm trying to reach Melanie Omar."

"Hello, this is Melanie speaking," she said very properly.

That's a good sign. *At least she doesn't talk like Jodi,* I thought.

"Hi, my name is Sollie. You gave my brother-in-law, well, soon to be, your business card, and I am in desperate need of a wedding planner."

"When is the wedding, Sollie?"

"Two months from today."

"Hold one second while I check my calendar. I'm available," she said returning to the phone.

"You are! How soon can we meet?"

"I can meet you now if you like. What is your address, sweetie?"

It's ten at night. She sure seems pressed. I thought

"Ms. Omar, now is not a good time. What about Sunday, at three?"

"Sunday, at three, is fine," she said, sounding disappointed. "What's your address?" she asked again.

"Everything is taking place at my mother's." I gave her the address and asked her to bring names of references and any photos she may have of her work. She hesitated, and then said, okay. "Thanks, Ms. Omar. I'll see you then."

"Sollie, please call me Melanie."

"Okay, Melanie, bye."

"It will work out just fine, you'll see. Now come over here and let's finish what the big girl interrupted." I didn't hesitate as I quickly removed my clothes and made love to my future husband.

Sunday came and my mother cooked a big dinner. Tyra met us there; she wanted to meet Melanie also. I invited my other girls over, but I told them to come at six. I really wanted to get a chance to talk with Melanie and see what her credentials were.

"Sollie, calm down," my mother said as I nervously kept looking out the window.

"Sollie, please sit down. It's only two. She's not coming until three. And where is her business card?" Tyra asked.

"It's right here. Why?" I said reaching into my purse.

"I just want to see it, that's all," Tyra said, taking the card out of my hand.

"I just hope she works out."

"I hope so too. You know B. and his taste in women. Either they look good and are tack heads or they look a hot mess and are still tack heads," Tyra said and we all laughed.

Three on the dot, the doorbell rang, and my mother broke her neck to answer it. Looking at her watch, she said, "She's on time. That's a plus."

Chapter Forty

I n walked a tall, very beautiful woman. Her complexion was a caramel color and her eyes were hazel; her hair was styled in a soft roller wrap, similar to mine. She could have easily been on the cover of a magazine. She had on a black Prada suit, and a sharp pair of black spaghetti-strapped Chanel stilettos. I stood up to greet her and said, "You're beautiful."

"Did you think I wouldn't be?" she retorted.

Wow! Sharp, and the bitch is conceded! I let that statement go. As long as she could get what I needed done to make my wedding as less stressful as possible, she could be conceded all she wanted to be. I looked at Tyra and the "Oh no, she didn't just say that" look on her face was priceless! I knew in that quick second Tyra had already formed an opinion of Melanie. I reached out to shake her hand. "I'm sorry, and no disrespect but I'm germaphobdic and don't shake others hands."

Tyra eyes widened "Well, I be…"

My mother called out Tyra name, and slightly shook her head.

Tyra apologized, and then glared at Melanie.

"I love your shoes," I said trying to break the tension that was now in the air. And when I complimented her shoes her eyes lit up like a child's on a Christmas morning.

"Let me guess, Lord & Taylor?"

"How did you know?" she asked, now smiling.

"I have the exact same pair."

I introduced her to everyone. We sat down and began to talk. She was very well spoken, articulate, but she really didn't have much experience as a wedding planner. She said that she was just starting out, but I definitely liked her style. Although she was a little strange, she had class! I asked her if she brought her references and she said that I could check out her Web site and read a few that are posted. Lamar and I excused ourselves and went into the kitchen and talked, and we decided to hire Melanie as our wedding planner.

When we walked back into the living room, I noticed Tyra was staring at Melanie with a strange look on her face, and I couldn't wait until Melanie left to get Tyra opinion.

"Well, Melanie, if you will accept, you're hired." We discussed her fee, which wasn't expensive at all. I wrote her a check, sealed the deal with a smile, and I excitedly asked if she brought anything with her.

"What do you mean?" she asked.

"You know magazines, samples of fabrics, anything. Although we pretty much have the basics, I'm always open to new ideas." She sat there looking dumbfounded as if she had no idea what the hell I was talking about.

"Melanie, were you born and raised here?" Lamar asked.

"Yes, I was. Why do you ask?"

"Your last name is very odd. I'm from Atlanta, Georgia, and I went to school with two brothers who have the same last name as yours."

"No, born and raised right here in Baltimore!" she said, nervously rubbing her hands together. "Where are you two going for your honeymoon?" she asked, somewhat agitated and unable to keep still.

I BE DAMN

"Jamaica mon," Lamar said, getting up and dancing into the kitchen.

"Are you leaving right from the reception?"

"No, the next morning," I said.

"So you are going to stay home on your wedding night?" she asked crossing her legs. And I could have sworn that I saw a black dildo inserted inside of her pussy. I shook my head thinking I must be tired.

I cleared my throat. "Actually, no, we're going to stay at the Drake Plaza hotel that night. As a matter of fact, where is that information, Lamar?" I asked looking through my papers.

"It's home, on the living room table."

I asked Melanie if she'd like to stay for dinner, and she accepted. All the girls came over and everyone ate and then just sat around in the living room talking about the wedding. Melanie didn't say too much, just sat quietly. She did ask if I could get her a glass of water because she had a headache. She then reached into her pocketbook and pulled out a bottle of pills. I have never seen headache pills that large, and I watched as she struggled to swallow the large blue pill.

My mother went to lie down, and Lamar left. He had to go and pick up little Terry from basketball practice. Lamar had become like a big brother to him.

Jodi came in and greeted everyone. I introduced Jodi to Melanie and they seemed to get along well, a little too well if you ask me. Her cell rang; she looked at the screen, and said she had to leave and that she would see us on Saturday. Just as she left out the door, Tyra came down the stairs.

"She's fine as shit! And fat as a motherfucker!" Jodi exclaimed watching Melanie's as she left.

"She is pretty, Tyra I have been dying to ask, what do you think?"

"There's something about her I don't like. And why was she asking all those questions about the honeymoon? Sorryyyyy, I don't like her. I was upstairs on the computer and you should see her Web site and just like her business card it looks as if it was just thrown

349

together," Tyra said handing me Melanie's card and then walking into the kitchen.

"Awwww man, go ahead wit dat! There you go. You don't even know her. Just shut up sometimes!" Jodi said rolling her eyes.

"Sollie asked my opinion, so I gave it to her. You mind your business, Mr. Man."

"And that's exactly what it is: your opinion. That don't mean jack shit!"

"Listen y'all for real, just chill out. Right now I don't have any other options, and besides, she's only here for a minute."

Tyra sat down and began eating her food.

"I know one thing. I'm going to get that ass, watch!" Jodi exclaimed licking her lips.

"Jodi, that woman is not gay, and besides she has a husband."

"That's what you think. A gay woman knows another gay woman! And who the fuck cares about her husband."

"Jodi, are you saying she's gay?" Mea asked in disbelief.

"I'm 99 percent positive that she is gay! Ya heard me? I bet I get that ass!"

"Y'all I wasn't going to say anything, but I swear when she crossed her legs I could have sworn I saw a dildo inserted in side of her?"

"What!" Mea blurted.

"You're joking right?" Tyra asked.

"Oh yeah baby It's on!" Jodi exclaimed smiling from ear to ear. "I'm out! I'll holla at y'all Saturday." Jodi said happily tossing her car keys in the air.

"Why are you coming to the fitting on Saturday?" Tyra asked.

"Why do you think I want that girl? That bitch is bad and she a freak!" she said leaving out the door and flipping her middle finger up at Tyra.

That coming week had come and gone so fast, there were only seven more weeks before the wedding. I was so excited as we all headed over to the bridal shop for the girl's second fitting and to pick up my wedding gown that was simply gorgeous. Everyone was smiling as I walked out of the fitting room wearing the beautiful dress that fit perfectly as if it was made just for me.

"Sollie, it's beautiful," my mother said. "You're going to be a beautiful bride."

"You need to fire her!" Tyra said, whispering in my ear, looking over at Melanie and Jodi. "She hasn't done anything but sit there since we have been here. I'm telling you, Sollie, I don't know what, but it is something about that woman I'm not feeling. I'm sorry, but she is nobody's wedding planner!"

The girls finished trying on their dresses. Everyone was pleased and paid their last payment. While we were all standing at the front, I looked back and yelled out loudly to Jodi and Melanie that we were done. Needless to say, they both jumped up and headed to the front of the boutique. Melanie asked me if I wanted to go to the florist. I told her no, and that we can go tomorrow. I asked her if she wanted to join us for lunch, and she said no. She said she had some things that needed to be taken care of that was long overdue. And Jodi was right on her heels.

"And where are you going?" I asked Jodi.

"I'm sorry. I have some things I need to take care of that's long overdue," she said laughing, after repeating what Melanie had just said. "What did I tell you?" she whispered. "I'm out, holla at you later!" Jodi bopped out the boutique behind Melanie.

We all left the boutique taking all the dresses to my mother's house and then headed for the restaurant. After we ate, I went over to Tyra's to relax. Tyra put on some old school Jill Scott. We opened a bottle of wine and just chilled. It was so relaxing until my cell rang again. "Oh Lord," I said looking at the screen.

"Yes, Jodi girl."

"Did I, or did I not, tell you I was going to get that ass!"

"Jodi, get the hell out of here! Get the hell out of here!" I said jumping up, and falling back down on the couch with my mouth hanging open in disbelief.

"Where are you, Sollie?"

"I'm at Tyra's."

"I'm on my way!"

I told Tyra what Jodi just said and she could believe it.

About thirty minutes later, Jodi banged on the door, and Tyra jumped up furiously.

"Why are you banging on the door like you're crazy?"

"Sorry, Mrs. Tyra," Jodi said walking past her, "I told you, I told you!" She said slapping my hand, looking like she just came off cloud nine.

"What happened, Jodi?" I asked anxious to get the dirt. "Where did y'all go, to a hotel?"

"Nah, we went to her crib," Jodi said sitting down next to me. "Now close y'all eyes and try to visualize what I'm about to say."

"Just tell the story, nasty!" Tyra snapped.

Jodi laughed, knowing she was pissing Tyra off even more.

"What does her place look like? I know it's nice!" I said.

"Actually, it's not. She doesn't have anything in there—no furniture, her mattress is on the floor, no food, nothing. She said she's buying a house, and that she was supposed to go for the settlement but it was postponed. So she had to put all her furniture in storage."

"That's bull. That doesn't even sound right!" Tyra said shaking her head.

"Oh yeah, She asked for your address."

"Don't tell me you gave it to her!" Tyra said.

"Why not? She's their wedding planner."

Tyra angrily shook her head. "If Sollie wanted her to have it, she would have given it to her."

"Tyra's right, Jodi, Cause she damn sure seems pressed to get over there."

"My, bad, anyway, listen. Here's how it went down. When I got there I was kind of skeptical, so I walked around the apartment and checking things out, you know, making sure that there were no signs of a man living there. So I walked over to a closet acting as if I wanted to hang up my jacket, but I was really checking to see if a man's coat was inside and just as I went to open the closet door, she rushed over and slammed it shut!

352

I BE DAMN

"Damn! What's in there, a dead body?" I asked.

"No! But that's where I keep my personal belongings. I'm very private." Melanie said taking Jodi by the hand and leading her into the bedroom. "I'll be right back." Melanie said. And when she returned she had a bag full of erotic toys. Sitting down on the blow up bed next to Jodi, they began to kiss. Jodi slid her hand up Melanie's skirt and was pleasantly surprised when she saw that Melanie wasn't wearing any panties. But there was a dido inside her. Jodi smiled as she happily removed the dildo, she was about to lay it to the side.

"Give me that." Melanie said taking the dildo from Jodi. Slowly she glided the dildo in her mouth and sucked her juices from off it. She then laid it next to her and looked at Jodi "Continue." She said.

Happily Jodi began fingering Melanie's wet pussy, Melanie moaned with pleasure. Jodi then reached behind Melanie slowly unzipping her skirt to make access to the ass much easier. After Jodi unbuttoned Melanie's shirt, she thought she would die when she saw her beautiful, plump, caramel-colored breasts. Slowly and seductively she began sucking Melanie's erect nipples, biting them just slightly enough to bring Melanie a little pain with the pleasure. Melanie loved every minute of it, begging Jodi to bite harder. And Jodi did. Melanie stood up from the mattress, and Jodi stared as Melanie stepped out of her skirt, and Jodi was in awe of her flawless body.

"You want me to fuck you?" Jodi asked with her mouth hanging wide open.

"I think that's why we're here!" Melanie responded sarcastically. She sat back down on the mattress, reached into her bag of toys, and pulled out a twelve-inch black dick.

"You can handle all that?" Jodi asked.

"Try me," Melanie said stretching her beautiful naked body across the mattress.

Jodi nodded her head smiling ready to turn Melanie out to the point where she had her wrapped around her finger like she had her other chicks. Little did Jodi know Melanie was a sex fiend and could fuck all night, and the only person that was going to get turned out would be Jodi. She got undressed, climbed into the bed, grabbed

Melanie's beautiful long legs, held them up, and gripped her fat ass, sliding down, taking her tongue straight to the spot. She sucked, licked, and devoured every part of Melanie's pussy. Jodi was sucking Melanie clitoris as if it was a lollypop, and Melanie couldn't take anymore.

"Fuck me, Jodi!" Jodi sat up and adjusted the strap on, climbed on top of Meanie, and began sucking both her breasts again, once again slightly biting Melanie's nipples.

"Bite them harder!" Melanie screamed.

"Shorty, if I bite them any harder they'll bleed!" Jodi said unaware that it was just what the sex fiend wanted, her nipples to bleed! Jodi climbed on top putting that twelve-inch dildo right where Melanie was dying for it to go, and she rode that ass like a cowboy riding a bull!

"Go deeper," Melanie pleaded. "Deeper!" She screamed. Trickles of sweat rolled down her beautiful face, her eyes rolled back in her head, pleasure filled her body as Jodi went deeper and harder. "I want in the ass, I need it in my ass!" She said breathing heavily. She was about to turn on her stomach, when she stopped "Do not question me about my back, do you understand?" She said.

Jodi looked at curiously "What are you talking about?"

Slowly Melanie turned on her stomach and Jodi eyes widened at the sight of the old scars on her back. "Shorty damn, what the…"

"I said don't question me." Melanie snarled.

"Fine." Jodi said shaking her head as she slid the dildo right into Melanie ass without hesitation.

"Oh baby, yes, yes, this black dick feels so good in my ass!" she screamed. Minutes later Melanie held out her hand and ordered for Jodi to stop.

Jodi came out, rolled over, and watched as Melanie sucked the dildo as if it was real, right before giving Jodi some head, sending Jodi into a state of euphoria. Jodi thought she was in heaven as she came all in Melanie's face. She lay there exhausted from what had just taken place. As Jodi tried to regroup and catch her breath,

Melanie reached into the bag and pulled some anal beads. "Oh were not done!" Melanie said.

Although exhausted from what had just taken place, Jodi tirelessly began putting each bead in Melanie's ass. While sucking Melanie's breast, she slowly began pulling out the beads. Melanie went nuts. And that's when the flashbacks began of her abusive childhood. The pleasure she was feeling was soon accompanied with pain as those un-wanted visions invaded her mind. "No, no." She yelled. "No please don't, stop it!" She screamed.

Jodi eyes widened "You want me to stop?" She asked noticing the painful look on Melanie face. "Melanie!" Jodi yelled out, bringing Melanie back to reality.

She stared at Jodi in confusion, as the vision she was having slowly dissipated.

"Damn, you good?" Jodi asked, although knowing this chic was nuts.

She tilted her head "Continue." She said.

"Yes, yes!" She screamed out in pleasure, raking her long nails across Jodi back and just as Jodi pulled the last bead, Melanie's cum shot out of her like a fountain.

"Damn, shorty, you could have told me you were a shooter"

"Well, I didn't, bitch!" Melanie snapped, jumping up from the mattress and quickly gathering her toys. She went in the bathroom to wash them. Jodi went to lie on her back but the sheets burned the deep scratches that Melanie had given her. She turned slightly to the side, took a deep breath, and smiled. Jodi knew the chic was nuts, but no one, had ever made her feel like Melanie just did. Jodi realized at that very moment Melanie was a woman and was definitely cut from a different cloth, and that she was not one of those hood rats that she had become accustomed to dealing with. She was ready to go home and break it off with LeLe and the other broads she was seeing. This girl was the one! she thought as she leaned over, reached for her jeans, and pulled out a wine -flavored cigarillo. Melanie walked back into the room, her eyebrows meeting, and her mug broke!

"Why are you still here? You can leave now!"

"Leave!"

"That's what I said, L-E-A-V-E!" Melanie yelled, spelling out the letters.

Jodi said she asked Melanie if she could wash up, and Melanie told her no. So she got dressed and as she was leaving out the door Melanie told her that what just happened stayed between them, and that she was not someone to be played with. Jodi said, as she went to respond, Melanie yelled, good night bitch and slammed the door in her face.

Chapter Forty-One

"Y'all—are—some—nasty—ass—people!" Tyra said frowning her face up at Jodi. "Talking about washing your ass, you need to wash your mouth! You don't even know that girl!"

"That's crazy! As sharp and classy as she is, I would have never thought she got down like that. So obviously that was a dildo I saw and B. said she had a husband."

"Yeah right, that bitch ain't married!" Jodi said. She then looked over at Tyra and asked for a glass of water.

Tyra got up and rolled her eyes. She went into the kitchen and came back with a bottle of warm water.

"Damn! Can I at least get some ice?"

"You sure can if it can fit through that hole. That's the only way you're getting it, 'cause you're not drinking out of no mug, cup, or glass from this house! Mmh, I don't think so!" Tyra said rolling her eyes again in disgust.

"You know what, Tyra, fuck you!" she yelled.

"Sollie, I'm out! I'll holla at you later," Jodi said as she stormed out the house leaving her bottle of water sitting on the table. Tyra snatched the water off the table, and followed quickly behind Jodi, and threw the bottle of water out the door.

"You forgot your water, you nasty bitch!"

I swear, when Tyra said that I stretched out across the couch and laughed so hard I was in tears.

"Tyra, Terry is probably rolling over in his grave hearing you cussing like that."

"I'm sorry, baby," she said blowing a kiss in the air. "Sollie, tell that other nasty wench her services are no longer needed. I'm serious."

"Tyra, calm down I need a wedding planner."

"Okay, then we will find another one. I'll even pay for it!"

"Tyra, the wedding is around the corner!"

"She hasn't done anything anyway!"

"Tyra, listen. We will talk tomorrow. I have to go."

"I'm going to make some phone calls in the morning to see if I can find another wedding planner." Tyra said.

"Whatever, Tyra, love you," I said as I walked out the door, and I laughed the whole ride home, still in disbelief of what Jodi had just told us. I wanted to tell Lamar, but I didn't dare. Even though he's my future husband, some things men don't need to know. When I got home, Lamar was sitting on the couch watching TV. I immediately walked over to him, sat down on his lap, and began kissing him. With the story Jodi just told still on my mind, I anxiously tried to loosen his drawstring pajamas.

"Baby, wait, what is wrong with you?" he laughed.

"I want you, Lamar."

"You know I want you too. But I have something to talk to you about."

"What is it?" I asked sucking all over his neck.

"I would like us to refrain from sex until we are married."

I couldn't believe what Lamar was saying. I looked at him as if he was crazy. "Are you serious?" I asked.

"Yes, I'm very serious."

I thought what Lamar was suggesting was very sweet. And I loved him even more for suggesting that we wait. I chuckled and asked, "Could we start refraining tomorrow?" We both laughed as I reached over and grabbed his drawstring again. Seeing that Lamar was serious I stopped.

"Okay, its fine," I said hugging him. "But I really don't think you will be able to hang!"

"Okay bet."

And we did. "The bet starts now," Lamar said, standing up and tying the drawstring to his pajamas back up, smiling at me. My cell rang, and it was Tyra.

"Hey, gutter-mouth," I laughed.

"Sollie, have you thought about what I said?"

"Tyra, chill out please!"

"Jodi doesn't make any sense. What is wrong with her? She needs to get her ass in church somewhere and turn her life around, and yes, so does my cousin."

"Tyra, listen! I'm really getting tired of hearing you talk about Jodi and her chosen lifestyle. It's her life, not yours. And you going on and on about her being gay is really getting tired. All you're doing is wasting a whole lot of energy on somebody else's shit! As long as what Jodi does doesn't affect Tyra Palmer, leave it alone. And you need to know that when you and Duce say your little jokes to her, it hurts her feelings, especially coming from two people who are supposed to be her friends, childhood friends, for that matter. Granted you and Jodi never got along even when we were kids, but we are grown now, so you have two options. Try and get along with her, or leave her alone totally. I can't speak about it, but Jodi has some very serious issues going on, so for real, just be easy with her." A few seconds passed and I didn't hear anything. "Tyra are you still there?"

I heard Tyra take a deep breath. "Yeah Sollie I'm here, and your right."

Tyra and I talked a little longer and said goodnight.

"Lamar I'm going to take a shower. Would you like to join me?" I said, unbuttoning my shirt in front of him, trying to make him lose the bet we just made.

"No thanks, I'll wait until you're done." Trying not to look at me, he reached for the remote and changed the channel. I giggled and went into the bathroom.

When Lamar finished taking his shower and walked into the bedroom, I was already in bed. He turned the night-light off and climbed in the bed, kissing me softly on my cheek; out of smartness, I backed my fat ass on him causing him to almost lose the bet.

"Sollie, why don't you stop playing?! You're trying to be smart!" he said laughing and turning over.

"Lamar, I'm not. You know this is how we sleep."

"No! This is how we sleep!" he said grabbing me, and playfully putting me in a head lock, we began wrestling like kids at a pajama party, and of course, he let me win! He eventually gave into the pain of me putting him in a Fort Nelson. After our wresting match, we both laid there in each other's arms, exhausted.

"Love you, baby." Lamar said.

"I love you too."

I lay there and the thought of Tyra and what she said about Melanie continued playing in my head. The last time she said she didn't trust someone, they were sleeping with my boyfriend, I thought as I drifted off to sleep. That morning, the phone rang, and it was Melanie.

"Good morning, Sollie."

"Good morning."

"Sollie, I need your address so I can come there and go over the floral arrangements."

"Didn't you . . ."

I quickly caught myself. I wasn't supposed to know that Jodi was over there yesterday. But she already has my address. Jodi gave it to her, I thought to myself.

"Are you there?" she asked.

"I'm sorry, Melanie. My thoughts were somewhere else. Just meet me at my mother's. Is two o'clock good for you?"

Once again taking a long pause, she said yes. I asked Melanie to call the tuxedo shop in Atlanta and make sure all the groom's men had been fitted for their tuxes. When I hung up, I wondered why in the hell does she seem so pressed to get over here. Lamar and I lay in the bed a little longer. Truth is, I could have stayed there all day. Planning this wedding was just as tiresome as it was exciting.

We missed the nine o'clock service, so we attended eleven o'clock service. After church service Lamar picked up little Terry, so they could hang out, and I headed over to my mother's to meet with Melanie. She arrived exactly at two. She walked in once again wearing all black. The outfit was sharp, but I wondered if black was the only color in her wardrobe.

"Where is your gorgeous fiancé?"

"He took Tyra son to the mall. He will be over later."

"Have you two known each other long?" Melanie asked.

"Long enough to know that he is the man that I want to spend the rest of my life with."

"Is Lamar your first man?" she asked, pulling a floral book out of a bag, the receipt fell on the floor, when I picked up the receipt, I noticed that she had just bought the book today. I handed it to her.

"No, he's not. Why?" I was getting very defensive as to why she was interested in knowing that. "Then again, yes, he is, because the other person I was involved with was very much a boy, as a matter of fact, he was a piece of shit!

Melanie's beautiful complexion suddenly turned red. Her voice began to tremble as well as her hands. She reached inside her pocketbook, pulled out the same bottle of pills, and asked if she could use the bathroom. I told her yes. Watching her go up the stairs, I leaned over and pulled the receipt from off the bag. "What kind of a wedding planner is she? She doesn't have anything."

I looked up, and Melanie was standing there, staring. I didn't even hear her come down the steps.

"Are you okay?" I asked.

"I'm fine. I have a slight headache."

She sat back down, picking up the book, and looking through it. Just as I looked up, I once again caught her staring at me with that strange look on her face. "Melanie, I don't know what the problem is, but I'm starting to feel that you are not really into the planning of my wedding, and if so, it's okay."

"I'm sorry. I just have a lot on my mind."

"I know how distracting that can be. Would you like to talk about it? It may help."

"I just recently lost a relationship that I cherished with all my life!" she said, placing her fingertips on the side of her head and slowly rubbing her temples.

"I'm really sorry to hear that. Was it serious? Well, obviously it was, if it has you this distracted."

"Yes, it was. He was everything to me!" she said loudly. "The only one who ever loved and took care of me."

"Melanie, listen, not long ago I was exactly where you are, and look at me now. I'm happier than ever. You will see it will get better. When it's time, you will find the right man." *Or the right woman,* I thought to myself.

"I'll never, ever be with another man!" she snapped, still rubbing her temples, and staring at me as if I had just cursed at her. Looking like she was about to cry she slowly lowered her head.

I noticed deep scars on her upper back that Jodi had mentioned. The scars looked very old, but they looked as if someone had literally beaten her with a whip. She raised her head slowly with a look that would kill, almost as if she had become someone else in just those few seconds.

"He asked me to fulfill one wish for him before he left. And I plan on doing just that!"

"I'm sorry. Did he pass away?" I asked, trying not to give her full eye contact. This chic was actually beginning to scare me.

"He might as well have!" she snapped.

I didn't dare ask her what the wish was, but I knew at that moment that once again, Tyra was right. This bitch was crazy! I quickly changed the subject. Picking up the floral book that she laid on the table, I said, "These calla lilies are really beautiful. Would you happen to know how much they cost?"

"No, I don't," she replied, still rubbing her temples.

I flipped through the pages. "Okay what about these?" I asked pointing to the peonies.

"I'm not certain." She began tapping her feet on the floor.

"Melanie, please excuse me. I need to take this call," I said getting up and walking into the kitchen.

"Hey Tyra."

"Hey, are you and the freak done yet?"

"Tyra, correct me if I'm wrong. Aren't wedding planners supposed to know every angle of wedding planning? I know when I hired her she said she was just starting out, but this is ridiculous!"

"Why, what happened?"

"This woman knows absolutely nothing!"

"Fire her! I'm waiting on a call now. I may have found you another wedding planner. I'm getting ready to take Trinity to my mother's house, and I will be right over there."

When I walked back into the living room, Melanie had quickly sat back down on the couch and it was obvious she was up to something, but what? Suspiciously looking at her, I asked if she had contacted the tuxedo shop in Atlanta. She said that she had forgotten.

I excused myself again and headed upstairs to use the bathroom. While inside the bathroom, I quickly made the decision to let Melanie go. As I came down the stairs to let Melanie know she was no longer needed, Melanie was gone! I looked around in the kitchen and the dining room. I then looked outside and I didn't see her car. I yelled back up the stairs and asked my mother if she would ride with Tyra and me to the florist. She said yes and that she would be down just as soon as she came out of the bathroom.

"Hey girl," Tyra said coming through the door. "Where is she?" Tyra asked whispering and looking around. I told Tyra what happened.

"Good! Let her stay gone!" Tyra said.

"Sollie, are you taking medication?" My mother asked as she came down the steps holding a large blue pill in her hand.

"No, Mommy. You know I'm not on any medication."

"I found this on the bathroom floor."

"It must be Melanie's. She pulled out a bottle of medication earlier."

"I'll take that, Mrs. Marie," Tyra said taking the pill out of her hand. Tyra walked into the kitchen, grabbed a small ziplock bag from the drawer, and put the pill inside of it.

"There she goes, Detective Palmer."

"That's right. I'm going to prove to you that woman is a nut case."

"Tyra, you need to volunteer full time at social service. You have too much time on your hand."

"You right!" she said smiling. "That's why I have decided to go to college and get my degree in criminology." She clapped happily.

"Are you serious?! I'm so glad for you," I said hugging her.

"That's great, Tyra," my mother said hugging her also.

"I was kind of nervous when I went to register."

"Why?" my mother asked.

"Mrs. Marie, I will be thirty soon!"

"And what does that mean?"

"That's kind of old returning to school, don't you think?"

"Listen baby," my mother said taking Tyra by her hand, "There is no age to acquire knowledge. You will be just fine, and this is obviously something that you are very passionate about. I remember, when you were a little girl, you would use up my ketchup and toilet paper for the blood and crime-scene tape. I wish you all the best."

Melanie knocked on the door. She walked in and spoke to Tyra and my mother.

"Melanie, why would you leave like that?"

"I apologize. I needed to get some air, so I went for a walk. May I sit down?" she asked appearing much calmer than she was earlier.

"But you didn't go for a walk. When I looked outside, your car was gone."

"I'm sorry, I meant a drive. I don't know what I meant." She shook her head in confusion.

"Melanie, I really appreciate you being available for us at such short notice, but I really don't think it's going to work out. I can pay you for your time."

"Pay her for what! She didn't do anything!" Tyra snapped and the look Melanie gave Tyra was such that if looks could kill, Tyra would be dead.

"Is there a problem?" Tyra asked standing up, and when my girl stood up, so did I.

"Girl, you don't want none for real!" Melanie said slightly laughing.

Tyra and I had fight in us, but this chic looked as if she was bred to fight.

"There will be none of that!" said my mother. "Melanie, thanks again. And sorry it did not work out." My mother extending her hand towards the front door, And Melanie left.

Chapter Forty-Two

We all headed over to the floral shop, and I prayed that the person Tyra had contacted would call. We arrived at the shop and with the help of the florist the flowers we chose were exquisite! I had mentioned to the florist that I was in desperate need of a wedding planner, and it just so happened that the florist's wife was one. He did tell us her business was just getting off the ground and that she had only done three weddings. He showed us some pictures of previous weddings that she had done. She was very good. After speaking with her briefly over the phone, and I met with her that evening, and I decided to go with her; we had no time to play around.

The weeks passed, and Mary, the new wedding planner, was doing an excellent job. Jodi was whipped after Melanie called her over for another freak session that totally blew her mind! And she was strung out, for sure! Tyra called her several times she wanted desperately to talk to Jodi and make amends, realizing she owed Jodi an apology. but Jodi wouldn't answer any of our calls.

Everything was coming together perfectly. Some of the guests were flying in on Monday and the others were coming at the end of the week. Most of them were staying at the hotel, and some at my mother's and Tyra's. I couldn't believe it was one more week before the wedding and still no word from Jodi. I called and left her several messages about the rehearsal, and that if she didn't show up; she was not going to be in the wedding. Mea said she heard Jodi had left LeLe, and was staying with her aunt. But when I went to her aunt's house, she said she hadn't seen Jodi in weeks.

"Hey cutie!" Lamar said coming in the door and running up behind me, pressing up against my ass.

"All right, Lamar, you better stop!"

"I am good. I can wait one week. Baby, you gaining weight, aren't you?" he said rubbing his hands along the sides of my hips.

"Not that much," I said, walking over looking at myself in the mirror. "Lamar, everything is going perfect with the exception of Jodi missing in action, which is unlike her. I just hope she is okay. I'm really starting to worry about her."

The next day, Lamar and I went to the mall to purchase gifts for our wedding party,

As we walked by the large fountain, I remembered the last time I was here; my life was such a mess then. This time I stopped and threw a quarter in and wished that everyone would be as happy as I was. We got to the jewelers and purchased the set to match my engagement ring. As we were walking out, we smiled at a couple as they walked by, happily strolling their baby.

"So when are we going to start our family?"

"Awwww, maybe ten, eleven years," I said jokingly.

"Sollie you're not serious, are you?"

"No, I'm joking. I guess when God is ready." I looked at him thinking how very much in love I was with him.

"You're right, when God is ready!" he said seeming to become distracted by something. "Sollie, Sollie, look!" He turned me in the direction of the food court. "Over there!" It was that simple ass Jodi sitting at the table feeding Melanie strawberries.

"I'm going to lay her ass out!" I said, as I attempted to rush over to the food court. Lamar pulled me back.

"Nope, not today Sollie."

"But Lamar, I haven't talked to her in weeks. I just want to make sure she is okay," I said although I was still going to lay her ass out!

"Sollie, from the looks of things, I'd say she's just fine," Lamar said taking my hand and walking in the opposite direction. "I just hope what my grandmother says doesn't stand true." He looked back at Jodi as we walked away.

"And what was that?" I asked.

"Never leave an old friend for a new one, because in the end you lose both."

We walked in the leather store and purchased the gifts for the groomsmen. Because all of Lamar's groomsmen were businessmen, we brought each of them a leather briefcase. I purchased each of my girls a gift card from Nordstrom's, and bought a Visa gift card for Duce. I really missed him, with everything that had been going on. I hadn't seen him much.

While Lamar was getting the groomsmen initials engraved into the briefcase's I snuck back over to the food court, but Jodi and that lunatic were gone. Lamar and I headed home.

Finally! I thought. Flopping down on the couch, I was beat, and I really didn't feel like meeting the girls for drinks tonight but Lamar talked me in to going. Dragging my tired body into the bathroom, I took a shower and changed. While I was in the room changing, Tyra called me and sounded really depressed, saying that she changed her mind and decided to stay at home. As I was coming down the hall, I heard Lamar talking on the phone in a very low tone.

"Who was that?"

"Oh, that was B. We're going to shoot some pool tonight."

While driving to meet the girls, Tyra called again, and sounded even more upset.

"Are you sure you're okay?"

"I'm fine. I just needed somebody to talk to. Just feeling a little lonely that's all."

"Where are the kids?"

"They're with my mother."

"Okay, let me call the girls and tell them I'm going to be a little late. I'll be right over."

"Sollie no, go and enjoy yourself."

"Yeah right, I'm on my way over there."

She probably missing Terry, I thought to myself. I pulled up at Tyra's and all of her lights were out. God, I hope she's not sitting in the dark crying. I knocked on the door, and she opened it with a very sad look on her face. As soon as I went to hug her, the lights came on and everyone screamed, "Surprise!"

"Why did y'all do this? I told y'all I didn't want a shower," I said crying and hugging everyone. "Lamar knew about this, didn't he?"

"He sure did. I just called him to see if you had left."

Tyra had every kind of food you could name. And I ate like a pig walking around there with my tiara on top of my head that read "Bride to Be" The photographer had to have taken a hundred pictures. Tyra gathered all of us around for the games we were about to play. She then handed Mea a spool of black thread and told her to take some and pass it around.

"How much to take, Tyra?" Mea asked.

"Take as much as you want. If you want a little, take a little. If you want a lot, take a lot."

I sat there looking, not knowing what Tyra was doing. After each person had taken some thread, Tyra explained the object of the game.

"Okay," Tyra said standing in the middle of the floor. "Take your string, and wrap it around your finger. While doing that, you must tell Sollie something in reference to her marriage, and you must continue until the string is completely wrapped around your finger. Okay, I'm first."

"Shit! That little-ass string you have, Tyra. All you can say is good luck," Mea said laughing.

Tyra looked at her string and smiled and began wrapping the short thread around her finger as she spoke: "Treat every day, every moment, every second with Lamar as if it is your last!" she said looking down at the thread that was fully wrapped around her finger and then she leaned over and hugged me.

I sat my drink on the table, all the girls came over to us, and we all wrapped our arms around one another.

"Okay, okay, enough of that," Mea said wiping her eyes. "I'm next." She held her thread in her hand.

She sat down in front of me and began wrapping her thread around her finger. "Fuck, fuck, fuck, fuck, and fuck some more!" she yelled.

Everyone eventually said their well wishes and we played some more games. After opening my gifts, Tyra's living room turned into a club as we all partied to the late great DJ K—Swift club mix.

Tyra came walking out of the kitchen carrying a round silver platter filled with jello shooters. "Jello shooter for the lady?" she asked, smiling and walking around to everyone. "Sollie, get the door please!" She yelled over the top of the loud music.

I walked over and opened the door and fell back against it laughing.

"Mr. Bob, where are your clothes!" I asked. Everyone was on the floor, falling all over each other dying laughing while Tyra's seventy-eight-year-old neighbor, Mr. Bob, stood there wearing black pants, no shirt, and a black bowtie around his neck with a whip in his hand. Bald head, five feet tall weighing only about ninety pounds, it was hilarious as he walked through the doors and started dancing. Everybody yelled, go Bobby! go Bobby! while he stood there shaking his frail ass acting like he was beating me with the whip.

"Got ya!" he said kissing me.

Tyra said that wanted to get me a real striper but she knew that I was not crazy about them.

Chapter Forty-Three

T   he bridal shower was over and Lamar came to help me with the slew of gifts I had gotten.

Back at the apartment, I showed Lamar my sexy lingerie that I had gotten. "I can't wait to see you in these," Lamar exclaimed while sitting on the couch and holding up the black lace nightgown that Mea had given me.

"Do you want me to try it on now?"

"No, I don't. Stop playing, Sollie. I know what you're trying to do."

"What am I trying to do, Lamar?" I said grabbing a few of my gifts off the love seat and running into the bedroom. When I came out wearing one of them, he wouldn't even look. Every time I stood in front of him, he turned his head in the opposite direction laughing. I reached for the remote and turned off the television, dimmed the lights, and put on Tank *"When we Fuck"* I began giving Lamar the lap dance of his life.

He pleaded with me to stop. Unable to control himself, he began rubbing his hand all over my body, and with each move I made he grabbed me tighter, now beginning to moan. "Sollie, stop!" he said as his breathing became heavier. With a look of sheer relief on his face, he began laughing and asked, "Why did you do that?"

"No, you didn't, Lamar!" I laughed.

"Yes, I did, Sollie," he said resting his head back, on the couch, and laughed.

"I won! I won," I sang.

"No, cheated is what you did." He walked to the bathroom to take a shower.

The next day, we didn't even go to church. We were both beat, and we stayed in all day and relaxed, because we knew that the week ahead was going to be hectic. Monday morning we met Mary at my mother's to go over last-minute details.

While sitting at the dining room, I was dozing off, I was so very tired! And I didn't feel well, you would have thought, relaxing all yesterday I wouldn't be as tired, but I was. My mother and Lamar even said that I didn't look good. I decided to call my doctor and make an appointment to find out what was going on with me, although it was probably nothing, just the stress of the wedding, or maybe even a cold coming on. And I wasn't telling Lamar or my mother that I was going to the doctor's because they both would have wanted to go.

"Sollie, I'm short of two RSVPs," Mary said looking again through her list just to make sure the names were not overlooked.

I looked inside my wedding-planner book and realized that I had left the list on the coffee table. I knew I was forgetting something."

"I'll run and get it," Lamar said.

"No, you two stay here and finish going over everything with Mary. Sollie, where are your keys. I'll go and get the list," said Tyra.

"Thank you, Tyra." I got up from the table and went and poured myself a glass of lemonade hoping that the bitterness would settle my upset stomach.

As Tyra pulled up into Lamar's apartment complex, she went ballistic when she saw Melanie leaving out of Lamar's apartment building, wearing a black sweat suit with the hood pulled over top of her head. "Oh shit! What the hell is she doing?" Tyra started to confront her but something in her gut told her not to. She slid down in her seat so Melanie wouldn't see her. Peeping over the steering wheel,

Tyra watched as Melanie quickly walked over to her car, jumped inside and sped out of the parking lot. Tyra reached inside her purse for her cell phone.

"Hey Sollie."

"Hi Tyra, did you get the folder?"

"Actually, I'm just getting here now. There was a traffic back up on Liberty Road. A crab truck turned over and, girl, it was hundreds of crabs crawling around on Liberty Road."

"Tyra, please." I said laughing at her.

"No, seriously, I'm on my way. But Sollie, what is Melanie's last name?"

"Oh Lord, why Tyra, and what are you up to?"

"What's her last name?" Tyra blurted.

"Omar why!?"

"And what Road was it that Jodi said she lived on?"

"Oh my god, Tyra, why?"

"Sollie! What was it Sollie?"

"I think she said those apartments were not too far from us. Look, I don't know!" Tyra insisted, and I blurted out "Dogwood Road!" I hung up, wondering what she was up to.

Tyra jumped out the car and ran inside the building. Standing in front of the apartment door, Tyra noticed chipped paint by the doorknob. Slowly turning the key, she entered into the apartment. Just as she grabbed the list of names off the coffee table, the door slammed shut! She turned, with her eyes wide, thinking that Melanie had returned. Holding her chest and breathing a sigh of relief, she realized that the wind had blown the door shut. She folded the paper, put it inside her purse, and ran out the door. Once inside her car, she drove around to Dogwood Road. Slowly she looked around, and then drove into the complex, parking her car behind the big green dumpster. She noticed a little old woman going inside one of the buildings. Tyra got out the car and walked over to her, cautiously looking around for any signs of Melanie.

"Hello ma'am, my name is Tyra Palmer. I work for the Department of Social Service, and I am looking for a woman by the name of Melanie Omar. She is maybe five feet five in height, with long beautiful hair. The old lady tried to think but she couldn't seem to remember. She wears black all the time," Tyra added, hoping that it may help the woman to remember.

"Oh yea, I know who you are talking about. She lives right over there, 2701," she said, pointing to the next apartment complex, "third floor, 3-A, as a matter of fact."

Goddamn! She must be related to Mrs. Johnson's! Sorry God, rest her soul. Tyra headed down to the next building, again looking around making sure Melanie wasn't coming around the corner. She noticed the mailman entering into the building and prepared herself for yet another Oscar-winning performance.

"Hi handsome, anything for me today?" she asked flirtatiously batting her big pretty brown eyes.

"Mmmm, muh!" the mailman said licking his nasty lips. "And how are you doing today?"

"Not too good," Tyra said sadly.

"What seems to be the problem?" he said with one eye going to the left and the other going to the right.

Tyra didn't know whether he was looking at her or the door. *Control those eyes, mister!* Tyra said almost laughing in the man's face.

"My husband and I are going through a very nasty divorce. He had the locks changed to the door and the mailbox. Do you think you could give me my mail?" she asked gently placing her hand on his arm and stroking it, causing his eyes to cross even more.

"Sure, baby," he said smiling. "What's your name?"

"Melanie Omar," Tyra said, wishing he would hurry up before Melanie returned. He dug through his mailbag and handed Tyra what he had. Tyra quickly went through it, and it was nothing but advertisements.

Disappointedly, Tyra asked, "Do you normally come at this time?"

"No, baby, this is not my route. I'm just filling in for someone else today. I have had the same route for the last thirty years. It feels kind of strange working this one, but that's okay. I'll be back on my regular route tomorrow," he said pulling a rag out of his back pocket and wiping the sweat from his brow.

"Listen, my husband is very abusive, and I'm really terrified of him. I'm waiting on a check, and I know if he gets it first I'll never see it. I normally would not ask someone to do such a thing but do you think you could get my mail in the morning before it leaves the post office, and I could meet you somewhere and pick it up? Please?" she asked once again stroking his arm.

"I don't know, ma'am. I would like to help you. My daughter just got out of a marriage with an old no-good dog like that. So I do sympathize with you."

Tyra sadly stared at him with those pretty brown eyes. "Please help me. I need to feed my kids."

"Okay, I'll do it, but just this one time."

"Oh, thank you, so much. Where would you like me to meet you?"

"Do you know where Rolling Road and Milford Mill meet at?"

"Yes, I do. That's not far from here, right?"

"That's right. That's my route, and it has been for the last thirty years."

"Thank you so much. I'll meet you there at 11:00 a.m. sharp!" Tyra said while running out the door.

"Good enough!" he yelled, "Listen, if you're looking for a sugar daddy I'm your man!" Tyra ran down the walkway, jumped into her car.

As Tyra bent the corner, she looked in her mirror and saw Melanie pulling into the parking lot, realizing she got out there just in time! *I'm going to find out who she is and what the hell she wants with Sollie.*

Chapter Forty-Four

"It took you long enough!"

"I'm sorry ya'll, traffic is a mess!" Tyra said, handing Mary the list.

Everything was finalized and there was nothing left but the rehearsal, rehearsal dinner, and then the wedding and I could not wait.

The next morning I made Lamar breakfast and served it to him in bed. Nauseated, once again I got dressed, and headed out for my doctor's appointment. My doctor said that from my symptom it sounded like a simple stomach virus, but he still took a urinalysis and blood work. She said she would call me in a day or two, but advised me for now to drink lots of fluid and try to get some rest.

Rest, yeah right, she's not getting married in four days. I drove back home and decided to change before we went to the airport to pick up Lamar's grandmother, and his aunt and uncle. In the meantime, Tyra was at the drug store where a guy we went to school with worked as a pharmacy technician.

Tyra

"Heyyyy, Sean," Tyra said, walking up to the counter.

"Hi Tyra, how have you been? I haven't seen you since the funeral. Your husband was really a good guy. You know he handled my brother's murder case, and my brother walked away a free man! I'll never forget him. We didn't have all the money for the attorney fees, but he worked with us. And in the end we still owed him five hundred dollars, and he told us not to worry about it."

"That's how he was." Tyra smiled. "So, Sean, how have you been?"

"I been well and I can't wait for Sollie's wedding. I know it's going to be beautiful. That's all everyone is talking about," he said excitedly.

"I can't wait myself. Listen, Sean, I need a favor. Can you tell me what type of pill this is, it must have gotten wet, the numbers on it are smudge and I can't make them out."

"Sure," Sean took the pill, and when he returned, he confirmed what Tyra had said from day one.

"Tyra, this is Haldol. This is prescribed to a person with severe schizophrenia disorder, and it's a very, very high dosage."

"What does that mean? They're crazy?"

"Professionally speaking no, coming from the hood hell yeah!"

Tyra looked at her watch and realized it was getting close to eleven. She told Sean thanks and that she would see him at the wedding and rushed out the store.

Sollie

Lamar was so happy to see his grandmother, and his aunt and uncle that I had heard so much about. They walked over to us. I hugged and kissed his grandmother. Lamar then introduced me to his aunt. And just as Lamar went to ask where his Uncle June Bug was, we heard his loud mouth walking over to us, wearing a pair of red plaid shorts sett, and a plaid hat, and to top it off, he had on a pair of white shoes. *Countryyyyyy!* I thought.

"Hey boy!" he yelled out loudly.

"That's Uncle June Bug," Lamar said shaking his head out of embarrassment.

"June Bug, stop being so loud. Act like you have a little bit of class," Lamar's grandmother said rolling her eyes at him.

"Boy, hell! You sure got yourself a fine one here. Yes sirrrrrr! Indeed, you do. She is goooood looking!" he said vigorously shaking my hand and kissing me on my cheek. "Now, I have had my introduction. All I need now is a liquor store. Boy! Where dat bighead brother of yours at? He still shooting pool?" He slapped Lamar on his back.

"Yeah, Unc, he's still shooting pool. He's at work. He will be over later."

He moved closer to Lamar and placed his arm around Lamar's shoulder. "I heard you and this pretty little thing here done struck it rich! Let me hold about fifty grand? Nah, I'm just joking, but I'll take about five, 'cause I ain't greedy, I aint greedy, now that's one thing I aint is greedy!" He had one rotten tooth hanging out his mouth.

"Oh, June Bug, please! For God's sake, that ain't none of your business! Tend to your own matters!" his grandmother yelled while shaking her cane at him.

"I will tend to my own matters just as soon as this boy gets me to the liquor store. I need a drink!" he snapped, and then mumbled something under his breath.

"Okay Unc, calm down. Let's get you settled in first and then I'll take you right to the store. And besides, it's only eleven in the morning."

"That is the time to start! The earlier it is the better. That way you got allllllllll day to drink! And I want me some absolute, you why Solet?" he asked whispering in my ear, pronouncing my name wrong, and smelling like he already had a drink.

"Why?" I asked frowning. The smell of liquor on his breath was turning my stomach.

"'Cause it gets me absolutely fucked up!" he said resting his tongue on his one tooth and smiling.

I tried not to laugh, but it was funny. Lamar's grandmother looked over at us knowing he had just said something crazy. She just shook her head as she held on to Lamar's arm, and we all departed the airport.

Tyra

In the meantime, Tyra pulled up at eleven on the dot. "Hello, I see you're here on time," she said to the mailman.

"That's right. I'm an on-time kinda man, and a good man if you need one." He took his cap off and wiped the sweat off his baldhead." It's a hot one this morning . . ."

"Was there any mail for me?" Tyra asked quickly cutting him off.

"I have it right here, all rubber band together." he said handing her the mail. Tyra rummaged through it and found a bank statement.

"Yes!" she yelled out.

"I take it that's what you were waiting for."

"Yes, thank you so much. I really appreciate what you have done," she said quickly walking off.

"Wait! Take my number, and give me a call!"

Tyra started to keep walking, but turned around and waited while he wrote the number down. He told her to call him that very night and that he guaranteed to show her the time of her life. As she got out of his view, she threw the paper, with his number written on it, away.

She jumped in the car and ripped open the envelope. She couldn't believe what the statement read, three hundred and fifty thousand dollars. And in the corner were the last four digits of Melanie's social security number. She then dialed Mike's number. He was a very close friend of Terry's, who was also a detective that Terry's law firm used occasionally.

"Hi Mike, it's Tyra Palmer."

"Hey, Tyra, how's it going? How have you and the kids been?"

"We have all been fine. Thanks for asking. Mike, I really need your help."

"Sure, anything for you. What's going on?"

Tyra explained the situation to Mike, and he agreed that it did sound strange. She gave Mike all the information she had from the bank statement and prayed that it would be enough to find out just who Melanie Omar really was. He told Tyra he would get right on top of it, but it may take a few days for him to get back with her.

By Thursday everyone who was arriving from out of town was here, and we had a ball, Uncle June Bug being the life of everything! That evening we had a fish fry. We all sat around the pool in my mother's yard and enjoyed the evening. Everyone was there except Jodi.

Rehearsal day was here. Mary began putting the wedding party with their partners, and I headed out the door to get some fresh air. When I walked out the huge church doors, I leaned up against the railing, took in a deep breath of fresh evening air, reached into my pocket book, opened the envelope, and gleamed with utter joy at the picture inside of it. Duce came out.

"Hey Duce, I missed you."

"I missed you too Shorty." Duce said hugging me tightly.

"Duce I'm sorry with the wedding and so much going on, I honestly forgot about your situation, are you doing okay?"

"Shorty I'm good, it comes and go, you know?" Duce said staring with a somber look on his face. He cleared his throat. "Are you happy"? Duce asked.

"Duce, I'm happier than you will ever know."

"I'm glad. And where's the little carpet muncher at?" Duce asked.

"Duce, don't start that. I don't know where she is. I left her several messages, and I can't believe she hasn't called me."

"Well, believe it! She's probably somewhere licking someone's . . ."

"In case you forgot, you are standing in front of a church!"

"My, bad, licking someone's booty," he said laughing.

This is really messed up. I would have at least thought she would have been here for the rehearsal. *Where is she?* I thought to myself.

Chapter Forty-Five

Melanie's Apartment

A fter another freak session, Melanie fell asleep, and Jodi figured this was the perfect time to see what the big secret in the closet was. Jodi eased out the bed, and tiptoed into the dark empty living room, looking back to make sure Melanie was still asleep. Little did Jodi know, all closed eyes aren't sleep. Trying to be as quiet as she could, she tiptoed slowly over to the closet, turned the knob, and opened the closet door just a little. It was so dark inside that she couldn't see a thing. She opened it wider and saw a black duffel bag, and a black briefcase. She looked back again thinking she heard Melanie. Turning back to the closet she eased the duffel bag out and slowly unzipped it. Jodi's mouth hung open when she saw nothing but stacks of hundred-dollar bills inside of it. "What the fuck!" she whispered. Quickly zipping the duffel bag, she slid it back to where it was. She turned, thinking again that she heard footsteps, but there was no one there. She then reached back inside the closet and pulled out the black briefcase and opened it. The noise from the locks sounded much louder in an empty apartment. "Shit!" she whispered. But still determined to see what was inside, she slowly opened it, and she saw

Uzis, .45s, 9s, and silencers neatly stacked inside. Jodi then noticed three pictures taped to the inside of the briefcase. One was of Dino with an **X** across his face, the other was of Remi with an **X** across her stomach, and the last picture was of Sollie.

Oh hell no, who the fuck is this bitch! Jodi said out loud as she bent over to get a closer look, and just then a clicking sound startled her. She slowly turned, and it was Melanie standing there wearing only a long black trench coat, totally naked. Jodi then realized the click she heard was Melanie putting the silencer on the .45 she was holding.

Jodi was lost for words as she followed the red dot that eventually landed in the middle of her forehead. And just that quick it was over, execution style! Jodi dropped to the floor. "Dumbass bitch!" Melanie said as she walked past Jodi's lifeless body to get a glass of water. As she walked out the kitchen, she stopped and stared at Jodi. She shook her head and said, "You obviously didn't know curiosity killed the cat"

Wedding Rehearsal

"Sollie still no word from Jodi yet?"

"No not yet. She may be caught up, but I just can't see her missing this rehearsal."

"You're right," Tyra said with a worried look on her face, and I knew just what she was thinking.

"Tyra, don't even think about it! You're not going over to that woman's house."

"But Sollie, something does not feel right. Listen, we really need to talk. I have to tell you something."

As Tyra was about to tell me what she had found out, Mary came to the door and called us inside.

"Come on, Tyra," I said pulling her into the church chapel, "We can talk later."

After rehearsal, we all left the church, and went to Ocean Air for our rehearsal dinner. All of us, especially the girls, had a good time. Mea and I teased our girlfriend Kim about her escort for the wedding 'cause that guy was ugly! Mea was pleased with her escort. He was a white guy and fine as hell.

We all left the restaurant, and the guys headed off to Lamar's bachelor party.

When we got home, I took Lamar's grandmother upstairs and helped her get settled into bed. "Listen sweetie, I'm not going to talk you to death, you have a big day tomorrow, but I need you to know one very important thing about your new beginning. Keep God first! And don't you ever forget that. And Lamar's parents would have adored you."

We all stayed up and talked half the night, knowing we had to get up early and be at Mea's shop by seven. I asked Tyra what was she about to tell me and she said it was nothing. Everyone eventually fell off to sleep except me. I was entirely too excited to sleep, and I couldn't wait to give Lamar his wedding present.

In the meantime, Lamar and the guys were at the bachelor party having the time of their lives, and needless to say the guys went crazy over the two beautiful topless waitresses wearing only panties. The waitresses took a break and walked over to the bar and ordered two Sex on the Beaches.

"Heyyyy sexy ladies!" Uncle June Bug said. Barely able to stand, he attempted to dance his way over to the bar. "Bartender!" he yelled. "Get these two beautiful women whatever their pretty young heart's desire!" And just as he said that he tripped and fell hitting his mouth on the chrome bar stool and knocked out the one tooth he had left! Everyone watched as the tooth rolled across the floor.

"And it's a strike!" Duce yelled out acting as if he was bowling. He fell over on the bar and laughed his ass off.

B. walked over and shook his head a Duce. "Man you haven't grown up yet? Come on Unc." B. said, picking his uncle up off the floor and walking him back over to the table. Lamar got a napkin and walked over to pick the tooth up from the floor and then took Uncle June Bug a tall glass of water.

"Sorry about that, ladies. I'll take care of those drinks," Lamar said.

The DJ yelled into the mic for Lamar to come to the dance floor. He hesitated at first knowing that the guys had gotten him a stripper, because he wasn't crazy about strippers either.

"Come on, man, one last time!" all the groom's men yelled out.

"For your ass be on lockdown!" Uncle June Bug yelled from across the room. "Believe me, I know. I have been on lockdown for the last thirty-five years! But at least you will be rich and on lockdown!"

Lamar went to the floor, and before he knew it, those two waitresses were all over him.

"Oh shit!" Lamar said laughing.

The guys went nuts as one of the women straddled him; she then grabbed his face and laid them on her breast.

"Baby girl, over here, got damn over here!" Uncle June Bug yelled to the other woman; waving a fifty-dollar bill in the air.

The other groomsmen pulled out their money, anxiously waiting for the girls to get to them. The woman danced over to Uncle June, bending her ass over in his face, while he put the fifty-dollar bill in her panties. The other woman was still with Lamar; she wanted to show him the business for real. Still straddled across his legs, she seductively whispered in his ear, "Would you like to meet me after your party? I guarantee I will make your last night as a single man unforgettable."

"Nah, I'm good," Lamar said pulling a long piece of her synthetic hair out of his mouth.

She rolled her eyes. "Your loss!" She said climbing off his lap and disappointingly danced her way over to the other guys that were waiting to spend their money. They partied until four in the morning, and they literally had to carry Uncle June Bug out the club. Once Lamar got home, he called me and asked about Jodi and said that if she didn't show up he had asked a cousin of his to fill in; and thank

God Jodi ordered her tux in a larger size. But like I told Lamar, I was really feeling that something was wrong. Jodi would have never done this to me.

I ended the call but not before telling one another how very much we couldn't wait to begin our lives together.

I love that man, I thought to myself.

As I went to turn over and go to sleep, I noticed Tyra laying there asleep with her cell phone in her hand.

Chapter Forty-Six

"I t's your wedding day!" my mother yelled out in happiness. We all took our showers and headed down to Mea's shop. Tyra was sitting under the hair dryer; I watched her take the phone out of her pocketbook looking at it. *What is up with her and that phone?* I thought curiously.

In the meantime, B. picked little Terry up and all the guys went to breakfast and then to the barbershop; they had it so easy.

Our hair, nails, toes, and makeup were done, and everybody headed back to my mother's to get dressed.

"Sollie, you have a telegram," my mother said walking into the room and handing me the envelope. "Open it, open it!" she said more excited than I was.

"I Never Break A Promise!" It read.

"Is it from Lamar?" my mother asked.

"I don't know. There is no signature on it."

Finally, all the girls were dressed, and they all looked beautiful as they stood there wearing long silk chiffon gowns. And now it was my turn. It took three people to help me get my wedding gown on.

Lamar's cousin yelled up the stairs letting me know that another delivery had arrived. I told her that I would be down in a few minutes. Finally my dress was on. I blushed as all the girls surrounded me.

386

"Sollie, you look absolutely beautiful!" Mea exclaimed backing away and staring.

I walked over to the mirror and stared at myself. The A-line beaded satin wedding dress was gorgeous. My hair was pinned up into a bun with soft squiggly curls hanging from it, and my makeup was flawless. I took a deep breath and smiled realizing that everything I had gone through in the past year, was to bring me to this very moment!

"Are you okay, Sollie?" Tyra asked as a tear fell from my eye.

"I'm fine. I'm actually fine!"

"Girllll, don't start it!" Mea said gently patting my eyes.

Tears filled my mother eyes as she walked over to me; she reached for my hands and held them tightly as she softly kissed my cheek and then stared into my eyes.

"This is the day that every mother dreams of for her little girl, and I thank God that he has blessed and allowed me to see it. At this very moment, I am so proud of you," she said struggling to hold back her tears. "With your strength and willingness to move forward, you made it through all those obstacles that came your way. You faced your past in order to be healed, and now your spirit is finally free, I know it is, because I can feel it. And what makes it even more beautiful, you are marrying a man that I know I can trust to take care of my baby, and that's truly a blessing! I often look at you in amazement and say wow to myself, that's my daughter! And I am honored and proud to say those words today. Sollie, from the depths of my soul, and every fiber of my being, today my heart not only beats, it sings for you."

I looked behind me, and Salique was standing in the door fighting back his tears.

"Awwww, look at my other baby," my mother said walking over and hugging him.

"Let's go, beautiful people. Time is of the essence!" Mary said to everyone, and we all headed down the stairs. Everyone stood at the bottom of the stairs waiting for me to come down. Tyra walked slowly behind me carefully carrying the eleven-inch train. I looked out the door, and there they were—one stretch Lincoln Town Car and a Rolls Royce waiting for my mother, Lamar's grandmother and Aunt Bessie. And I knew Lamar and the guys were showing off in their stretch Hummer. I then looked up and down the street at the neighbors standing outside their houses patiently waiting for me to come outside.

"Sollie, here is your delivery," Lamar's cousin said.

"I hope this one has a name on it," I said. And it did. It was a small black velvet box with a white ribbon tied around it. I opened it and inside was a necklace with two small diamond hearts. And the card read, "Today Our Hearts Become One."

My mother gathered everyone in a circle and said a prayer. The girls all headed out the door. I told Mary that I needed to talk to Tyra for a quick second. She looked at her watch, raised her eyebrows, and said, "Just a second." She walked out the door.

Laying my train down, Tyra walked around to me and asked, "What's wrong?"

I held Tyra's hand. "Nothing wrong, everything is perfect. I just wanted to say thank-you for being my very best friend for the last nineteen years. You have been there for me through the good times and bad since I can remember. And this past year has been pretty rough on both of us and with all that you had to endure, you still stood by me, and I truly thank you for that. My mother used to say when I was younger that I better hope God allows me to live long enough to have a true best friend. And how blessed am I, because he has. And there is no one that I would rather have standing next to me than you. I you love, Tyra Palmer."

"I love you too, Sollie." We hugged each other and we both began to cry. "Now look at our faces. We need to get our makeup touched up."

"Come on, ladies, we have to go!" Mary said coming in the door.

We all headed out the door. Tyra and me laughed as I held my hand in the air and waved to all the onlookers as if I was Miss America.

"What in the hell happened to y'all makeup? Y'all get on my damn nerves, all this crying and shit!" Mea said stomping her feet and reaching for her makeup bag.

By the time we arrived at the church, Lamar and the groomsmen were already there. Mary got out of her car and walked over to the limousine as we pulled up and told us to wait a second. She wanted to make sure Lamar was where he was supposed to be, so I could enter the church without him seeing me.

I looked through the tinted window of the limousine and I saw my father and his friend walking into the church. I also saw George, his wife, and Ms. Susie and her granddaughter. So many people were arriving that Mary told the limousine driver to drive around the back of the church so that I wouldn't be seen by anyone.

"Sollie, it's time!" Mary said clapping her hands together as she walked into the room. "Ladies, line up and get ready to meet your partners."

"Sollie, you ready?" Salique asked, excitedly walking into the room.

"Okay, Sollie, take a deep breath. This is it. The flower girls are walking down the aisle as we speak, and you are simply gorgeous. It has been such a pleasure working with you and Lamar," Mary said smiling, and giving me a hug.

Salique proudly held out his arm, and I wrapped my arms around his. "Sollie, I'm glad you and your father made amends, but I am equally glad you chose me to give you away."

I could hear Meet Me On The Moon playing as I made my way to the entrance of the chapel. Duce walked over and kissed me on my cheek. "Your beautiful." He said.

Duce and Lamar cousin open the huge wide wooden doors. I stood back waiting for the music to start but it didn't. I looked over at Mary standing in the corner. "When are they going to start the music?" I whispered to her, Mary smiled as she gestured for Salique to walk me to the entrance, he did. And Lamar began to sing, You Are So Beautiful To Me. "Oh my God!" I said as my eyes watered with tears. Salique began walking me down the aisle. I couldn't believe what Lamar was doing. Everyone was in awe of my entrance, and the fact that he was singing to me made my entrance even more special.

"She's beautiful!"

"Look at that dress!"

"I wonder how much that cost. She looks like a princess," someone else said as the flashes from cameras and cell phone kept coming.

All I wanted to do was to get to Lamar. Once I was in front of him, he began crying, while continuing to sing. He reached into his pocket and pulled out a tissue and wiped his eyes. When he finished singing, everyone was in tears.

"Who gives this woman to this man?" Rev. Martin asked.

"I do!" Salique said proudly.

Salique shook Lamar's hand and gave me a kiss. Lamar quickly took my hand and smiled at me. I reached over and wiped his tears.

"I love you!" Lamar said trying to whisper and realized he didn't when our guest whooed and Awwwed!

"Good people Lamar is already expressing his love to Sollie," Rev. Martin said smiling. "That's all right, son, that is alllll right! Tell her you love her every day! And Sollie, you tell Lamar the same. Love is beautiful, yes it is, but as I'm about to tell you, it's going to take more than just love to keep this marriage strong! Oh yeah, I'm going to tell you the truth! There are going to be times when you are going to want to wring each other's neck! Sometimes you may even want to pack your bags and leave. And then there's the temptation that will sometimes stare you right dead in the face! And y'all know what I mean about temptation! Those ones out here that don't care nothing about these sacred vows you two are about to take! But today, today, is such a beautiful day, the joining of two people who truly do love each other, and look good together too, I might add! But this day will end just as the honeymoon will end, and before you know it, years will have passed and nature and time will not allow Sollie or Lamar to look like they do at this very moment. So you see, it's going to take much more than love to keep this union strong. And as you change over the years, you two laugh at the fact that you can't get up the stairs as quick as you once did, and the wrinkles that you're sure to get! But pray! Pray that your marriage makes it that far, and it's not going to make it because of the love you feel right now! That's right. The only way you two are going to make it is if God is smack dab in the front! Ah hah! Y'all good people thought I was going to say smack dab in the middle. That is what the saying says, but I took the liberty of changing it, because God can't be in the middle of nothing! Amen! God has got to be in the forefront!"

"Yes, he does!" Lamar's grandmother yelled, waving her hands in the air.

"So many marriages have failed because of people failing to put God first! And it—is—a—must! Now listen, I am not saying to you that while God is at the forefront of your marriage, there won't be any rough times ahead. There are going to be, but if you keep God first, I can almost guarantee you will be just fine. And when rough waters come, don't take it to the girlfriend, the homeboy, Mommy, your coworker, or the stranger on the street. Take it to God! And for God's sake, keep your business to yourself! And folks get mad when they find out somebody is discussing their business! If you keep your mouth shut, they wouldn't have anything to talk about. And another thing, don't forget those in-laws! Don't let those in-laws become outlaws! Even though y'all are going to be family, don't tell them nothing either! It ain't none of their business! Amen!" Everyone said, "Amen!"

"Okay, I am not going to talk y'all to death. I know y'all trying to get to the reception, so you can do the electric slide, and what the young folks say, turn up!"

"Is that right, Sollie?" he asked.

"Yes, Rev. Martin, that's right," I laughed.

"So, Lamar, you be Sollie's pillar of strength, and Sollie, you be Lamar's," Rev. Martin said without a smile on his face, "and by all means keep, I say again, keep God first, and you two will be just fine. And while you're sitting in your rocking chair holding your grandkids, or taking long slow walks in parks together, that's when you know that you were and still are highly favored by God, because

391

what God puts together, let me say it again, what God puts together stays together! 'Cause can't no man take it apart! So today, folks, pray, pray that God allows these two lovely souls to get to that point. And after speaking with this lovely couple on several occasions, I think they are going to be just fine. Now let's join these two souls into one."

Rev. Martin was a trip, and you wouldn't believe he was a white man!

Chapter Forty-Seven

T he ceremony continued with mixing of the sand to join the two families, and we had a brief moment of silence as we rang a bell for each name called of family members and friends who were no longer with us. Duce walked up to the mic and began to call out the names. I was startled when I heard a loud noise at the back of the church. Everyone turned, and it was Uncle June Bug falling, trying to walk out the door. Lamar and B. were furious, and so was their grandmother.

It was time for the exchanging of rings. When we placed them on each other's fingers, Rev. Martin said, "That's a lot of bling! God is good. Amen." As soon as Rev. Martin told Lamar he could salute his bride. Lamar lifted my veil and kissed me, and everyone stood and clapped.

Duce walked down the aisle and laid a beautiful rose-covered wicker broom in front of us; that was important to us to pay tribute to our ancestors. After jumping the broom, we happily walked down the aisle. After we greeted everyone we took what seemed like a million photo's, and I couldn't wait to get to the reception. I was starving, exhausted, and my feet were killing me. As much as I loved Lamar, I really didn't think our marriage would be consummated tonight. I was beat!

We headed for the reception. Once inside, Mary led Lamar and me to a room filled with all types of appetizers, champagne, and a beautiful chocolate fountain with fresh fruit lying around it. The wedding party was in the other room with the same complimentary spread.

"You guys relax. I am going to make sure everything is going smoothly with the seating arrangements, and give you guys some privacy. I'll return when it's time for you two to make your entrance," Mary said moving quickly out the door.

Tyra knocked on the door and came inside. "Y'all's married now," Tyra said copying a scene from Color Purple.

"I sure is!" I said pulling her down on the couch next to me. "Where is the phone? I'm surprised you didn't walk down the aisle with it! You sure slept with it last night. Who are you waiting for to call you?" I asked.

"My phone is in my purse, where it is going to stay. She smiled warmly. "I was waiting on a call."

"A call from who?" I asked curiously.

"A friend of Terry's, and I will explain everything when you return from your honeymoon. But Sollie I still can't get over Jodi not showing up," Tyra said.

"Well, I guess she was where she wanted to be." I shrugged.

Tyra left the room.

"I can't wait to get you out of this dress," Lamar said, kissing me. "Sollie, if there is such a thing as perfection, right now, at this very moment, my life is perfect! And I will thank God for you until the day I die!"

"Lamar, don't say that word."

"Baby, we are going to be together for a very long, long, long time."

Mary knocked on the door, and it was time for us to make our grand entrance as husband and wife.

Mary began to call the wedding party's names and had to call Mea and her partner's name twice. They both came flying around the corner, Mea running her hands through her hair and smoothing out her dress to get the wrinkles out.

"Freak!" Duce said.

Mea chuckled, grabbed her partner hand and they walked into the champagne room. The wedding party was all standing at the head table and finally, it was our time to enter.

"It is my pleasure to introduce for the first time Mr. and Mrs. Lamar Lane Jr."

Oh my god, I thought, as we entered the ballroom. It was simply beautiful. Everyone stood and clapped as we walked in. We made our way to the dance floor and began to dance our first dance, and as *Make Tonight Beautiful* played I laid my head on Lamar's chest, and I thought he was right; My life felt absolutely perfect!"

Dinner was ready to be served, and twenty chefs came out with their white crisp chef uniforms and tall white hats on, holding our covered dinner plates in the air. They stood there in uniform formation for about a minute, and then proceeded to serve the head table. Everyone was eventually served, and after eating, the party began. After two hours of dancing, mingling, cutting the cake and other stuff, I was beat. Carrying the train to gown, I made my way over to Tyra.

"Tyra, have you seen Mary?" I asked looking around the room.

"I'm sorry, Sollie. I forgot to tell you she left her gift she had for you and Lamar so she went to get it. Go mingle with your guests."

"Mingle my ass. I'm tired, and I'm ready to go!"

Tyra laughed looking at how irritated I was becoming.

"Sollie, it's almost over." She looked at me. "You do look really tired."

Tired wasn't the word. All I wanted to do was get out of here and take my heavy wedding gown off, climb in the bed, and go to sleep.

Tyra and I walked her Mother and kids to the door. Tyra hugged the kids tightly and told them to be good and that she would see them in the morning.

"Mommy when am I going to get married. when I become a big girl?" Trinity asked.

"Never, I won't let you!" Lil. Terry blurted.

"Oh Lord." Tyra said. As we all laughed.

Drake Plaza Hotel

"Hello, I'm Mary Zifer. I'm the wedding planner for Mr. and Mrs. Lamar Lane. They have the honeymoon suite booked for tonight," she said smiling at the hotel clerk.

"Ah yes, I have their reservations right here. How may I help you?" the perky blonde-head clerk asked.

"Is it possible to get in the room? I have a few things I need to do before they arrive." She held up a bag to the clerk. "I want to make sure the room is perfect for them, you know, really romantic. I would have done it earlier, but with so much going on, time would not allow."

"Ms. Zifer, we really aren't supposed to do that."

She took a fifty-dollar bill out of her pocketbook, laid it on the counter, and slid it to the clerk. The clerk's eyes widened. She looked around and took the fifty-dollar bill.

"Here you are," the clerk said, handing her key to the room.

"Thank you so much. I shouldn't be long."

"Okay," the clerk said smiling.

She quickly walked to the elevator, looking at her watch, checking the time.

Reception

Meanwhile, Uncle June Bug had laced his coffee with Hennessey. Lamar and B. had to take him into one of the sitting rooms to try and sober him up. Mea and her partner were on the dance floor grinding, I mean really grinding, my guest stared in disbelief, and when Mea eyes rolled back in her head, I knew that slut had just had an orgasm.

"Did you see what I just saw?" Tyra asked in disbelief staring at Mea.

"Yes the fuck I did!"

Duce walked over to us "Yo go get that nasty ass girl of the dance floor!"

Drake Plaza Hotel

The clerk was becoming very impatient. Looking up at the clock, she knew that her relief would soon be in, and she needed that key back before someone noticed it was missing. She placed a sign on the desk that she would be back shortly. She took a duplicate key from the drawer and headed up to the honeymoon suite.

"Ms. Zifer, are you in here?" the clerk asked knocking on the door. "Ms. Zifer, are you in here?" she asked again. The clerk heard a strange noise inside the suite. She slid the key in the slot. Opening the door, she walked into the huge honeymoon suite, and what she saw next, blew her young mind. The woman was lying on the couch, naked, wearing nothing but a long black trench coat, holding a dildo inside of her with one hand, and a loaded .45 Magnum in the other!

The clerk didn't know the woman she gave the key to had many personalities and that she wasn't Mary Zifer, the wedding planner, but Melanie!

"Fuck me, Ahmaun, please fuck me," she said ramming the dildo deeper inside of her while thinking about the love of her life! Trying to release all the pain she was feeling since the only person who ever understood and showed her any kind of love ever since she was a little girl, had been taken out of her psychotic life. She loved Ahmaun and would do anything he asked her to do ever since he saved her from the burning apartment building across from his aunt's house that her notorious brothers had set and left her to die inside to teach her a lesson.

Ramming the dildo harder inside of her, she began having flashbacks of her life, feeling pain and pleasure at the same time. She thought about her brothers and how they had both abused her. It made her angrier. She thought about how she watched them so many times kill numerous people, remembering the first time they made her pull the trigger to take the life of an innocent person walking through the park, and how angry they both became when she missed! And because of that they beat the living hell out of her with an iron cord until she was unconscious. They were determined to make her a professional killer like themselves, and they used seven innocent victims for her to kill until she killed with perfection!

She then remembered the day she put three bullets in Ahmaun Aunt head, after he begged her to kill her, knowing with his Aunt being dead, he would be able to come back to Baltimore. Remembering how they both stood watching his aunt beg for help until she took her last breath.

She thought about her most recent murders, Dino and Jodi, and how she beat Remi half to death because there was no way in hell she was going to let Remi have Ahmaun's baby. She was in so much emotional pain. All the mental institutions she had been placed in, all the medication she was on, all psychiatrists she had seen, were unable to help her. Only one person understood and loved Melanie, and that was Ahmaun. And now he was gone! Sollie had taken him from her, and she was determined to make that dumb ass bitch pay!

Chapter Forty-Eight

The clerk stood there pissing on herself unable to move, not knowing what to do. She couldn't take her eyes off that huge .45 Melanie was holding, but she knew she had to get the hell out of there! She took a deep breath and slowly turned and moved toward the door, startling Melanie with her movement. Melanie's eyes widened as she raised the .45 with the silencer on it. The clerk tried to run to the door not realizing she didn't have a chance against a professional, and within a second it was over. The clerk lay there dead with a gunshot wound to the back of her head!

Melanie jumped up snatching the huge dildo out of her and throwing it on the beautiful Italian couch. She buttoned her trench coat, tied the straps tightly around her, and ran to the door. Opening it, she looked up and down the hall, making sure no one was around. She then dragged the clerk's lifeless body down to the exit door and pushed her body down two flights of stairs, staring at the dead body rolling down the stairs while showing no remorse! "Dumbass bitch!" she said angrily.

As she walked back to the suite, a couple was coming out of the room next door. She was so angry that she was ready to take them out!

"That's a bad coat you're wearing, miss," the lady said, saving her and her husband from catching a hot one to the head.

Little did they know that because of the ridicule Melanie received from her brothers as a child, she loved when someone complimented her.

"Thank you," she said going back into the room. As she was shutting the door, she heard the lady ask her husband was that blood in the hallway floor.

Melanie ran into the bathroom grabbed a towel and wet it, ran back out into the hall, and quickly tried to wipe off the blood. But she couldn't get it all, so she rushed to set up everything, and she could finally carry out what Ahamun asked her to do. Even in his absence, Ahmaun was determined that another man would never have Sollie. But in Melanie's eyes she was killing the woman that he would never leave her for, and who had ruined her life forever! Even if B. didn't fall for the setup that she and Ahmaun had planned, Sollie would have still been killed! Looking at her watch, she knew she had no time to waste!

Reception

Mary met Lamar and me as we made our way down the soul-train line and giving us a beautiful statue of a black couple jumping the broom with our names and the date of our wedding engraved on the front.

I went to change, and Tyra and me had the hardest time getting me out of my wedding dress. Back in the ballroom, we went over to say good-bye to my mother, and she hugged us tightly.

"Mommy, you act like we are leaving tonight for the honeymoon! You will see us in the morning."

"Oh hush!" she said hugging us again. "I love you two. Have fun. See you at the airport in the morning."

Lamar and me went over to the DJ and got on the microphone telling everyone goodnight and thanks for coming and sharing our special day with us, and also that we would not be accepting any phone calls tonight. Everyone laughed and all the groomsmen held up their glasses in delight! Lamar grabbed my hand and we ran out the door and jumped into the limousine that was waiting for us.

Drake Plaza Hotel

"This behavior from Dena is no longer acceptable," the hotel manager said angrily to the other clerk. "This is the third time she has disappeared. If Dena is in the kitchen eating again, that's the last straw. She will be terminated tonight!"

Reception

"Duce, will you go with me tomorrow to look for Jodi?" Tyra asked Duce as they were leaving the reception.

"Hell no! The lawn mower is obviously where she wants to be!"

"Duce, seriously, I'm worried about her, and we both owe her an apology."

"For what?!"

"For how we have been treating her, and all the hurtful things we have said to her since she came out."

"I don't owe—"

"Yes, we do," Tyra said quickly cutting Duce off. "We have all been friends since we were kids and how we treated her wasn't right! And truth be told, these last few weeks that we haven't seen her, I miss her. I just hope she will forgive us.

Duce looked at Tyra. "I hate to admit it, but you're right. We probably do owe Shorty an apology, but if her ass start's running her mouth, I'm going to hit her straight in it. Come on Shorty, let me take you home," he said putting his arm around his childhood friend and walking to his car.

"Oh well, it's over," Tyra said standing there waiting for Duce to unlock his car door. "And thank God, my intuition this time was wrong."

"Why you say that T.?"

"No reason."

"What the hell is that beeping noise?" Duce asked.

"Oh, it's my phone," Tyra said reaching into her tiny silver clutch noticing the "battery low" indicator flashing on the screen. She saw that she had twenty-three missed calls. "What the hell" She said. And just as she went to see who had called the phone went completely dead. "Damn it! It's dead!" she said angrily stomping her feet.

"What did you expect? Sollie said you slept with it all night. It does run by battery, dummy! Who were you waiting for to call you?"

"Duce, shut up and give me your phone." She slightly chuckled.

"Shorty, I didn't bring it with me."

Tyra rubbed her hand across her forehead and nervously began rocking her leg, frustrated, because she knew something was wrong.

"Duce, please, drive faster!" she said looking at every corner they passed for a pay phone. "This is unbelievable. No pay phones anywhere."

"What is wrong with you?"

"Just get me home!" she said. She tapped her hand on her knee and tried to remain calm. The closer Tyra got to her house, the more nervous she became. As Duce pulled into the driveway, Tyra reached inside her clutch and pulled out her house keys yelling for Duce to let her out the car!

"Girl, at least let me park!" Tyra jumped out, ran to the front, and anxiously looked through her keys trying to find the house key. Unlocking the door, she opened it and ran inside grabbing the cordless phone off the base, and began checking her messages. Duce went in behind her. The way she was acting he knew something had to be wrong. He stood there watching as Tyra frantically began listening to her messages.

Tyra, this is Mike. You need to call me immediately. I have the information that you requested, and it's not good! So ple—" Tyra didn't even listen to the whole message. She quickly dialed Mike's number. "I knew it, I knew it!" she yelled stomping her feet, looking over at Duce, who was still standing at the front door.

"Knew what, Tyra? What the hell are you talking about?"

"Wait, wait," Tyra said waving her hand in the air at Duce after hearing the other line pick up. "Mike, hi, this is Tyra"

"Thank God, I have been trying to reach you all day! Tyra, this woman Melanie Omar is dangerous! How do you know her?"

"Mike, please just tell me what you know?" Tyra pleaded as she began pacing the floor.

"She's from Atlanta, Georgia. She is the youngest child of the notorious Omar brothers. She—is—treacherous! She's wanted for several murders in the Georgia area dating back fifteen years ago. She has also been in and out of mental institutions under different aliases and has been on escape for almost a year. She's even wanted for questioning by the FBI for possibly harboring a fugitive, Ahmaun Moore, who I also researched. He's from Maryland. Tyra, if you know the location of this maniac you need to contact authorities immediately. This woman is dangerous! Her brothers, who were hit men, taught her very well! And believe me when I tell you, she could kill ten people at one time, in the blink of an eye!"

"Oh my God," Tyra yelled. "Mike, listen. Call the police and tell them to come to the Drake Plaza!"

"Is she there?"

"I am not sure, but I know who is," Tyra said hanging up the phone.

Chapter Forty-Nine

"T yra, what is it!" Duce asked again.

Tyra ran up the black spiral stairs, ran down the hallway, and into her bedroom. She ripped off her beautiful gown, kicked off her shoes, opened the closet door, and snatched a sweat suit off the hanger. She slipped on her tennis shoes and raced into Terry's office. Grabbing the chair from under the desk and pulling it over to the closet, she slid her hand across the ledge on the closet door feeling for the key to the safe. "Shit, where is it?" She reached her hand further down to the end. After finding the key, she opened the red box that sat high up on the shelf, pulled out a .32 Magnum, and loaded it, "Let's see how crazy this bitch really is." She ran back down the steps and ordered Duce to come on.

"Tyra, what the fuck are you doing with that gun?!" Duce asked looking at her as if she had lost it.

"My father said the only time you pull a gun out is if you're going to use it!" she said running out the front door.

"Man, shit!" Duce said following behind his childhood friend. They both jumped in the car, and Duce began backing out of the driveway. "Where are we going?"

"To the Drake Plaza," she yelled, laying the loaded .32 on her lap and reaching down to tie her tennis shoes.

"That's where Sollie and Lamar are, right? Are they in trouble?"

"Yes!" Tyra yelled! Hearing that, Duce began driving like a maniac!

Drake Plaza Hotel

Lamar reached for my hand and helped me out of the limousine.

"Excuse me, sir, you left something," the limo driver said reaching inside and handing me my clutch that had Lamar's wedding gift inside.

"Oh, thank you, your gift is in here," I told Lamar.

"It's mighty small," he said playfully trying to take it from me.

"Stop, I'll give it to you later." He wrapped his arm around me, and we headed inside the hotel.

Thank God we already had our key to the room. As we stood there waiting for the elevator that seemed to take forever, laying my head on Lamar's chest, I was struggling to keep my eyes open.

"Dam baby you're really tired, I had no idea a wedding was this exhausting," he said kissing me on my forehead.

We stood in front of our honeymoon suite. "What is that smell? It stinks. It smells like some kind of cleaner," I said, as I waited for Lamar to unlock the door. He lifted me up and carried me into the room. It was so beautiful; candles were everywhere.

"Who did this?" I asked looking at all the candles that had obviously just been lit. They hadn't even started to melt yet, and the fragrance from them was so relaxing.

"Wow," Lamar said looking around. "Maybe Mary requested the hotel to do this," he said playfully reaching for my clutch to get his gift.

Tyra and Duce

"Will you drive?!" Tyra yelled at the car in front of them. Duce went as fast as he could swerving into the other lane and pressing the gas, taking the speedometer to a hundred, while looking over at Tyra holding the loaded .32.

"God, please let everything be okay," she said rocking back and forth.

"Shorty, calm down. They're good."

"And poor Jodi I know that she did something to her. I know it!"

Drake Plaza Hotel

Lamar and I stood in the middle of the suite as he undressed me, and he was pleasantly surprised when he saw the beautiful white bridal-laced baby-doll lingerie I was wearing. I then began to undress him, and smiled as I looked over at his gift that I had laid on the couch.

"I adore you, Sollie Lane," he said looking into my tired eyes. But I still went with the flow. He then took my hand and led me into the bedroom.

I stopped and grabbed my clutch off the couch. The bedroom was huge. It had a king-sized bed with a white satin comforter on it, and a single red rose laid in the middle of the pillows, while rose petals covered the white satin spread; the candles were burning and the lights were dim, and the reflection from the candles on the wall made the room so romantic. Lamar led me over to the bed and then went over and turned the music on.

Tyra and Duce

"Mr. and Mrs. Lane!" Tyra yelled out to the front desk clerk.

"Excuse me!" the clerk said, already pissed because they couldn't locate one of their employees.

"Look bitch, this is an urgent matter. We need to know what room they're in!" Duce said yelling at the clerk.

"I'm not at liberty to disclose that information!" the clerk yelled back.

"The hell you can't!" Tyra said raising her left hand so the clerk could see the .32 she was holding. Duce proceeded to go behind the desk and get the information himself.

"Okay, okay, I'll give it to you," she said nervously typing in the last name. "They're in room 113."

Tyra and Duce ran over to the elevator, and the clerk dialed 911. "Come on, shit!" Tyra yelled waiting for the elevator to come. It finally came, and it was full of people getting off with several pieces of luggage.

"She has a gun!" the old lady yelled causing everyone to go back into the elevator. Duce looked around and noticed the stairway.

"Come on, Shorty," he said pulling Tyra by the hand, realizing they needed to make it up thirteen flights to get to the room. As they proceeded to run, they heard police sirens coming from a distance.

Lamar and Sollie

Lamar and I stood in the middle of the floor, slow dancing. A warm breeze came in through the room. I looked around and noticed that the sliding doors to the balcony were open.

"Did you open those, Lamar?"

"No, I didn't. Do you want me to close them?"

"No, it feels good," I said watching the breeze blow the sheer white curtains in the air.

Tyra and Duce

"Come on, T.!" Duce said reaching out for her hand and at the same time trying to catch his breath while noticing they had four more flights of stairs to go.

"I'm coming!" she said stopping and heavily breathing as she held on to the banister.

They began running again, tirelessly making it up another flight, and then they heard loud footsteps coming behind them; they paused for a minute and looked down as far as they could and saw that it was the police. They began running even faster;

"Oh shit!" Duce blurted, falling back into the wall.

"What's wrong?" Tyra asked out of breath and began vomiting when she saw the hotel clerk's body lying there with a hole in her head.

"Come on, Shorty, don't look!" he said turning her in the opposite direction of the dead body. They began running even faster knowing that Melanie was probably behind the killing.

Lamar and Sollie

"Are you ready for your gift?"

"Yes I been ready." I reached over and grabbed my purse, opened it, and pulled out his gift. Holding it behind my back, I told Lamar to close his eyes. I took his hand and laid the tiny gift inside of it.

"Okay, you can open your eyes."

"What is this?" he asked looking at the sonogram.

"I hope it's your son!"

"Sollie, you're not . . . !"

"Yes, I am. Three months to be exact." Lamar picked me up and swung me around, got down on his knees, and laid his head on my stomach.

"Thank you, God," he said crying, "thank you, for my second blessing."

I noticed a red dot on the wall traveling through the reflections of the candles.

"Lamar, what is that?" He looked over and slowly stood up. We both looked over at the balcony, startled. We saw someone standing there naked wearing only a long black trench coat. Lamar stepped in front of me. We couldn't see the face but when she spoke, we both recognized the voice.

Chapter Fifty

"I   told you I never break a promise," she said softly, while the breeze became stronger, blowing her silk trench coat in the air. I screamed as the dot that traveled the wall eventually landed in the middle of my forehead.

"Oh shit!" Lamar yelled grabbing me, throwing me on the floor and covering me with his body.

As Duce and Tyra ran down the hall they looked back and noticed about five officers running behind them ordering them to stop. But they didn't. Hearing me scream, they had no intentions of stopping.

"Give me the gun T.!" Duce said taking the gun out of Tyra hand. He backed up and shot two rounds breaking the lock on the door. "T. stay out here!" Duce yelled as he ran into the suit, and into the bedroom. Seeing Melanie he began shooting, and so did she. After the gunfire ceased, four people were on the floor, their bodies riddled with bullets. Frantically turning my head from side to side, I cried out for Lamar, Tyra, and Duce," But no one answered. Slowly I opened my eyes; my body trembled, and my heart ached with pain knowing that someone I loved was probably dead. *What!* I thought in total disbelief. I closed my eyes and reopened them I couldn't believe who I was seeing. It couldn't have been, it can't be! It wasn't Lamar, Tyra, Duce, or even Melanie. It was Ahmaun! "No!" I yelled, snatching the covers from off me. I jumped out of bed and ran over to the window, quickly pulling back the curtains in hopes of seeing a BMW parked out front. But there wasn't.

I turned to Ahmaun with my eyes widened and eyebrows raised and asked in a very loud tone. "Where is my BMW?"

Ahmaun rose up out the bed, stretched his arms out, and yawned.

"What the hell are you talking about a BMW?! You don't even have a fuckin license." He laughed as he lay back down. Still in disbelief I ran over to the closet frantically rummaging through my clothes in hopes of seeing Giuseppe, Christian Dior, Gucci, Jimmy Choo, but I didn't. Only thing I saw was my hand-me-down from the local thrift store. Leaning up against the closet door, I thought, *I know*. Anxiously making my way over to my dresser, I opened the wooden jewelry box in search of my beautiful teardrop diamond ring, and of course, it wasn't there. Reality quickly began to set in. I slowly backed away from the dresser and sat down on the bed. *How could it have been? It all seemed so real,* I silently thought.

"Girl, come over here and tell big daddy what your dream was all about. I must have been putting it on you Shorty. One minute you were laughing and the next you were crying and shit."

You wish, I thought silently. You see in reality I was a timid, shy, plain Jane who didn't have a voice and the self-esteem that I lacked had played a pivotal role in the woman that I was. But no more! I thought as I angrily stared at him, realizing that the dream was only confirmation to what I have known in my heart and mind for a very long time. Shaking my head I thought about the eleven wasted years of being with him, eleven years of my life that I will never get back.

I looked at the time on the alarm clock, thinking that Duce was probably at work by now; I was just going to have to wait until he got off so that he could be here with me when I tell Ahmaun that I wanted him out of my house and my life. It was time...

Staring at the wall I began to think about my dream that was fading away as each second pass. Chills went through me as I thought about the parts of the dream that were nothing less than nightmares. And then I thought about him, I began to smile as my heart tried desperately to hold onto the fairytale. Wondering could there really be a man out here like Lamar.

"Sollie what's up, can a nigga get some ass or what?" Ahmaun asked while gripping his erect penis.

Just looking at Ahmaun made me sick! I wanted to vomit. I rolled my eyes as turned my head.

"Come on, what's up? And I know you ain't holding out on a nigga, you need to be glad that I fucks wit you for real, cause don't nobody want you, but me!"

"Somebody wants me," I softly whispered.

"I heard what you said; somebody wants you, yeah right." He chuckled. "Then again, I'll bite. Who the nigga and where he be so I can pull his ass up! I'm so fucking jealous." Ahmaun laughed sarcastically.

His name is Lamar Lane and you will never ever find him, I thought while praying that one day I will. ***I BE DAMN!*** Why did it have to be a dream?

I Be Damn 2 available now

About The Author

Dawn lives in Baltimore, Maryland. As a child Dawn loved to read, unaware that years later her love of reading would ultimately bring out the creativity that was etched in her creative mind, giving her the tools to write three in your face novels, that most can relate too. After completing her third novel; she has now written a stage play titled "Loving Me". Dawn's life is simple; she finds perfection in her imperfect life, and she loves it.

Order Form

Facebook: Dawn Barber
Instagram: damn_dawn3
Twitter: Dawn Barber
Snailmail:

Dawn Barber
PO. Box 2942
Baltimore, Maryland, 21229

$12.99 $13.99 $13.99

Name:_____

Address:_____

City:_____ State:_____ Zip:_____

Amount		Book Title or Pen Pal Number	Price
		Included for shipping for 1 book	$4 U. S. / $9 Inter

This book can also be purchased on:
AMAZON. COM/ BARNES&NOBLE. COM/ CREATESPACE. COM

Made in the USA
Columbia, SC
21 January 2025

51419600R00250